INTRODUCTION

The Criminal Procedure Law of 1979 (extensively revised in 1996 and again in 2012) installed an inquisitorial model of legal process in China similar to the civil law tradition of continental Europe.

England and Wales and the United States, for example, use an adversarial model where the prosecution and defence argue their respective positions before a neutral judge or jury, where the judge or jury have no prior knowledge of the case.

Under the inquisitorial model, however, facts are discovered through a coordinated process led by officers of the state – police, prosecutors and judges – all of whom are involved in a theoretically impartial effort to get to the truth.

In China, the majority of criminal investigations are conducted by the People's Police – the Public Security Bureaus (PSBs). The police have powers to gather evidence and detain suspects, though the formal arrest of a suspect is subject to the approval of the People's Procuratorate. If the police deem a case serious enough to be dealt with by a court, it is forwarded to the People's Procuratorate. The police also have the power to impose administrative punishments for various, usually minor, offences. Except for special units, or in special circumstances, the police usually conduct their work unarmed, though because of increasing violence in Chinese society this is beginning to change.

The People's Procuratorate handles the prosecution of a case. Procuratorates have the power to interview suspects, witnesses and victims. They may also order further investigation work to be done by the police. It is the responsibility of procuratorates to draw up a Bill of Prosecution detailing the charges laid against a defendant and to present the case in the People's Courts. Procuratorates have the power to investigate those cases considered too sensitive or too complicated for the police to handle. They also supervise the work of the police and the courts to prevent errors in the administration of justice.

There are four levels of criminal People's Court: Basic Court, Intermediate Court, Higher Level Court and the Supreme People's Court. Less serious cases will be heard in the Basic Court; those, such as murder, for example, heard in the Intermediate Court. Cases are heard in public unless matters of state security or private affairs relating to individuals are to be discussed. Any death sentence pronounced by a court must be approved by the Supreme People's Court.

It should be noted that the police, procuratorates and courts can each investigate criminal offences, interrogate suspects and collect evidence. It is possible for a trial judge to preside over a case in which he was the lead investigator.

Political and Legal Committees supervise the work of the police, the procuratorates and the courts at all levels. If a Political and Legal Committee 'recommends' a certain trial outcome then that outcome is generally accepted by the court.

The People's Armed Police Force (PAP) is a paramilitary organisation under the joint command of the Central Committee of the Communist Party of China and the Central Military Commission. The CAPF's main duties are border and forest protection, fire-fighting, road construction and specialized transportation, the guarding of vital installations and VIPs, and the provision of anti-terrorist SWAT teams. The PAP often works alongside the People's Police and would be deployed to counter instances of mass social unrest. Unlike the blue of the uniforms of the People's Police, the PAP wear pine-green uniforms and have a similar rank structure to the army. They therefore often get mistaken for army personnel.

The Ministry of State Security (MSS) is responsible for foreign intelligence, counter-intelligence and domestic security. It has the same powers of detention and arrest as the police. It is also subject to supervision by the procuratorates and the courts.

THE WILLOW WOMAN

A PHILIP YE NOVEL

LAURENCE WESTWOOD

LISA!

Hope you enjoy!

Laurence Westwood

SHIKRA PRESS

21/2/22

1st Edition, January 2019

Published by **Shikra Press**
An imprint of Shikra Press Limited
Stratford-upon-Avon
United Kingdom
www.shikrapress.com

E-Book ISBN: 978-1-9164569-3-8

Paperback ISBN: 978-1-9164569-4-5

Hardback ISBN: 978-1-9164569-5-2

Cover design by www.samwall.com

Cover photograph copyright © Philippe Lejeanvre

For more information about the author and forthcoming titles:
www.laurencewestwood.com

Ranks of the People's Police

- Commissioner-General
- Deputy Commissioner-General
- Commissioner (1st Class, 2nd Class, 3rd Class)
- Supervisor (1st Class, 2nd Class, 3rd Class)
- Superintendent (1st Class, 2nd Class, 3rd Class)
- Constable (1st Class, 2nd Class)

CAST OF CHARACTERS

In the People's Republic of China, a person's given name usually follows their family name. When a woman marries she usually keeps her father's family name rather than take her husband's family name. Any children from the marriage take their father's family name.

(SC) = Shanghai Clique

The Family Ye

- **Philip Ye** - Superintendent (1st Class), Homicide Section, Chengdu PSB
- **Ye Zihao** – Philip's father, former mayor of Chengdu
- **Ye Yiwei** – Philip Ye's paternal uncle, in aerospace
- **Ye Peng** – Philip Ye's paternal uncle, in pharmaceuticals
- **Ye Lan** – Philip Ye's half-sister, restaurateur
- **Ye Yong** – Philip Ye's half-brother (deceased)
- **Qu Fang** – Ye Lan's husband
- **Qu Peng** – Ye Lan's elder son
- **Qu Gang** – Ye Lan's younger son
- **Day Na** – 'aide' to Ye Zihao
- **Night Na** – 'aide' to Ye Zihao
- **Zhou Jin Jing** – Zihao's former wife, deceased
- **Philippa Wilson** – Philip Ye's mother, lives in the U.K.
- **Isobel Grainger** – Philip Ye's fiancée, deceased

Chengdu Political Leadership

- **Cang Jin** – Mayor of Chengdu (SC)
- **Li Zi** – Chengdu Party Chief (SC)
- **Wu Jing Zi** – Party Secretary; Chair, Chengdu Political and Legal Committee

Chengdu People's Procuratorate

- **Gong Wei** – Chief Prosecutor
- **Xu Ya** – Prosecutor, Legal and Disciplinary Procuracy Section
- **Deng Shiru (Fatty Deng)** – Special Investigator
- **Madame Ko Yi-ying** – Senior Legal Clerk
- **Hong Jia (Mouse)** – Legal Clerk

Chengdu Public Security Bureau (PSB) - Criminal Investigation Department

- **Di Qi** – Chief of Police
- **Miao Qing** – Chief Di's secretary
- **Ho Feng** – Commissioner (1st Class), Head of Robbery Section (SC)
- **Ji Dan** – Commissioner (1st Class), Head of Internal Discipline (SC)
- **Wei Rong** – Commissioner (2nd Class), Head of Homicide Section (SC)
- **Wang Da** – Commissioner (2nd Class), Head of Legal Affairs Section (SC)
- **Han Fei** – Supervisor (1st Class), Legal Affairs Section
- **Maggie Loh** – Supervisor (1st Class), Homicide Section
- **Meng Bo** – Supervisor (1st Class) (SC)
- **Cai Jing (Strike Hard)** – Supervisor (2nd Class), Narcotics Section
- **Long Ping (Clever Long)** – Supervisor (2nd Class), Economic Crime Section
- **Zuo Lu** – Superintendent (1st Class), Homicide Section
- **Tan Yang (Boxer Tan)** – Superintendent (1st Class)
- **Cao Cao** – Superintendent (2nd Class), Homicide Section
- **Wang Chao (Big-Mouth Wang)** – Constable (1st Class)

- **Yong He (Squint-Eye Yong)** – Constable (1st Class)
- **Wu Ping (Baby Wu)** – Constable (2nd Class)
- **Ma Meili** – Constable (2nd Class), Robbery Section
- **Dr Kong Ai** – Forensic Pathologist / Medical Examiner
- **Dr Wang Xing** – former Forensic Pathologist / Medical Examiner

People's Armed Police Force (PAP)

- **Wang Yan Zhang** – Major-General, C-in-C Sichuan Province
- **Wang Jian** – Captain, son of General Wang

Chongquing Public Security Bureau (PSB) - Criminal Investigation Department

- **Min Fu** – Commissioner (1st Class), Homicide
- **Lang Tao (Wolf)** – Supervisor (2nd Class), Homicide

Fatty Deng's Apartment Building

- **Deng Mei** – Fatty Deng's mother
- **Aunty Ho** – neighbour
- **Uncle Ho** - neighbour

Aunty Li's Apartment Building

- **Aunty Li** – Owner and businesswoman
- **Gao Yi (Old Man Gao)** – father of Junjie
- **Gao Junjie** – son of Old Man Gao, missing
- **Zhu Yi** – barman, The Singing Moon
- **Wang Li** – rural migrant
- **Han Fan** – rural migrant

The Family Fu

- **Fu Bi** – wealthy businessman, Chairman of FUBI International Industries

- **Fu Lu (Lucy)** – businesswoman, daughter of Fu Bi

- **Ni Peng** – night concierge
- **Gan Yong** – day concierge

- **Professor Ou Dong** – Director of Teaching
- **Madame Xiong Lan** – Head of Administration
- **Professor Xiong Yu** – visiting lecturer
- **He Dan** – student
- **Zhang Lin** – student
- **Pan Mei** – student

- **Xu Da** – Xu Ya's father
- **Yu Xiaoli** – Xu Ya's mother
- **Qin Qiang (Beloved Mister Qin)** – Xu Ya's former law tutor (deceased)
- **Bao Ling** – owner, The Singing Moon bar
- **Fan Yao** – employee of Bao Ling
- **Freddie Yun** – local gangster
- **Brother Wang** – associate of Freddie Yun
- **Han Ying** – school headmistress
- **Tingting** – young girl
- **Yao Lin** – Zhu Yi's former girlfriend
- **Wang Jiyu** – Secretary Wu's wife
- **Yu Jianguo** – Xu Ya's husband (deceased)
- **Yi Li** – Professor Xiong Yu's wife (deceased)
- **Nattapong Mookjai** – Thai businessman (deceased)
- **Han Yue** – Lang Tao (Wolf)'s wife
- **Lang Xiu** – Lang Tao (Wolf)'s daughter
- **Yoyo** – Ma Meili's pet cat

CHENGDU
SICHUAN PROVINCE
PEOPLE'S REPUBLIC OF CHINA

SPRING

CHAPTER ONE

Thursday

I n the near distance, in the grey light of dawn, Philip Ye saw her, plodding toward him on the other side of the road, a giantess, a veritable woman-mountain, not an ounce of fat on her, at least a head higher than most everybody else. The mass of people, travelling directly to work or first taking their children to school, flowed about this woman – a slow-moving river around a large boulder. Few made eye-contact with her. Those who did looked away quickly, not liking what they saw, wanting nothing to do with her.

She moved closer, seemingly not in any hurry, her eyes flicking this way and that. She scrutinized everyone and everything about her: the pedestrians, the street-vendors and road-sweepers, as well as the cars, buses, mopeds, and cargo tricycles driving by. She reminded him of a very old story told by the Venetian traveller, merchant and arch-fantasist Marco Polo. The story concerned a Tartar princess named Aiyaruk, which means 'Bright Moon'. The princess, so the story goes, had such physical strength and possessed a mind of such independent bent that she had agreed only ever to marry that rare man who could best her in a bout of wrestling. There had been many contenders but Philip Ye was at a loss to recall if any had proved worthy. He smiled at his remembrance of this remarkable tale, wondering if indeed any part of it was true. That Marco Polo had actually reached China, he thought possible (if not necessarily proba-ble), but which of Marco Polo's many stories were actual reportage, or hearsay, or downright fantasy, he was not knowledgeable enough to say. What he did know was that the woman moving toward him was most unusual. He also knew what she was, and that it was she he had come to find.

A few hours before, Philip Ye had woken, the sky still dark and the air about him gone chill. He had fallen asleep while reading, the lamp at the side of his bed still illuminating the room with a dull yellow glow. There was fresh smoke in the air: an aromatic tobacco, fruit-scented, seeping under the door. As always during the night, his father was up and about, smoking his pipe, wandering the great house. He could hear his father's voice, just a faint murmur, speaking, he presumed, on the telephone.

But it was not his father who had disturbed his sleep. With the familiar feeling of the hairs rising on the back of his neck, Philip Ye rolled out of bed, drew a silk dressing-gown about him and took a seat in his favourite leather armchair. He closed his eyes and began to breathe. He held it to be a truth that the rate at which thoughts cross the mind is directly proportional to the rate of respiration. If the breathing is slowed and regulated, so the mind is slowed and regulated. And when the mind is regulated, so the emotions are diminished, and the fear that lurks within is brought under control.

Inhale, counting eight heartbeats; hold for four heartbeats; exhale for eight heartbeats.

He repeated the cycle.

And then again.

He whispered to himself, "In breath, there is life; in breath, there is serenity; in breath, there is clarity."

He opened his eyes.

In the centre of the room stood a translucent figure, a ghost, an old man, blinking, as if surprised by this encounter with the physical world, unsure, it seemed, not only of his whereabouts but also about what he was doing here. Philip Ye pushed aside all thought of the Chinese unwritten rule of millennia – the living were the living, and the dead were the dead, and never the twain should meet – and opened his mouth to speak.

"I am Philip Ye, a superintendent of the People's Police, how may I be of service to you?"

The old man frowned, more definite in form and in purpose now. He pointed toward the north. "Wukuaishi…you must go to Wukuaishi…that is where you will find her."

The old man disappeared then, still pointing toward the north as he faded from view. Wukuaishi was an area in the north of the city, in the Jinniu District, famous for its tea market but little else.

Philip Ye telephoned his friend Superintendent Zuo. "Any trade tonight?"

"No."

"Wukuaishi?"

"Not that I've heard. Bad dreams? Can't sleep?"

"Something like that."

Philip Ye terminated the call. He checked the clock. It was a few minutes after four. He showered and shaved quickly. Was time of the essence? He didn't know. He selected a dark blue wool suit, cream silk shirt, crimson tie and handmade black patent leather shoes polished to a brilliant shine. A pale grey raincoat to finish, he briefly examined his appearance in the tall mirror before exiting his rooms. His father was nowhere to be seen. But he found Night Na lounging in a comfortable seat in the main sitting-room, some kind of investment magazine open before him.

"Where's the fire?" Night Na asked. In fine humour, he showed almost every one of his teeth.

"Wukuaishi," Philip Ye replied, not stopping to chat. It was pointless trying to explain.

He closed the front door behind him and, with the night mist swirling around him, jumped into the Mercedes. As he steered out of the long driveway and headed north, he picked up his phone and dialled, a sense of dread in his heart, a feeling that a tragedy was imminent, impossible to divert.

"Wukuaishi Police Station!"

"This is Superintendent Ye, Homicide – any trouble?"

"No sir, but if you wish to speak to—"

Philip Ye dropped the phone on the seat and concentrated on his driving. His destination was a long way off, the other side of the city. He pushed the car onward, the early morning traffic not yet heavy enough to slow him down. Wukuaishi was not exactly a small area. Once there he would have to make a decision about where to go, where to park up and wait. And, if his intuition gave him nothing at all, then…well, he'd cross that bridge when he came to it. No ghost had ever misdirected him before.

After what seemed an age of driving, and of gnawing indecision, he finally parked up on the Yusai Road, happy at least to find a space, somewhere to be still for a while, to breathe, to think, to contemplate just what it was the ghost had said. He was to look for a woman…or maybe a girl. But what was she: victim, witness or criminal?

Briefly he stepped out of the car to look about him, to stretch his legs, to get a feel for the area. It had been some time since he had been in this part of the city. However, he soon got back inside the car, disliking the exhaust fumes in his nostrils and the clamour of the awakening city around him. He closed the door, happier in his mechanical cocoon. He rubbed his tired eyes and settled himself down to wait.

It was after seven, his patience almost at an end, when he spotted in the distance across the road, through the gaps in the passing traffic, the largest woman he had ever seen. It offended him that she was dressed so poorly: faded smock, ill-fitting jeans, knock-off Nike training shoes that looked as if they had already walked a thousand miles. But, while he was reflecting on her lack of care for herself, a commotion caught his eye across the road from him. He twisted in his seat to get a better look, wrenching his neck in the process. An old man was holding a long knife aloft while clasping a young girl to him, trapping her in the crook of his free arm. The girl, in a pretty school uniform, at most eight or nine years old, was hysterical, screeching, struggling to get free. Nearby, a young woman, just as hysterical, whom Philip Ye took to be her mother, cried out to the passers-by to help.

Philip Ye had time to move, to intervene. He could have jumped out of the car and run across the road in seconds. But he recognised the old man. He thought him already dead, the exact physical likeness of his ghostly visitor from only a few hours before. And that recognition gave him pause, glued him to his seat.

How was this possible?

Had his ghostly visitor an identical twin?

The old man was shouting. Philip Ye couldn't hear him above the din of the traffic and from within the safety of the car. Frozen in his seat, his neck twisted around at a painful angle, Philip Ye could only watch the violence unfold, the old man waving the knife around like a crazy man.

Then, pop! pop!

The old man fell, his face contorted in mid-shout, bright-red arterial blood pumping from wounds that had blossomed suddenly on the side of his head. The young girl, still screaming, disentangled herself from the old man as he fell, to be caught in the waiting outstretched arms of her distraught mother. Then the giantess was there, leaning over the old man, pistol in hand, staring down at the now lifeless body, her expression blank, puzzled even, devoid of any emotion.

A truck pulled up to a halt beside the Mercedes, obscuring the scene. Not that it mattered. Philip Ye had already closed his eyes and settled back into his seat to ponder all that had just transpired.

CHAPTER TWO

There is an ancient tradition, probably born more of philosophers than of the native beliefs of the people, that the body is animated by two souls: the *pò* and the *hún*. After death, the *pò* – known as the white-soul or moon-soul and aligned with the feminine or *yīn* principle – returns to the ground with the body; and the *hún* – known as the cloud-soul or breath-soul and aligned with the masculine or *yáng* principle – soars up to the heavens. In the sixth century BCE, Zi Chan, Prime Minister of the state of Zheng, put forth the theory that if a man (or woman) suffered a violent death then the *pò* and the *hún* might linger, bound together in the physical world, uneasy and unhappy, unable to progress to their respective realms – in essence, to remain as a ghost.

Philip Ye had doubts about Zi Chan's theory, that violence was essential for the formation of a ghost. He believed there were other reasons a ghost might appear to the living. And he personally suspected there was only one soul, not two. But he had always taken it for granted that those ghosts he had seen were representations of – or indeed simulations of – the bodies of men and women already dead. Never before had he seen the ghost of a person still alive. And never before had a ghost given him a presentiment of events that were yet to come. He knew the theory, of course, of astral projection but—

A knock on the car window.

Roused from his meditation, Philip Ye glanced up to see a

familiar face. He dropped the window. "Boxer Tan, how the devil are you?"

Boxer Tan, or Superintendent Tan to give him his proper title, was for all intents and purposes responsible for law enforcement in and around Wukuaishi Police Station. It was common knowledge that Supervisor Meng, the actual commanding officer at that station, had, in the last few months, taken to spending his entire shift locked in his office, neither giving nor receiving orders in any manner that could be described as reasonable or professional. Quite admirably, Boxer Tan had stepped into the breach – not that a promotion for him was in the offing; or an official censure for Supervisor Meng, for that matter. Supervisor Meng was Shanghai Clique, and therefore untouchable.

"Mister Ye, have you come to take charge?" asked Boxer Tan.

"No, I was just passing," replied Philip Ye, the lie coming surprisingly easy to his lips.

Philip Ye looked across the road. It was full daylight now but the day that was promised would be dull, cold and heavily overcast. A small crowd had gathered. People were taking pictures with their phones. Fortunately, someone – probably a nearby shop-keeper – had had the common decency to cover up the old man's body with an opaque plastic sheet. Of the distressed schoolgirl there was no sign. The giantess stood off to one side, the crowd keeping their distance from her, her face as devoid of expression as before, her large eyes staring off into the distance.

"What's her story?" asked Philip Ye.

Boxer Tan, quite used to explaining most kinds of trouble in official reports, scratched his head, unsure as to where to start. It was a hell of a mess. He had felt no small relief when he had noticed the black Mercedes with the police plates parked up across the road. Deciding it best to begin at the beginning, he pointed to the giantess. "That's Constable Ma Meili. She's Robbery. She was assigned to us for…uh…"

"Reasons you don't quite understand?"

"Yes, Mister Ye."

"She answers to Commissioner Ho then?"

"I suppose so," replied Boxer Tan. "She was sent to us last September. Works nights. Patrols the streets on her own. She brings the occasional lost drunk to the station, breaks up a fight or two, and—"

"What was that? She patrols on her own?"

Embarrassed, Boxer Tan replied, "Mister Ye, I have no orders otherwise. And she isn't exactly sociable. She hasn't spoken a word to me in the last six months. Not a fucking word. A real miserable bitch! Only Baby Wu has taken a liking to her."

"Why is she armed?"

Boxer Tan shrugged. He couldn't speak about what he didn't know. Apart from high risk operations, when senior officers would authorise the use of weapons, the vast majority of police out and about in Chengdu carried out their duties unarmed – the only exceptions being the SWAT teams located at various points across the city. How long this situation would last was anyone's guess. Violent crime levels were rising. And, more specifically, there was the increasing threat from Islamic extremists unhappy with the political situation in the Xinjiang Uyghur Autonomous Province. Most believed it was only a matter of time before pistols were issued on a permanent basis, which would make a mockery of a police force that prided itself on being: 'Of the people, for the people!'

"And the old man?" asked Philip Ye. "Who was he?"

"That's just as complicated, Mister Ye." Boxer Tan beckoned over a fresh-faced constable who looked young enough to still be in school. The constable arrived at a run, dodging the traffic that was slowly beginning to move again, before coming to attention and saluting.

"Baby Wu, tell Mister Ye what you know about Old Man Gao," said Boxer Tan.

"Yes sir, it's a sad story," began Baby Wu. He leaned in close so Philip Ye could hear his soft voice over the traffic. "Old Man Gao's son, Junjie, vanished last October. I was manning the reception desk when Old Man Gao came in to make a complaint. I'm the most junior so that's my job. But I don't mind. So when—"

"You know we hardly ever take missing persons reports, Mister Ye," interrupted Boxer Tan, wanting to speed things up. "Not unless there's some evidence of foul play. Old Man Gao could tell us nothing except his son went out one day and didn't come back."

Baby Wu continued with the story after receiving a nudge from Boxer Tan. "Old Man Gao returned to the station at least once a week after that. His wife is dead or run away…we don't know which…and he swears he has no other relatives to turn to. Sometimes he would just sit and cry. I would make him a cup of tea to cheer him up."

"How old was the boy?" asked Philip Ye.

"Seventeen, sir," said Baby Wu.

"But the boy was an idiot…soft in the head," said Boxer Tan, tapping his temple. "Couldn't really take care of himself. He probably jumped on a bus one day just because he fancied the idea and got himself lost. Anyway, last week we heard that Old Man Gao had gone to the Mayor's Office to deliver a petition asking for help in finding his son. But Old Man Gao just got thrown out on his arse for his trouble. Rumour has it that he hadn't been right in his mind since – not eating, not drinking, shouting terrible abuse out of his window."

"Do you think he meant to hurt the schoolgirl?" asked Philip Ye.

"Does it matter?" asked Boxer Tan. "I just don't know what to do next. I've sent for an ambulance to take the body away but what am I to do with her?" He pointed at Constable Ma again. "I phoned Robbery but Commissioner Ho hasn't arrived for work yet. And Chief Di is tied up in yet another meeting."

Philip Ye thought swiftly, about practicalities, about procedure, deferring further contemplation of his own – as yet unexplained – part in this simple tragedy for later. There was no point in Boxer Tan waiting for Commissioner Ho. In the last few years Commissioner Ho had become infamous for partying almost every night. Though Shanghai Clique, Commissioner Ho had taken with unbridled enthusiasm to the Chengdu pastime of consuming enormous quantities of an unholy mixture of Chivas and green tea. If he staggered into the office by lunch it would be a miracle. As for the review of the shooting itself, that would be placed in the unsafe hands of PSB Internal Discipline, with oversight provided by the Legal and Disciplinary Section at the Procuratorate. If it was decided that Constable Ma had acted beyond her powers, she could find herself in a lot of trouble. Police shootings did not play well in the media these days.

He was about to suggest that Boxer Tan take Constable Ma back to the station, give her a cup of tea and take a brief statement from her, when he saw someone stumble drunkenly out of the crowd toward her. This man began to abuse her, shouting angrily, shaking his fist in her face. Not a novel occurrence for the police in Chengdu. Most people were never short of a word or two if they saw something they didn't like. But what made this instance so unusual was that the abuser was wearing the new pine-green uniform of the People's Armed Police Force, or the PAP for short.

Philip Ye was out of his car in a heartbeat, running across the road, stopping protesting cars with an outstretched hand. As he reached the confrontation – Constable Ma remaining stoic and unblinking to a fault – he heard what the officer, a captain by his insignia, was shouting at her.

"The police are supposed to defend the people! The police are supposed to be heroic! The police should not be shooting down old men in the streets like dogs!"

About thirty years of age, fine-featured, and with an army-style buzz-cut, Philip Ye didn't recognise the officer. Not that it mattered. He pushed him backwards, away from Constable Ma, smelling the drink upon him.

"Go home – you're a disgrace to your uniform!"

The captain stumbled, almost losing his footing. He was stunned by the shove, by the force of Philip Ye's command. With senses dulled by far too much alcohol, his eyes red-rimmed and unfocused, the captain only slowly absorbed Philip Ye's unusual appearance: the piercing green eyes, the prominent nose, and the expensive suit. The utter confidence behind those eyes shocked him, as did the arrogance of Philip Ye's aggressive stance.

"Do not touch me, *lǎowài*!" the captain sneered, swaying as he tried to hold his ground. "Don't you lay a stinking finger on me!"

Lǎowài.

Foreigner.

It was an easy mistake to make.

But Philip Ye was no foreigner. He was a *hùnxuè'ér*: a person of mixed blood.

"Go home!" repeated Philip Ye, the little patience he possessed already exhausted.

The captain then made the unfortunate mistake of moving his hand toward his belt as if to draw a pistol from a holster that mercifully was not there. But that gesture, impotent though it was, was more than enough to condemn him. Philip Ye stepped forward and hit the captain hard on the jaw, just the once, putting him straight down on the ground.

CHAPTER THREE

F atty Deng was so nervous, his hands shaking so much, his mother had to help him with his tie.

"Be strong," she said. "And when you think the time is right you must invite her to dinner."

Invite her to dinner.

What a joke!

Neither he nor his mother could cook worth a damn. And Prosecutor Xu was not the sort of woman who would give him a second glance. Very few women did.

"Mother, I don't think relationships are allowed at work," he said, intent on dissuading her from telling the neighbours that a wedding could soon be in the offing.

"Nonsense," she replied, pushing him out the door.

Well, for all he knew, his mother could be right. After the longest of winters – five whole years of unrelenting misery – the wheel of fortune had finally turned.

He didn't know why.

Who could explain fortune – good or bad?

But turn the wheel certainly had.

Fatty Deng had been collecting debts in the area for a local gangster, name of Freddie Yun. Not that he'd ever actually met him. He had been employed by a lowlife intermediary – Brother Wang – who told him the names and addresses of those who owed money to Freddie Yun, how much money was owed, and by which date the said money had to be paid (plus interest). Only a few weeks into the job and Fatty Deng had already been cursed, spat at, punched, and one time threatened with a rusty knife. He'd also seen enough human suffering to make him sick to his stomach. But, because of his size – he wasn't called Fatty for nothing – and because of his resolute politeness in explaining to the debtors that a visit from him was as good as it was going to get, he'd already collected a fair chunk of cash. Which had pleased Brother Wang immensely.

"Fatty Deng," he said, "you're our sort of guy."

Our sort of guy.

That didn't bode well for the future. He could hardly look himself in the mirror as it was.

Then the wheel of fortune had begun to turn.

He had arrived home one day, washed the muck of the city off his face and hands, eaten whatever it was his mother had scraped up, and reluctantly examined a letter that had arrived through the post.

It looked important.

It looked official.

Opening it with some trepidation, he almost choked when he saw the embossed seal of Chengdu People's Procuratorate at the letter-head. He was certain someone had informed on him, that he'd been spotted conversing with Brother Wang, that he was going to be sent to some nameless shit-hole of a labour camp on the border with Mongolia until he croaked.

But the letter was not what he expected.

"This must be a mistake," he told his mother.

Attached to the letter was an application form, already made out in his name, just requiring his signature. The Procuratorate, so the letter said, was intent on modernization, wanting to introduce new people into its workforce – people with proven skills.

"A justice system for the 21st Century!" the letter proclaimed. "A justice system the people can rely on!"

Which made him laugh.

"Is it genuine?" asked his mother.

A difficult question to answer in China at the best of times. But he thought so, yes.

"You must still have friends!" his mother announced gaily, the weight of the world temporarily lifted from her shoulders.

"No, I'm sure I don't," he muttered in reply.

The application form was made out for the post of 'Special Investigator', to be attached initially to the Legal and Disciplinary Section. He curled up his lip in distaste. Then he saw the salary.

5000 *yuán* per month!

Which was more than he had ever earned when he'd actually been police.

"We will be able to live like human beings again," said his mother.

Unable to solve the mystery of who had not only sent the application form but who had also mostly completed it for him, Fatty Deng decided to sign it anyway. What harm could it do? His mother said she'd post it back the very next day.

A week later, another letter.

He was invited to attend an interview in three days.

A hand-written page of briefing notes was attached to this second letter. It was a rough history of Chengdu People's Procuratorate, with some intelligent comments on its ten year mission statement, and a few potted biographies of its most senior personnel. He memorized every word of it, puzzled as to why someone would go to this much trouble for him.

Fatty Deng phoned around and was able to borrow an old suit from a similarly-sized cousin. Not that his mother didn't have to spend many hours sewing, making the necessary alterations. The night before the interview he hardly slept at all. In the morning he skipped breakfast, unable to face food of any sort.

"Don't take the car," advised his mother.

Which was wise. It was nothing but an old Japanese bag of bolts. He didn't want to break down halfway. He walked from their apartment in Wukuaishi to North Train Station and caught the Metro into the city. Far too early, he killed time by staring into shop windows at all the things he might one day buy, then hopped on a bus that took him west into Wuhou District. By the time he walked into Jule Road, he was still early – by almost an hour.

He sat on a bench and stared up at the imposing Procuratorate building, unable to figure out how all of this had come to pass. He had no friends in the Procuratorate – or enemies for that matter. He'd never been that important.

"Sometimes good things do happen to good people," his mother had said earlier that morning.

Maybe that was just the truth of it.

When it was time he approached the forbidding entrance. Some idiot working security, who probably couldn't even read, checked over his interview letter, frisked him with unnecessary roughness, and pushed him inside. He was forced to sign in at reception and told to wait, that someone would soon come for him.

Which she did eventually.

A young woman, so short at first he thought her a child on a work placement, led him into the bowels of the building and then up the stairs to the fourth floor. Which was very fortunate. He hated lifts and didn't want to embarrass himself sweating with fear. He couldn't tell if she was pretty or not. She wouldn't properly show him her face. But her voice was kind. She told him not to worry, that his interview was with Prosecutor Xu who was very nice. None of the questions he would be asked would be beyond him.

"Just be yourself," she said, "and you'll be fine."

He doubted this but he thanked her for her confidence in him just the same.

Their destination turned out to be an office off a long and deserted corridor. She knocked on the door for him as if not trusting him to have the nerve to do it and then ran off without even a backward wave. Her perfume had been pleasant though, leaving him with a good memory.

"Come in." A woman's voice.

He opened the door and then, quite unexpectedly, fell in love.

"What was Prosecutor Xu like?" asked his mother, some hours later.

He told the truth. "Beautiful...a real lady...and very, very smart!"

Uncle and Aunty Ho, their good neighbours, had come to visit, to join in the celebration. Uncle Ho had brought a small bottle of *báijiǔ*. He poured a drop into four small cups, only a sip of which burned Fatty Deng's mouth and tongue. It tasted like Uncle Ho had distilled it himself.

"So will you be working directly for Prosecutor Xu?" asked Aunty Ho, excited.

"Yes," Fatty Deng replied. "As her personal investigator. She's not taken up her post properly yet. She's still in the process of transferring in from Chongqing."

"That rats' nest!" exclaimed Uncle Ho, screwing up his wrinkled seventy-year-old face with distaste.

Fatty Deng remembered that Uncle and Aunty Ho had lived in Chongqing many years ago. Evidently they didn't have fond memories.

"Is she married?" asked his mother, giving Aunty Ho a sly wink.

Fatty Deng didn't know. Not for sure. But he didn't think so. He hadn't seen a wedding ring on her finger. There was also something she said, about her life being dedicated to the law, that made him think there was no husband. And he had noted a fragility about her, a subtle loneliness beneath her professional manner, that made him suspect that her life outside of work was not so happy. But that impression had been fleeting. And, not wanting to seem disrespectful, he had tried to keep his eyes down, away from her exquisitely made-up face.

She had been very patient with him.

She had given him plenty of time to answer her questions about what he'd been doing the last five years – that is, to concoct a great many lies – and passed him a glass of water when his mouth became incredibly dry. He noticed her fingernails then, long and superbly manicured; her perfume too, different from the child-like woman who had guided him through the building; lighter, the essence of some kind of rare flower, he thought – and so, so expensive. She had family money, he guessed, a prosecutor's salary not that great.

She'd had his old police file open on her desk. His record was immaculate, she said. This was news to him. She wanted someone who understood police methods: all their tricks, all their scams; someone who had experience collecting evidence, taking statements; someone who had an intimate knowledge of the criminal underworld, especially its many connections to corrupt police. He thought of Brother Wang and almost laughed.

"I don't know why the police let you go," she said.

He nodded, not wanting to speak, not wanting to remember what had been the worst day of his life.

She asked him what he knew of the Procuratorate, what he understood of the work that was done here. He reeled off the handwritten notes, all that he had memorized, silently thanking the kind heart – the mysterious heart! – who had provided him with all he needed to know.

Prosecutor Xu listened to him carefully, choosing not to ask questions or interrupt him. When he was done, somewhat pleased with his performance – he had never been so prepared for a job interview in his life – he contemplated his own fingernails, chewed down to the quick, as she turned her attention back to his police file. He wasn't sure what this hiatus meant. The silence soon became interminable.

"Mister Deng," she finally said, "you do understand that within the Legal and Disciplinary Section we may be tasked with investigating the legality of police investigations, including the conduct of the police themselves?"

"Yes, Prosecutor Xu," he replied, finding himself suddenly short of breath.

"And that would pose no problem for you?"

"No, Prosecutor Xu – not at all."

She made him wait another seemingly interminable time before saying, "Then I would like for you to have the job."

And that was that.

No mention of other candidates.

No waiting period.

No second, third or fourth interview.

No mound of bureaucracy to wade through.

No medical, no extra background checks.

The job was his.

Fatty Deng had heard of nothing like it before in his life.

Prosecutor Xu had taken him to have his photograph taken and then walked him out of the building, stopping just before the doors to shake his hand – her little hand, so delicate, so soft-skinned, entirely engulfed by his big paws. He tried not to hurt her, not to squeeze too hard, or to stare into her eyes like a lovesick puppy.

A real lady.

No doubt about that.

Uncle Ho passed around the *báijiŭ* again. His mother cried, as did Aunty Ho.

That evening, he went out with Brother Wang and got drunk. He told Brother Wang he'd been offered a proper well-paid job working security for an American electronics company that had just opened up offices in one of the new high-tech industrial parks to the south of the city. Brother Wang understood. Brother Wang knew all about the wheel of fortune. Brother Wang cried. Brother Wang had really liked him. Brother Wang asked if he would put in a good word for him. Though it could pay well from time to time, working for Freddie Yun was no real sort of life, he said. Fatty Deng promised, feeling really bad about the lie he had told.

Four days later, a parcel arrived by courier. A brand new Procuratorate badge and ID, complete with a set of glossy business cards.

Fatty Deng felt as if the sun was shining out of his chest.

His mother cried with joy again.

His cousin said he could keep the suit, that he never liked it anyway. Another cousin, a mechanic, did his best with Fatty Deng's car on the promise that payment was sure to follow in good time. Then a phone call from the Procuratorate, a legal clerk named Ms. Hong. His first day of work would be Thursday, she explained. Prosecutor Xu needed a few days to settle into her new apartment first. Fatty Deng said Thursday would be just fine.

And so the day arrived, his mother having to help him with his tie because his nerves were so bad. The car started first time. He had to take a short detour as the Yusai Road was fouled up for some reason but he still made it on time. He flipped his gleaming new badge at the idiot security men, ready to give them a piece of his mind if they tried to frisk him again, told the receptionist he remembered the way, climbed the stairs to the fourth floor telling himself the exercise was good for him, stood in the still empty corridor for a few moments to catch his breath, and knocked on the door.

She was standing, leaning up against her desk, watching the TV on the wall, long glossy hair pulled back into a pony-tail, conservative dark grey jacket and tight pencil skirt, sharp-pointed stilettos on her dainty feet.

"Investigator Deng, look at this," she said. "This has been playing on the local news this last half-hour."

He stared at the TV. It was a recording she was watching. She ran it back and played it from the start. The footage was unfocused and shaky, taken he guessed from someone's phone. But he could see well enough the old man clasping the child to him while waving a knife in the air. He recognised the Yusai Road not far from where he lived. So this was the reason for the traffic foul-up. The old man was shouting but about what Fatty Deng could not tell. Unfortunately the recording was silent. The old man looked as if he had lost his mind. Then he was down, blood everywhere. Fatty Deng forgot to breathe. The camera panned around and Fatty Deng saw what had to be the largest woman in the world, a pistol in her hand.

"Do you know her?" asked Prosecutor Xu, freezing the image with the remote.

He shook his head.

"She's police," said Prosecutor Xu. "Is it any wonder some of the people think the police are brutal and ill-disciplined? She could have tried to negotiate with the old man, done something other than shoot him dead. She acted with reckless speed, discharging a firearm on a crowded street."

"Yes, Prosecutor, I can see that," he said, not sure if he did. He had been troubled more by the old man's strange behaviour.

"This happened early this morning," said Prosecutor Xu. "It is to be our first case. We need to identify her, get her file, and then begin work immediately. Chief Prosecutor Gong wants answers quickly. We shall be liaising with Commissioner Ji of PSB Internal Discipline."

"Yes, Prosecutor." Fatty Deng wondered quite what he had gotten himself into.

"There is something else I want you to see," she said.

She ran the footage on. He saw the crowd gather like vultures around the body of the dead man. He saw a uniformed PAP officer appear from nowhere and start gesticulating angrily at the overlarge policewoman. And then a familiar figure appeared and the PAP officer was suddenly out cold on the ground.

Fatty Deng laughed out loud.

But Prosecutor Xu wasn't smiling. "Investigator Deng, do you know him?" she asked, sharply, turning angry but wondrous eyes upon him.

Fuck, what had he done? He was working for the Procuratorate now. He had to watch every thought, every word, every daft expression that crossed his fat, stupid face.

"Only by reputation, Prosecutor."

"Superintendent Ye?"

"Yes, Prosecutor – that's him."

"Not a friend of yours?"

Try as he might Fatty Deng couldn't keep from laughing again. "No, Prosecutor, I have never—"

"Moved in such rarefied social circles?"

She smiled then and he belatedly realised that he was being teased. He flushed and looked down at his shoes.

CHAPTER FOUR

Thursday

I t made no sense to Philip Ye.

Even if he dismissed the odd chronology – the soul's separation from the body *prior* to physical death – the question remained why the ghost of Old Man Gao had singled out Constable Ma for attention rather than asking for his help in finding his missing son Junjie.

Why would the ghost do that?

Had the ghost been hoping he would intervene and save the life of its physical body?

Constable Ma had acted quickly – some might argue pre-emptively – before Old Man Gao had had a chance to hurt the young girl. In the past, Philip Ye had seen a knife drawn across a throat in a blink of an eye. It took no leap of the imagination to say that Constable Ma had, in all likelihood, saved that young girl's life. It did not matter that Old Man Gao's life-story was tragic, or that he had not received adequate help from the police or the Mayor's Office in finding his missing son. He had threatened the life of an innocent young girl. And, ghost or no ghost, that was that.

However, Philip Ye remained unsettled by the morning's events. He continued to turn the matter over in his mind rather than open the current crop of murder files laid out upon his desk. The cup of tea he had prepared for himself he let go cold. He wished, and not for the first time, he could put a direct question to a ghost – and receive a direct answer in return. He was weary of partial, confusing and often cryptic one-way communications.

He was alone in the office, one of only two homicide detectives assigned to the brand-new glass-clad edifice that served as headquarters for Chengdu PSB. The other, his friend Superintendent Zuo, worked nights. Superintendent Zuo was probably already in bed by now, their paths usually crossing only briefly at shift changeover, or in those rare instances when the exigencies of a manhunt required their combined attentions. Philip Ye had arrived too late at the office to see Superintendent Zuo this morning. But his friend had left him a little pencil sketch: two pugilists squaring up to each other, one waving a British Union Jack, the other the flag of the PAP. The caption read:

The Third Opium War?

Superintendent Zuo meant nothing by it. He liked his history. And he liked trying to get under Philip Ye's skin, making fun of Philip Ye's mixed ancestry. Philip Ye screwed the sketch up and threw it in the bin. It hadn't exactly been his finest hour.

They usually shared the office with Commissioner Wei, the head of the Homicide Section, boss to the far too few homicide detectives scattered at various stations throughout the city. But he was off on long-term sick, taking up a bed in the Sichuan Cancer Hospital, not expected to return anytime soon.

The door opened softly and Chief of Police Di walked in, a thin, stooped man, prematurely aged by overwork and bad fortune, a cigarette dangling from his lips. Small, tinted spectacles concealed tired, sad eyes. Unlike Philip Ye, he wore the standard blue uniform of the People's Police.

Philip Ye stood to attention but was waved back down into his seat. Chief Di leaned up against the window, looking out through the accumulated grime at the city below. He took a long drag on his cigarette, letting the ash fall to the floor. He chain-smoked Panda cigarettes, an expensive brand, once favoured by Sichuan's most famous son, Deng Xiaoping.

"How is your father?" asked Chief Di.

"Well, sir – as well as can be expected."

Chief Di continued to gaze at the people on the streets below, his mood hard to read. Once famous for his volcanic temper, these days he was more prone to long silences – and headaches too, so bad they sometimes kept him off work for days.

"Philip, you must call Major-General Wang," said Chief Di.

"Of course, sir – who is he?"

"Our new PAP provincial commander. It is his son, Captain Wang, you were fighting with this morning. It appears that Captain Wang is quite the hero…just finished a long posting in the Tibet Autonomous Region. He's here to take up a position on his father's staff. Major-General Wang spoke to me not long ago. He is most distressed. He has seen the media reports on TV and misunderstood them. He thought you were an American…a tourist or a business-man. He wanted you arrested and deported. I explained that you actually didn't think much of Americans; that you're half-English, quite famous in Chengdu, the son of former mayor, Ye Zihao; and that you were, on occasion, a half-useful detective. He was most surprised. Lost for words, I should say. But still, you must call him to apologise."

"Of course, sir."

"I have also just got off the phone with Chief Prosecutor Gong. He wanted to know what you were doing in Wukuaishi this morn-ing. He also wanted to know what kind of insanity overtook you when you began fighting with a PAP officer in front of a crowd of people carrying phones with cameras, and – I believe this question was directed at me – what was Chengdu PSB doing employing some great pig of a peasant farmer's daughter to patrol the streets of his beloved city. The man is a two-headed snake but he does have a point, I think."

"Sir, I—"

"I don't wish to know what you were doing, Philip. As far as I am concerned…and I told this to Chief Prosecutor Gong…your presence in Wukuaishi was purely coincidental. So there will be no further questions for you to answer. But I suspect you will be required somehow to build bridges with the PAP. So I suggest, once you have called Major-General Wang, you go home, take the rest of the day off and consider carefully your response. You have worked too many days straight as it is. As for Constable Ma, I don't think I know her."

"Robbery, sir."

"Ah, that may explain it – Commissioner Ho's wayward little army. What did you do with her?"

After he had knocked Captain Wang unconscious, Philip Ye, still in a foul temper, had ordered Constable Ma into the car. Leaving a protesting Boxer Tan to clean up, he had driven them both into the city. She had opted to sit on the backseat, to stare sullenly out of the window, refusing to answer any of his questions. Her lack of any obvious remorse disturbed him. Warranted or not, the killing of a man should evoke some human emotion, some empathy for the dead. Her large eyes, when he managed to glimpse them in his rear-view mirror, were dull – as lifeless as the long, lank hair that fell about her massive round face. Her clothes smelt of the mist, of the smog, of the city. He found her very presence in his car depressing.

"I left her in the canteen, sir – to await further orders."

"Is that her weapon?"

Philip Ye nodded. He had taken her pistol from her. It was now lying on his desk sealed in a plastic evidence bag for safe-keeping. Presumably the Procuratorate would want to examine it whenever they got their act together; which could be days, months or years.

"There is nothing I can do for her," said Chief Di. "Chief Prosecutor Gong wants to make an example of her."

"Sir, she did nothing wrong."

"Some in the media are saying otherwise. People are beginning to feel a lot of sympathy for the old man. It seems he got into some trouble at the Mayor's Office last week."

"He was trying to deliver a legal petition asking for help to find his missing son and got beaten up for his nerve."

"Philip, some commentators are saying we were out to get him, had singled him out as a troublemaker. True or false, the Procuratorate want to demonstrate our accountability to the people. They are determined to curb excessive use of force – and no doubt to prove in the process that Constable Ma is not up to the job. What is she… about thirty years old? It is a pity she is not young and pretty, more sympathy might be shown her then."

Which was an undeniable truth.

Last summer Chengdu PSB had run a 'beautification campaign' to improve the image of the force among the people. A small number of very attractive young women had been recruited, the idea being – and it had some perverse merit – that if the force looked good out on the streets, then it must *be* good. Mayor Cang, enthused by the plan, had happily granted the small increase in budget to support the campaign and the salaries of the newly recruited personnel. Unfortunately, what Mayor Cang was not so enthusiastic about was granting the police the necessary funds to make it a really professional body, able to properly enforce the law in a modern, growing, and truly international city – which is what Chengdu was set on becoming. A few pretty girls in uniform would not cut it. The police needed better pay, better training, better equipment, better forensic capability and at least an intake of five hundred new cadets to face the rising levels of crime with any confidence. Another budget meeting was set for Sunday morning to discuss this problem yet again. No one in Chengdu PSB was holding their breath.

"What do you make of Constable Ma?" asked Chief Di.

The question surprised Philip Ye. These days Chief Di showed so little interest in the rank and file. He found himself at a loss for anything sensible to say.

"I'm not sure, sir."

Chief Di didn't seem to mind the lack of any intelligent reply. On the way out of the office, he said, "Don't forget to call Major-General Wang before you take the rest of the day off."

Philip Ye was indeed tired – bone-tired. And he had been sleeping poorly recently. An afternoon at home might do him some good, might give him some valuable time to meditate on the morning's visitation. But first he locked Constable Ma's pistol in his desk and went down to the armoury to have a chat with the guys there. That done, satisfied by what he had discovered, he returned to the canteen. Constable Ma was where he had left her, sitting hunched over the table, shunned by all, staring down into her tea-cup. Nobody had come down from Robbery to collect her. He doubted now if anyone would.

"Constable Ma, you are under procuratorate investigation," he said. "Go home and wait for them to summon you."

If he expected any meaningful response – emotional or otherwise – he didn't get it. She got up from the table and lumbered off, the canteen a much lighter and brighter place after she'd gone.

He felt guilty but he didn't know why. In the car-park two uniforms gave him the thumbs up, mimicking boxing-stances as they did so. He would be very popular for a day or two. In the car, driving home, he realised he had forgotten to call Major-General Wang.

CHAPTER FIVE

I t had always been said – not least by the family Ye – that the fortunes of the city of Chengdu and that of the family Ye were inextricably linked, each a part of the other's foundation.

Ye – meaning 'leaf' – was a clan name during the Spring and Autumn Period of the Eastern Zhou Dynasty. It referred to the then city of Ye, which would, in time, give its name to Ye County in the modern province of Henan roughly nine hundred kilometres from Chengdu. For reasons that will probably forever remain obscure, one day a branch of the clan Ye decided to journey across China. They crossed the formidable mountain ranges that acted as a protective barrier around Sichuan, sailed treacherous rivers, and walked bandit-plagued roads, just so they could set up shop in Chengdu.

When was this expedition made?

According to the family Ye, in the 11th century, early in the Song Dynasty, when Sichuan was already famous as 'Heaven's Store-house' – a land of opportunity and plenty. If asked, Ye Zihao, Philip Ye's father, would state fervently that the family Ye possessed all the necessary documents and references to prove its long historical attachment to the city. But, so precious were they, all such materials were kept safely under lock and key, unfortunately unavailable to public scrutiny.

As for the independent historians – it is believed that there are one or two in Chengdu – they have only ever been able to trace the genealogy of the family Ye in Chengdu back to the 19th Century, during the final decades of the Qing Dynasty, perhaps arriving as refugees from the ravages of the Taiping Rebellion.

What all agree on, however, is that, since the beginning of the 20th Century, the family Ye have either occupied, or being close to, the seats of power in Chengdu; have always chosen their friends wisely; have always made the correct alliances at the correct times, and have survived all of the terrible convulsions of the last hundred years more or less unscathed.

When Ye Zihao returned to Chengdu from a prestigious posting to London as a technology attaché at the Embassy of the People's Republic of China – remarkably with a small half-English boy in his arms – he and his two brothers set about lobbying Beijing on behalf of the city.

An economic 'open door' policy had just been announced for the geographically favoured cities of the east coast. It didn't take a Daoist soothsayer to predict that the cities in the interior of China would soon lag far behind. The persistence of the three Ye brothers (though they should not take credit alone) led to Chengdu being approved by the State Council as an 'open city' – to become a beacon for foreign investment, a place where China's embryonic high-tech industries could claim a safe foothold.

One Ye brother moved into aerospace, another into pharmaceuticals. However, Ye Zihao, the youngest of the three, had set his heart on a greater prize. A talented communicator and networker, exuding unflagging confidence and charisma, and with a useful background in civil engineering and city-planning to boot, Ye Zihao rose quickly through local Party committees to become mayor. This was just in time to welcome the Party's 'Go West' programme, which actively encouraged even greater investment in the cities of central and western China – cities such as Chengdu. With Mayor Ye Zihao in charge, and as he said it himself, "putting Chengdu not only on the map, but also on the world stage", international capital and expertise began to flood in. A quaint city with a grand and ancient history was transformed into a burgeoning metropolis of glass and concrete, ready to make money hand over fist. Which it did – as did the family Ye.

So, all was as it should be, Heaven and Earth each in their rightful places, the family Ye firmly in the ascendancy, until everything was suddenly turned upside down.

. . .

The earthquake took the lives of upwards of 90,000 people, wiping whole communities, especially in the remoter areas, off the map. Miraculously, the city of Chengdu was relatively undamaged. But there were some terrible aftershocks to come. Especially for the family Ye.

Had the family Ye overstretched themselves?

Had they perhaps rubbed someone important in Beijing up the wrong way, the perceived inadequate relief response from Chengdu after the earthquake providing a useful excuse?

Or had the media reports, impossible to fully silence, of badly built apartments, of schools collapsing like stacks of cards upon the studying pupils within, been far too dreadful for even the hardest Party stomach to ignore? After all, Mayor Ye Zihao was famed for his links with the construction industry, not only in Chengdu but across all of Sichuan. If someone was to be blamed, then why not him?

Or was there some other reason, as yet to be uncovered, that had brought the wrong sort of attention to Chengdu and therefore to Mayor Ye Zihao?

Whatever the truth, as the glorious soldiers of the People's Liberation Army parachuted down to distant hills to lend assistance to the bereaved, the homeless and the traumatized, a fresh team of municipal executives and administrators, originating mostly in Shanghai, was parachuted – metaphorically, this time – into Chengdu. These men and women were soon to be known as the 'Shanghai Clique.' And they soon invited many others from Shanghai and other cities – consultants, advisors, contractors, police and security personnel – to join them, much to the utter dismay of the people of Chengdu. Presumably, the problems the initial team found in the management of the city were so vast and systemic that nothing but a thorough house-clearing would do.

Wisely, the Ye brothers in aerospace and pharmaceuticals kept their heads down and their mouths shut. They withdrew from public life to concentrate on what they did best – making lots of money. The Party had no argument with that.

Mayor Ye Zihao, however, was marched out of his office in handcuffs, suspended from the Party (he had simultaneously occupied the post of Party Chief), and placed under house-arrest to await formal charges; charges that should have inevitably led to a very public trial and, his enemies hoped, his swift execution. And yet, for reasons nobody could properly explain, years later, Ye Zihao, as well as his enemies, were still waiting.

It was a source of some pride to the majority of the people of Chengdu that Ye Zihao had not buckled as would weaker men.

Forbidden to leave his house, he hadn't resorted to poison, or gone insane, or sought solace in alcohol, or dabbled in exotic religious beliefs. If anything, his determination to clear his name of any wrong-doing, and to return himself to the Mayor's Office, had become more pronounced with every passing day. As had his hatred of the Shanghai Clique. In his view – and no other view was tolerated under his roof – the Shanghai Clique was sucking the lifeblood out of Chengdu, by fair means and foul. And Mayor Cang Jin, currently occupying *his* desk, was the greatest *jiāngshī* – vampire – of them all.

Ye Zihao had coined the name 'Shanghai Clique' himself, shouting it out loud when he was carried bodily from the Mayor's Office. One would think, as the majority of the new personnel did indeed originate in Shanghai, that this naming was no great feat of the imagination. But Ye Zihao had been very clever, very clever indeed, the name an allusion to an infamous past. In 1976, just after the death of Mao Zedong, a group of four individuals, led by Mao's wife Jiang Qing, and soon to be known as the 'Gang of Four', had tried to seize power. They were arrested and put on trial, blamed for the chaos and worst excesses of the Cultural Revolution. Never much of a gang, and not really responsible for the Cultural Revolution – it was not politically expedient then to blame Mao Zedong directly – these four were swiftly found guilty, the verdicts underscoring not only the rise to power of Deng Xiaoping and the pragmatists but also their determination to repudiate the majority of Mao's social and economic policies. Since then the 'Gang of Four' had become a byword for treachery and vaulting ambition. Each of the four had had important links to Shanghai – very useful to Ye Zihao in his hour of need. Not wanting to be so obvious as to call the new arrivals a 'gang', by calling them the 'Shanghai Clique' Ye Zihao was well aware that the people of Chengdu would quickly get his meaning.

Unfortunately for Ye Zihao, Chengdu actually began to grow from strength to strength under the leadership of the Shanghai Clique. And, as the days, months and years began to pass, the Shanghai Clique began to be accepted by many of the people as the new face of Chengdu. However, this meant nothing to Ye Zihao. To him, that some of the Shanghai Clique turned out to be excellent executives and administrators was nothing but smoke and mirrors; that many of the Shanghai Clique had come to look upon Chengdu as their adoptive home, nothing but blatant lies – a mere public relations exercise. Ye Zihao alone knew the real truth of what the

Shanghai Clique was really about: its shadowy ventures; its infiltration of every local Party committee, every public concern, and every private company – becoming more corrupt and more malign and more dangerous as it burrowed deeper and deeper into the body of the city. And, as for Mayor Cang, Ye Zihao would happily tell any who cared to listen that there was no evil he was above perpetrating – not even the ordering of the brutal killing of a harmless old man.

"Philip, you must investigate," said Ye Zihao, jabbing the stem of his pipe in his son's direction to reinforce his point. "I've been taking calls all morning. Mayor Cang had that old man beaten up last week just for trying to deliver a petition. And today he's had him killed... shot in the head, just like that!"

Philip Ye hadn't yet taken off his raincoat. He had returned home to find his father in the kitchen, apron wrapped around his waist, about to start work preparing the vegetables for lunch. Day Na sat nearby on a stool, his eyes twinkling. He liked it best when father and son argued.

"There's nothing to investigate," said Philip Ye.

"Have you no eyes?" spat Ye Zihao. "Have you no independent mind? She's been on TV – that monster that Mayor Cang hired to do his dirty work." He turned to Day Na for support.

"You have to admit the big girl does have skills," said Day Na, nonchalantly picking at his teeth.

"This is ridiculous," said Philip Ye. "She is police – and anyway, she's already under investigation by the Procuratorate."

"The Procuratorate!"

This came out almost as a curse. Ye Zihao had never hidden his disdain for that particular organ of law enforcement even when he'd been in office. But, before he could say more, his phone rang. He walked out of the kitchen, phone to his ear, listening intently to whatever it was he was been told.

"I was there," said Philip Ye to Day Na. "Constable Ma saved the young girl's life."

"Maybe," said Day Na.

Philip Ye went to his private rooms, changed his clothes and sat down to watch the TV. The local station was replaying the incident again and again, together with footage of a press conference hosted by the Procuratorate. Chief Prosecutor Gong said, quite blandly, that the people should not be concerned, that the policewoman was under formal investigation, and that the child taken hostage was quite safe. The girl was, in fact, already back at school and working hard at her lessons. He said nothing about Philip Ye's altercation with the PAP officer, which was some blessing.

The footage of the shooting incident itself was more intriguing, more disturbing than Philip Ye had expected. Two different sequences were shown, apparently taken by two different mobile phones. Philip Ye watched, and watched again, feeling chilled. From his vantage point sitting in his car across the road he realised he had hardly seen anything at all.

"A lot of knife-waving, a lot of shouting, but not much else," said Day Na, appearing in the doorway. "That old man was never intending to hurt anyone."

"It doesn't make Constable Ma a murderer."

"No, but did you see the speed her pistol came to hand? She was expecting trouble."

Philip Ye, like it or not, was forced to agree. The old Type 77 pistol with which she had been armed required a round to be chambered before it could be fired. On the TV he watched her again and again withdraw the pistol from the holster on her belt underneath her smock and shoot immediately, demonstrating that the pistol had been holstered with a round chambered, held on the safety, against all regulations. This made no sense. She was either careless with her firearms discipline or, as Day Na said, expecting trouble. And she did not seem the careless type to him; plodding and methodical, unfeeling and lacking remorse maybe, but not careless.

"Jesus," said Philip Ye, out loud.

Not understanding English, but appreciating the sentiment, Day Na laughed.

Day Na, and his twin brother Night Na, had arrived in Chengdu a few weeks after the earthquake, not long after Ye Zihao had been placed under house-arrest. Distrustful of the Chengdu police, many of whom were about to be dispensed with as surplus to requirements anyway, the Shanghai Clique decided to put the matter of Ye Zihao's confinement in the hands of the Ministry of State Security. State Security, in turn – worrying about residual local loyalties – thought it best to put the matter into the hands of private contractors. So the brothers Na were summoned from the industrial port city of Dalian in the north-east, so far away that they would have little if any knowledge of the political turmoil in Chengdu and too disinterested to take sides.

Hard men, armed to the teeth and supremely physically confident, one brother would sit in the car watching the house all day, while the other would do the same all night. Not quite identical, Philip Ye had come to name the twins Day Na and Night Na to tell them apart – names they had loved and had adopted ever since.

State Security, either out of incompetence or just having more important fish to fry, had failed to properly brief the Na brothers on just who it was they were watching. Hard men they might be, they were more vulnerable than anybody knew.

After a few days, with the pattern of their independent vigils fixed, Ye Zihao began to personally take Day Na and Night Na cups of tea. The household staff, too frightened of their own possible arrest by the Shanghai Clique and any requirement there may be to give evidence against their former master, had long since fled the house. The constant supply of hot tea surprised the Na brothers. Once they got over their initial shock, it was always gratefully received. A month later Ye Zihao was busy preparing them breakfast, lunch and dinner, standing by their car for a moment or two after delivering it for a friendly laugh and a joke. And then, one humid summer evening, Philip Ye returned home exhausted from work to find Day Na and Night Na sitting at the kitchen table, eating like pigs, being royally entertained by one of his father's most colourful stories, unsuspecting prisoners of his immense charm and wit.

A few months after that, the brothers had moved permanently into an empty wing of the house and were running errands for Ye Zihao – some legitimate, some probably not so – and almost certainly on the family Ye payroll. They bought provisions for the house, ferried house-guests back and forth – including some of Ye Zihao's lady friends – and often disappeared, probably up to no good, at the strangest of hours.

Whatever the details, Philip Ye chose not to know. He was pleased only that his father now had some company in the big house, both day and night – for the brothers kept to their distinct sleeping and waking hours – and that the Na brothers were now focused on threats from without the house rather than from within. They had become devoted to his father, hanging onto his every word, absorbing and adopting every facet of his idiosyncratic worldview. In effect, they had become family.

After six years, were they still employed by State Security?

Philip Ye did not know. He hadn't seen fit to ask the Na brothers and they hadn't seen fit to tell him. It could be that they had quit, State Security losing interest in whether Ye Zihao defied his house-arrest or not. Or, quite possibly, there were elements in State Security supportive of Ye Zihao's cause and comfortable with the Na brothers' transfer of allegiance. The workings of State Security, both domestic and foreign, were often hard to fathom.

However, Philip Ye suspected incompetence on State Security's part rather than any active intention to support his father's return to the Mayor's Office. Whatever the truth, he had come to trust the Na brothers, happy to leave them with that little bit of mystery. They never spoke of any family in Dalian, any wives or children. They spoke only of Chengdu, how they had fallen in love with the city – and of the Ye family mansion as their home.

Philip Ye turned the TV off. He didn't want to see himself knock the PAP officer down yet again.

"Constable Ma is off-limits to me," he told Day Na. "But I might take a closer look at the old man."

"That will please your father," said Day Na.

"There will be nothing to find."

Day Na smiled. "Lift any rock in China and something nasty will come crawling out."

"You talk like a frightened old woman," said Philip Ye.

"And you hit that PAP prick like a girl."

CHAPTER SIX

P hilip Ye slept some and meditated some that afternoon in the quiet of his private rooms. His father had made his point about Mayor Cang and expected action. But Ye Zihao should also know his son. What Ye Zihao expected was not always what he got.

Philip Ye had come to no firm conclusions about the death of Old Man Gao. Except one, that is: Old Man Gao had tired of living.

Sad though this was, Philip Ye could see no way forward for any investigation. Old Man Gao, frustrated in his search for his missing son, frustrated in his search for justice, had chosen to die. And Constable Ma had been on hand to grant him his very wish. What else was there to learn? But the more Philip Ye meditated on the events of the day, beginning with the visitation from Old Man Gao's ghost, the more dissatisfied he became. He was convinced he was missing something. But what?

He sat down to dinner with his father. They were joined by Day Na and a newly risen Night Na – who thought nothing of eating a full dinner as his breakfast. Despite the strange day, and his father's earlier intensity, the talk around the table was convivial. The Na brothers liked their sport. The form of the local Chengdu football team had of late been not so hot, so they discussed instead the English Premier League of which they were both avid fans. Ye Zihao, never short of an opinion on anything, happily chipped in. Philip Ye, though, ate in silence, not just Old Man Gao and

Constable Ma on his mind, but the drunken Captain Wang of the PAP also.

Just before dinner he had had a strained conversation with Major-General Wang, not only the Captain's senior officer but father also – no nepotism there then. Apologising for hitting his son, Philip Ye made the excuse that a batch of PAP uniforms had been stolen a month or so ago – actually, a real event – and he assumed, by Captain Wang's odd behaviour, that he was not PAP at all. Major-General Wang accepted this explanation without comment. Major-General Wang – his loss of face being almost unimaginable – explained that since returning from Lhasa his son had not been very well. Philip Ye could believe it. Policing Tibet was known to be detrimental to the health of both the heart and the mind. Philip Ye said that if he could ever be of service to either of them he would be happy to oblige. Major-General Wang thanked him for the call with more grace than Philip Ye had any right to expect, leaving Philip Ye feeling oddly guilty for giving his son a smack in the first instance – deserved or not.

After dinner, Philip Ye retired once more to the quiet of his rooms. He phoned Wukuaishi Police Station. Baby Wu was still on duty. The young constable enthusiastically gave directions to Old Man Gao's apartment block located just around the corner from where the shooting took place. It meant another long journey to the north of the city. Not that Philip Ye had any other plans. He picked a much darker suit for the evening and a red and blue striped silk tie.

"Be careful," said his father.

Putting on his raincoat, Philip Ye replied, "Mayor Cang has nothing to do with this." But, by his father's stony expression, he was not to be believed.

As he drove across the city, Philip Ye recalled the one time he had met Mayor Cang, not long after the Shanghai Clique had taken control. Mayor Cang had visited PSB headquarters to address all the detectives who had been summoned from all over the city. Many were hoping for a pep talk. The removal of Mayor Ye had been deeply unpopular throughout the PSB. Some were also worried for the fate of Chief Di, whose career it was said was hanging in the balance. Philip Ye had stood with the others, feeling self-conscious in his crisp blue uniform, his Western features singling him out in the crowd.

Mayor Cang marched out in front of them, a drab, fat little man. His speech, thankfully not in old Shanghaiese, was still made almost incomprehensible by his thick accent. Not that he spoke for very long. This was the gist as Philip Ye and the others interpreted it: "You police officers are just like the rest of the people in this dirty backward city – lazy bastards! I'd sack all of you if I could. Fortunately I've brought some proper police officers with me…real crime fighters…proven black bashers!"

By 'black' he meant *hēishèhuì* – literally 'the black society', the criminal underworld.

An hour later, upon every notice board in every police station across the city, a list of police officers was posted: those to lose their jobs immediately, to make way for the enforced intake from Shanghai and other places, a clear-out soon to be known as 'The Purge'. Philip Ye checked the list, expecting. But his name wasn't there. Nor was Superintendent Zuo's. He breathed again.

"It's because you're half-English," said Supervisor Cai of Narcotics.

"They don't want to risk bad press in the Western media," added Supervisor Long of Economic Crime.

Both were safe, both had good connections in the Party and in other government agencies. But they had made a show of checking the list anyway.

"If it was up to us…."

"…we would have got rid of you."

"You're too pretty to be police."

"Too pretty by far."

Funny guys.

Friends.

Good guys to know.

He called Superintendent Zuo, who was at that time at home recovering from serious injuries, two bullet wounds to his leg. Superintendent Zuo was sleeping, still on painkillers, so Philip Ye spoke to his wife. "It's okay," he said. She, out of relief, burst into tears.

Later that day he was summoned to Chief Di's office. Chief Di was standing, looking nervous. Behind the Chief's desk sat someone Philip Ye was already familiar with, his face in every local newspaper – Chengdu's new Party Chief, Li Zi. He had the look of a reptile and was smoking a cigarette in an intricately carved ivory holder. Standing to attention, Philip Ye struggled to keep the distaste off his face.

"So you're the mongrel, the half-breed?"

"Yes, sir," Philip Ye answered.

"You look more English than Chinese?"

"Yes, sir."

"That is all, Superintendent Ye."

He guessed that Party Chief Li had just wanted to take a close look at Mayor Ye's famous *hùnxuè'ér* son. Nothing happened after that. At home, still coming to terms with the shock of his rapid fall from power, his father was exultant that his son had somehow kept his job.

"This is their first mistake!" exclaimed Ye Zihao. "The dozy bastards! Now you can keep an eye on them from the inside, uncover all of their dirt!" He was trembling with nervous energy, his pipe shaking in his hand. "Together we'll soon bring those Shanghai fuckers down!"

That Philip Ye, in the following months and years, showed no such enthusiasm for investigating too deeply into what the Shanghai Clique was up to around the city, was soon to stick deeply in his father's craw. Their relationship, always tense, became difficult, often strained. Never openly accusing him of treachery, there were times around the dinner-table when Philip Ye would catch his father looking at him with cold and untrusting eyes, as if his son was a stranger in his house. But then, soon enough, his father would begin laughing and joking again, lighting and relighting his pipe, as warm and as exuberant as ever, telling the Na brothers the most outlandish stories.

Philip Ye was able to park his car in the same space on the Yusai Road he had used that morning. Despite the evening hour and the darkness and heavy fog that had descended, many people were out and about on the streets. He turned the collar up on his raincoat and made his way across the road. He stood for a short while on the spot where Old Man Gao had died. Nothing remained as evidence of his passing, not even a speck of blood. Old Man Gao's life had been washed away. Feeling depressed, he followed Baby Wu's directions and walked around the corner. A couple of minutes later he had arrived at the entrance of a run-down apartment block.

"Watch out for Aunty Li," had warned Baby Wu.

Apparently, Aunty Li was known to the police. She owned the building and was not to be trifled with.

Inside, the air smelt bad. It was also dank and felt a good ten degrees colder than the outside – a legacy of Mao Zedong's cruel and arbitrary decision to deny heating to any construction south of the Huai River, that river taken to be the dividing line between North and South China. There was rubbish piled up in the hall. An old woman was sweeping out her room, adding to the pile.

"Grandma, where did Old Man Gao live?"

She peered up at him with bad eyes. "Who are you?"

"Police."

She came closer, her broom at the ready, curious. "Āiyā!" she exclaimed. "I know you. You are the *lǎowài*, Mayor Ye's English son!"

"Yes, Grandma, can you help me?"

"Your father is not forgotten. I pray for his return every day. He is a good man – the very best. Those in power now are just rats and snakes."

"Old Man Gao – did you know him?"

"It was terrible what the police did to him…shot him down in the street like a dog. But that was Old Man Gao for you. He had bad luck all his life. His wife…ah, she was a vicious bitch…ran out on him… left him with that fool of a boy."

"Where did he live, Grandma?"

She gestured with her thumb. "Around the back, up the stairs, on the first floor. But don't go there! This place is full of gangsters now. I pray each day for your father's return. He would free us from this life of bitterness."

Philip Ye left her mumbling to herself. He went around the back of the building, treading gingerly between puddles and more piles of rubbish, anguished that he was dirtying his shoes. The light was so bad he had to take a small torch from his pocket to find his footing. The doorway at the back was open and unlit. He played his torch within. Stairs led up and down. He grimaced as he heard voices rising up from the darkness below, from what he guessed must be an illegally built basement. The poorest of the poor would be down there, living a subterranean existence when not out looking for work. His quest, thankfully, took him upwards. The concrete steps were damp and slick. He watched his footing as he ascended, careful not to slip. He pushed open a fire-door almost hanging off its hinges and found himself in a short, narrow corridor, a single stark fluorescent tube lighting the way. A lot of noise emanated from the apartments on either side, a baby crying, a TV blaring. At the end of the corridor, sitting on a stool and facing toward him but engrossed in a magazine, sat a rather fat man, dressed in a poor excuse for a suit. Philip Ye remembered the old woman's warning about gangsters.

"Who are you?" he asked.

Startled, the fat man almost fell off his chair. He steadied himself and looked up, his face breaking out into a toothy grin.

"Mister Ye, sir – what are you doing here?"

"You know me?"

"Yes, sir – it's me, Fatty Deng." Fatty Deng stood and put out a fleshy hand. "I was a constable a few years ago – at Wangjiang Road Station."

Philip Ye shook his hand briefly, not remembering him. "So you are retired now?"

"They got rid of me with the others...after the earthquake."

"Ah." The Purge.

"But I'm with the Procuratorate now," said Fatty Deng, proudly showing off his badge. "It's my very first day."

Philip Ye was suddenly wary. "So you're taking a closer look at Old Man Gao?"

Fatty Deng nodded. "I'm waiting for Prosecutor Xu. She's due here any moment."

Philip Ye was incredulous. "A prosecutor is coming here?"

Prosecutors often re-interviewed victims and witnesses, not always trusting the police's version of events. But the current crop of prosecutors usually did this without ever leaving the office.

"Prosecutor Xu's new...from Chongqing...a real lady," said Fatty Deng. "A looker too."

"What does she expect to find?"

"I'm not sure. Some clue as to why Old Man Gao took the child hostage, I suppose – or what really happened to his missing kid, Junjie. Did you know the old man was beaten up outside the Mayor's Office last week? I've been asking around. People say it was the *Chéngguǎn* who beat him. The poor bugger was only looking for help in finding his son."

The *Chéngguǎn* – short for the Urban Administration and Law Enforcement Bureau – enforced the city's bylaws: markets, environment, sanitation, health and safety etc. But they were often little more than thugs and used in the main for Mayor Cang's own private purposes. Philip Ye hated them, as did most other police – including some who were Shanghai Clique.

Fatty Deng pointed inside the room he'd been guarding. The door was wide open. "Someone's been here this afternoon...an hour or so before I got here. Turned the whole place over. Smashed the only light bulb. Not sure why. Prosecutor Xu will be furious. An old lady downstairs told me it was local gangsters. Her neighbour told me it was the *Chéngguǎn* again."

"Difficult to tell the difference sometimes."

Fatty Deng laughed, his ample belly moving up and down. "Doesn't make sense, though, Mister Ye. The old man had nothing. There's fuck all here. My guess is that Aunty Li – she's the owner of this dump – sent her own men round looking for back rent or anything to steal to make good her loss."

"May I go in?"

Fatty Deng pursed his lips. He had his orders. Prosecutor Xu had been adamant.

"I promise not to touch anything," said Philip Ye.

"She could be here any moment," protested Fatty Deng. "I really need this job, Mister Ye."

But Philip Ye, not wanting to be put off, and personally doubting that any lady prosecutor, once she had seen the outside of the building, would dare to step inside, pushed past Fatty Deng. He shone his torch around, lighting up the mess that Fatty Deng had referred to: clothing strewn around the floor, cooking utensils spilled, pots turned upside down, bedding piled up in one corner. He doubted there had ever been anything worth stealing. Maybe the old man had had his savings, paltry though they may be, hidden under the mattress. There was only one bed. Philip Ye suspected the old man had once shared that with his son. There was no toilet. The people in the building probably had to share or walk to find a public convenience. Philip Ye decided that if he'd lived here, he would have contemplated suicide himself.

Fatty Deng played his own torch across the walls. "See the pictures, Mister Ye. "According to the neighbours the missing kid was a bit of an artist."

The pictures, sketches in black or coloured charcoals, taped to the walls around the whole room, were good, showing some talent.

"I thought he was a fool."

"They call it 'learning difficulties' now, Mister Ye. From what I've been told he was a good boy…harmless…much like the old man. But he was always drawing, anything that caught his attention."

Philip Ye saw that. The pictures depicted all manner of subjects: different makes of cars; motorbikes; youths in sunglasses lounging against a wall; young women laughing, out shopping together; old people practicing *tàijíquán* or dancing together in the street as is the current fashion; a black and white cat; a man walking a dog on a lead; a small hawk perched on a power-line pole. Philip Ye was impressed; and unsettled also. Drawn just in black charcoal, it was difficult to identify the exact species of hawk. Nevertheless difficult memories arose, memories Philip Ye fought quickly to suppress.

"Look at the spaces on the walls, Mister Ye. I think some of the pictures are missing."

"Perhaps the kid took them with him when he ran," said Philip Ye.

"Maybe," said Fatty Deng, looking unsure.

"Is the Procuratorate gunning for Constable Ma?" asked Philip Ye, sharply, wanting to change the subject, feeling suddenly exhausted by the room, tired of Old Man Gao's squalid life, of the damp and the cold, of the sadness that seemed to bleed from the walls.

"I think so," replied Fatty Deng, sounding glum.

"Constable Ma was just doing her job."

"It didn't look good on TV, Mister Ye. She didn't give the old man a chance to drop the knife."

Not knowing now why he had come, what he had hoped to achieve, Philip Ye offered Fatty Deng his hand again. "I've seen enough. Good luck with the job," he said. With that, he turned and left.

CHAPTER SEVEN

On the street, on the way back to his car, his father called.

"What have you found out?"

"Nothing," replied Philip Ye.

"You mustn't give up!"

"I'll see you later, Father."

He switched off his phone, content to be unreachable for an hour or two. He sensed someone behind him and turned to see a squat, middle-aged woman with a face fixed into a permanent scowl and dressed in a motley array of clothing against the cold: a thick black ski jacket over a pleated red skirt, heavy brown fur-lined boots, all topped off with a garish orange bobble-hat.

"You police?" she asked.

"Superintendent Ye."

"People call me Aunty Li. How long are you going to be bothering my tenants? I have a business to run. I don't want people frightened away. That fat man has been snooping around all evening and—"

"He's not police, he works for the Procuratorate. So don't mess with him, Aunty Li, or you'll bring a whole heap of trouble down on your head."

She took a few steps nearer, her eyes bright, her mind churning. "All this for one daft old man?"

"He was shot on TV – makes people nervous. Was it you who searched his rooms?"

"Āiyā! Who do you take me for, policeman? I am no thief. Anyway Old Man Gao had nothing. He was three weeks behind with the rent. He spent so much time looking for that idiot son of his, he lost his job. I said to him, 'Old Man Gao, do I look like a charity?' He told me he would get the money to me when he could. But I said to him—"

"When did Junjie go missing?"

"October, I think – but who cares? The boy was useless. So what if he got up one day and went for a walk and never came back? Some days he couldn't even remember his own name and—"

"He could draw."

"Pah! What a waste of money that was. Old Man Gao used to fritter all of his spare change away on paper and charcoals for that boy. It would have been better if he'd found him a job in some stinking factory where you don't need a brain to get on. Old Man Gao earned little enough as it was. He was a janitor at the school until they'd had enough of him crying over his missing boy and chucked him out. I said to him, 'How are you going to pay the rent now?' And he would cry and cry, just like a baby. People have no common sense these days."

Philip Ye passed her his card. "Call me if anything strange happens."

"Like what?"

He left her standing in the street squinting at his card. Back in his car, not wanting to face his father just yet, he decided to make a short detour before heading home. He drove into the city and parked around the corner from The Silver Tree. The restaurant was busy, every table full. He skirted the entrance and went around to the side door which led directly into the sweltering kitchen. As he entered, the over-worked but happy kitchen staff, all pouring with sweat, began to wave and grin at him – all except his half-sister, Ye Lan, whose restaurant it was. Hair pulled back tight under her protective cap, sleeves rolled halfway up her fleshy arms, she threw down her cleaver, and hurried over to him, her head reaching no higher than his chest. She punched him hard on the arm, angry.

"Handsome Boy, what's the matter with you? I saw you fighting on TV. I called Father but he wouldn't talk to me – you know how he is. I've been worrying all day."

"Little Mother, the fight was nothing…just a misunderstanding." He allowed her to hug him briefly. "If you were so worried, you should have called me."

"And disturb you at work? Why would I do that? Now listen to me, that temper of yours—"

"It was nothing," he repeated.

A young and nervous cook made a slight bow to him and pressed a steaming bowl of *dàn dàn miàn* – spicy noodles, made to his sister's secret recipe – into his hands. Though Philip Ye had only eaten dinner a few hours before, when the wonderful aroma filled his nostrils, he began to wolf the food down.

Ye Lan pulled him to one side, away from the hustle and bustle of the cooks and young waitresses running back and forth. She whispered to him. "Handsome Boy, last night I had a dream. Ah, it was terrible. I don't remember much of it. Just that you were in big, big trouble. I saw bright, sharp knives in the darkness. When I woke I switched on the TV and saw that big ugly peasant-girl shoot the old man dead. And then I nearly fainted when I saw you fighting. I thought you were going to be shot too. Speak to my husband. He'll tell you. My nerves have been jangling all day."

Her husband, Qu Fang, who worked the front of house, appeared briefly in the kitchen, nodded in Philip Ye's direction and disappeared back out again. He and Ye Lan had a good marriage. Qu Fang was calm, untroubled by life, happy to do whatever Ye Lan asked of him. Philip Ye liked him immensely.

"Little Mother, you mustn't worry. Nothing is going to happen to me," Philip Ye assured her again.

"Handsome Boy, if you got hurt or died, our father would never recover."

"That's nonsense, and you know it. Where are the boys?"

"Upstairs, doing their homework. Don't you get giving them more money! They have to learn what hard work is for, what it takes to succeed."

Careful not to trip over boxes of produce, Philip Ye made his way up the narrow stairs to the living quarters above the restaurant. In the lounge, he found the two boys sitting at the table, both hard at their studies even though it was now getting late. They eagerly threw down their pens and ran towards him.

"Uncle! Uncle!"

"We saw you on TV!"

"With the monster woman!"

"And fighting with the soldier too!"

The boys, Qu Peng and Qu Gang, eight and seven years old respectively, wanted to wrestle. But he kept them at arm's length, annoyed that they'd been allowed to watch the news on TV. Better for them to remain children for a little while longer, he thought. He slipped them each a twenty-*yuán* note, sending them both scurrying into their bedroom to hide the money from their mother as he settled into a comfy armchair. They were both good boys but Philip Ye worried about how hard Ye Lan pushed them at their schoolwork, intent on careers for them as either civil engineers like their grandfather or as computer scientists, hopefully working for one of the new electronics companies now bringing so much money into Chengdu. Slaving in the kitchens was not for them. Nor was dangerous police work.

The boys returned quickly to sit back at the table, wanting him to tell them more about the monster-woman, why the old man had gone mad with a knife, and why their uncle had been fighting with a soldier. They had mistaken the pine-green PAP uniform for that of the army.

"You must not speak of Constable Ma like that," he cautioned them. "She is not a monster. She is police and you must be respectful."

As for the other questions, he deflected them with ease, suggesting that maybe on Sunday, if he could get time off work, he would take them to the zoo again. He got a great deal of pleasure from taking them to see the animals and they assured him, though he was never completely certain they were telling him the truth, that they enjoyed it as much as he did.

"But first, you must finish your homework," he told them, closing his eyes as they set about their studies with renewed vigour. This ability they had to refocus always amazed him. He had never been that attentive to his studies when he'd been their age.

His mind wandered back to the events of that morning, to Constable Ma. He wanted to know her story, what she'd been thinking at the time of the shooting, and what she was thinking now, whether she had regrets, any second-thoughts, over what she'd done.

Ten minutes later, the older boy, Qu Peng, ran down to the kitchens to tell his mother that Uncle Philip was fast asleep and could not be woken even when pinched.

CHAPTER EIGHT

Prosecutor Xu had shown even less interest in the pictures on the walls than Philip Ye. She had been more concerned with what Fatty Deng had learned from the neighbours, about Old Man Gao's many fruitless trips to Wukuaishi Police Station looking for assistance in finding his son. Fatty Deng was forming the distinct impression that Prosecutor Xu didn't think much of the police and was going to be deaf to anything that took her away from her intended track. Not even the beating up of Old Man Gao outside the Mayor's Office had left any impression on her.

"This is all about Wukuaishi Station," said Prosecutor Xu, repeating herself for about the twentieth time that day, moving some of Old Man Gao's upended belongings with the toe of her shoe.

Fatty Deng shone his torch at the pictures, trying to make her see. "Prosecutor, some of the people the son has sketched might well have information—"

"We haven't the authority yet to do a full investigation into the failures of Wukuaishi Station," said Prosecutor Xu. "But, once we have dealt properly with Constable Ma, I don't think either Chief Prosecutor Gong or Commissioner Ji could refuse a request to widen the scope of our investigation."

Scope of our investigation?

Fatty Deng wasn't quite sure what she was talking about. He had tried in vain, throughout the long day, to explain to her – once information had trickled in about the circumstances of Old Man

Gao's death – that in respect of police tasking, missing persons reports were unashamedly at the back of the queue. But, because Constable Ma had been based there, Prosecutor Xu had taken vehemently against Wukuaishi Station. She had also begun to openly refer to Constable Ma as a 'peasant'; which, despite the big girl's unfortunate size and distinctly rural looks, Fatty Deng thought a tad unfair.

"This is about justice, Investigator Deng," Prosecutor Xu had said back at the Procuratorate. "People do not just vanish in China. Wukuaishi Station must be held to account for its failings."

Fatty Deng had nearly spilt his tea.

It was his first day. He didn't want to appear a smart-arse. Nor did he want to correct his new boss. She had been kind enough to hire him, to give him the opportunity to get his life back on track. So he kept his mouth shut. But still he had to marvel about how little Prosecutor Xu seemed to know about life outside of her office.

People vanished in China all the time; men, women and children. And for a multitude of reasons. Most went in search of a better salary, learning that a new factory had opened in some far off city. There were also the more adventurous – or more desperate – sorts who were prepared to go into thousands of *yuán* of debt to pay snakeheads to smuggle them to another life in a country far, far away. Then there were the others who wished to escape a difficult family situation or who just preferred a nomadic existence. And finally there were the victims, those taken by force or lured off the street, thrown into a life of slavery, working up to twenty hours a day in conditions that would astonish and appal.

Was this what had happened to Junjie?

Was he now being worked hard somewhere, treated like a dog?

Fatty Deng didn't know. But the neighbours had described the youth as a healthy seventeen year old, of average height and build, with a slow and impressionable mind. He'd be useful to someone. Fatty Deng was convinced that one of the people depicted on Junjie's sketches might have some idea of where he had ended up – that's if he hadn't indeed just jumped on a bus heading out of the city, got himself lost wandering some lonely country lane, and was now lying dead in a ditch.

Fatty Deng had been prepared to say more about the pictures, shining his torch on some of the more unsavoury-looking characters that Junjie had drawn. But then Aunty Li had arrived and all hell had broken loose and the chance was missed forever. Once Prosecutor Xu had tired of the argument and gone –with Aunty Li pursuing her all the way down the stairs – Fatty Deng had had to content himself with taking all of the pictures down from the walls and slipping them inside an evidence bag for consideration at some other time.

On the way home, to celebrate his first day on the job, he picked up some *tàibáijī* – chicken pieces mixed with scallions and chillies in a spicy orange sauce – from a cheap restaurant to eat with his mother. She accepted the food gladly. But, before they could sit down together at the table, she made him apologise for not phoning to tell her he would be late, for making her worry. The TV given to them by Brother Wang had blown up after a couple of days. But she had heard about the shooting on the Yusai Road that morning from the neighbours. So her nerves had been worse than usual that day and she had been worried sick about him. The *tàibáijī* was very good though, worth the slight delay.

"Uncle and Aunty Ho will be over soon," his mother said. "Cards or *májiàng*, the choice is yours tonight."

Not much of a choice. Good neighbour though Aunty Ho was, she would always find a way to cheat, whatever the game.

"I spoke to Philip Ye today," he said, in between mouthfuls.

His mother was amazed. "Āiyā! Has he aged?"

Fatty Deng shook his head. Philip Ye had been as impossibly handsome as ever.

There had been a time, before the earthquake, before the Year of Calamities, when his mother hadn't been able get enough of the doings of the family Ye, their lives a heady mixture of glamour and tragedy. She never missed an episode of what became known in Chengdu as the 'Ye Family Opera'. She was first at the news-stands when Ye Zihao had returned from England, most mysteriously, with a baby in his arms – and with no sign of the mother. The boy seemed so English in his features that a number of muck-raking journalists, sanctioned by the then political establishment in Chengdu, actually accused Ye Zihao, because of his fascination with all things English, of kidnapping a full-blood English baby – a *lǎowài* – to raise as his own.

It was not true, of course, but rumours continued for years and the '*lǎowài*' appellation had stuck. Left in the hands of maids and baby-sitters, not much of the boy was seen as Ye Zihao pursued a punishing work schedule, negotiating the rocky road to financial and political success. But the few photographs that were released of the growing Philip Ye to the clamouring media – Philip Ye sitting at his father's desk, Philip Ye reading *The Romance of the Three Kingdoms*, Philip Ye standing proudly with his father watching the foundations to the new family Ye mansion being laid – pictured a smiling, happy boy with the most marvellous blend of both Western and Eastern features.

"That boy will become a real lady-killer," said Fatty Deng's mother at the time.

A lady-killer – wasn't that the truth.

Some newspapers had it on good authority that before Philip Ye was ten years old, Ye Zihao, to his great pride and amusement, was already receiving letters of proposal from mothers with daughters of about the right age.

But first, before there was to be any discussion about marriage, the young Philip Ye had been sent to a private school and then to a university in England – a decision which had caused much discussion in Chengdu, about the state of education in the city, about whether one day, when Ye Zihao had made enough money and invested it safely abroad, he would make a run for the West himself. Not that life in England had proved golden for Philip Ye. It was said that he and his estranged English mother did not see eye to eye. Furthermore, in his final year at university, a romance with an English girl had been struck by tragedy. First, the newspapers said that his father – by then Mayor of Chengdu – had forbidden the lovers to marry. Fatty Deng's mother had shed many tears over that, over the cruelty of men. And then, with the engagement entered into in spite of his father's wrath, Philip Ye had lost his English flower to some dreadful disease.

"Money can never buy happiness," Fatty Deng's mother had said through her tears, temporarily reversing the only philosophy she'd ever had.

The media continued to follow Philip Ye's progress after returning to China, through four years of law school in Wuhan, his earth-shattering decision to join the police in Chengdu, the embarrassment he'd caused his father by enlisting without permission – not to mention the bust-up between Chief of Police Di and Mayor Ye Zihao over the matter – and how Philip Ye had been thrown out of his father's home to end up living with his half-sister in one of the rooms above her new restaurant, The Silver Tree. It had taken months for Mayor Ye Zihao to forgive Philip Ye, to ask him to come home – a photographer conveniently on hand to capture that very moment when Mayor Ye embraced and took his beloved son back. There was not a dry eye among the women in Chengdu that day, so it was said.

The procession of photographs of Philip Ye came thick and fast then, probably encouraged by Mayor Ye himself, wanting to show the pride he supposedly felt in his son keeping the peace on the city's streets, devoting his life to Chengdu *as the family Ye had always done*. Fatty Deng's mother had kept many of the photographs in a scrap-book – page after page of them: a photograph of Philip Ye directing traffic in his brand new uniform as young women swooned in the background; a photograph of Philip Ye posing at the wheel of a police-car; a photograph of Philip Ye sharing a joke with fellow police in the canteen; a photograph of Philip Ye making an arrest of a pick-pocket, the thief smiling for the camera, glad of his few fleeting moments of fame before being sent to prison.

There were so many photographs that Fatty Deng, a policeman himself back at that time, soon ceased to care.

Who could compete with Philip Ye?

A photograph of Philip Ye taking a young actress out to dinner; a photograph of Philip Ye being promoted to Superintendent Third Class in record-breaking time; a photograph of Philip Ye working for Robbery, no longer in his crisp blue uniform but in the most expensive of handmade suits; a photograph of Philip Ye holding up a merit award for all to see; a photograph of Philip Ye smiling in hospital after having being hurt single-handedly apprehending a trio of house-breakers.

From Superintendent Third Class to Superintendent Second Class to Superintendent First Class, a succession of glossy photographs, in each Philip Ye more handsome, more self-assured, than the last.

"Even the most beautiful woman pales in comparison to him," had said Fatty Deng's mother, studying a photograph of Philip Ye out on the town with Lucy Fu, the stunning daughter of the industrialist Fu Bi – reputedly the richest man in all of Sichuan. "This is why Philip Ye will never marry. What woman can ever look for so long at a face more beautiful than hers? Lucy Fu will dump him, just you wait and see."

Fatty Deng had laughed out loud, annoyed by his mother's stupidity. Surely the woman had not been born who would refuse to marry into the family Ye. However, his mother had been proved right. The romance with Lucy Fu had flared, stuttered and died.

But by then it was already the Year of Calamities. Tensions flared in the Tibet Autonomous Region, the unrest soon spreading to Chengdu. The police, Fatty Deng included, were never busier, shift merging into shift, sleep a forgotten luxury.

Philip Ye's older half-brother, Ye Yong – The Nomad, the society magazines called him – who had married a Tibetan woman against the express wishes of Ye Zihao (or so it was said) was killed with his wife in the April of that year in a mysterious flaming car-wreck on the outskirts of Chengdu. A photograph of the family Ye, sombre, gathered together at the funeral, was printed on the front of every newspaper. This was the last time Lucy Fu was seen at Philip Ye's side.

The horrific shoot-out on the Zhimin East Road came no more than three weeks later. Philip Ye, in Homicide by then, together with his new partner Superintendent Zuo, were ambushed by the suspects they were hunting as soon they got out of their car. Superintendent Zuo went down, badly injured, bullet wounds to the leg. A journalist, soon to be awarded for his skill and good fortune, took the photograph that would serve as the apogee of Chengdu's love affair with Philip Ye. The photograph was a close-up of Philip Ye as he knelt, pistol in hand, protecting Superintendent Zuo with his own body, his face bloodied, cut by flying glass, his physical beauty marred by the stress of the moment, well aware that the suspects were about to rush him, that his life and the life of his partner hung by a thread.

Bang! Bang! Bang! Philip Ye, heroic son of Mayor Ye Zihao, icewater in his veins, the heart of a tiger beating in his chest, refusing to leave his fallen comrade, stands tall and shoots three desperate and wicked men stone dead.

So the caption to the photograph in one of the newspapers read.

However, it was the last hurrah for the family Ye – if it could be called that.

The earthquake struck a few days later, the curse that some said had been cast against the family Ye taking a stranglehold.

Somehow Philip Ye kept his job in the police. Nobody knew how or why. There were no more stories featuring the family Ye, no more photographs of Philip Ye – presumably on the orders of the Shanghai Clique. But by then Fatty Deng's mother had ceased to care about the travails of that family. Fatty Deng was her only child, his job as a police officer the pride, the very foundation, of her life. Having just been accepted into detective school, his life's dream, Fatty Deng had discovered his name on the list of those to be purged. The bad news had hit her like a hammer blow. She had lost her own job as a hotel cleaner through nervous collapse. Fatty Deng, to make ends meet for them both, had been forced to take on every filthy job he could.

"How old is Philip Ye now?" Fatty Deng's mother asked. "He must be thirty-six or thereabouts."

Fatty Deng did not know. He guessed that was about right. He himself was thirty-four, feeling older.

"Still good-looking?" asked his mother.

Fatty Deng nodded. "Women would think so."

There was a knock at the door. It was just after nine. That would be Uncle and Aunty Ho. Fatty Deng was tired but he knew he had to show willing. The Hos had always been good neighbours. Two years back they had given his mother enough money to pay the rent for that month and had never once asked for it back. Good people, the best, despite Aunty Ho cheating in every game she played.

As his mother welcomed them inside, Fatty Deng's mind drifted back to Old Man Gao's room, how Philip Ye had unselfconsciously checked his gold pocket watch by his torch, pulling it from his waistcoat pocket and opening the dial cover with the elegant movement of a well-practised hand. The pocket watch was rumoured to be a rare antique. What was it was worth? Twenty thousand *yuán*? Thirty thousand *yuán*? More? When alive, working as a school janitor, Old Man Gao would have been lucky to take home more than a thousand *yuán* a month. To Fatty Deng this signified all that was wrong with the world.

CHAPTER NINE

E arly morning, the chill of winter was still in the air. The sky was low and dark. Driving into the city, already late for work, Philip Ye took a call from Boxer Tan.

"Mister Ye, there's a rumour that Internal Discipline are about to inspect Wukuaishi Station."

"Just get all your files in order."

"We shouldn't be held responsible for Constable Ma."

"Concentrate on your files, Boxer Tan."

"Supervisor Meng tried to hang himself last night – from the light fitting. He brought half the ceiling down. Broke his leg. There's plaster dust everywhere."

Philip Ye laughed.

"It's not funny, Mister Ye. If Internal Discipline come today—"

"Boxer Tan, stop worrying."

Boxer Tan rang off, despondent.

Philip Ye was still laughing when another call came in. He answered without checking the number, his eyes on the road, the cars moving erratically around him. "Yes?"

"Hey, Policeman – this is Aunty Li. There's big trouble!"

Philip Ye's heart sank, his amusement over Boxer Tan's misfortunes fading away. "What kind of trouble?"

"Big trouble! In Old Man Gao's room. You must come quick!"

And then she was gone.

He realised it was his haste to get away from Wukuaishi last evening that had caused him to be so stupid as to give Aunty Li his card. He drove on for a short while, prepared to ignore her, until he remembered the unease of the night. There had been no more visitations. But he had woken time and time again with the impression that he had unfinished business with Old Man Gao. He swung the car around to the north.

He found Aunty Li in Old Man Gao's room speaking to a young couple. The man and woman stared at him fearfully. Recent country migrants by the dark tone of their skin. Fresh fodder for Aunty Li. The young woman was heavily pregnant.

"Hey, Policeman, where've you been?" asked Aunty Li, visibly irritated, her face flushed. She was dressed in the same motley collection of all-weather clothing of the evening before. "We've been waiting for you. These people need a place to live. The baby's coming soon." She pointed to the young man. "He's fit and strong. He's just got a good job as a groundsman at Chengdu National University up the road. Unlike Old Man Gao, he can pay the rent."

"So what's the problem?" asked Philip Ye, furious that he'd been dragged all this way just to help Aunty Li run her business.

"The problem is that stuck-up bitch!" exclaimed Aunty Li, hands on her hips. "You know, the prosecutor…the fat man's boss-lady… that haughty, cold-faced cow. After you left last night, she came in here, tottering around on her high-heels like some princess, telling me…telling Aunty Li!…what I can and can't do with my own building. I say to her I have a business to run. She tells me there's been a crime and Old Man Gao's room must stay the way it is. I say to her, 'What crime? I can't see any crime.' But she wouldn't listen to me. I felt like twisting her scrawny neck like a chicken."

Philip Ye looked around him. Old Man Gao's meagre belongings had been piled up in one corner. The walls were now bare. "What happened to all the pictures?"

"How should I know, Policeman? Maybe the fat man took them. He was okay. He didn't cause me any trouble. But that skinny perfumed slut—"

"Give these people the room."

Aunty Li clapped her hands together with glee. "You really mean it, Policeman?"

"Yes."

Despite his father's protestations to the contrary, Philip Ye felt there wasn't anything to be investigated here – certainly no criminal conspiracy featuring Mayor Cang. And, putting aside his feelings of unease that he wasn't yet done with the spirit of Old Man Gao, he wasn't going to return to this dump by choice. Nor did he think that Prosecutor Xu or Fatty Deng would bother to do so either. Better a young family used the room and put a roof over their head.

Philip Ye walked out, wanting nothing more to do with Aunty Li. But she followed him, grabbing something off the pile of Old Man Gao's belongings as she did so.

"Wait, Policeman!" She pushed a tatty school exercise book into his hands.

"What's this?"

"That fool boy used to draw in it all the time. You can give it to the fat man so he doesn't have to come back," she said.

Then she was gone, back to the young couple, certain to fleece them blind for the room.

Philip Ye flicked through a couple of pages, seeing rough charcoal sketches. Junjie probably carried it about with him as an aide-mémoire. He would refer to it when he returned home to draw what would become the finished version. In his car, Philip Ye tossed it to one side, forgetting about it in an instant. He started the engine, pushed out into the traffic, and headed off at speed.

In the office, Superintendent Zuo, usually long gone by now, was sitting at his desk writing, surgical mask firmly in place, the mask his considered defence against the influenza outbreak that was spreading across the city. Hooded eyes stared at Philip Ye, red-rimmed and tired. Superintendent Zuo looked all of his forty-five years.

"I hear you caught some trade last night," said Philip Ye.

"Tibetan Quarter," said Superintendent Zuo. "Some mutt – no ID – got a knife put through his neck. Scorpion tattoo on his arm. Never seen anything like it before – the tattoo, I mean. Don't think it's gang-related but I've asked Organised Crime to take a look. And Narcotics. Witnesses say he's ethnic Yi. Don't know his name. He had a girlfriend with a similar tattoo…also ethnic Yi. Both arrived on the bus from Xichang last week. I am told she has a temper and a liking for sharp objects."

"Your kind of woman?"

"I'll let you know when I find her."

"Coming to the party this evening?"

"Can't get cover," replied Superintendent Zuo, shuffling his papers into one pile, calling it a night. "Xia and Pu at Tiaosanta Station were my best bets. But Xia says he's going this time and Pu has just fallen over with the flu."

"My father is cooking Tibetan spicy mutton."

"Nice – but I've called everyone I know. Anyway I need to go hunting for this crazy Yi girl tonight. I'm expecting her to break cover and run."

"Where are your priorities?"

"Where are yours? Are you going to do the decent thing and marry her? She's good for ten kids if your father is willing to pay the fines."

Philip Ye was momentarily perplexed. Then he realised Superintendent Zuo was speaking about Constable Ma.

"The Procuratorate picked her up this morning," Superintendent Zuo continued. "It seems her pistol has gone missing and Commissioner Ho, in fine form as usual, has disowned her. Oh, and the Procuratorate has been chasing you as well this morning. There are five messages on your desk, each one slightly more hysterical than the last. I told them I didn't know where you were, that I didn't have your phone number, that I was not your fucking mother, and that frankly the PSB would be better off without you."

"You are such a charmer."

"Chief Prosecutor Gong wants you for a photo-shoot. You're to kiss and make-up with the PAP."

Unsurprised, Philip Ye unlocked his desk and brought out the small cardboard box he placed there the day before.

"What's that?" asked Superintendent Zuo, standing and putting on his coat. "A gift for that PAP idiot you decked yesterday?"

"No, Constable Ma's pistol and a copy of the armoury log from last September."

Superintendent Zuo whistled. "It won't be enough to save her job. She's not pretty enough…not camera-friendly like you. No one wants her patrolling the streets anymore."

"She was stupid," said Philip Ye.

"Stupid for not realising the old man wanted to die, or stupid for not being born a little easier on the eye?"

"Both."

An hour later, Philip Ye found Fatty Deng slouched against the outside wall of the Procuratorate smoking a cigarette, looking disconsolate, wearing the same bad suit from the day before. He stood and brightened somewhat when he saw Philip Ye approaching.

"I hear you've got Constable Ma inside," said Philip Ye, not in the mood for preamble.

Fatty Deng's downcast expression returned. "We picked her up just after dawn. It was some to-do, Mister Ye. I could have collected her peaceably and driven her in on my own. But Prosecutor Xu wanted to be there…as did Commissioner Ji and some of his boys."

Commissioner Ji was Head of PSB Internal Discipline as well as Shanghai Clique. A cold fish, Philip Ye had never found the need to exchange a single word with him.

"Two of the Internal Discipline boys tried to put cuffs on her," continued Fatty Deng. "But she laid them both out cold. Didn't know what to think about Commissioner Ji before then but he had the good sense to back off and just order her to get into the back of the car. They're working her over now, trying to get her to speak. Chief Inspector Gong has even slapped her about a bit but she's having none of it. Hasn't said a word…not a word. I couldn't stand it so I came out here for a smoke. Her pistol's gone missing, Mister Ye. And Commissioner Ho of Robbery has given us a statement saying that he's never even seen her before. He doesn't know how or why she came to be armed or who posted her to Wukuaishi Station. We're now thinking that she brought a pistol from her time with the police in Pujiang County. Prosecutor Xu is looking to charge her with every offence she can. All this and it's only my second day, Mister Ye."

Philip Ye held the small cardboard box out to him. "Inside you will find Constable Ma's pistol, my statement relating how and when I disarmed her, and where the weapon has been securely kept until now. There's also a copy of the armoury log for the issue of that weapon last September. I was concerned the log might go missing overnight. You will find Commissioner Ho's signature most prominently and legibly displayed."

"Fuck me," said Fatty Deng, taking a last drag of his cigarette before throwing it to the ground.

"What I can't tell you is why she was armed or why she was posted to Wukuaishi Station. I'll leave that to you to discover. Do you want the box or do you wish me to take it inside?"

Philip Ye watched the cogs turn behind Fatty Deng's eyes. Always the investigator's dilemma: is it worth uncovering what your boss might prefer you do not find?

But Fatty Deng took the box, which pleased Philip Ye. Fatty Deng had some strength, some integrity.

"Constable Ma may have poor judgement," said Philip Ye, "but she is not a criminal."

"Yes, Mister Ye – I agree."

"And Commissioner Ho is Shanghai Clique so…"

"Absolutely, Mister Ye," agreed Fatty Deng, grinning.

CHAPTER TEN

Inside the Procuratorate, Philip Ye was kept well away from the interrogation rooms. An unfriendly clerk took him to a conference suite on the first floor. Captain Wang of the PAP was already waiting, sitting in full dress uniform, his posture straight-backed, very military. Philip Ye took a seat opposite him, content with the silence. Captain Wang had gone within himself, face impassive, revealing nothing of what he was thinking. Philip Ye suspected he was well practiced at this, except in those times when he had had so much to drink that what was so tightly contained within forced its way out. Occasionally, Captain Wang's eyes would subtly flick over to where Philip Ye was sitting. But, apart from those odd occasions, he may as well have been a statue.

Philip Ye used the time to meditate more on the problem of Constable Ma. After giving her pistol and the copy of the armoury log over to Fatty Deng, he wondered if he had any further duty to her. He was coming to the tentative conclusion that the visitation by the ghost of Old Man Gao could possibly be an expression of forgiveness toward Constable Ma, and him the instrument of that forgiveness. It made sense, a great deal of sense, if one chose to ignore the inconsistent chronology of the ghost appearing before the shooting event. But Philip Ye was nagged by a feeling of incompleteness, that there was more to this story to come to light. Why had she been keeping her pistol on the safety? Why had she been expecting trouble? And why was she refusing to talk to Chief Prosecutor Gong?

He was still considering all of these questions when Chief Prosecutor Gong walked in, followed closely by a young official photographer. Chief Prosecutor Gong was sweating and flustered, his tie slightly askew. But he greeted them both cheerfully, shaking each of them by the hand.

"Captain Wang…Superintendent Ye…I am glad you could both attend, that you have put your past differences aside."

The photograph was then taken with Chief Prosecutor Gong standing between them beaming at the camera. He explained, quite straight-faced, that the caption would read, 'New Combined Task Force for Peoples's Police and PAP'. The explanatory text to follow would announce that exercises had already begun, one of which had already been caught on camera at the time of the shooting, Captain Wang playing the part of a drunken trouble-maker jumping out from the crowd.

It was nonsense but someone would believe it.

Outside the Procuratorate, Philip Ye turned up the collar of his raincoat against the deteriorating weather. The tops of the tallest buildings were obscured now by a thick mist and a slight drizzle was beginning to fall. Captain Wang touched his arm.

"Superintendent, I want to apologise for—"

"Captain, understand this," said Philip Ye, brushing Captain Wang's hand away. "You may have been a king in Tibet, but in Chengdu you're just another idiot in a uniform. Abuse a police officer again and you'll end up in a hole in the ground."

Philip Ye left him standing there, blinking in surprise.

But, in the car, driving back to PSB HQ, Philip Ye began to regret his words. Captain Wang was interesting. There were so few people he had met who were comfortable with silence. In China, it seemed, almost everybody had something to say and could not help saying it at every opportune moment of the day. But Captain Wang had maintained his self-control and his fortitude in the midst of great loss of face – at least until they were both outside of the Procuratorate. It would have been useful to learn some more about him.

Back in the solitude of the office, Philip Ye set about the tedium of reviewing all of his current files, making notes, trying to be creative with the few leads he had, struggling to conjure up new paths of investigation. However, each and every case was dying its own peculiar lingering death. Suspects had either never been identified or were long gone, or the evidence, against those suspects he was certain of, extremely weak. And one suspect was so well-connected that the Criminal Procuracy Section at the Procuratorate had advised against picking him up for interview until there was evidence that could be deemed overwhelmingly substantial – which was never going to happen.

He had received no communications from the afterlife for any of these cases: no visitations, no spectral forms, and no whispers in the ear. He had no idea why this was. He had asked for help enough times. He had actually taken the photograph of one young dead girl to a local Daoist temple and had prayed and lit incense in the hope that she would appear before him. But nothing. Not a word. Not even a cool breeze that would raise the hairs on his neck. It was enough to make him very sceptical of Prime Minister Zi Chan's contention, back in the 6th Century BCE, that violent deaths give rise to unhappy ghosts. More likely that the spirits of the dead from the files on his desk no longer cared about their earthly lives – or earthly modes of justice for that matter. Or maybe they were content to await their assailants' appearance before the spirit-judges in the courts of the Netherworld.

By mid-afternoon, however, he felt he had made some progress: a discrepancy in a witness statement in one case he hadn't noticed before; a newly delivered phone record creating a fresh line of enquiry in another.

Then he took a call. The voice was hesitant, weak. "Philip… would you visit me this afternoon?"

"Of course, Commissioner Wei."

Commissioner Wei had arrived with the rest of the plague from Shanghai. He had taken over a Homicide Department that was undermanned – more so after The Purge – lacking in morale, and in desperate need of leadership. Superintendent Zuo was still at home then recovering from gun-shot wounds. Philip Ye, though he would admit it to no one, was still in shock from shooting three men dead, their ghosts visiting him one after the other, on consecutive nights, having nothing to say, their manner more curious than threatening. None of the Homicide detectives were hopeful about the future. They were all summoned from their respective stations across Chengdu and squeezed into Commissioner Wei's office. Commissioner Wei sat behind his desk, hunched over like an angry bear, glaring at each of them in turn. "What we do is hunt," he said. "If you do not want to take part in this hunt I shall understand. It is not for everybody."

Two eventually did resign, unable to cope with the new intensity Commissioner Wei brought to homicide investigations, as well as the modern protocols and techniques he demanded to which they were all required to adhere. Much more than a breath of fresh air, Commissioner Wei proved to be a human dynamo, smoking constantly, working at a feverish pace from early morning until late at night. In this one instance at least, Shanghai's loss was Chengdu's gain. Not an easy man to get to know, Commissioner Wei avoided friendships outside of the office – which included the rest of the Shanghai Clique. But in the office he was supportive, ever-willing to offer good advice and never prepared to give up on any victim. All unsolved cases were to remain open. And he remained deaf to determined protests from Chief Di, the Procuratorate and a small delegation from the Chengdu Political and Legal Committee, concerned about how the city's clear-up rates would compare to every other metropolis in China.

After two months of working for Commissioner Wei, Philip Ye said, at home one evening, "Father, though he is Shanghai Clique, I really admire this man."

Ye Zihao slapped him hard across the face, the betrayal so deep and so vast he would not speak to his son for three days.

Philip Ye left the office before his shift was done, fearing Commissioner Wei was ailing. In a private room at the Sichuan Cancer Hospital, Commissioner Wei was being treated for Acute Myeloid Leukaemia – an aggressive cancer of the blood – with a potent mixture of chemotherapy and traditional herbal medicine. Nobody knew what the prognosis was. Commissioner Wei wasn't talking. Most blamed his constant smoking and the exhausting hours he worked – not yet forty-two, he looked ten years older – but Philip Ye was more inclined to point the finger at Commissioner Wei's family, his wife and son. They had refused to travel to Chengdu with Commissioner Wei. They had preferred to keep their old lives in Shanghai, to effectively break off all contact with him – his grief over this betrayal being as sure a cause of his disease as his heavy intake of nicotine.

Philip Ye found him propped up in bed, reading, his weight loss and hair loss in the last few weeks dramatic, his suffering under the poisonous treatment regime profound. His eyes were still bright though and his welcome fulsome.

"Thank you, Philip, for coming…thank you."

Philip Ye passed him a gift he had picked up on the way, a couple of bright red packets of Chunghwa cigarettes, Commissioner Wei's favourite. Scented with plums, they had been the preferred brand of Mao Zedong. If the Panda cigarettes smoked by Chief Di and the

Chunghwa cigarettes smoked by Commissioner Wei could be considered as metaphors for the absorption of Deng Xiaoping Theory and Mao Zedong Thought, then Chengdu PSB – as the Americans would say – had all the bases covered.

Commissioner Wei accepted the cigarettes without comment. He held up the document he was reading. "Look at this."

Philip Ye took the document from him and sat down next to the bed. It was an internal memo from the Procuratorate printed on expensive glossy paper. The Procuratorate appeared to have more money than sense these days. He quickly scanned the cover, seeing nothing that should immediately grab his interest: good news on a few recently tried cases; yet more legal guidance offered by the Supreme People's Procuratorate in Beijing on the correct interpretation of anti-bribery law.

"Other side," said Commissioner Wei.

Philip Ye turned over the memo and saw a large announcement for a new member of staff. There was a photograph of a young woman sitting behind a desk, her hair pulled back conservatively behind her head. He could see nothing of her figure, but she looked to him the model of an ambitious lawyer, immaculately turned out, her cosmetics evident but restrained.

"Prosecutor Xu Ya," said Commissioner Wei.

"So it says."

"Attractive, isn't she?"

"I suppose."

"Just transferred in from the Procuratorate in Chongqing."

"Ah."

"Do you remember her?"

"Should I?" asked, Philip Ye, passing the memo back to Commissioner Wei.

"She studied law at Wuhan at the same time as you."

"Is that so?" said Philip Ye, puzzled. He had no memory of her at all.

Commissioner Wei tried to sit up straighter in bed. Philip Ye helped him plump up the pillows.

"She is the future, Philip. Thirty-three years of age, fluent in English, studied comparative law in America before Wuhan, destined in a few years to be a judge."

Destined to be judge.

Commissioner Wei said this not as a possibility but as a certainty. Philip Ye wondered who on the Chengdu Political and Legal Committee, which decided such important appointments and promotions, was the source of this information. Probably Secretary Wu, the Committee's chairman.

It was indisputable that the judiciary in China had no choice but to evolve. It was no longer appropriate to recruit judges straight from the army; men and women often with little education and certainly no grounding in the law. Once, such former senior officers had served a use, the military discipline supposedly giving them the backbone to make tough but necessary decisions – *and the good sense to follow orders when required*. But, as China had become more outward and internationalist in its viewpoint, and its legal system had developed at breakneck pace so it could meet acceptable international standards (or at least give the impression that this was so), a new approach had been needed. Prior to 1983, no legal training at all had been required to become a judge – and unfortunately many of those historical appointees still lingered in post. But, these days, legal qualifications and experience was a requirement; and, since the Judges Law of 2001, prospective judges were required to pass the National Judicial Examination as well. This did not mean there were not some who slipped onto the judges' bench through the back door, but things were better than they had been.

"What is our interest in her, sir?"

"Philip, I wish you to extend protection to her, as you protected that big farmer's daughter yesterday. Don't think I didn't see you brawling on TV. I was so ashamed. I spend most of my day here trying to convince the nurses that you are not the man of their dreams. But young women these days have so little ambition. They see a grown man fighting on TV – a man who should have more decorum, who has been taught better – and squeal with delight."

"Why does Prosecutor Xu need protection?"

"It is not important…let us just say that she is considered, at present, vulnerable."

"Vulnerable to what or to whom?"

"I cannot answer that."

"Is she family?"

"No…no…nothing like that."

"Is this you asking me or Secretary Wu?"

"Does it matter, Philip?"

"It does to me."

"Then I ask it as a personal favour. Prosecutor Xu has taken an apartment in Tranquil Mountain Pavilions. Do you know it?"

"Yes, of course, but—"

"Philip, all I ask is that you keep a watchful eye over her – at a distance. She is not to know."

"But—"

"You will find a way."

Philip Ye nodded, accepting the inevitable. "Am I required to like her?" he asked, mindful of Prosecutor Xu's present persecution of Constable Ma.

But the question remained unanswered. Commissioner Wei was asleep, his energy spent, the Procuratorate memo clutched tightly in his hand. On his way out of the hospital, Philip Ye was so deep in thought, so troubled by the unusual request, that he didn't notice the group of giggling nurses that brushed by him in the corridor.

CHAPTER ELEVEN

Early evening, the grim, damp, cold and misty day turned into an equally grim, damp, cold and misty night. Fatty Deng sat in a quiet bar, glumly drinking a beer. He was not ready to go home quite yet. He had known it was going to be hard, working a proper full-time job again. But during the long five years of doing any sort of dirty job he could get his hands on, he had forgotten the bad feelings involved in policing, in investigation work, the sense of never really succeeding at anything, the profound depression that could wash over you from time to time. Working for the Procuratorate was infinitely better than working for Brother Wang and Freddie Yun. It was all just a bit of a shock to be back on the front line. And, to cap it all, he owed Philip Ye a favour for the contents of that cardboard box – a favour that could be called in at any time. It was not the position in which he wanted to find himself at the end of his second day.

The police brutality case was over, such as it was. He had called them out of the interrogation room and placed the cardboard box down on a table before them. Chief Prosecutor Gong reached for the pistol, Prosecutor Xu the statement made by Philip Ye, and Commissioner Ji the copy of the armoury log. Chief Prosecutor Gong's face turned an odd puce colour, Prosecutor Xu bit her lip and Commissioner Ji said pretty much what everybody was thinking. "Commissioner Ho is a lying, drunken bastard." He then slapped Fatty Deng on the back. "Good work, Investigator...good work. Now leave Commissioner Ho to me."

Commissioner Ji then left to return to PSB Headquarters, presumably to confront Commissioner Ho, and Chief Prosecutor Gong and Prosecutor Xu locked themselves away in an office to discuss what else could be done. It surprised Fatty Deng to get praise from Commissioner Ji. Shanghai Clique he might be, but Fatty Deng decided Commissioner Ji was a decent sort – especially as it was the only praise he got.

Fatty Deng glanced into the interrogation room. Constable Ma was sitting at the table, her head slightly bowed, holding the inflamed side of her face where Chief Prosecutor Gong had struck her. Fatty Deng wanted to hate the prosecutor for his violence but could not. There was something about Constable Ma, something unsettling, something profoundly irritating. He didn't know whether it was her obstinate silence, her intimidating size, or the dark cloud of misery that seemed to hang about her, but he couldn't spend long in her presence without feeling sick. He chose instead to wait in the corridor outside Prosecutor Xu's office for something to happen.

When Prosecutor Xu did return, almost a full half-hour later, she wasn't best pleased. Fatty Deng followed her inside her office. As she sat at her desk he noticed a slight tinge of red on her cheeks – a flush of temper – thinking how attractive this made her look.

"It is an impossible situation," she said. "Our hands are tied. I could charge Constable Ma under Article 22 of the Gun Management Regs, for discharging her pistol in the midst of a crowded street, but... and this is the problem...Article 20 of the Criminal Law provides her with a useful defence and..." She threw her hands up in exasperation. "All I can do is write a recommendation for Constable Ma's transfer back to the police in Pujiang County. So we will be hopefully rid of her by the end of next week. She shall be on suspension until then."

Which, though Fatty Deng didn't quite follow all the legal stuff, was what he had already figured out would happen.

"I have an idea though," said Prosecutor Xu, her mood lightening in an instant, her lovely eyes shining. "In Chongqing we have begun auditing the city police stations. I wasn't directly involved but the theory is simple. So, apart from writing Constable Ma's recommendation for transfer, I am going to start work on an audit proposal today to be put on Chief Prosecutor Gong's desk by Monday morning. We will bring all the police stations in Chengdu under proper managerial control."

Good luck with that, thought Fatty Deng.

"And this audit won't just cover personnel management," continued Prosecutor Xu, "but all of the functions carried out by the police."

She's lost her mind, thought Fatty Deng.

If the Procuratorate was going to get into a wrestling match with the PSB there would only ever be one winner. Prosecutor Xu could quote as many laws and regulations as she liked but the one unwritten rule of law enforcement is that you fuck with the police at your peril. And that applied to the Courts and the Procuratorate as well as the criminals. Police have long memories. Police bear grudges. Police make bad enemies.

Prosecutor Xu started scribbling notes down on a pad at lightning speed, Constable Ma already forgotten. Fatty Deng was upset she hadn't even asked him how he had come by the cardboard box and its contents. Even if he didn't truly deserve it, a little bit of praise from her would not have gone amiss. He was about to sit down and take the weight off his legs when she suddenly looked up and pointed at him with her pen.

"Go and make a snap inspection of Wukuaishi Station. That will wake them up."

His mouth dropped open.

"You were police once, Investigator Deng. You know every trick in the book, I expect. Just go in, have a good nose around. We're not really pushing our brief. The Legal and Disciplinary Section exists to make sure the judiciary, prosecutors *and* the police follow lawful procedures. You're bound to find something wrong with how they do things there. Start with how they record complaints from people who just walk in off the street. This was how Old Man Gao was let down in the first instance. Monday morning we'll put our heads together to finalise the audit plan. What you find today will give us all the justification we need to go ahead."

"Shouldn't we speak to—?"

"No, you can go in on my authority. It's just a fishing trip, so nothing to worry about. I spoke to Commissioner Ji the other day. He says he is all for new ideas." She waved him out of the door. "Go! Go! And get me some good news."

Outside her office, he leaned up against the wall, his bowels turned to water. Did she understand what she had just asked of him? Did she have a fucking clue?

Unlike most police forces around the world, in China the police had a whole multitude of tasks to worry about. Yes, they had to go out on the streets and keep the peace (always remembering to complete the necessary paperwork on their return), but they also had to: maintain traffic safety and respond promptly to accidents; fight and prevent fires; control the use of firearms, knives and explosives; supervise regulated occupations and the licensing of clubs and bars; provide personnel to guard installations and important personages; administer the *hùkǒu* – the household registration system; deal with matters of nationality, with foreigners coming in and out of the country (who was staying in what hotel and so on); enforce certain penalties against offenders and supervise those offenders on parole; control and monitor parades and demonstrations; and just about anything else that could be thrown at them when the shit hit the fan.

It was true that not all of these things were being done by the officers at Wukuaishi Station. The strutting PAP did a lot of the guarding of important buildings. And there were dedicated fire personnel with their big, fancy bright red trucks ready to deal with major fires. But pretty much everything else would be happening in and about Wukuaishi Station. How in Heaven's name was he going to inspect all of that?

He pushed the nightmare to one side for the moment, remembering Constable Ma was still in the building. Someone was going to have to take care of her. Prosecutor Xu's sharp but restless mind had already moved on to more fertile ground. He went down to the interrogation room and found Constable Ma unmoved, the atmosphere in the room oppressive, suffocating.

"You're free to go," he said.

He backed away as she stood, not sure that he had the strength to match her if she turned violent. He pointed her toward the exit, following her to make sure she left the building safely. The idiot security guards gave her lots of space, demonstrating they had at least a modicum of common sense. Outside, the drizzle had turned to light rain. She had no coat. No one had thought to tell her to bring one.

Fatty Deng said to her, "You're still on suspension. By the end of the week you'll be transferred back to Pujiang County."

If she heard him, she gave no sign of it. She trudged off into the rain without looking back. He began to feel guilty. If he was going to make his inspection he could have dropped her off. She lived but a brief walk from Wukuaishi Station. He didn't even know if she had the bus fare to get home. But he reminded himself that he had problems enough, that she wasn't his responsibility. And, perhaps more importantly, he wasn't sure the ageing suspension in his car would support the weight of both of them.

· · ·

By lunchtime, Fatty Deng was sitting in a small restaurant within sight of Wukuaishi Station, trying to plan his next move. He had retrieved his old briefcase from the boot of the car to make himself look more official, had written a few notes in his notebook about what he was trying to achieve and had consumed a bowl of hotpot to settle his stomach. He had also bought himself a raincoat to cover his suit, much as he'd seen Philip Ye wearing. But his raincoat was so cheap-looking in comparison that he had laughed to himself when he'd tried it on, staring into the mirror, imagining the contempt on Philip Ye's face if they ever met again. Then his laughter had ceased when he remembered the favour he owed Philip Ye for the contents of that cardboard box. It was well known the family Ye rarely did kindnesses. Something was always expected in return.

He finished the last mouthfuls of his hotpot and walked out into the rain. In a few thumping heartbeats he was stepping over the threshold of Wukuaishi Station with his shiny Procuratorate badge and ID open in his hand.

"This is a Procuratorate snap inspection!" he announced forcefully to the young constable manning the reception desk.

The constable's eyes rolled to the back of his head. He slipped off his chair and hit the floor with a thud. A few minutes later, Baby Wu was being revived with some tea, Fatty Deng feeling worse than ever.

"It's not your fault," said Boxer Tan. "He's my cousin's son. I got him into the police as a favour. He's good with people, doesn't bat an eye at the sight of blood or vomit, but sudden shocks are a problem for him. Are you going to put this in your report?"

Fatty Deng shook his head. "I don't even know what to report. This is only my second day."

"Last I heard you were working as door security for a gay bar in the city," said Boxer Tan.

"That was three years ago," said Fatty Deng. "The job was good but I had to quit. My mother doesn't like me out late at night. Her nerves…"

"It was bad what they did to you," said Boxer Tan, meaning The Purge. He helped Baby Wu to sit up, while shooing away a couple of female officers trying to fuss over the young constable. "You were at Wangjiang Road, weren't you? How did you get the Procuratorate job?"

"Don't really know," admitted Fatty Deng. "Dumb luck, I guess. Maybe I interview well."

"The Legal and Disciplinary Section?"

Fatty Deng nodded, hating himself. "They wanted someone who

understood policing, someone who'd also been out of the job a few years. No close ties, if you understand what I mean. This morning we were just dealing with Constable Ma and suddenly I'm sent here. Prosecutor Xu – she's new, from Chongqing – thinks the police in Chengdu are running out of control."

"The police in Chongqing are a bunch of fuck-wits compared to us – nothing but blood-sucking bandits."

"I know, but she doesn't listen," admitted Fatty Deng. "She's nice though, and really good-looking." He opened his briefcase and took out the Procuratorate memo he had initially picked up to show his mother. He passed it to Boxer Tan and pointed out her photograph.

Boxer Tan whistled. "She married?"

Fatty Deng shrugged. "Don't know anything about her."

"What's going to happen to Constable Ma?"

"Suspension and transfer back to Pujiang County."

Boxer Tan sighed. "I suppose it's for the best." He left Baby Wu to recover in the chair and took Fatty Deng to one side. "Look, what do you want to do this afternoon? How do you want to play this stupid inspection?"

Fatty Deng knew Boxer Tan from old. The man was a legend. He had got his name fifteen years before when he had been confronted in the street by five thugs wanting to try out some *wǔshù* moves they had learned from the movies. Cool as you like, Boxer Tan had put them down one by one with his fists.

"How about if you just show me round," suggested Fatty Deng. "I'll make some notes about the usual problems …not enough training, shitty equipment, computers breaking down all the time, low morale, not enough storage space for paper files, evidence lost being moved back and forth to the Procuratorate and the courts, and not enough hours in the day to do everything that has to be done. I'll even mention the slow response times from the Procuratorate when legal advice is needed or formal authority required for an arrest. And then on Monday morning I'll do my best to explain to Prosecutor Xu how the world really works."

"Telling the truth might lose you your new job, Fatty."

"She might have forgotten about this audit by then and be working on something else. She's really smart but a bit flighty, I think."

Relieved, Boxer Tan asked Fatty Deng if he could keep hold of the memo to show Prosecutor Xu's photograph to the other guys at the station. Fatty Deng agreed. He could get another for his mother anytime. He also felt very proud that his new boss didn't resemble the back end of a bus.

Boxer Tan gave Fatty Deng the full tour. It felt good to Fatty Deng – too good, perhaps – walking around a police station again. Painful memories of loss arose in him, the feeling of a united purpose, of a camaraderie he'd never experience again. They even had a laugh together when Boxer Tan pointed out the damage to the ceiling in the office where Supervisor Meng had tried to hang himself.

"If he'd told us what he was going to do we could have helped him," said Boxer Tan, shaking his head.

At the end of the tour, having made copious notes – all of which had been read and agreed by Boxer Tan – Fatty Deng raised the subject of Old Man Gao and his missing son.

"What do you think really happened to Junjie?"

"Personally, I think he's dead," replied Boxer Tan, seriously. "And, I think, in his heart, Old Man Gao knew it too. That's why he stepped out in front of Constable Ma."

Fatty Deng had the same depressing feeling. But, after the tour was done, very pleased with the notes he'd taken and the friend he'd made in Boxer Tan – they had promised to meet up for a drink in a week or two – Fatty Deng sat in his car and sorted through the pictures he'd removed from Old Man Gao's walls. He wasn't content with the obvious explanation that Junjie had walked off and got himself lost, or that he'd been picked off the streets by a recruiting gang and taken to some hellhole to work eighteen hours a day as slave labour without anyone noticing. It didn't smell right. Someone somewhere surely would have seen something.

He checked his watch. It wasn't even late afternoon. He could go home and put his feet up, or he could go hunting.

He picked out a couple of Junjie's pictures where the faces had been drawn with enough detail to be instantly recognisable, the locations in the background too. They were mostly near to where Junjie lived or in the vicinity of the campus of Chengdu National University just up the road. He began to walk the familiar streets of Wukuaishi with Junjie's pictures in hand, the pictures protected from the rain by plastic wallets he'd filched from the Procuratorate for just this very purpose.

Three miserable hours later he had stumbled into the bar with sore feet, feeling very sorry for himself. He had discovered nothing, found nobody from the pictures. Fatty Deng had asked around about Junjie. Some people had known him and been willing to talk. But none had any idea about what had happened to him. Most had only wanted to comment on the cruel way Old Man Gao had been shot down by the police.

It was the elderly in the main who were happy to speak to him, the young rushing past him, unwilling to be stopped by a fat man in a dodgy raincoat, their phones glued to their ears. Chengdu had been so much better in the old days, the elderly told him. In the old days everybody knew everybody else's business. In the old days proper respect was shown by the youth to their parents and grandparents. In the old days the people hadn't given themselves over to the obsession with making money. In the old days the city had been a beautiful place before the traffic had clogged up the streets and the air filled with smog and before the massive redevelopment that had made Chengdu as ugly as every other modern Chinese metropolis.

"What's one missing boy among all this shit?" asked one particularly bitter old man, laden down as he was with his groceries for the weekend.

What *was* one missing boy among all this shit?

A valid question, Fatty Deng mused, sipping his beer. A valid question indeed.

CHAPTER TWELVE

Friday

The parties had been Philip Ye's idea.

After the earthquake, after his father's house-arrest, after the arrival of the Shanghai Clique, Philip Ye had become worried for his father's mental health, the signs of a deep despondency creeping in. So he had made the suggestion to his father.

"They will not come," was Ye Zihao's bitter reply.

"They will."

"The maids have run away."

"You will cook and I will serve drinks."

"There will have to be rules," said Ye Zihao, not wanting his reputation or his house sullied despite his loneliness.

"Of course."

"No women."

"Agreed."

"Suits only, no uniforms."

"Agreed."

"The more senior officers only."

"Agreed."

"All alcohol will be consumed in the English way, water only with spirits if required, wine and beer in the appropriate glasses."

"Agreed."

"And no gambling."

"Agreed also."

"Philip, do you think they will really come?"

"I do."

And they did. A trickle at first, but come they did. Philip Ye was relieved to have correctly judged the mood of Chengdu PSB, the deep-seated resentments left by the random purge of the ranks to make way for the influx from Shanghai. And, as the monthly parties began to swell in size – the Shanghai Clique either too weak as yet (or too uncertain) to punish or warn off the attendees – Ye Zihao's fleeting brush with despondency became just a distant memory, to be replaced with a real inner fire, a firm resolve that one day he would return to power.

Of the old guard only Chief Di was never seen at the house. Nothing to do with the Shanghai Clique, this was personal. He and Ye Zihao had been the greatest of friends once, inseparable, until a woman had come between them.

The Ye family mansion was located in the prestigious Wuhou District of Chengdu. On his return from his posting at the Embassy in England, and after he had made enough money from his local business dealings, Ye Zihao had bought a large tract of land in the city. After demolishing what was there before, an architect was employed – flown in especially from Hong Kong – and a gang of highly-skilled workmen recruited from all across China. Ye Zihao had himself constructed an exact replica of a Victorian manor house he had once visited on his travels in England.

The house soon became the talk of Chengdu. It was named by the people as the 'Ye family mansion' though out of the extensive family only Ye Zihao and his half-English son lived there. The house made Ye Zihao a man to watch, a man with international credentials – a man soon to be mayor. There were those who criticized the blatant Englishness of the house until, that is, the first tours were organized for friends and business partners. They saw the interior and were very pleased. It was absent of Victorian soft-furnishings and clutter, decorated sparsely instead in the Chinese style: a few ornaments here and there, the occasional exquisite watercolour hanging on a wall. And the house had the capacity to still impress today, many years on, minus its household staff, with only the Na brothers now answering the door and serving drinks, and with Ye Zihao cooking in the kitchen, holding court as he did so, always with a story to tell, a lecture to give – as passionate as he'd always been, sometimes irrationally so.

"Mayor Cang had that poor old man murdered," said Ye Zihao to the mass of men squeezed into every corner of the kitchen. "Shot him down in the street like a dog for having the nerve to try to deliver a petition. That may be how it's done in Shanghai but in Chengdu…"

And so on.

His words had force, his perspective seemingly eminently plausible. It made no difference that his audience was mainly comprised of police officers who already knew the facts. Or thought they did. Many would leave the party that night distrusting their own minds. And not a few would convince themselves that Ye Zihao had a point.

Dismayed with the continuation of his father's obsession with the death of Old Man Gao, and with the smoke from so many cigarettes choking his lungs, Philip Ye took his glass of mineral water out into the garden. The rain had lessened, a heavy night mist come down. He found his two friends, Supervisors Cai and Long, standing under a canopy at the edge of the large ornamental lake. Supervisor Cai was throwing chunks of stale bread he had brought from home. He was fascinated by the massive silver fish that rose up from the depths to gobble up the bread under the light cast by the coloured lanterns the Na brothers had hung about the garden. The fish were mirror carp, not indigenous to China, imported at great expense from a lake in England. Supervisor Cai, like most everybody else attending the party, lived in a high-rise apartment block. He loved the house, the expanse of gardens, and the fish so much there were sometimes tears in his eyes.

Supervisor Cai was known throughout the PSB by his nickname of 'Strike Hard' after his very vocal opposition to the periodic Strike Hard politically-inspired anti-crime campaigns, thankfully not so common as of late. It was not that he was viscerally opposed to the mass round-ups of suspects, or the parading of these suspects before crowds of people, or the fast-track 'kangaroo courts' that convicted these suspects sometimes on the flimsiest of evidence. Supervisor Cai just believed such campaigns were a waste of time and money, detrimental to true crime-fighting, taking him and the rest of the police away from their proper day-to-day tasks – the tasks that kept them close to the people, gaining useful intelligence, and disrupting criminal activity at its root. The crime statistics backed up Supervisor Cai's view but few others were so vocal in their criticism of these campaigns – including Philip Ye. Supervisor Cai, though, was considered untouchable. He had been working narcotics in the city for fifteen years. He knew things – many, many secrets. Important people feared him, within and without the Shanghai Clique.

Supervisor Long was even more of an unknown quantity. 'Clever Long' to his friends, he not only understood the complex mechanisms of economic crime, but he also possessed unparalleled political nous, never moving against any suspect until he got the green-light from above and beyond Chengdu, from one of his shadowy contacts in the National Supervision Commission. He always knew how far up the food chain his investigation should go. It was rumoured that the Shanghai Clique – who were doing their level best to extend their tentacles, their business interests, throughout Chengdu – were terrified of him. Chief Di kept away from him too, leaving him to manage his own time and resources. And, at these parties, Ye Zihao always treated him with the utmost respect.

What Supervisors Cai and Long actually thought of the family Ye – or suspected – was anyone's guess. Philip Ye never spoke to either of them about family concerns. But he had been grateful that they had been the first to agree to attend his father's parties and had remained so ever since. He joined them under the canopy.

"Philip, I hear your over-large girlfriend is leaving you," said Supervisor Cai, throwing another chunk of bread out onto the lake. "Back to Pujiang County, so I hear."

Philip Ye maintained his silence.

"It's probably for the best," said Supervisor Long. "Constable Ma doesn't look to be the city type."

"This morning I heard an odd story though," said Supervisor Cai. "Your mate Zuo was asking around about a scorpion tattoo. He thought it might be gang-related...some new players in town. So I met with an informant – not well connected but he travels and picks up enough stuff to earn himself a good meal once in a while. He saw your girlfriend – the ogre, he called her – shoot the old man on TV."

"As did most everybody else in Chengdu," muttered Philip Ye.

"Just wait – this story is worth hearing," said Supervisor Long.

"My informant had seen her before," said Supervisor Cai. "Last summer he was in Pujiang County, doing the odd job or two, helping out at some of the remote farms. The circumstances are unclear but he had occasion to visit one of the police stations there...you know the type, a dingy little stone building in the middle of nowhere, manned by a couple of clowns, and guarded day and night by a flock of geese. My informant told me that was where he had seen her, not in uniform but in one of the cells."

"He is a liar," said Philip Ye.

"Just listen, Philip," said Supervisor Long.

"Some of the local peasants told my guy her story," said Supervisor Cai. "It seems there was once a family of poor pig-farmers, who had had the misfortune to birth three daughters and no sons. The older daughters got married and went off to manage poxy little farms of their own. The third daughter, however, grew up to be unusually big and strong, with a face and a naturally unhappy disposition that didn't exactly invite suitors. Daughter Number

Three grew up tough enough to work the farm when her father and mother became too old and feeble. Worth keeping around, you understand. The problem was that Daughter Number Three had other ideas. She wanted to be police. Born stubborn as well as strong, she threatened her parents that if she wasn't allowed to enlist she would hot-foot it to the city. Now the senior constable in the area was not only related to the family, but he was also a reasonable man. How reasonable we shall soon discover. He didn't want her father and mother to suffer without their daughter. But he also didn't want to miss out on a potential recruit who would not only cook and clean at the station, but who was also prepared to work unsociable hours, who would…without complaint…walk miles and miles up and down muddy country lanes in any weather on patrol, and who was powerful enough, and intimidating enough, to knock thick peasant heads together when needed, who was skilled at rounding up runaway pigs and—"

"I get the picture," said Philip Ye.

"So a deal was struck," continued Supervisor Cai. "Daughter Number Three was to work part-time at the farm and part-time as police. Which she did, thoroughly imbued with the spirit of Lei Feng."

Lei Feng was the hardworking and selfless young soldier who had supposedly died in an accident at the age of twenty-one in the early 1960s and held up by the Party as an exemplar of the ideal socialist man – a model of devotion to the Party and to the people. There was some doubt these days whether he had ever actually existed, whether he was just a figment of a propagandist's imagination. Lectures were still given at the PSB on his life and times, the attendees exhorted to live their lives as Lei Feng once had. Attendances were not what they once were.

"But all was not rosy in Pujiang County," said Supervisor Long.

"No, indeed," said Supervisor Cai. "Because, so my informant tells me, this backward slice of the country hides a dirty little secret. Hidden away in the forest is a meth lab. And the local constabulary – to augment their poor salaries, you understand – provides armed protection for this lab and the movement of its product from time to time."

"I don't want to hear anymore," said Philip Ye, seriously.

"You must," said Supervisor Long.

"Now our new recruit, Daughter Number Three," said Supervisor Cai, "is a bit slow on the uptake. She only learns about the lab after some years in the job. Then, after one sleepless night, the spirit of Lei

Feng coming to her in a dream, she pulls a pistol on her fellow police and tells them that they are all under arrest."

"A big mistake," says Supervisor Long.

"Unfortunately," Supervisor Cai continued, "while levelling a gun at her corrupt comrades in blue, she forgets to do a proper head count and gets smacked from behind by a large piece of wood. She ends up in one of the cells, which is where my informant saw her, leaving our reasonable senior constable with a pig of a problem…if you'll excuse the expression."

Supervisor Long laughed. Then he said, "Keep listening, Philip, the story is about to get weirder still."

"The local drug barons," said Supervisor Cai, "wanted our reasonable senior constable to put a bullet in the back of the head of Daughter Number Three and bury her deep in the forest. But he actually likes her *and* is related to her, remember. Her parents are also by this time causing all sorts of trouble, throwing rocks at the station, crying and pulling out their hair, wanting Daughter Number Three returned to them. She was supposed to be helping them run the farm, not get herself locked up. So what to do? Luckily, this senior constable is a resourceful man. He had just heard about our police beautification campaign. So he phones up Chengdu PSB, gets an application form, concocts a story about Daughter Number Three's ten years' impressive experience in the Pujiang County police and – much more importantly and quite brilliantly – attaches a photo of some starlet cut from a magazine and then posts off the form. A week later, Commissioner Ho, drunk as always, is fooled by the picture, approves her transfer, and Daughter Number Three is on her way to Chengdu."

"Jesus," said Philip Ye.

"It gets better," said Supervisor Long.

"At the bus stop, our reasonable senior constable warns her never to return," continued Supervisor Cai. "If she does, it won't be just her ending up with a bullet in the head but her parents too."

"We thought you should know," said Supervisor Long, with a wry smile. "It appears she has a lot of baggage. Not necessarily wife material."

Philip Ye now understood why she had been patrolling the streets with her pistol held on the safety and why she had kept her mouth shut under interrogation at the Procuratorate. She had been terrified. And now, for doing her job, for shooting dead Old Man Gao, she was to be transferred back to Pujiang County to face certain death. In her place, he would run. This very night, he would run.

"It's just the word of an informant," said Supervisor Cai, with a shrug.

"But the story is so ridiculous…so very Chengdu…it may well be true," said Supervisor Long.

Supervisor Cai threw another chunk of bread out on the lake and both he and Supervisor Long gasped as the largest fish they had even seen came up the surface to swallow it whole. Neither saw the grim expression that had settled on Philip Ye's face.

CHAPTER THIRTEEN

Friday

The law, being the dark side of social control, is governed by the *yīn* or the feminine principle – as is occult phenomena, including the appearance of ghosts.

Xu Ya, newly appointed prosecutor to Chengdu People's Procuratorate, believed in the law. Her life was dedicated to the law. She did not, however, believe in ghosts.

In the 6th Century, the scholar Yan Zhitui had compiled a collection of supposedly true stories entitled *'Tales of Vengeful Souls'*. In one of these colourful accounts a young man is returning home to attend the funeral of his father. On the way he is waylaid by his father's former retainers, robbed and drowned. With his body missing, no one knows what has become of him. And, as there is no evidence of a crime, there is nothing for the authorities to investigate. But, later that night, the young man appears to his mother in a dream. He tells her what has happened to him, how he has been murdered, that even now as he speaks to her his corpse is being thrown about by the river. In the morning, when the mother awakes, she takes this information to the local officials who, through their investigations, are able not only to confirm the death of her son but also to apprehend his murderers.

A true story?

No.

There was no such thing as ghosts.

But, to Xu Ya, such stories pointed to a deeper truth: that, when the people are failed by the organs of law enforcement, they will look elsewhere for justice – even resorting to praying to non-existent gods, spirits and ancestors, and engaging in all manner of wild superstition.

That, for Xu Ya, would not do.

She wanted – no, needed! – China to continue its path of scientific and socialist modernisation. If there was to be no reversion to medievalism and backwardness, then everybody in law enforcement had to do their job – including the doltish police of Wukuaishi Station. It sometimes amused her, though (and she knew it was hypocritical of her), to imagine the spirits of the dead standing next to her, for example, when she was preparing a Bill of Prosecution for a homicide case. Such a practice, though childish and ultimately ridiculous, kept her focused, reminding her that she was dealing with the lives (and deaths) of real people, not just abstract concepts of law. The law owed a duty to the dead, to the relatives of the dead. The law owed a duty to Old Man Gao.

The facts of the case, as ascertained by Investigator Deng, were very simple.

Junjie, the son of Old Man Gao, had vanished in October last year. Old Man Gao had gone to Wukuaishi Station to file a complaint. The police at Wukuaishi Station had refused to accept that complaint, citing the lack of evidence of any criminal wrongdoing. There was no legal basis for this refusal. The police at Wukuaishi Station had been derelict in their duty, their eyes probably on the time-honoured problem of crime clear-up rates. They doubted their ability – probably with good reason – to ever find out what had happened to Junjie and thereby clear the complaint. No complaint, no crime – a scandalous solution practised by the majority of police forces the world over.

Last week, according to witnesses, Old Man Gao had even tried to deliver a petition to the Mayor's Office. He was following the ancient Chinese tradition of delivering 'a petition to the Emperor' when the local authorities had refused to help. With no emperor these days, and with Beijing far away, Old Man Gao had decided, quite properly, that the Mayor's Office would suffice. Unfortunately, in trying to deliver his petition he had been beaten up by assailants unknown, though the *Chéngguǎn* was suspected. This beating was the last straw for Old Man Gao. He chose to break the law himself. He took a young girl hostage, and threatened her life with a knife. Whereupon Constable Ma, a plain-clothes officer of the PSB Robbery Section, ironically working out of Wukuaishi Station, took it upon herself to shoot him stone dead.

For all of this, Xu Ya's fury knew no bounds.

She had begun the day, she thought, with very achievable ambitions. Constable Ma, for her callous inability to consider any other option except shooting Old Man Gao dead, was to be arrested and charged with whatever offence was deemed most appropriate. This done, Xu Ya would draft a clarification of the *Regulations on Public Security Organs' Use of Guns in the Provision of Civil Service* – usually referred to as the Gun Management Regs – so the police would have no excuse not to understand what they could and could not do in respect of arming themselves and discharging their weapons. (For reasons best known to them, the police in China had yet to properly appreciate that the law actually applied to their work and that some knowledge of the law might, at times, prove useful). Once that clarification had been issued, she had hoped to descend upon Wukuaishi Station herself, let them feel the lash of her tongue and warn them of the consequences if properly made complaints were not taken in the future. That none of these things had come to pass had left Xu Ya not only with a sense of intense frustration, but also a feeling that in Chengdu, as she had once done in Chongqing, she was fighting a war quite alone.

She had also barely contained her temper with Investigator Deng and was now reconsidering the haste with which she had hired him. The cardboard box he had produced as if from thin air in front of Chief Prosecutor Gong and Commissioner Ji had ruined everything. If he had called her to one side, shown her the contents of that box first, she would have had a chance to come up with an alternative plan. Instead, taken aback by the contents, Chief Prosecutor Gong had advised her to kick Constable Ma loose. And Commissioner Ji – whom she had been ordered to trust by Secretary Wu, no less – had decided quite unilaterally to confront the drunken liar Commissioner Ho all by himself.

Xu Ya had tried to argue her position in Chief Prosecutor Gong's office. "Constable Ma's recklessness is just the tip of the iceberg," she had said. "We cannot let all this be swept under the carpet by Commissioner Ji. Commissioner Ho not only issued a weapon to the ignorant Constable Ma and dispatched her without proper management control to Wukuaishi Station, he blatantly and arrogantly lied to us about it. You must order his arrest!"

"No, Ms. Xu, you do Commissioner Ji a disservice," replied Chief Prosecutor Gong. "Let us trust him. He will ascertain the facts about Commissioner Ho and put them before us when the time is right. Then we will take the appropriate action."

"But—"

"Commissioner Ji has given us a free hand with Constable Ma though. Just return that peasant to the country. With her off the streets, we can at least restore public confidence in the police."

"Then I want to visit Wukuaishi Station and—"

"No."

Her face glowing red-hot, Xu Ya waved Philip Ye's statement in front of Chief Prosecutor Gong. "And what about this? We do not even know what this officer was doing at the scene."

"Leave Superintendent Ye to me," replied Chief Prosecutor Gong. "The politics of Chengdu are complicated."

Defeated, Xu Ya had sat down and put her head in her hands.

"You must not take all this so personally, Ms. Xu," said Chief Prosecutor Gong. "Getting Constable Ma off the street will be a real achievement for us. It's not that we want old men taking young girls hostage but the speed of Old Man Gao's shooting, and its ruthlessness, has shocked the city. The media are talking more and more about his missing son and—"

"How about an audit?"

"An audit?" Chief Prosecutor Gong raised his bushy eyebrows.

"I could develop a comprehensive audit tool that can be used by police standards inspectors – us or Commissioner Ji's men – when visits are made to police stations. That way we can bring Chengdu PSB under some consistent control."

Chief Prosecutor Gong nearly leapt out of his seat with excitement. "You can do this? Mayor Cang loves audits. He speaks about them all the time."

"Yes, it should not be too difficult."

Chief Prosecutor Gong ordered her to come up with an outline of what she had in mind by Monday morning, by which time he would have returned from his golfing excursion to Shenzhen.

Golfing excursion!

In China?

Xu Ya had thought she was hearing things until Chief Prosecutor Gong showed her a photograph of himself proudly standing on a golf course with some of his businessman buddies holding what he described as a 'nine iron'. It was a pity he was flying out this evening, he said, or he would have invited her to a discreet club he knew to discuss the audit tool further with her over drinks and a fine meal.

Relieved she hadn't had to use one of her prepared excuses (both her friend Mouse, and Madame Ko Yi-ying, the senior legal clerk at the Procuratorate, had warned her about Chief Prosecutor Gong's predatory instincts) she had escaped back to her office. There she had sent a shaken Investigator Deng to conduct a preliminary assessment of Wukuaishi Station – revenge for him producing the cardboard box in front of Chief Prosecutor Gong and Commissioner Ji without showing it to her first. She had spent the rest of the day thinking and working on the audit tool and then gone home.

She checked her watch. The evening was getting late. It was after ten. She hadn't heard from Investigator Deng since that morning. She was conscious she was fretting, like a mother concerned for an errant child. He should have reported in after completing his inspection of Wukuaishi Station. He was supposed to call her, not she chase after him. Come Monday morning, she was going to have to explain the way things worked to him. Then, if by the end of the week his performance hadn't improved, she was going to have to let him go.

She sipped from her glass of red wine – a habit she had picked up while travelling across Europe on her way to her year of study in the United States. Tea had been the drink of her childhood. She had never known anything else. So it was with some surprise on her return to China that she had discovered a hitherto unknown (to herself) wine industry. One glass an evening she allowed herself, the current open bottle a dry red Cabernet Sauvignon from Ningxia, to the south-west of Beijing.

She was sitting at her desk in the study of her new apartment in Tranquil Mountain Pavilions. Open before her was Constable Ma's personnel file that had been sent across from Chengdu PSB. She was putting the last touches to the Recommendation for Transfer document, the intention being to return Constable Ma to the backwoods where she belonged. It pained Xu Ya that she could do no more. However, after she had signed the transfer document with a flourish and was about to slip it inside the file, she was astonished to note that the photograph attached to the file was not of Constable Ma at all. She put her hand to her mouth, not knowing whether to laugh or cry.

"Āiyā!" she said out loud. "Why are the police so stupid?"

The photograph could not even have been of Constable Ma's sister. Constable Ma was big and, in Xu Ya's view, monstrously ugly. The woman in the picture looked like a svelte model – brainless, of course, and probably with pretensions of becoming an actress or singer, but a model nevertheless. Xu Ya looked at the date that Constable Ma had been accepted by Chengdu PSB and she knew immediately what had happened. Last summer, she had read with outrage and incredulity about Chengdu PSB's beautification campaign – a recruitment drive to get more attractive women to join the police, the thinking behind it being that if the police looked more attractive out on the street then the people would consider it a more attractive force and appreciate it more. It was hard to fathom the mind-set and archaic sexist attitudes of the grey men in suits who dreamed this nonsense up, or the seeming lack of awareness that the women they might recruit – pretty though they might be – might have brains like turnips or might indeed possess evil intent. Thankfully the campaign was now over, the report on its success yet to be published. But this was how Constable Ma must have slipped through the net, her application to transfer to Chengdu PSB approved by some officer in personnel leering at the picture, or by the drunken Commissioner Ho himself. No wonder Constable Ma had been exiled to Wukuaishi Station on her arrival.

Xu Ya made a note to phone Commissioner Ji on Monday morning and tell him what she had discovered. Then let him tell her what he was going to do about that idiot Commissioner Ho! She closed the file, somewhat satisfied, glad she was going to inflict some injury on Constable Ma by not only sending her back where she came from but by – with Chief Prosecutor Gong's approval – charging her with making a false declaration on her application in the first instance. She was about to research the relevant offence when her phone rang. Hoping it was Investigator Deng finally remembering to report in, she was dismayed to find herself talking to her father instead.

"Butterfly, have you had a productive week?"

"Yes, Father, a police brutality case – an unnecessary shooting."

"And everything else is well?"

"Yes, Father – quite well. Now you must not worry. I have got good people working around me."

"And that investigator you hired?"

"A bit slow and maybe a bit soft-hearted. We had to take a police-woman into interrogation yesterday and he looked decidedly uncomfortable. But I hope he will yet turn out well."

"Good, good, but your mother is concerned that—"

"Father, please, I must go. I have to be up early tomorrow morning. I will call next weekend, or maybe come and visit. I will tell both of you all about my first impressions of Chengdu."

He rang off distinctly unhappy. Xu Ya couldn't do anything about it. She was sick and tired of them both worrying and trying to run her life. She had to make a fresh start, prove to herself that she could live alone.

She put the phone down and found herself standing, staring at the only picture she had been able to mount upon the wall so far. It was a photograph of her graduating class from the School of Law at the University of Wuhan, her younger self, sitting front and centre, much more confident of the future then – a different person before the darkness had taken hold of her. But it was not her own face that consumed her attention. At the edge of the group, *staring away from the camera*, stood a young man. She touched her finger to his face, smudging the glass, thinking back to the footage being played over and over again on TV of that elegantly dressed police officer knocking the PAP captain to the ground.

"What has happened to you, Melancholy Ye?" she asked out loud. "What has happened to you?"

She turned suddenly, feeling there was someone standing in the doorway to her study, the ghost of Old Man Gao perhaps. But she laughed at herself when she saw no one there. It was just an odd shadow cast by her desk-lamp. With shaking hands she lifted her glass and took another sip of her wine, returning to her contemplation of the young, and impossibly handsome, Philip Ye.

CHAPTER FOURTEEN

B reathe.
     In for eight beats, hold for four, out for eight.
     Breathe.
In breath, there is life; in breath, there is serenity; in breath, there is clarity.

So much to consider.

Constable Ma.

Prosecutor Xu.

Old Man Gao.

Junjie.

Philip Ye had retired early to his rooms, the party still in full swing. Supervisors Cai and Long had already made their excuses, each returning to their respective homes and families, neither seemingly in the mood for enjoying themselves. Though the story of Constable Ma's past had been told with good humour – just another tale of modern life in China, no more bizarre than any other – the telling of it had, it appeared, robbed the evening of all enjoyment for them. So, with his friends gone, and tired himself, Philip Ye had refused a game of cards with Supervisor Bai from Jiulidi Station, said good night to as many as he could, and taken himself off to bed.

He tried to sleep but found his mind drifting to the meth lab in the wilderness of Pujiang County. Conflicted as he was about Constable Ma's shooting of Old Man Gao, if it was in his power to do so he would not see her suffer at the hands of corrupt police and drug dealers. But there were a million such tragedies in China every day. What else could he do except advise her to run? He had no leverage with the Procuratorate, no favours he could call in. Only the ignorant and the deluded believed the family Ye had any *real* influence in Chengdu these days.

As for Constable Ma's nemesis, Prosecutor Xu, it troubled him that he did not remember her from Wuhan. There were reasons, of course. Looking back, those four years were a blur, full of grief over the loss of Isobel – anger too – and the shock of the first visitations from the ghosts of the dead. For a time then he had thought he was going insane. He had made no friends there, remembered no faces. It was a miracle he had come away with a qualification at all.

And then there was Old Man Gao and his missing son Junjie.

What duty, if any, did he still owe them?

What had actually become of Junjie?

What dark road had that boy walked along to vanish into thin air?

Not long after two, Philip Ye gave up on sleep. He pulled his robe about him and sat in the armchair and began to breathe, hoping the practice would clear his mind. He breathed and breathed and breathed.

One problem at a time.

He considered Commissioner Wei's unusual request of him, to extend some sort of protective umbrella about Prosecutor Xu. She was the future, he had said. She was destined to be a judge, he had said. She was vulnerable, he had said.

But vulnerable to what or to whom?

Maybe it didn't matter.

Maybe it wasn't his business.

He had a duty to fulfil Commissioner Wei's request and that was all that counted, certainly not any antipathy he might feel towards Prosecutor Xu in light of her treatment of Constable Ma.

Had Prosecutor Xu really been in his class at Wuhan?

Wouldn't he have noticed such an attractive woman?

He gave up on breathing and phoned Maggie Loh. The phone rang twice. She picked up, bright as a button.

"Hey, babe – I thought you were partying tonight," she said in perfect English.

"It's fizzling out," replied Philip Ye.

"Saw you on TV the other day. You looked good but that PAP officer looked even better. Now him I thought really tasty."

"Are you working tonight?"

"Double-shift – Chen and Chu both called in sick. Flu. We're dropping like flies."

Chen had been at the party looking fine. Philip Ye chose not to mention this.

Maggie Loh was ex-Hong Kong police, a detective there for fifteen years. Then four years ago, as much a shock to her as to anybody else, she had met a businessman from Chengdu. She had fallen in love, married and quit the force in Hong Kong, following her husband back to Chengdu to make a different life for herself. Unfortunately, she bored easily. She had money and a good apartment and an interesting social life. But Maggie Loh was not born to be a hostess or a housewife. With her husband's full support, she sent an application in to Chengdu PSB, only to be turned down flat. The assessor either thought she would be a trouble-maker – hailing as she did from Hong Kong – or was under the mistaken impression that she had nothing useful to offer. Maggie Loh knew otherwise. She tracked Chief Di to his house and brazenly knocked on the door.

"I have skills," she told him. "I speak English and Cantonese and I'm getting better at Mandarin every day. I don't need much money as my husband earns enough for both of us. And I'm a good detective…the best…ferocious in pursuit."

Chief Di sent her to Commissioner Wei, who hired her on the spot. Six months later she had caught The Night-club Killer almost single-handedly, impressing everybody with her energy, aggression and single-mindedness – especially Mayor Cang, who had made sure a photograph of Maggie Loh had appeared on the front page of every local newspaper.

"She is the future of Chengdu policing," Mayor Cang said to the gathered journalists, meaning it, daring any to say otherwise.

Maggie Loh's career moved forward then in leaps and bounds, unlike Philip Ye's, frozen since the Shanghai Clique had come to town. However, he did not mind that Maggie Loh out-ranked him now. Her experience in Hong Kong counted for a lot. And everybody liked Crazy Maggie Loh. Some of the younger policewomen even worshipped her.

"Tranquil Mountain Pavilions – that's on your patch, isn't it, Maggie?"

"Could be…what's caught your interest there?"

"Nothing much…nothing I can speak about."

"Ah, the secrets of the family Ye. You know who owns that building, don't you?"

"The family Fu – I used to date the daughter."

"Oh, you are full of surprises. Tell me more!"

"There's nothing to tell. It lasted only a few weeks. The family didn't like me and she soon got bored."

"You, boring – never!"

"It's true – now will you help me, Maggie?"

"What do you need?"

"Eyes and ears in the building."

She whistled. "You don't ask for much."

"It's important, Maggie."

"Babe, I don't know anybody who has an informant in that building. It's locked down tight. All the staff are vetted. They're loyal only to the family Fu. And as for the tenants, they're either rich Chinese or richer *gwáilóu* who'd sooner stick their heads up their own arses than talk to the police. Maybe State Security has someone in there but you don't want to go messing around with those shifty bastards."

Gwáilóu.

Cantonese for foreigner – in the past derogatory, but not so much these days. Philip Ye didn't take offence.

"Maggie!"

"Give your old girlfriend a call, babe. Or rent yourself an apartment there. I'm sure your old man has the cash."

"The family Fu would tear up my application."

Maggie Loh laughed. "Tell me what's got you so hot about that building and I'll see what I can do."

"Find someone for me, Maggie...and then I might tell you."

"Okay, give me a few days...but no promises."

She rang off. She'd come through if anyone could.

Feeling like he'd done at least something, he climbed back into bed. He needed to sleep. He was back in the office in the morning. He closed his eyes. He thought he slept and dreamed, imagining himself back in England for a time, cycling down a country lane with Isobel.

The phone rang. The clock said a little before three.

"Maggie?"

"Sorry to disappoint," said Superintendent Zuo. You sober?"

"Naturally."

"We have trade."

Philip Ye sat up. "Where?"

"Wukuaishi."

For some reason Philip Ye thought of Junjie. "I'll be with you in under an hour."

CHAPTER FIFTEEN

Saturday

Fatty Deng woke up drenched in sweat. He reached for the packet of cigarettes he kept at his bedside only to stop halfway. Five cigarettes a day was his limit. He didn't want to use one of those cigarettes up some hours yet before dawn.

His mother knocked on the door. "Are you alright? I heard you shouting?"

"Don't worry…go back to sleep," he replied. "It was a bad dream, nothing more."

It had been the same dream as always. Wangjiang Road Station. He had just returned from patrol. On the noticeboard was a list of names, those to be purged to make way for the Shanghai Clique, his name at the very top. In the dream he would stare at the list for hours and hours, wondering what he was going to tell his mother, how he could explain to her that his whole life had turned to shit.

He heard his mother shuffle back to her room. Sometimes her nerves were so bad, her medication so ineffective, she would not sleep at all. He had hoped his new job at the Procuratorate would settle her down. Not a total cure, not a miracle, nothing like that – but some change for the better at least. Unfortunately, she had seen the haggard look on his face when he'd walked in, his mind so preoccupied with the missing Junjie he'd forgotten to put on his usual act. She had begun to sob uncontrollably.

"No, don't cry," he told her, hugging her. "Nothing's gone wrong.

I'm just tired, that's all. It's been a long day. I was even commended this morning for my good work."

To cheer her further he told her about his inspection of Wukuaishi Station, how warmly he had been received, how Boxer Tan had invited him out for a drink with the boys.

"Mother, you remember Boxer Tan, don't you?"

She nodded through her tears.

His mother remembered all their names, the good and the bad. She had lived his ten years on the force vicariously, enjoying every minute of it, all the stories he had had to tell. She calmed down as he cooked for them both – ground pork, with pickled beans he'd prepared a few days earlier – but she continued to stare at him as they ate their food and all through the late-evening game of *májiàng* with the Hongs, well aware something was amiss. He hadn't the heart to tell his mother that, good-looking and smart as Prosecutor Xu was, he had a feeling she and he were not born to see eye to eye.

After the beer at the bar, before returning home, Fatty Deng had made one last stop at the local school – not only his old school but Junjie's also. He found Headmistress Han at her desk, working late as always, as diligent and dedicated as ever. Eager to help, she rifled through all of her old files and, with a sharp shout of satisfaction, produced a small photograph of a smiling Junjie taken early the last year.

"I am pleased you are looking for him, Investigator Deng," she said, passing the photograph to him. "If anyone can find out what happened to Junjie then it's you. As a child you always looked out for the lonely, the unfortunate and the disadvantaged. In your class, you were my favourite."

He flushed, not wanting to hear her words, staring hard at the photograph. It was his first look at Junjie, the smile, the vacant expression, the nothingness behind the eyes.

"I am so glad you are back on your feet again," Headmistress Han added. "I've been so worried. And to think you now have an important job at the Procuratorate! Do you remember Mouse? She is working there too…in the archive. She only came to visit me a few months ago. Oh, she and I did laugh. It seems like only yesterday you were both here. She would follow you around as if she was tied to you and—"

"When was Junjie last at school?" Fatty Deng asked, staring hard at the photograph, trying to etch Junjie's likeness into his brain.

"Oh, maybe early last year," replied Headmistress Han. "I let him come and go as he pleased. It seemed for the best. He was never going to learn much here anyhow. All he did in class was sit and draw. A sweet boy. He took after his father and not his mother, thank goodness. Did you know Old Man Gao was the janitor at the elementary school down the road? I couldn't believe my ears when I heard that he'd died. Did the police have to shoot? I do not know much about such things but—"

"Headmistress, are you sure you haven't seen Junjie since last year?"

"I am certain of it. When I heard a few months ago…October or November, I think…that he'd gone missing, I asked around…spoke to the other parents…some of the older boys too. But you know how it is in China: when someone is infirm or not right in the head, unable to perform their responsibilities to the family, they may as well be invisible."

Invisible.

Fatty Deng knew all about that. For the last five years he'd been nothing but.

Headmistress Han then unexpectedly took his hand. "Go find Junjie, Investigator Deng. Old Man Gao loved him so much. Go find Junjie and set Old Man Gao's troubled spirit to rest."

Such a good woman.

Fatty Deng owed her. His mother too nervous, his father not even a memory, Headmistress Han had helped him fill out his application form for the police all those years ago. Then she had accompanied him to the recruiting office, happy to tell the personnel officer what was what.

And, in a way, he owed Junjie too. Invisible people had to stick together.

Fatty Deng got out of bed and dried the sweat off his back with a towel. He sat down at the small desk where he had struggled with his homework all those years ago. He knew then he would never be the sharpest tool in the box but he had never given up, just scraping the qualifications he'd needed to join the police. He switched on the desk-lamp, lit a cigarette despite his initial resolve not to, and began to flip through all of Junjie's drawings again looking for something he might have missed. He did this over and over, staring intently at the faces of the people Junjie had drawn, the scenes of life Junjie had decided needed to be captured.

And then, his cigarette burned almost down to the filter, Fatty Deng slapped his head viciously with his own hand.

"I am one stupid fat fuck!"

He put all the pictures to one side except for three, all portraits of the same little girl, bright eyes, cheeky smile, pig-tails tied with ribbons. He couldn't believe how stupid he'd been. He had ignored these pictures earlier in the day. All he had done was follow in Old Man Gao's footsteps, looking for the adults who might have seen Junjie, failing as Old Man Gao had done. But Headmistress Han had said it. To the adults Junjie was invisible, a non-person, unworthy of consideration or remembrance. His passing by would have left no trace in their minds. But the children, they were a different matter. It wouldn't have occurred to Old Man Gao to ask them. Children were often invisible too.

"Big mistake," said Fatty Deng, with a laugh. He lit another cigarette to celebrate.

Children see everything.

CHAPTER SIXTEEN

Saturday

As the flashing blue and red lights guided Philip Ye the final part of the way, he reminded himself for what seemed like the thousandth time that he would not be looking down at the body of Junjie. The youth had disappeared months ago. He was long gone, never to be seen again. His body wouldn't just turn up now. Baby Wu came running over with an umbrella, an unseasonal heavy downpour underway. Spring was supposed to be a dry season.

"What do you know, Baby Wu?"

"Not much, sir – Superintendent Zuo isn't talking." Baby Wu shivered, either with excitement or the cold. He wore no coat, just his thin police tunic over his shirt.

Philip Ye walked with Baby Wu up to the tape sealing off one end of a narrow alley from curious onlookers – that's if there had been any. At this time of night and with the heavy rain there were only police to be seen. The alley was no more than a cut-through between ageing apartment blocks. Detritus from crumbling walls and litter was scattered all over the ground. Philip Ye was careful where he stepped. Rainwater was running in rivulets from the alley. A police car had been positioned so as to shine its headlight beams to illuminate the scene. At the far end there was more tape and another police car facing him, its beams also doing their best to break through the gloom. At the point where the headlights beams almost touched, he could see the silhouette of his friend Superintendent Zuo, torch in one hand, umbrella in the other, leaning over to examine what, from a distance, amounted to nothing more than a shapeless mound.

"Who found the body?" Philip Ye asked of Baby Wu.

"That was me, sir," replied Baby Wu, proudly, trying not to smile, to respect the gravity of the scene.

"Where's Boxer Tan?"

"I'm not sure, sir – maybe with some of the other guys having a good look around."

Philip Ye put his fingers between his lips and whistled. Superintendent Zuo stood up, stretched his back, and came limping toward the tape. His bad leg always gave him pain, he said, when it rained. Philip Ye had to smile when he saw the surgical mask still fixed to his face.

"You're going to catch something worse than flu standing out here in this weather," he said.

Superintendent Zuo grunted, not in good humour. He checked his watch anxiously. It was a quarter after four. "I can't stay. I caught a whisper a few hours ago that scorpion tattoo girl is going to make a run for it, heading to North Train Station sometime before dawn. I've got a SWAT team on standby. If I don't get there soon to watch over them there could be mayhem."

"This is not our patch, what's special about this body?" asked Philip Ye. Baby Wu lifted the tape for him and he moved under it, exchanging the protection of one umbrella for the other.

"It's not the street robbery it seems, which is why I thought of you," replied Superintendent Zuo. "Watch where you walk. There's rubbish everywhere. I swear a rat ran over my shoes a short while ago. The street-sweepers seem to be frightened of this idyllic little spot."

Philip Ye stayed close to Superintendent Zuo as they moved slowly up the alley, careful where he put his feet, trying not to soil his shoes in filthy puddles of rainwater or on discarded food wrappers and, of course, not wishing to disturb potential evidence – what little remained, that is, after the rain had done its worst.

At the body, Philip Ye took his own torch out of his pocket. Though he had no idea about Junjie's appearance, one glance was all it took to realise it wasn't him. Even in death, with eyes already beginning to cloud over, Philip Ye sensed an intelligence about the features of the young man who lay curled up almost in the foetal position, his mouth half-open to the sky. The hair was short and fashionably cut. The clothing was also modern and relatively expensive, a leather jacket over blue jeans. The hands were small, almost feminine, the nails tidy, the palms free of callouses. No manual worker this. No defensive wounds either. The attack had been savage, taking the victim by surprise. The jacket was open at the chest, the shredded and bloodied remains of a white shirt underneath easily seen. He had been stabbed multiple times, the knife the weapon of choice in China. Philip Ye guessed he had bled out quickly, dying at the very spot he'd been attacked – not that much blood was now evident, dispersed and diluted as it had been by the rain.

"Has the knife been recovered?"

"Not yet," said Superintendent Zuo. "Boxer Tan and his boys are still looking, checking all the nearby streets. They will have to comb the area again in the morning. Let me talk you through it so I can get away. The call was received at 2.17AM by the 110 control centre. The system has crashed again so no Caller ID. And the dispatcher got so excited she didn't ask any of the right questions. So, a fucking shambles from the off. Fortunately for us, Boxer Tan was just coming back on shift when the dispatcher called Wukuaishi Station to say there was a body on the Yusai Road, about twenty metres from the Happy Times Tea Shop. The caller was only about fifty metres off. Anyway, as I was saying, lucky for us Boxer Tan was on duty. Any other station would have taken one look at the weather and decided to wait until morning." Superintendent Zuo pointed back at Baby Wu staring at them from behind the tape. "The kid there found the body. Stepped in the blood, but not much else – not that it matters because of the weather. The kid's got promise though. He told me exactly how he walked up the alley, what he did and didn't touch. Boxer Tan sees it's an ugly one and starts ringing around looking for whoever's on duty. Some thick bastard at Chengbei Station – I don't know who but I'm going to find out – told him to dump the body at the morgue and just mark it down as a robbery gone wrong and wait for someone to pick up the paperwork. Happily, I was already nearby, waiting for scorpion girl to turn up. I heard the commotion over the radios so I came to take a look. Body was warm when I touched it, so death in the past two hours." He reached into the pocket of his coat and pulled out two small plastic evidence bags. He held the first up for Philip Ye to see. "This wallet was lying next to the body, as if placed. Money gone and credit cards gone too – if there were any in the first place." He passed the wallet in the bag to Philip Ye. Then he held up the other bag. "Student ID for our victim from Chengdu National University, two years out of date. The photo's still a good likeness though."

Philip Ye took that bag off Superintendent Zuo as well and shone his torch onto the ID to study the photo. There was no doubt it was the victim, the eyes large and clear in life, the face sensitive – too sensitive perhaps – with thin unsmiling lips. Zhu Yi was the name printed on the card. On the reverse was an address.

"Don't get excited," said Superintendent Zuo. "Boxer Tan's been over there already. It used to be cheap student accommodation but a family has been living there for the past year and a half, no known connection to our lad here."

"Phone?"

"Not recovered so far. So what do you think?"

Philip Ye put the light from his torch back on the body. "This alley was either his usual route home at this time of night and the assailant knew it, or our boy was lured here for some sort of meeting. No defensive wounds so he was surprised and overcome quickly. No stab wounds to neck or face, so possibly former friend or lover? I agree – this is no simple street robbery gone wrong. By the mess made of his chest our assailant really meant him never to get up again."

"I thought with your new-found affinity for Wukuaishi this little mystery would be just up your street," said Superintendent Zuo. "Could there be a connection to the shooting of that old man by your new oversized girlfriend the other day?"

Philip Ye did not reply but he had already been thinking along the same lines. The murder rate in China, and therefore in Chengdu, was well below the global average. What were the chances of two very violent events happening on almost consecutive days and almost within shouting distance of each other? Coincidences did happen but it was a line of enquiry definitely worth pursuing.

"Is Doctor Wang on the way?" Philip Ye asked.

"Didn't I tell you?"

"Tell me what?"

"He went on holiday to Macao last week, probably to gamble away all that remained of his life-savings. The old fool got into some sort of fracas with a pair of fancy chickens and—"

Chickens, prostitutes.

Philip Ye was incredulous. "Doctor Wang?"

"My wife says it's always the quiet ones you have to watch. Anyway, he isn't returning anytime soon. He is supposed to have beaten them up quite badly. The court date is not for a month or so and he is looking at doing some serious time. So I called Doctor Kong."

"Who's Doctor Kong?"

"Did I forget to tell you about her as well? She arrived three days ago, direct from Beijing. She's fully qualified, spent a year or two in America and England studying the latest techniques. She assumed she was coming here to get experience working with Doctor Wang. Mayor Cang had met her at some law enforcement conference in Hangzhou – don't ask what he was doing there, because I don't know – and invited her to come and study under the great man, all expenses paid. Believe it or not, he told her that Doctor Wang was some sort of forensics pioneer. She should have done her homework before accepting the invitation. Anyway, if one were the suspicious type, one might come to the conclusion that her arrival in Chengdu and Doctor Wang's altercation with a couple of chickens in Macao had been very carefully choreographed. I met Doctor Kong when she came out to look over scorpion girl's handiwork the other night."

"I liked Doctor Wang."

"Don't lie to me, Philip. We're well shot of that old fool. He only ever told us what we wanted to hear. Believe me, Doctor Kong's first autopsy report was a revelation – clear, concise and plausible; everything that Doctor Wang isn't. Mayor Cang might have actually done us a favour for once. So don't you go upsetting her! Use some of that fabled Ye family charm. She's a little bit touchy. Being from Beijing she doesn't understand much of what any of us are saying yet and our spicy food is upsetting her stomach. She is also of the opinion that our forensic facilities date from the Ming Dynasty, and she doesn't have much faith in the intellectual abilities of the police. But apart from that she is an absolute peach. Mind if I go now? I have a scorpion to catch."

"Sure – but watch yourself. I don't want to have to explain to your wife how a little girl put a knife in your neck. And check the back seat of the car. I brought you some of my father's Tibetan spicy mutton from the party."

Superintendent Zuo waved in acknowledgement and Philip Ye was left standing in the rain. He began to take pictures of the body from multiple angles using his phone. They would have to do until Doctor Kong and her official photographer arrived.

"Mister Ye!"

He turned and saw Boxer Tan waving to him, standing next to Baby Wu. Philip Ye, his work done at the body for now, gingerly retraced his steps to join them, happy to be shielded again by Baby Wu's umbrella.

"Boxer Tan, any joy?"

"No, Mister Ye – no witnesses, no murder weapon, and no fucking blood trail because of all this rain. Whoever did this must be covered head to foot in blood after what he did to that poor bastard. And don't ask about CCTV coverage around here because there isn't any. The nearest camera is at the hotel down the way and that's been broken since a party got out of control at the New Year. I've already run the victim's name – no criminal record and his temporary student *hùkǒu* has lapsed, so he's been working as a ghost. We'll knock on doors in the morning but…." He shook his head, already resigned to the fruitlessness of the exercise.

"Any local gang trouble?"

"Nothing recent," replied Boxer Tan.

"Who uses this alley?"

"Students mainly, spilling out of the clubs and bars, a short-cut home to their dorms at the university. But they're usually long gone by now. Just a few local people walk their dogs here late at night. But other than that…."

Philip Ye saw the frown on Boxer Tan's brow. "What is it?"

"Just an idea, Mister Ye. You know we don't get out on patrol as much as we used to. I can't remember the last time I walked up this alley. Until tonight, I'd forgotten it existed. But Constable Ma has been patrolling all around here these last six months or so. You could set your watch by her, night after night. I bet she knows the streets and the people better than any of us now. She might even recognise our victim if he lives or works nearby."

Philip Ye felt a tremor run through him. He sensed the spirit of Old Man Gao nearby. He looked around him but saw nothing, not a shadow that shouldn't be there, not a shimmer of silvery light.

"I know she's been suspended," continued Boxer Tan, "and is due to be sent back to the country by the end of the week…and she might not be keen to help after what's been done to her but…well, Baby Wu knows where she lives."

Baby Wu nodded vigorously. "It's not far, sir."

Philip Ye stared back up the alley at the body, lost in thought. He felt the rightness of Boxer Tan's suggestion, the unseen approval of the spirit of Old Man Gao loitering nearby.

"Mister Ye?"

He turned back to Boxer Tan. "It's worth a try. You wait here for Doctor Kong. Don't let her take the body away until I've returned."

"Who's Doctor Kong?" asked Boxer Tan, confused, but Philip Ye and Baby Wu were already jumping into the Mercedes, taking the only umbrella with them.

CHAPTER SEVENTEEN

I n 2011, Chengdu had unveiled its new logo: four golden birds circling a whirling sun – a copy of an artefact fabricated in gold three thousand years ago by the people of the Shu and excavated recently from the Jinsha ruins in the Qingyang District of Chengdu. It was said to represent the eternal longing of people desirous of a better life.

And Xu Ya wanted that better life.

She needed a new beginning, free of the nightmares of the past.

How then had she ended up in Chengdu?

How had she ended up in *his* orbit yet again?

Unable to sleep, Xu Ya pressed her hands against the cold, rain-streaked glass of the window of her apartment. She stared out across the confluence of the Fu and Nan rivers – recently named as one, the Jinjiang River, by the Chengdu Municipal Government – toward the city centre. It was a grim night, the rain falling, the mist hanging in thick shrouds about Tranquil Mountain Pavilions, occasionally obscuring the bright lights of the city, and casting odd reflections on the river water below. He was out there. She could feel it. He was awake and working. Somewhere in this vast city of over seven million souls – fourteen million if one counted the greater Chengdu area – the rain was falling upon Philip Ye.

Did he lift his face to the skyline?

Did he see her face staring from the window?

And, if he did, did he care?

· · ·

Two months previously she had had no future at all. Living with her parents again, she had wiled away the hours of each day, reading books, watching TV, and contemplating – to her parents' horror – a permanent move abroad. Then a letter had arrived, addressed to her in the strictest confidence. The letter, written in ink, the calligraphy excellent, purported to be from the Chair of the Chengdu Political and Legal Committee, a Secretary Wu Jing Zi – a man she had never heard of and certain she had never met. He requested a meeting with her, to be held – again in the strictest confidence – in a location of her choice.

Intrigued but wary, she chose a very public place, a bench near to the Orangutan House at Chongqing Zoo. She knew the zoo well, visiting it often these days, finding some inner peace laughing at the antics of the animals.

A short, well-dressed man in his late middle years, seemingly content in himself, she discovered Secretary Wu to be very direct.

"Ms. Xu, we have an opening at the Procuratorate in Chengdu for a woman such as you."

"I have been inactive for the last five years," she replied.

"That is not important, Ms. Xu."

"Also, you do not know me."

This was not true, he explained. Years before, he had observed her at work. She had been presenting a case, a rape-homicide, in the Intermediate People's Court in Chongqing. He had been very impressed. So much so that he had never forgotten her name. He explained further that the post he had in mind for her in Chengdu was anything but ordinary. She would be attached to the Legal and Disciplinary Procuracy Section, concerned in the main with the legality of police investigations and their gathering of evidence. In reality though, once she was bedded in, her tasking would be more specialist and much more important.

"To investigate and prosecute very serious crimes, Ms. Xu – by officers of the PSB, the Procuratorate and the Courts, not to mention all levels of the municipal and provincial government."

Chengdu was the provincial capital of Sichuan Province. And, as such, the provincial government was based there. Chongqing, though larger and also located in Sichuan Province, had been one of four cities granted, in terms of its governance and administration, separate 'provincial' status – the others being Beijing, Shanghai, and Tianjin – and thereby governed directly by Beijing.

Xu Ya had been stunned by the job offer. "You would wish me to operate in secret?"

"Yes – as a special prosecutor."

"Answering to?"

"Me – and a minority of members of the Political and Legal Committee. In the short term, nobody in the Procuratorate, not even Chief Prosecutor Gong, will be informed of your true status."

"This is most unusual. Do you not trust the appropriate sections of the Procuratorate?"

"We live in unusual times, Ms. Xu. I must also insist that if you accept this post you do not inform anyone of the true nature of your work – and this includes friends and family."

"Of course."

"You will be given licence to hire your own staff, including an investigator, but I suggest you wait until you are fully satisfied with them until you brief them properly on the nature of the work you are to do. Naturally, you will not be operating in a total vacuum. I will expect you to liaise as you see fit with the local representatives of the National Supervision Commission, the Central Organisation Department and the Ministry of State Security – though I will leave it to you to decide whom you should trust and whom you should work with. I must warn you that the work will not be easy and might involve some personal danger."

"How do you know I have the facility for such work?"

He smiled at her as if he thought the question ridiculous. He gave her his card. "Call me when you have decided. You will be required to make a presentation before the whole Political and Legal Committee as you would if applying for an ordinary prosecutor's post. But this will just be a formality. Be yourself, Ms. Xu, and I am sure all will be well."

Back home, her father unhappy, aware only that a prosecutor's post was been offered to her, asked, "What is there about Chengdu that could interest you?"

"A new life," she replied, her mind full of possibilities, her heart dancing.

Her mother, more astute, and with a better memory, took her to one side, speaking quietly but sharply to her. "Don't be a little fool!"

"Mother, I am thirty-three years old. I can decide for myself."

"Haven't you suffered enough at the hands of men?"

"The family Ye are no longer in power in Chengdu. And the city is so big there is little chance I would bump into—"

"The family Ye is like a weed, the roots of which are so deep and so far-reaching that it can never be destroyed no matter what is done to it. It will continue to spread and grow – in the darkness if need be – leeching the life out of everything and everyone it touches."

"Mother, I am no longer a child."

"You are worse than a child because you do not learn. You are but a moth to a flame – and you will get burned up!"

Stubborn as she had always been, and determined not to pass up on the incredible opportunity Secretary Wu was offering her, Xu Ya ignored her parents. A few days later she took the fast train to Chengdu to make her presentation before the Political and Legal Committee there.

She chose not to speak about herself, about the qualifications she had gained, her proficiency in the English language and her year's study of comparative law at Harvard University in the United States. Nor did she linger long on her accomplishments at Chongqing People's Procuratorate, the startling improvements she had made to the administrative processes there, the complex cases she had worked, the lectures on law she had delivered.

Instead, she chose to speak about the history of law in China – and its potential future. She spoke of dynastic law, that strange amalgam of Confucianism and Legalism; of the struggle to reform the political and legal system at the end of the Qing Dynasty, leading to the creation of an independent judiciary and the adoption of modern Western and Japanese laws; of 1949 and the revolution, the creation of the People's Republic of China and the subsequent revival of the judiciary and its body of laws, and the establishment of a new political system based on Marxist-Leninist ideals which viewed the law as a means of state domination and where all crimes were seen as 'political acts'; of the Cultural Revolution from 1966 to 1976, where, arguably, there was no law at all; of the year 1978, during the 3rd Plenary Session of the 11th Central Committee, where the decision was made to replace class struggle with economic development, which led, in the following years, to the drafting of thousands of laws and the recovery of the legal institutions: the PSBs, the Procuracy, and the Courts.

But her presentation was no mere chronology of the history of law in China. That recounting was to serve only as the basis for the argument she was about to make. She spoke of the present day, on the ongoing debate about what is meant by *fǎzhì* – 'Rule of Law'; of the bitter clashes between the rightists and the leftists; of the positions held by the Constitutionalists, the New Confucians and those still wedded to Marxist-Leninist theory; and finally she spoke of her personal commitment to the law, to maintaining social order, and to Chengdu – that is, if they would have her.

"We have to be pragmatic," she said. "If China is to take its place, as it should, as one of the leading nations of the world, then our legal system must be transparent and our laws rigorously upheld if we are to attract continuing foreign investment and trade. China must be a state in which it is safe to do business. However, though I am a firm believer in legal reciprocity, in that Western interests in China should be as protected as our interests are in the West, this does *not* mean that Western values and principles are Chinese values and principles. Legal common ground must always be found for the sake of trade and international relations, but the beating heart of our law must always remain Chinese!"

The Committee was silent for a brief moment and then stood as one to applaud her. Secretary Wu, looking very pleased and proud, introduced her personally to every member. One woman, whose name Xu Ya instantly forgot in the excitement, took her hands in hers and said, "Ms. Xu, you are like a bright new star in the sky!"

In the weeks that followed, despite her parents' unhappiness with her decision, more pieces fell into place. She phoned Mouse and was overjoyed to find her old friend still working in the Chengdu People's Procuratorate archive. After a stuttering start, Mouse in tears of delight, they were soon chatting away as if five years hadn't passed by at all. Mouse told her not to worry about finding an investigator. Mouse said she had access to the personnel files, old and new, of all the organs of law enforcement. She would find someone suitable, she said, someone Xu Ya could rely on.

Xu Ya then found herself attending a banquet with her parents – a birthday party for an old friend of the family – and was seated next to Fu Bi, Chairman of FUBI International Industries, reputedly the richest man in all of Sichuan, whose complicated business networks radiated like spokes of a bicycle wheel out of Chengdu. Not only did he show genuine interest in her appointment as a prosecutor in Chengdu, but he also revealed that he had an apartment available in one of his luxury developments – Tranquil Mountain Pavilions – which she could lease, if she so wished, at a highly preferential rate.

Xu Ya accepted immediately. Fu Bi was famously a good man, admired by his friends and clients the world over. His daughter, Fu Lu – though she preferred to use her adopted Western name of Lucy even in China – was seated next to him. A sharp businesswoman in her own right, she was dripping in diamonds, with a short, almost severe, hairstyle and eyes like crystals – distant and coldly condescending.

"I also keep an apartment at Tranquil Mountain Pavilions," she said to Xu Ya. "Perhaps you and I could be friends."

I don't think so, thought Xu Ya, smiling and nodding politely.

Lucy Fu was famous for once having dated Philip Ye.

Wuhan.

Fourteen years ago.

Where had the time gone?

Philip Ye had arrived late to their first lecture at the School of Law, his entrance quiet and unassuming, just silently taking his seat at the back. All the girls took notice, though; none had ever seen such a beautiful man. He was tall and slim, his muscle lean. With brilliant green eyes and a face that had taken the very best the East and West had to offer, it was hard not to stare at him for hour upon hour. He was older than most too, having already gained a degree in physics in England. But it was what he carried about with him that really made the girls shiver – an air of loneliness and sadness, a pervading sense that his mind was always elsewhere.

It was Xu Ya who named him.

Melancholy Ye.

The other girls said to her, "You go talk to him. You're sophisticated. You've been to Europe and America."

She refused their urgings as well as her heart's own. Intuitively, she already knew, even before she had learned anything about the murky history of the family Ye, that Philip Ye was far, far beyond her – of a more subtle, much darker, much more complicated world.

Such inner knowledge, though, did not prevent her day-dreaming, finding excuses to pass close by him, to sit next to him in lectures, to study the way he held his pen, to attempt to guess his thoughts as he stared out of the window as their lecturers droned on. She was also moved to do private research into the genetics of eye-colour, trying to figure out the probability (and failing) of whether she and he would produce a green-eyed child. She also found his melancholia infectious. Always bright and bubbly as a child, she now found herself often waking in the middle of the night, crying for no reason, her dreams confused and disturbing. Some days she would find it impossible to study and would take herself off for long walks, her mind overwhelmed with such a deep sadness that she began to wonder if her life was worth living at all.

Her vacations, much to her parents' annoyance, were full of talk of Philip Ye and his family.

"Who are they to us?" her mother would ask.

And her father would say, "Mayor Ye Zihao is known to be a man of limitless ambition and questionable morality. He would never be welcome in this house. So stay away from this Philip Ye. As the father is, so shall the son be."

Their advice, however, proved to be redundant. Not once during the four long years Xu Ya shared a class with Philip Ye did he speak to her or give her any sign that he had noticed her at all. Nothing she had tried, acting cool and aloof or outrageously flirtatious, or regularly changing the way she dressed, or the different cosmetics and hairstyles she experimented with, brought her any attention at all. Nor did any other girl have any better luck. Philip Ye was apparently unmoved by every woman at the University of Wuhan.

It was Mei-Mei, one of the girls Xu Ya hung around with, who discovered Philip Ye's tragic secret. She had a relative in Chengdu who told her the whole story. It seemed Philip Ye had been engaged to an English girl during his time in England, against the wishes of his father, only for her to die of some terrible disease.

"Oh," said Xu Ya, moved to tears.

"He is better off without her," said Ju, another friend. "Philip Ye is more Chinese than English. A Chinese man and an English woman, that never works. But an English man and a Chinese woman, now that is something else entirely."

Mei-Mei disagreed. "Look at his face, surely he is more English than Chinese."

"No, he's not!" exclaimed Ju.

That particular argument raged until their graduation party.

Her degree gained, Xu Ya returned home to Chongqing with the graduation photograph under her arm. Her mother asked her to point out Philip Ye, taking a magnifying glass to his face. After some long moments, her mother said, "Be glad he never noticed you, Butterfly. Such a man would have destroyed you."

Butterfly.

Her parents' pet name for her.

Not quite a moth.

Six months into her practice year with a law firm in Chongqing, Xu Ya had received a phone call from Mei-Mei.

"Have you heard?"

"Heard what?"

"About Philip Ye?"

Xu Ya's heart skipped a beat. She imagined something dreadful, an air-crash, or a hasty and ill-considered marriage, or that he was returning to England, leaving China for good.

"He's now police," said Mei-Mei.

Xu Ya, stunned, said, "Don't be stupid."

"No, it's true," said Mei-Mei, getting upset. "I heard it from Ju."

"Ju is a little liar!"

"No, she swore it. She's just returned from a shopping trip to Chengdu. She saw him on the street, in uniform, directing traffic."

Police.

It made no sense. Philip Ye had two degrees. A police career was for those with few brains and no ambition.

Xu Ya did some research of her own. She contacted a newspaper in Chengdu and found out it was all true. After Xu Ya agreed to a subscription, the newspaper sent her a back issue. The photograph on the front page was of Philip Ye in uniform at his passing out parade from the police college, as handsome as ever. Full of rage about his mistake, Xu Ya sat down and drafted a very long and passionate letter, wanting him not to waste his education, needing him to understand that his life could be so much more.

She almost sent it. Somewhere she had it still, the paper long since discoloured with age.

She passed the bar exam first time, at the very top of her year. It was Chongqing People's Procuratorate that actually approached her, appointing her immediately to the post of prosecutor. She was grateful not to have to spend a couple of years learning the ropes under the guidance of some ageing prosecutor about to retire who probably knew less about the law than her mother's pet dog. Through her work, though she made no good friends among her colleagues, Xu Ya found an excuse to make phone contact with an artless young legal clerk at Chengdu People's Procuratorate who worked in the archive there. Her name was Hong Jia, though she was known to one and all – because of her size, she said – as Mouse.

Mouse, though shy at first, overawed that she was speaking to an actual prosecutor from Chongqing, loved to talk. Xu Ya was always able to steer their frequent conversations around to the latest gossip about the family Ye while never revealing that she and Philip Ye had attended university together. Mouse told her that Philip Ye was doing well in the police. Mouse told her that though his decision to join the police had at first infuriated his father, Ye Zihao going as far as to throw him out of the house, all was forgiven now and Philip Ye had moved back into the family home. And Mouse told her that Philip Ye was dating a string of aspiring models and actresses, each more beautiful than the last.

Xu Ya laughed with Mouse about this but was privately disgusted. So much for his never-ending grief.

As Xu Ya's work at the Procuratorate in Chongqing became more and more demanding, the phone calls between her and Mouse inevitably became less frequent. There was no falling out between them – it was perhaps Xu Ya's longest, and closest, friendship to date – it was just that with the passing of time, images of Philip Ye intruded less and less on her mind and her heart did not hurt so much. And perhaps there was the loss of hope too, a growing realisation that, compared to those actresses and models, she would always be considered a rather common flower.

Then came the Year of Calamities.

Without a word from her in months, Mouse telephoned in some distress. "There's been a shoot-out with some criminals on the Zhimin East Road," she said, through her tears. "The police radios are going crazy. A homicide detective has been killed, they say. There's a man I once knew from school…a constable…I just heard his call-sign. He is responding on foot. Oh, I'm so frightened, Prosecutor Xu. I will call you when I know more."

Mouse, it seemed, had, for some reason, a police radio set up in the archive. Xu Ya closed her office door, put her head in her hands, tried to control her breathing and ignore the pain in the pit of her stomach, and waited for Mouse to call back. Philip Ye had not long been transferred to homicide.

"Bang! Bang! Bang!" exclaimed Mouse, a few days later, when the full story of the Zhimin East Road shoot-out had emerged. Thankfully, Xu Ya had not had to wait that long. Mouse had phoned back within the hour of that first phone call to confirm that Philip Ye had been there but had survived unscathed as had that constable she knew.

"Bang! Bang! Bang!" Mouse shouted again down the phone. "And some say there are no heroes left in China anymore."

Mouse sent Xu Ya some of the newspaper clippings – Xu Ya had long since ended her own newspaper subscription – including the soon-to-be famous photograph of Philip Ye, pistol in hand, protecting a fallen colleague with his own body.

Philip Ye.

Hero.

It was hard to believe.

But studying the photograph closely, following her mother's lead with a magnifying glass, Xu Ya saw it was not her Philip Ye at all. The melancholy had gone. The sombre indifference to the world had vanished. He had evolved into a different creature entirely.

Xu Ya had no one to share this knowledge with. Ju had stayed in Wuhan and married well. Mei-Mei was working abroad for a Western conglomerate. Besides, as was her way, Xu Ya had fallen out with both of them. Not that it mattered. Neither of them had found Philip Ye as fascinating as she.

The calamities kept coming.

The Tibet Autonomous Region in uproar, bodies of ethnic Tibetan and ethnic Han alike lying on the streets of Lhasa. Riots across Sichuan, a Tibetan neighbourhood in Chengdu in lockdown.

Mouse sent more newspaper clippings.

Philip Ye's half-brother, Ye Yong, killed in a car-crash, along with his ethnic Tibetan wife, the circumstances unclear, if not suspicious. A photograph of the funeral, the whole extended Ye family captured by the camera. The text accompanying the photograph said that Philip Ye had been unwell, had taken a few days off work for the first time in his police career. The text also clarified that the woman arm-in-arm with him was the 'renowned beauty, businesswoman and philanthropist Lucy Fu'. Xu Ya took a magnifying glass to her face too, grimacing as she did so.

Mouse phoned a few days later in high spirits, to tell her that Philip Ye's affair with Lucy Fu was over. "He is too physically beautiful," laughed Mouse. "People are saying that Lucy Fu couldn't stand the competition."

Then the ground shook and the whole world turned upside down.

Remembering Lucy Fu's famous philanthropy, Xu Ya decided to take time off work to help the victims of the earthquake, to give blood, to raise money for charity. It was a decision so unlike her – and, maybe because of this, it cost her dearly. She never got to hear from Mouse what happened next in Chengdu: the removal of Mayor Ye Zihao from office, the coming of the Shanghai Clique, the purge of Chengdu PSB. She had problems enough then of her own. For, while raising money for those afflicted by the earthquake, she had met a most charming man and fallen into a terrible darkness. It would be a full five years before she communicated with Mouse again.

She pressed her forehead against the glass of the window to cool the heat of her skin, trying to peer through the drifting mist to the heart of the city.

"I have made such a mess of my life," she said. "I have wasted years pining after one man, only to be ruined by another."

But Secretary Wu had given her a chance at a new life. Did not Chengdu mean 'Successful City'? She was here to begin again, to prove herself again. She was still young, at least relatively so.

That she knew Philip Ye was somewhere out in the city tonight should not matter. That he was as fascinating as ever – and as handsome – should not matter. That, by some quirk of fate, he had been involved – if only on the periphery – in her first case should not matter. If he had not noticed her in four years at Wuhan, why should he notice her now?

She sighed.

It had occurred to her, sitting on that bench with Secretary Wu at Chongqing Zoo, that as a special prosecutor it might be intended that her brief might ultimately include ending that curious legal limbo of Ye Zihao's house-arrest, to lay formal charges against him, to finally bring down the family Ye, to make herself a lifelong enemy of Philip Ye.

It was a possibility.

Maybe even a probability.

And yet she had still accepted Secretary Wu's offer of employment.

And yet she had still come to Chengdu.

Like a moth to a flame.

CHAPTER EIGHTEEN

Despite Boxer Tan's assurance, Baby Wu didn't know where Constable Ma lived – not exactly. It turned out he only knew her apartment block. Back in September Baby Wu had seen her take an 'apartment to let' advertisement down from the noticeboard, the leaflet placed by a landlord better disposed to the police than most – or at least liking some muscle in the building he could call on when necessary.

"The apartment is on the fifth floor," Baby Wu said, as they drove. "Or maybe the sixth. But she definitely lives in that building. Only the other week I saw her return there from the market with a big ginger cat in her arms. So if we see a ginger cat we will know we're in the right place and…Stop! Stop! This is it!"

Outside of the car, the apartment block looked dark and forbidding, though perhaps a step up from the accommodation offered by Aunty Li. The stairwell was free of litter and the air, though frigid, did not smell bad. Baby Wu took the stairs two at a time and Philip Ye followed on as quickly as he could.

Baby Wu stopped at the fifth floor. There was an array of doors off each side of the corridor but no sign of any ginger cat.

"If we listen," said Baby Wu, "we might hear it miaow."

"In Pujiang County they buy cats to eat," said Philip Ye.

Baby Wu looked askance at Philip Ye, unsure whether he was being teased. Boxer Tan had told him to watch out for Superintendent Ye, saying that he could be a bit sharp, that his humour wasn't quite right – more English than Chinese.

"Well, which apartment, Baby Wu?"

Baby Wu was forced to shake his head. "I have no idea, sir."

Philip Ye checked his pocket watch. It would be hours yet before someone turned up to work in the Personnel Office in PSB HQ and could access Constable Ma's file. Fatty Deng could have told him but Philip Ye had not exchanged phone numbers with the Procuratorate investigator, seeing no need at the time; and, if he were honest with himself, not wanting Fatty Deng to consider him a friend.

Determined not to give up, and about to resort to waking all the families on this floor by thumping on their doors, he noticed the last door on the left to be slightly ajar. Up close he saw the door was dented in a number of places and actually broken at the lock. Police handiwork, he guessed. Fatty Deng hadn't said so but it seemed as if Commissioner Ji's boys had opted to kick in the door. Good for Constable Ma, he thought, that she'd laid a couple of them out.

Philip Ye pushed the door open. Damaged hinges creaked loudly. The atmosphere within had a sterile quality, almost unlived in. He sensed straight away there was no one home. He found a light switch. A single naked bulb hanging from the ceiling flared into life. It illuminated a small lounge with a kitchenette off to one side. A door opened into the only bedroom and a shower-room.

They were in the right place. On the wall was taped a tatty Manchester United team poster. Philip Ye recalled she had worn a faded Manchester United fabric badge on the front of her smock. An English Premier League fan. She would get on well with the brothers Na. Philip Ye looked around the room, a single table to eat off, one large moth-eaten comfy chair to sit in, and a tired looking TV in the corner to watch. The kitchenette was clean. In the bin he saw the remains of her last meal, leftover food wrapped neatly in a plastic bag so it didn't begin to smell, a single plate left by the sink to dry. Her fastidiousness intrigued him. He wondered how long it had taken her to decide she had no option but to run.

Baby Wu went exploring and emerged from the bedroom with her police badge and ID in his hands, obviously upset. Boxer Tan had mentioned that Baby Wu had actually quite liked her.

"Her clothes are gone. Where is she? Why did she leave her badge behind?" he asked, bemused.

"It's complicated," replied Philip Ye, not wanting to burden the young officer with the misery of Constable Ma's life story, or the unfortunate truth that sometimes it was hard to tell the difference between police and criminals. "Are you sure you don't have a phone number for her?"

"No, Mister Ye – I never saw her with a phone. She might not have even owned one. She only took the radio we issued her when she went out on patrol and I don't remember her ever using that."

"Does she have any relatives in the city?"

"None that I know of, Mister Ye."

Philip Ye took the badge and ID off Baby Wu and put them in his raincoat pocket. If she had left early on Friday, immediately after her interrogation at the Procuratorate, she would be long gone.

His phone rang. It was Superintendent Zuo.

"Any joy?" Philip Ye asked.

"Not yet," said Superintendent Zuo. "But you know me, optimistic as always. I'm at the train station. Someone else here has caught my attention. Now far be it for me to get myself involved in any of your romantic entanglements but—"

"Don't let her leave!"

"I'm not going anywhere near her. Even the SWAT team are frightened of her," replied Superintendent Zuo, laughing as he terminated the call.

Ten minutes later, Philip Ye and Baby Wu arrived just in time to see Superintendent Zuo and five heavily armed SWAT officers carrying a struggling, screaming teenage girl with a colourful scorpion tattoo inked on her neck out of North Train Station. Superintendent Zuo was breathing heavily, but elated. One of the SWAT officers had a fresh cut to his face; another was limping almost as badly as Superintendent Zuo.

"The big girl's still in there," Superintendent Zuo gasped. "We could have done with her help."

"About time you retired, old man," said Philip Ye.

"And then what would I do?" he replied in all seriousness.

In the station concourse, Philip Ye spotted Constable Ma sitting on the floor, her back propped up against the far wall, a suitcase and a small holdall next to her. She was staring at something in her hands, a small piece of paper, perhaps her ticket to take her far away. The piece of paper disappeared into a pocket the moment she noticed him watching her. She had tremendous awareness. He liked that. He advanced slowly across the concourse toward her, Baby Wu at his side.

"My name is Superintendent Ye, do you remember me?" he asked, when he reached her.

Eyes full of fear stared up at him. Her massive hands now rested on her knees, her knuckles white with tension. He had forgotten the potential brute power of her. He imagined, if she so chose, she could jump up and snap his spine with consummate ease.

"I remember you," she said, flatly.

"A young man has been murdered in an alley off Yusai Road. I have been informed that you used to patrol that area, that there is a chance you might recognise this man. Would you accompany me to the scene to take a look?"

"I am suspended," she said.

"You would be just helping me with my enquiries."

"I don't know anything about murders."

"Constable Ma, all I need is for you to examine the body. Once you are done I will bring you back here. Unless there is somewhere else you want to go."

"Chongqing," she said, bluntly.

"Why Chongqing?"

"I read the police are recruiting there."

Chongqing – not for nothing had it always been known as the 'Chicago on the Yangzi'. Organised crime there was endemic, the police there as corrupt and disaffected as any in China. It was doubtful an honest peasant girl from Pujiang County would prosper there.

"If that is what you want," said Philip Ye. "But there are better places to be a police officer. Help me tonight and I will see what I can do for you."

"You would help me?" The fear in her eyes had been replaced with hope.

"If I can," he replied, unsure if he could, holding her badge and ID out to her.

He saw the indecision in her eyes. But he did not have to wait long. She clambered to her feet and took her credentials from him. A mewling arose from the holdall and a fuzzy ginger face pushed its way out of an opening in the zip.

Baby Wu, visibly relieved, reached down to stroke the cat. "Ah, Constable Ma, you didn't eat it after all!"

The look Constable Ma gave Baby Wu was a complex mixture of puzzlement, anger and disbelief. Philip Ye found himself smiling for the first time that night.

Back at the alley, Philip Ye discovered Boxer Tan arguing with a small, rather interesting looking woman, not yet thirty years of age, with intelligent eyes, thin lips, a hint of make-up and hair pulled back into a tight bun. Near to them stood the official photographer, a shy young man with bad skin whose name Philip Ye could never remember, blinking rapidly as he watched the argument flow back and forth. Next to him were two bored ambulance crew, waiting to take the body away.

"What's the problem here?" asked Philip Ye.

"She wants to remove the body because of all the rain," said Boxer Tan. "I told her to wait but—"

"I am Doctor Kong," the woman said, "and I will say when a body is to be removed and—"

Philip Ye ducked under the police tape, beckoning for Constable Ma to follow him, leaving the new pathologist open-mouthed.

"Watch where you place your feet," Philip Ye instructed Constable Ma. "Just step as I step."

He lit the way with his torch. The rain had finally stopped but the alley was still awash with puddles and little streams. Glancing behind him, he was glad to see Constable Ma doing as she was told. He also saw the frown on Doctor Kong's face and heard her hiss with exasperation. Not that she wasn't right. The sooner the body was removed the better.

He shone his torch on the victim's face so Constable Ma could see. He studied Constable Ma as she leaned over the body, keeping her eyes away from the bloody mess that was his chest, searching his face only.

"Is this your first body?" he asked her.

"My grandfather."

"Murdered?"

She shook her head. "Died in his sleep."

"Do you recognise this man?"

"I think so."

Think so or know so?"

"Know so – he works around the corner at The Singing Moon."

"What's that – a club or a bar?"

"A bar," she replied, standing upright again. "The students go there from the university. They drink too much. I've looked in the window many times. This man used to work there."

"Serving drinks behind the bar?"

"Yes – but it will be shut now. It closes at midnight."

"And the staff leave soon after…when they've cleaned up?"

"Yes."

Philip Ye was satisfied. The chronology made sense. Most likely

Zhu Yi had been on his way home when he had had his fateful encounter with his killer.

He asked her, "Is there ever any trouble at this bar?"

"I haven't seen any."

"Have you ever seen this man outside of the bar, speaking or fighting with anyone?"

She shook her head. Then he sensed her breathing quicken and saw that her big eyes were glistening with excitement. "But I know where he lived," she said.

CHAPTER NINETEEN

Philip Ye had the distinct impression that someone – maybe the spirit of Old Man Gao – was playing tricks on him. He was right back where he started.

"Are you sure?" he asked.

"Yes, Superintendent," replied Constable Ma.

"I believe her," said Boxer Tan. "I believe every crazy thing this city throws at us."

Leaving Baby Wu to oversee the removal of the body from the alley with Doctor Kong – Boxer Tan had had enough of her – Constable Ma had led them on foot from the scene of Zhu Yi's murder to the building where she said he had lived. It had been a short, ten-minute walk in the rain. Now they were standing on the street staring at the front of Aunty Li's crummy little apartment block, the building looking even more uninviting and decrepit than Philip Ye remembered. Not a single light burned in a window.

"I've seen tombs more welcoming," said Boxer Tan, shaking his head.

"Around the back there's another entrance," said Constable Ma. "Down the steps there's a basement where some country people live."

Philip Ye was astonished. "Zhu Yi was living with migrants?"

"Yes, Superintendent."

Boxer Tan got on the radio to call in reinforcements, concerned the migrants might cut up rough and run. Philip Ye, perplexed and impatient, finding it hard to believe that a barman with a steady income would choose to live with the poorest of the poor, opted not to wait. He took off walking at pace around the side of the building, careless now as to whether he stepped in piles of accumulated refuse or puddles of filthy water – his shoes were already beyond repair. He entered the unlit entrance at the back and paused for a moment in the stairwell to listen. Constable Ma was right behind him, as was Boxer Tan, cursing under his breath. A faint light emanated from below as did the low murmuring of voices.

"Best wait," said Boxer Tan, trying to get Philip Ye to err on the side of caution.

Philip Ye ignored him and carried on down the stairs followed by Constable Ma, with a hint of a smile on her face.

Philip Ye found himself in a room larger than he had expected, of shabby and hasty construction, with walls of bare breeze block and a single electrical cable snaking across the ceiling to a bare light-fitting. An honest building inspector would have found numerous violations. Apartment blocks in China had collapsed before because of landlords wanting to maximise their profits by excavating basements where no basement was meant to be. Philip Ye wondered how much Aunty Li was charging her tenants for the pleasure and risk of living here.

He counted fifteen or so heads, all men, fully dressed against the cold. Most were lying down on cheap wooden-framed bunk beds or bare mattresses laid out on a floor of hard packed earth. Three of the men were crouched around a small stove, brewing what looked like their first tea of the morning. Soon enough it would be dawn and these men would be out all day doing the jobs nobody else wanted to do, or queuing up at the Labour Exchange competing against each other for whatever work they could get.

Philip Ye held up his police badge. "Does Zhu Yi live here?"

Silence.

Some woke and turned their heads toward him, some already awake turned their heads away. The remainder stared not at him but at Constable Ma, abject fear in their eyes. Whether this was due to her imposing presence or because they had encountered her before, Philip Ye could not tell.

"Zhu Yi – does he live here?" he asked again, more insistent this time, pushing Zhu Yi's old student ID in the face of the nearest man, a leather-skinned old-timer with an ugly white scar on his jaw.

Scarface squinted at the ID in the wan light of the room, so Philip Ye helped him out with a flash of the torch. Scarface nodded. "He works at The Singing Moon."

"I asked if he lives here," said Philip Ye.

"Yes," admitted Scarface, twisting around and pointing at an empty bunk near the back of the room. "He should have returned by now. What's he done?"

Philip Ye ignored the question, moving deeper into the room, stepping over mattresses and prostrate bodies. He shone his torch over every man he saw, looking for signs of violence, bloodstained clothes and hands. But all he saw was the usual dirt and grime, and faces aged prematurely from a life far too hard, from the long hours of work – or the long hours of no work – and from the pain of separation from their loved ones back in their home villages, a separation that could extend from months to many years. On Zhu Yi's bunk he found a small suitcase which, when opened, revealed some clothing and a couple of paperback books – nothing of any great value. It made no sense. Was this the sum of Zhu Yi's life? What had happened to him after dropping out of university that had caused him to end up here?

He turned to Scarface. "Anyone missing besides Zhu Yi?"

"No, sir – the weather's been so bad none of us have been going out until after dawn."

Philip Ye was about to give the order to Boxer Tan, who was standing expectantly at the foot of the stairs, to have them all escorted to Wukuaishi Station for formal interrogation when he noticed Constable Ma staring at what he took to be a poster on the wall. The poster was partially obscured by the wooden frame of a triple bunk bed, each of the bunks still occupied.

"What have you found, Constable Ma?" he asked.

"Superintendent, it is nothing, just a picture."

"Move!" he commanded the occupants of the bunks. The men all jumped out of the way just in time as Philip Ye yanked the bunk bed away from the wall so he could get a better look at what Constable Ma had found. The poster was the one incongruity in the room – something he should have noticed himself.

At first he had assumed it to be an old-style propaganda poster, perhaps a print from before the Reform Era. But, up close, he saw it was a painting of some skill, done in ink and colours – and not too old either. The thick artists' paper was curling up at the edges from the damp of the basement, but the colours looked as fresh as the day it was painted, which might have been only a few days before. Not that this meant anything. There were many in China who could make old things look new and new things look old. Still, Philip Ye was astonished by the painting and found his eyes drawn to the woman at its centre. She was dressed in a green Sun Yat-sen suit and sitting by the bank of a river, beneath the hanging branches of a willow tree.

Sun Yat-sen was known to history as the 'father of the republic'. He had not only been instrumental in negotiating the end of the Qing Dynasty but had become the first elected president at the end of 1911. He had had – so the story goes – an old Japanese army uniform adapted for himself to wear as civilian dress. This 'Sun Yat-sen suit', as it came to be called, soon became one of the symbols of the nationalist revolution. It was to be quickly adopted by the political elite *of both the left and the right* and became a statement for those men and women wearing it – militaristic, militant and revolutionary – during the tumultuous decades of the early to mid-20th Century. But it was also a refutation of China's dynastic past, of dynastic fashions – and, by implication, the wider dynastic culture. And so it was, when Mao Zedong appeared atop the Gate of Heavenly Peace in Beijing on the 1st October 1949 and formally announced the founding of the People's Republic of China, he wore the Sun Yat-sen suit (afterwards to be known in the West as the Mao-suit) rather than old-style Chinese dress or – probably even more reprehensible to him – a Western-style two or three-piece suit.

By the cut of the Sun Yat-sen suit in the painting, Philip Ye thought the image dated from the late 1950s or early 1960s – maybe even as late as the Cultural Revolution. As for the woman herself, her face, though beautiful, was heavily stylised. A halo of suffused yellow light shone about her head. This made the painting seemingly more religious than political in theme. Her face was so soft and forgiving, she reminded Philip Ye of the many images he had seen of Guanyin, the Buddhist goddess of compassion. Properly framed, and the paper in perfect condition, he would have happily hung it on the walls of his own rooms at home – if it were not for the ugly Sun Yat-sen suit she was wearing. As it was, the painting would be valuable to someone. It was not something he would have expected to be in the possession of struggling migrants.

Philip Ye turned to Scarface again. "Where did this painting come from?"

"Zhu Yi, sir."

"Did he buy it or paint it?"

Scarface looked confused by the question. "He just came back with it one day."

"What does it represent?"

"Ah, she is The Willow Woman," replied Scarface, feeling on safer ground. "Zhu Yi came to live with us so he could teach us about her. He was instructing us on how we should pray to her. He says she has the power to make our lives better. He says if we give our lives over to her, she will make a better China for all."

"Do you really believe that?"

"Maybe," replied Scarface, with a shrug, looking to the other migrants for support. When no one else spoke up, he added, "When Zhu Yi returns he will tell you all about The Willow Woman."

"I doubt it," replied Philip Ye, his eyes on the painting again. "Zhu Yi is dead."

CHAPTER TWENTY

Saturday

It seemed to Xu Ya that she had just fallen asleep when her phone rang. She had been dreaming. She had been flying like a bird, soaring over mountains and forests, skimming the rooftops of Chengdu. She sat up in bed, anxious and disorientated, surprised by dawn's pale light filtering through the window blinds.

She picked up her phone. "Yes?"

It was Investigator Deng. "Prosecutor, I must speak to you urgently."

She had been half-expecting this call, though not, she had to admit, until Monday morning. The Procuratorate was not for everyone, the work difficult and challenging – draining intellectually, morally and emotionally. She had noticed how Investigator Deng had reacted when Constable Ma had been arrested. She had seen his distaste when Chief Prosecutor Gong had slapped Constable Ma's big insolent face. Xu Ya did not approve of violence, and Chief Prosecutor Gong had technically committed an offence, but it was Investigator Deng's walking out of the interrogation room that most disturbed her. It had occurred to her then that he might not have the stomach for the job. If the simple interrogation of a dumb peasant upset him, how would he get on working for her in her role as special prosecutor, when they may well have to operate in the shadows and interrogate people off the books so to speak?

It had been her own fault, of course. Wanting to get things done quickly, she had asked a favour of Mouse. So Mouse had dug through the archives for her, read through numerous old PSB personnel files and, of the few files Mouse had placed on her desk, Investigator Deng's had been at the top of the pile.

"Are you sure?" she had asked Mouse.

"Yes, Prosecutor – there is none so trustworthy. He is a safe pair of hands. Mister Deng is former police. He has been out of the force five years and therefore is more or less forgotten. He has no proven or suspected connections to organised crime, has no known vices, has lived in Chengdu all his life and so knows the city like the back of his hand – and, most importantly, is very, very good with people."

Xu Ya regretted being so influenced by Mouse. She should have gone through those personnel files herself. It wasn't as if there hadn't been time. Secretary Wu had promised to let her bed down into the Procuratorate before he began her true secret tasking. A month or two to find the right investigator would not have been a problem.

Xu Ya agreed to meet Investigator Deng within the hour at the Starbucks nearest to Tranquil Mountain Pavilions. She found the address quickly on her phone. The timing of the meeting annoyed her. She had planned for herself a day of self-indulgence, playing the tourist, taking in the sights of the famous Jinli Street, visiting the thatched cottage once lived in by the Tang Dynasty poet Du Fu, and then spoiling herself with a mini-shopping spree along the Chunxi Road and maybe even booking an excursion to the famous Wolong Nature Reserve to see the pandas there. But perhaps it was best that she accepted his resignation now, away from prying eyes at the Procuratorate (his employment *had* been a misjudgement on her part) and just in case there were any unfortunate emotional scenes. She could then attend the evening's reception at the Mayor's Office she'd been looking forward to – 'Women in Law Enforcement' – with a clear mind and a lighter heart, and then start the search for a new investigator nice and early Monday morning.

Her main difficulty was deciding what to wear. Not wanting to imitate the formality of the office – to put Investigator Deng at his ease – and not wanting to doll herself up too much – this was not a date! – she opted for slim-fitting black jeans, a warm top, and a long navy-blue coat she had treated herself to just before leaving Chongqing. A swift glance out of the window proved her choices correct. The rain had stopped but a heavy mist still hung over the city and it looked none too warm.

By the time she was dressed and ready there was no time for a leisurely breakfast. Imagining she could pick up something sweet and sustaining at Starbucks, she exited her apartment, descended in the lift to the lobby, waved goodbye to the day concierge, Mister Gan

– a polite, watchful and reassuring man – and walked to her rendezvous.

In Starbucks, she found Investigator Deng already there, dressed as always in that awful crumpled suit of his, sitting at a table in a gloomy corner well away from the other customers, dark shadows under his eyes. Before she could speak, he struggled out of his seat – his excess weight not helping him – and offered to buy her anything she wanted. Embarrassed by his kindness, especially in light of what they were about to discuss, she accepted a hot chocolate and a raspberry and lychee mooncake. As he wandered over to the counter she sat down at the table. He had laid out a pile of charcoal sketches as if he had been studying them. Puzzled, she glanced over and saw him chatting amiably to the waitress as he made the order – not a hint of emotional distress in sight. A jolt of electricity ran through her. Investigator Deng was not about to quit. He had been working.

When he had placed the drink and cake before her and retaken his seat opposite her, she spoke to him sharply, trying to recover her composure.

"You should have called me yesterday afternoon."

"Forgive me, Prosecutor, but I—"

"Did you actually get to Wukuaishi Station?"

"Yes, but—"

"Let me see your notes."

Reluctantly, he pulled his notebook out of his inside jacket pocket and handed it over. She flipped it open and began to read, expecting to be dismayed. Instead, to her astonishment, she found comprehensive notes made in a very fine hand. It was not quite what she was looking for, more a catalogue of problems at Wukuaishi Station rather than an analysis of management failures. But it was a start and it would do for now. And to be honest, it didn't matter too much. She had been thinking of the future when she had conceived the audit. The audit would provide investigative cover – a useful excuse – for her to visit any PSB station or office in Chengdu when she so chose. Not that Chief Prosecutor Gong needed to know that just now.

"You really should have called me," she insisted.

"Forgive me, Prosecutor…I lost track of time."

"If we are to learn to trust each other we must converse. If we have been separated for some hours, would it hurt you to check in with me? I will always answer my phone – always. Take today, for instance, you appear to be working but—"

"Prosecutor, please, let me speak…I have discovered something important about Junjie."

"Who's Junjie?"

He stared at her as if she had gone mad. "Prosecutor, Junjie is Old Man Gao's missing son. He vanished in October of last year, remember? The police at Wukuaishi Station did nothing to help."

"Of course, please excuse me...I didn't sleep so well last night." She looked down at the charcoal drawings on the table, suddenly remembering where she'd seen them before – stuck on the walls of the hovel Old Man Gao had called home.

"Prosecutor, look at this girl." Investigator Deng held up a portrait of a smiling young girl with pig-tails. "Her name is Tingting. She lives in the apartment building next to Aunty Li's. She's given me new information about Junjie's disappearance. Old Man Gao never thought to speak to the children. Tingting actually tried to speak to him but he ignored her, as did her own parents who didn't want to get involved. I thought I would have trouble finding her. The children have been playing inside their homes because of the bad weather. But I had a stroke of luck. There's been a murder and—"

Xu Ya's mind came into focus. "A murder?"

"A barman from The Singing Moon in Wukuaishi. It's just a student bar – no trouble there usually. One of the local police told me that the barman had been attacked on his way home and robbed. Anyway, the police raided a basement in Aunty Li's building and took a bunch of migrants in for questioning."

"Always the easiest people to blame," said Xu Ya, biting into her mooncake.

"Prosecutor, I have sympathy for migrants too. But we cannot ignore the fact that some of them are criminals. Anyway, the commotion had brought out a crowd to see what was going on, including the girl Tingting. So I spoke to her. Now I know I did wrong, Prosecutor, as her parents weren't around, but she told me an interesting story. As you can see from these charcoal drawings, Junjie was a very good artist. Tingting told me that last year some students from Chengdu National University...girls...had invited him into their dorm to draw pictures of them and—"

"What kind of pictures?"

Suddenly lost for words, he took a swig of his tea.

"Immoral pictures?" asked Xu Ya, pressing him.

"Prosecutor, Tingting called these university girls sluts. You see, Junjie was harmless. He didn't really know right from wrong. The girls supposedly gave him money and sweets...and his father was always out working, leaving him to his own devices."

"What did these girls do with the pictures?" asked Xu Ya. "Put them on the walls to admire themselves?"

"Maybe, but I have a theory, Prosecutor. You know how some

girls take photographs of themselves and send them to their boyfriends. I think it was the same with these pictures. A sketch or a drawing is a bit classier, yes? And some of these students have rich boyfriends in the city who might appreciate them. You should see the expensive cars that arrive to pick them up from the campus for dates. Some of these guys are gangsters – violent men, maybe jealous men."

"Are you saying Junjie was murdered in a jealous rage for drawing one of these girls in the nude?"

"Tingting told me that the last time she saw him, Junjie was on his way to the university to draw a girl called Poppy. That was back in October. He never returned. Whatever happened that day, this Poppy probably has useful information for us."

Xu Ya felt a frisson of excitement. "Have you been down to the dorm?"

"The security is too tight there. It's not easy to talk to the girls without attracting a lot of attention. And I thought you should be informed first. I didn't want to mess with a university without permission. There's also something else. Remember how someone had searched Old Man Gao's room before us. I was thinking robbers at the time. But I noticed a couple of pictures had been taken down from the walls. I didn't understand it then. Now I'm thinking they were pictures of Poppy. I haven't quite worked it out in my head, Prosecutor, but I reckon when Constable Ma shot Old Man Gao, someone got nervous…very nervous. They guessed we'd come snooping round to take a closer look at how the old man lived. Someone wanted all connections between Junjie and Poppy gone. If we don't move quickly, Prosecutor, and visit the university today, then maybe more evidence might vanish…maybe even Poppy herself."

"Do you trust the word of this child?"

"Yes, Prosecutor."

"Little girls have big imaginations."

"She's only nine years old but she seems to have far more sense than Junjie ever had. Tingting told him not to go to the university. She warned him he would get himself into trouble."

"Did Tingting ever see Poppy?"

"No, Prosecutor."

"Pity."

"Prosecutor, let's take those girls at the university by surprise."

This was not quite as easy as it sounded. Investigator Deng had been right to be cautious and right to seek her permission before going on a fishing trip into the girls' dorm. Any investigation into a missing youth or into immoral pictures hanging on the walls of the girls' dorm at Chengdu National University was well outside her brief. Moreover, investigations at universities had to be conducted very discreetly and sensitively. Some of the students would be the sons and daughters of important people. And the Board of Directors of the university would invariably include senior Party cadres. One would have to tread very carefully indeed. But the information Investigator Deng had provided intrigued her. She would enjoy finding out what had really happened to Junjie and embarrassing the idiot police at Wukuaishi Station with the facts – not to mention giving some immature girls a good talking to.

"We would need Chief Prosecutor Gong's authority to approach the university," she said. "He's on a stupid golfing trip to Shenzhen this weekend. He has a photograph of him with his golfing buddies on his desk instead of his wife."

"He actually prefers a brothel in Meishan to his wife," said Investigator Deng, finishing off his tea.

Her expression hardened. "Is that old PSB gossip or a fact?"

Investigator Deng didn't blink. "A fact, Prosecutor."

She put her hand to her mouth. And not because of what she had learned about Chief Prosecutor Gong but because Investigator Deng had surprised her again. Had Mouse been right after all? Was this seemingly overweight and nondescript man going to be a font of useful knowledge and a mule for hard work?

"Prosecutor?"

"Let me make a phone call," she said.

CHAPTER TWENTY-ONE

Saturday

The painting of The Willow Woman baffled and fascinated Philip Ye in equal measure. He had never seen anything quite like it. He had carefully taken it down from the wall in Aunty Li's basement, not trusting the ham-fisted forensic technicians to do so without ripping it. It was now laid out on the table of a cramped interrogation room at Wukuaishi Station. Philip Ye stood over it, determined to unravel the mystery of its origins, feeling that The Willow Woman – or at least the worship of her – had somehow contributed to Zhu Yi's violent death.

"Are you sure you haven't seen this painting before?"

"No, Superintendent," replied Constable Ma.

She was sitting in the corner of the room feeding some of her breakfast – *bāozi*, steamed buns filled with spicy pork and beansprouts – to her pet cat. Much to Boxer Tan's annoyance, Philip Ye had insisted on not only buying breakfast for Constable Ma and the uniforms still conducting a fingertip search for the murder weapon out on the damp streets, but also for the migrants they had detained for further questioning.

"You're setting a dangerous precedent, Mister Ye," said Boxer Tan. "We're the police, not a fucking charity."

But Philip Ye had remained unmoved. Personally convinced there was no murderer lurking among the migrants, he thought they might be more talkative with their bellies full of good food rather than the usual prisoner slop.

However, for now, it was the painting that held his attention. And it was the Sun Yat-sen suit The Willow Woman was wearing that unsettled him the most – the military-style attire so at odds with the otherwise religious nature of the scene. Or was that his personal prejudice clouding his judgement? He had always considered such 'uniforms' ugly – representations of an ugly time. It was hard not to see The Willow Woman's clothing as political rather than religious in meaning. The other symbolism in the painting was just as uncertain. The willow tree, underneath which woman was sitting, could represent loss or separation, as could the river at her feet – the river a 'flow of tears'. But artists, through the years, had also used the willow tree to symbolize the season of spring, or feminine beauty, or even to act as a ward against evil.

"What does the painting mean?" asked Constable Ma.

"I don't know," Philip Ye replied. "But we Chinese do like our female deities. Did you know that at the end of the 16th Century when Matteo Ricci came to China – he was from Italy, a Jesuit, a kind of Christian priest – he found us more receptive to images of the Virgin Mary than to those of Jesus on the cross? He was clever enough, as most Jesuits were then, not to take issue with our peculiar tastes. This may have been a mistake in the long-run, though. For many years we Chinese thought the Christian god a woman. As for lifelike representations of Jesus on the cross, we were so horrified by them that allegations of black magic were lodged against—"

"I am not religious," said Constable Ma, bluntly.

This made Philip Ye smile. "Maybe not, Constable, but as police we must be aware that many people do believe in all manner of gods and spirits...sometimes fervently so...and such beliefs can occasionally lead to conflict and murder."

"Then these people are stupid," said Constable Ma.

Philip Ye smiled again. "I have met many clever people who believe in the afterlife."

"Well, I do not," she replied, turning her face from him.

Thinking the time now right for this question, he asked, "Are you sure you never spoke to Zhu Yi while you were out on patrol?"

"Very sure, Superintendent."

"How did you know he was living in that basement? The stairs leading down to it are not visible from the road."

"I don't remember," she replied, continuing to avoid his gaze. She ripped off another chunk of a steamed bun to push into the mouth of her mewling cat.

It was a lie, of course.

But the reason for the lie would have to wait. Philip Ye had more important matters to attend to. He rolled up the painting, put it to one side and phoned Supervisor Long.

"Clever, I need a favour."

"Can it wait? I'm cooking breakfast for my wife."

"Why did you marry such a lazy cow?"

"I don't have a rational explanation – now what do you want?"

"There's a student bar…The Singing Moon…not far from Chengdu National University. I need to know who owns it…and then who really owns it."

"Philip, what are you doing back in Wukuaishi?"

"Stemming the black tide of lawlessness all on my own. Get back to me today, if you can. I'll be in the office later."

There was no hurry. According to Boxer Tan, the bar didn't open until midday. The interviews with the owner and the staff could wait.

Philip Ye took a quick bite from one of his own steamed buns, opened his notebook, and then shouted for Baby Wu to bring in the first of the prisoners – Scarface, the most talkative. Constable Ma stood to leave, but Philip Ye indicated with a shake of his head that she should stay. The fear she engendered in the migrants would serve as a useful counterpoint to the gentleness with which he was going to put his questions. Moreover, the law now required that all interrogations were conducted by at least two officers being present. She was as good as any other.

Baby Wu brought Scarface in and sat him down. Scarface didn't look too happy about Constable Ma being present. He seemed especially frightened of her cat. Baby Wu placed a packet of Golden Hair Monkey cigarettes and a cheap lighter in front of Scarface as Philip Ye had earlier instructed him to do. Scarface looked first to Philip Ye for approval and then greedily reached for the packet. He lit up and blew a cloud of smoke into the air, pretending more confidence than he had.

"Name?"

"Han Fan, sir – originally from Xinjin County."

"Tell me about Zhu Yi?"

"Tell you what, sir?"

"Everything you can remember."

Puffing on his cigarette, Han Fan was happy to talk. One of the other migrants – he couldn't remember which – had bumped into Zhu Yi at the Labour Exchange. Zhu Yi had already got a job at The Singing Moon but he wanted somewhere cheap to live. They all thought it a bit odd. But Zhu Yi was so likeable that nobody objected to him moving in and paying some of the rent. He was good at fixing stuff too – electrical stuff. He even helped rewire some of the building for Aunty Li. Not sure if she ever paid him, though. Did Zhu Yi know Old Man Gao? Sure, everyone knew Old Man Gao, explained Han Fan, his eyes nervously flicking over to Constable Ma and back to Philip Ye again, not wanting to say any more about that. But Zhu Yi, he was a lot of fun on his good days. Good days? Yes, he was a bit moody, some days he was happy and smiling but on others he was very depressed. Maybe it was something to do with missing his family or breaking up with his girlfriend. Zhu Yi wasn't a Chengdu native. He was from Mianyang. But he wasn't going to go back there. Zhu Yi said he'd completely split from his family. As for the girlfriend, Han Fan had never seen her. But he'd heard she visited the basement one day soon after Zhu Yi had moved in and that they'd had a furious row. One of the others might remember more about her. Zhu Yi was well into his religion though – wouldn't stop harping on about The Willow Woman, how The Willow Woman was going to bring them all good fortune, how The Willow Woman was going to make sure the people were equal, that no one would be poor any longer. Some of the others prayed with him but religion wasn't for Han Fan. A man made his own luck, didn't he? Did he or any of the other migrants ever meet any other believers in The Willow Woman? No, none of them did, but Zhu Yi always said there were many. No, he had no idea where the painting had come from. Zhu Yi had come back with it a couple of weeks ago. Zhu Yi never said where he got it. No, none of them had ever drunk at The Singing Moon. Students only, ethnic minorities and migrants not welcome. But sometimes Zhu Yi brought food and beer back for them all, which was really appreciated. The only problem with Zhu Yi was that he thought too much. People who think too much get depressed, don't they? A university drop-out. Really? Han Fan was surprised. He had had no idea.

After Han Fan, Philip Ye had the others brought in one by one. Some smoked, some didn't – some proved too frightened to say anything much at all. None of them contradicted what Han Fan had had to say though. Zhu Yi was very religious. The Willow Woman was his life. Everybody liked him. He had no enemies.

And so on, and so on, until the last of the detainees – Wang Li.

"His girlfriend's name was Yao Lin," said Wang Li.

"Are you sure?"

"Absolutely," said Wang Li, nodding furiously. "He spoke to me about her a lot after they broke up."

Philip Ye could believe it. Zhu Yi and Wang Li would have been of an age. They could even have been brothers if not, as was explained, for the fact Wang Li had been brought up on a farm, had never attended school and now collected waste paper to scratch out a meagre living.

"Did Zhu Yi own a phone? We didn't find one on his body."

Wang Li shook his head.

"Are you telling me the truth?"

Wang Li lit a cigarette though he had refused one earlier. "Why would I lie? He told me The Willow Woman disapproved of phones. I personally think he was hiding from his family in Mianyang. Maybe he got a girl pregnant there."

"Tell me about his girlfriend in Chengdu."

Wang Li explained that the girlfriend, Yao Lin, had broken up with Zhu Yi because she didn't like him working at the bar or living in the basement. Which Wang Li understood. Zhu Yi was smart. He could have done so much better for himself. Was she religious? Wang Li didn't think so. But the police could ask her. He knew exactly where she lived, in the east of the city. Zhu Yi had decided to visit her just after the New Year and Wang Li had gone with him to keep him company. But at Yao Lin's door, Zhu Yi had chickened out. He was really depressed that day, said Wang Li, almost as much as he was the day Old Man Gao had been shot down in the street like a dog.

Philip Ye stopped making notes. He stared at Wang Li, but Wang li had already covered his face with his hands, hiding himself from Constable Ma's fierce glare.

"Constable Ma, step outside for a moment," said Philip Ye, ruing his decision to let her sit in on the interviews.

She went silently, taking her cat with her. As soon as she had shut the door behind her Philip Ye felt the atmosphere in the room lighten and the tension – tension he had until then been unaware of – leave his body. Wang Li dropped his hands from his face and grinned bleakly.

"Tell me about Zhu Yi and Old Man Gao," said Philip Ye.

Wang Li shrugged. There wasn't much to tell. Everyone in Aunty Li's building had known Old Man Gao. A sweet old guy. They had all felt sorry for him when his idiot son had gone missing back in October. They had all promised Old Man Gao they'd keep an eye out for him. Not that Junjie had ever been seen again. Zhu Yi had been especially depressed by Junjie's disappearance. Wang Li remembered that very well. And then when Old Man Gao had been beaten up outside the Mayor's Office, it had been Zhu Yi who had cooked him some broth and spent some of his own cash to buy Old Man Gao some groceries. And then the other day, when Old Man Gao had been killed, Zhu Yi had refused to get out of bed he was so upset. It had been Wang Li who had persuaded him the last evening that he must go back to his job at The Singing Moon.

"If I hadn't done that then maybe he wouldn't have got murdered," said Wang Li, seeming genuinely upset.

"And Constable Ma...what about her?"

Wang Li frowned, drawing deeply on his cigarette.

"Speak! You won't get into trouble from me," insisted Philip Ye.

"We have always kept clear of her," Wang Li replied, not willing to say any more, which explained everything and nothing.

CHAPTER TWENTY-TWO

The drive to Secretary Wu's house in the south of the city was anything but a pleasurable experience for Xu Ya. She had been hoping to get to know Investigator Deng a little better, learn something of his family background, his time in the police, the reason he remained unmarried. But unfortunately the short journey was fraught from the start. Her tiny sports car was not exactly suited to his girth. He made a stupid fuss about squeezing into his seat, encroaching on her space as he did so. And then, when the car had picked up speed and she had begun to weave through the traffic, he had thought it amusing to feign fear. By the time they reached their destination, she was fuming. So, instead of inviting him into the house to meet Secretary Wu as she had originally planned, she told him to wait in the car until she was done.

However, her mood improved considerably when, after being let into the house by a maid, Secretary Wu came to greet her personally, taking her hand briefly as he did so.

"Are you well, Ms. Xu?"

"Very well, Secretary Wu – thank you for receiving me at such short notice."

He showed her into a fabulous reception room decorated in cream and soft yellows with an ornate crystal chandelier suspended from the ceiling. The attention to detail was such that Xu Ya detected a woman's hand in the room's design. If she ever met Secretary Wu's wife, Wang Biyu, she would offer her heartfelt compliments.

"And your parents…are they well also?" asked Secretary Wu, directing her to a leather sofa.

"They are in the best of health, thank you," she replied, taking her seat, regretting now not changing into something more appropriate for the house. Her black jeans seemed uncouth, out of place. Secretary Wu, though at home and on a Saturday morning, was dressed in a light-grey suit.

Secretary Wu took his seat in an armchair facing her. He delayed his speaking again until the maid had served tea, bobbed slightly, and left the room.

"How are you settling in at the Procuratorate?" he asked.

"I could not have been made more welcome."

"And Chief Prosecutor Gong?"

"Very generous with his advice."

"I am pleased to hear it, Ms. Xu. He is a bit rough around the edges but should never be underestimated. He has a fine mind. In the summer, perhaps, we will sit down with him and instruct him on the true reason for your appointment. There may well be personal relationships he needs to sever so he can be fully supportive of your work."

Xu Ya nodded, glad to learn that Chief Prosecutor Gong would not be her first object of scrutiny. She did not want the reputation as the prosecutor who took down her own boss.

"Now, before we discuss the reason for your visit," continued Secretary Wu, "tell me the outcome of your investigation into the police shooting in Wukuaishi."

Xu Ya had been prepared for this inquiry and spoke slowly, choosing her words with care.

"Secretary, the Procuratorate has deemed the shooting of the citizen Gao Yi, known locally as Old Man Gao, as lawful. Constable Ma, the officer who discharged her pistol, was properly authorised to carry a firearm and was not impaired by alcohol or any other factor at the time of the shooting. By her quick action, a criminal was stopped in his tracks and his hostage released unharmed. This is beyond dispute and so no disciplinary measures shall be taken against Constable Ma. However, it is my personal view that she was overly hasty in opting for lethal force and somewhat reckless in discharging her firearm in a crowded public place. I am also sympathetic to the public disquiet over the apparent callousness of the shooting and to the unhappy personal circumstances that led Old Man Gao to taking the young girl hostage. Moreover, I have found that the vetting and assessment of Constable Ma's application to transfer from the police in Pujiang County last summer to be fundamentally flawed. The Procuratorate has taken the view that her continued patrolling of the streets of Chengdu would be detrimental to public confidence in the PSB, and in the Party, and, as such, she should be transferred as soon as practicable back to Pujiang County. I drafted the Recommendation for Transfer Order last evening."

Secretary Wu nodded. "Excellent, Ms. Xu – I agree entirely. And Commissioner Ho?"

"Commissioner Ji of PSB Internal Discipline was to speak to Commissioner Ho directly. I am hoping to learn the outcome of that meeting sometime on Monday."

"Good – and what about Philip Ye?"

Xu Ya flushed. "Forgive me, Secretary Wu – what about him?"

"I believe he was present at the time of the shooting."

"Yes, indeed he was," said Xu Ya, annoyed at herself. It was easy to forget that Secretary Wu – perfectly mannered and with a most engaging smile – was one of the most knowledgeable and astute men she had ever met. The TV footage of Philip Ye brawling with a PAP officer would not have passed him by.

"Did you interview Philip Ye, Ms. Xu?"

"No, Secretary, it was deemed unnecessary. Chief Prosecutor Gong spoke with Chief of Police Di over the telephone. Superintendent Ye was indeed in the vicinity of the shooting, but quite by coincidence and his line of sight to the incident obscured by passing traffic. It was decided he had nothing substantial to offer our investigation."

"I am quite relieved, Ms. Xu…though I would have been interested to hear your opinion of him. Philip Ye is a most unusual man."

"So I have been led to understand." said Xu Ya, breathing again, taking a sip of her tea, willing herself to relax.

"But that fracas with the PAP officer, that was unfortunate," continued Secretary Wu, his eyes becoming distant and unfocused. "Philip has always had a temper. In that, if in nothing else, he takes after his father. The mother, now she is very different. I met her once: restrained, elegant – somewhat cold. She is an academic at the University of Oxford in England, a professor of chemistry. I often ponder how Philip would have turned out if she had taken a greater interest in his life."

"Do you know the family well, Secretary?"

Secretary Wu returned from his reverie, for a moment surprised by the question, "Ah, Ms. Xu, how quickly I have forgotten that you are not Chengdu born and bred. To answer your question, yes, I am very well acquainted with the family. Philip's father used to be one of my closest friends. The Year of Calamities changed all that. Ye Zihao was removed from the Mayor's Office due to allegations of impropriety and negligence in the wake of the earthquake. You should understand that as Chair of the Chengdu Political and Legal Committee it was my duty to remain impartial, to await formal charges to be instituted. For some reason, we are still awaiting these charges. It saddens me that Ye Zihao hasn't spoken to me since the day of his arrest, perhaps believing erroneously that I had the power to prevent his removal from office and as a friend should have done so."

Xu Ya made sympathetic noises but sensed Secretary Wu was not being fully open with her. The interminable house-arrest of Ye Zihao, well publicised in Chongqing, had always baffled her – Ye Zihao's comeuppance not quite final, the takeover of Chengdu by the Shanghai Clique not quite complete. Was Secretary Wu somehow preventing those charges being put against his old friend? Did the new status quo suit him? He was, after all, one of the few Chengdu natives to retain his post after the Shanghai Clique had taken over. Or did Ye Zihao still have some very powerful friends in Beijing? She put the thought to the back of her mind for further consideration.

"Is something troubling you, Ms. Xu?"

"I was just thinking about friendships, how difficult they are to maintain when the law must take precedence."

"This is one of the reasons I chose you, Ms. Xu. You are one of the few to realise that law and public order *must* always take precedence – that is, if we are to break the cycle of gangsterism, and the abuse of family, social and business relationships that so plagues our city and our nation."

He was, of course, speaking of *guānxì*, that web of social connections through which a person could achieve various ends. Simply put, if one did someone a favour, one could, at some future time, ask for a favour in return.

It was, however, much more complicated than that. Everybody in China existed in such a web of relationships. And though, as Xu Ya saw it, the current rise of individualism in China seemed to present an argument against the continuing practice of *guānxì*, she did not envision its obsolescence anytime soon. Some legal scholars saw *guānxì* as being incompatible with the Rule of Law. Xu Ya took a more nuanced view. The exchange of gifts or favours did not have to involve the breaking of the law. She had to admit, though, that her thinking on this subject was not fully done. Even if the law might not be broken by the doing of favours, it would be a fairer and better country if one progressed through life on merit and personal accomplishment than because of whomever one knew. But wasn't that also true of every other country in the world and not just China?

"Life is a difficult road," Secretary Wu continued. "And sometimes it is others, our families for instance, who suffer as a consequence of our morally correct actions. Consider Philip Ye again. What I have not told you, Ms. Xu, was that he was once like a son to me and my wife. We have no children of our own, you understand. Years ago, when his father was away on business, Philip would stay with us – often for days at a time. Since the removal of Ye Zihao from office, since the breaking of my personal friendship with him, Philip has not returned to our house or spoken to me or my wife. Again, I do not blame Philip for this. A son should always be loyal to his father. But for my wife it is a personal tragedy. Her heart is shattered and I fear it will never recover. She writes to Philip twice a year, on his birthday and at the New Year – not once has he replied."

"Maybe he doesn't understand how much hurt he inflicts by not communicating," said Xu Ya, carelessly, her mind floating back to the past. "He hardly spoke to anyone at Wuhan."

Secretary Wu was startled. "What did you say, Ms. Xu?"

Unable to take back her words, she stumbled on. "In Wuhan…the School of Law…Philip Ye was in my class."

Secretary Wu shook his head at his own stupidity. "You should think me a fool, Ms. Xu. Your résumé is still on my desk. It never occurred to me that you were at Wuhan at the same time as Philip." He stood and held out his hand to her. "Please, come with me."

She followed him down the hall and into a small room which she assumed he used as his library and study. There was a desk and chair placed next to a large window that looked out onto a beautifully cultivated garden. As for the walls, shelves filled with books ran from floor to ceiling. From the desk Secretary Wu picked up a photograph in a silver frame and passed it to her. The picture was of Philip Ye, looking hardly more than twenty years of age, standing arm in arm with a proud and smiling young *lǎowài* woman – not as handsome as he, but striking nevertheless, her presence reaching out of the photograph and into the room.

"Isobel," said Secretary Wu.

"Who is she?" asked Xu Ya, knowing full well.

"Philip's fiancée from England – a real force of nature." Secretary Wu smiled to himself as if he were remembering good times. "Philip's father was infuriated by the engagement. I am sure he had his reasons, probably thinking Philip too young. But Philip always had a mind of his own. When Philip brought her to Chengdu to visit, Ye Zihao refused to let her in his house. So she stayed with us. I have to admit that my wife and I were ready to dislike her. But she was like a whirlwind, full of energy and life, lighting up every room she entered. It was a great pity. She died less than a year after this photograph was taken. A cancer of the bone...painful but mercifully quick. It is hard to believe that fifteen years have gone by. After the funeral Philip returned from England a desperately sad young man. He was quieter than ever...more turned in on himself. My wife is convinced he will now never marry. She says he prefers to commune with shadows, with ghosts, rather than with the living. I am inclined to agree. This was my real reason for asking if you had interviewed him about the shooting in Wukuaishi, after that stupid fight with the PAP officer. I would have valued your opinion, how he is these days in his heart and in his mind."

Isobel.

A force of nature.

A whirlwind.

Xu Ya felt so small, so insignificant, she wanted to run from the room.

Secretary Wu took the photograph from her and replaced it with another. This photograph was older still, of Philip Ye as a boy, a small hawk on his outstretched arm. Philip Ye was not looking at the camera but at the hawk – in wonderment and adoration. It was the hawk that stared into the camera. It seemed to stare directly into Xu Ya's soul. She shivered at the wildness of its eyes.

"Shikra," said Secretary Wu.

"Pardon?"

"It is the species of hawk, Ms. Xu. It is a bird of southern climes, rare I believe around here in Sichuan, but common enough across all of South-East Asia and India – and Africa too, if my memory serves me well. Philip adored that bird for the short time it was in his possession."

"He lost it?"

"In a manner of speaking, Ms. Xu. Come let me introduce you to my wife."

They found her in the kitchen, sitting at the table with a cup of coffee, Western-style, a book open before her. Xu Ya had been expecting, after all that had been said, to meet a woman beaten down, embittered by life. Wang Jiyu was anything but. In her late middle-years, her eyes and smile still dazzled.

She stood and shook Xu Ya's hand, saying, "I have heard much about you, Ms. Xu. Welcome to Chengdu. You caused quite a stir with your presentation before the Committee."

"Oh, in a good way, I hope," replied Xu Ya, very flattered and very pleased.

"We should invite Ms. Xu to dinner," said Secretary Wu.

"Indeed we should," said Wang Jiyu.

"Your house is so lovely," said Xu Ya, wanting to return a compliment.

"Thank you," said Wang Jiyu.

"Ms. Xu knew Philip at Wuhan," Secretary Wu told his wife.

It was then that Xu Ya suddenly saw the loss flare in Wang Jiyu's dark eyes.

Xu Ya flushed again and began to stutter out an explanation. "When I said I knew him…I did not mean to say…he was just in my class…not a friend as such, if you understand."

"Do not be embarrassed, Ms. Xu," said Wang Jiyu. "I don't believe anybody knows the real Philip Ye. He revealed little about himself as a boy, even less I should think now he is a man. But I would like to hear about your time in Wuhan."

Xu Ya agreed to set a date for dinner in the near future. She hoped Wang Jiyu, though of an older generation, would become a close friend – a woman with whom she could properly converse.

Back in the reception room, with more tea poured for them by the maid, Xu Ya was finally able to explain to Secretary Wu the reason for her visit. She spoke about what Investigator Deng had discovered – giving him full credit – and that she needed the authority to approach Chengdu National University, not only in regard to the possible immoral behaviour of some of its female students but also to track down the student Poppy who may have information for them concerning the fate of Junjie.

Secretary Wu considered the problem for a few moments and then asked, "Do you know how many children go missing in China every year, Ms. Xu?"

"I haven't done that research."

"Maybe 70,000 a year, possibly many more. It is a national scandal that defies an easy solution. Some children are given away, or sold by their parents to make ends meet. Others are kidnapped off the street by gangs to work in factories, or forced into the sex industry, or the more fortunate sold to couples lacking children of their own. I will happily put you in touch with Professor Ou, the Director of Teaching at the university. He ought to be made aware of your concerns about the behaviour of some of the young women there. But I would ask you not to expend much energy searching for this

Junjie. He could be anywhere in China by now. He is nothing but a minnow in a very big river. Remember, Ms. Xu, it is the big fish we are after...the big fish. If we bring the big fish to justice then surely the minnows will have nothing then to fear. Do you understand?"

She did.

CHAPTER TWENTY-THREE

No murder weapon was recovered during the fingertip search of the area or anything else that could be construed as useful evidence. No witnesses were found from the canvass of all the local apartments either. It seemed no one had heard or seen anything, except one old woman who said she had heard shouting from the street during the night – or maybe it was the night before, she wasn't quite sure. The forensic team had thoroughly swept the basement where the migrants had been living. They had come up empty-handed also, not a speck of blood to be found. Needing his people to return to their usual tasking, Boxer Tan had said enough was enough and ordered everybody back to Wukuaishi Station.

Alone now in the interrogation room, Philip Ye quickly completed his notes from the interviews with the migrants and considered his next move. Disregarding the possibility (for now) that there was a violent psychopath loose on the streets targeting people at random, he had to assume that Zhu Yi knew his killer – or at least his killer knew him. That it was a homicide made to look like a robbery lent credibility to this view. It was time to return to PSB HQ. He needed space and time to reflect on what he'd learned so far, and to make enquiries about The Willow Woman.

Neither Wukuaishi Station nor PSB HQ was the place for Constable Ma. Wukuaishi Station was too close to the bus and train station. Boxer Tan and Baby Wu would eventually take their eyes off her and she could easily slip away, never to be found again. And that would not do. There was much, Philip Ye was convinced, she had yet to tell. As for PSB HQ, there were too many eyes and ears there. Constable Ma was on suspension. If she was seen with him, he would have questions to answer. Not difficult questions admittedly – she was helping him with his enquiries – but questions he didn't wish to be bothered with right now. He needed to find another place for her to stay.

He poked his head into Boxer Tan's office. Boxer Tan was struggling with a mountain of paperwork of his own.

"I'm leaving but I might be back later," said Philip Ye.

"And the big girl?"

"I'm taking her with me."

Boxer Tan looked relieved. "What about the migrants? Shall I kick them loose? It's Saturday. I'll need the space in the cells tonight."

"I'll let you know."

This was not the answer Boxer Tan had been hoping for.

Philip Ye found Constable Ma sitting by the reception desk with her cat on her lap and her luggage by her feet. Baby Wu, full of life despite the long night, was chatting away to her, not that she was paying much attention. Her big eyes found Philip Ye as soon as he emerged from the back offices, wary of what he was going to say or do.

"Constable Ma, you are to come with me," he said, choosing not to explain himself. "Leave the cat here. It will be fine, won't it, Baby Wu?"

"Yes, Mister Ye – I'll take good care of Yoyo."

Constable Ma stood, looking uncertain, clutching the big ginger cat to her chest.

"That's an order, Constable," said Philip Ye, wanting to be off.

Baby Wu came around for the desk and took the cat from her, demonstrating some talent with animals. The cat made no complaint and began to purr in his arms. With a single threatening glance back at Baby Wu – a warning that if anything bad happened to Yoyo there would be consequences – Constable Ma picked up her luggage and followed Philip Ye out onto the street. He took the luggage from her and put it in the boot of the Mercedes. She was about to take the back seat again when he said, "No, you sit up front with me."

He drove them into the city. He did not speak to her again until he parked up outside the front of The Silver Tree.

"This is my sister's restaurant. I want you to stay here for now. Later, I will return and we'll go looking for Zhu Yi's former girlfriend Yao Lin. I need to know if you recognise her and if you have seen her recently near to The Singing Moon. I hope to learn much from her about Zhu Yi's background, how he came to be living with the migrants. But we must also remember that, for reasons we are yet to determine, she may have had a hand in his murder or be the murderer herself. We must consider all possibilities until further information comes to light."

Constable Ma listened carefully, taking all of this in. She asked no questions. She got out of the car and took her luggage from the boot and followed him obediently down the alley at the side of the restaurant and in through the door to the kitchens. The preparations for the long day of cooking to come were suddenly suspended as all the cooks stopped what they were doing and gawped at the immense woman Philip Ye had brought with him, her head almost brushing the low ceiling.

"Handsome Boy, what are you thinking bringing *her* here?" asked Ye Lan, horrified, remembering Constable Ma from the TV.

"It is just for a few hours, Little Mother…she needs a place to rest."

"Has she no place of her own?"

"She will be out of the way in the spare room. I'll be back for her by lunch, I promise."

"No, Handsome Boy…this is not right! This is my business, my home. What will the customers say?"

"Little Mother, please…she is police. She'll be no trouble."

Ye Lan sighed. She could only protest so much. She had never been able to refuse Philip Ye, ever.

Philip Ye took Constable Ma up the stairs to the living accommodation above the restaurant. The boys, Qu Peng and Qu Gang, met them at the top of the stairs, well aware that something was up. When Constable Ma rose before them to her full size and height, they backed away, their mouths dropping open.

"Boys, this is Constable Ma. She is going to rest in the spare room. I don't want you to disturb her."

The boys nodded as one, still open-mouthed.

Philip Ye took Constable Ma to the spare room. It was filled with stacks of cardboard produce boxes which he moved to one side so she could get in and set her luggage down on the single bed. He doubted the bed was big enough for her but it would have to do.

"She does not want me here," said Constable Ma.

"Ye Lan? Ah, do not mind her. She has lots of worries, that's all. It is difficult running your own business. But there is no bigger heart in all of Chengdu."

"She does not look like your sister."

"She's my half-sister. My father divorced her mother a few years before I was born. When I was very young Ye Lan often used to look after me."

Constable Ma sat down on the bed, the old mattress giving way somewhat under her weight.

"So, you promise me you will stay here for now?" he asked.

"Yes."

"Good – I will return in a few hours and then we will go hunting for Yao Lin."

He saw indecision in her eyes. "What is it?"

She shook her head, not wanting to speak.

"Constable, if I am to do my job properly you must tell me everything. I will not shout at you or hit you."

"Superintendent, what if Zhu Yi was a bad man?"

"Bad man or not, I will do my utmost to hunt his murderer down."

"What if Zhu Yi deserved to die?"

"Constable, it is not your place or mine to say if someone should live or die. That is for a court to decide."

"He hurt Junjie."

"Are you sure of this?"

"No, not sure – but I think so."

She reached into her pocket and pulled out a small photograph. She held it out to him, avoiding his eyes as she did so. He took the photograph from her. He thought at first it a picture of two of her male relatives, an old man and a youth, both laughing, making silly faces at the camera – just a happy family snapshot. It only slowly dawned on him that the face of the old man was familiar to him. It was Old Man Gao. And the awkward-looking youth next to him had to be Junjie. It was this photograph Constable Ma had been holding in her hands when he found her in the train station concourse, that she had swiftly hidden from him then.

"So you knew them?"

Constable Ma closed her eyes, squeezing forth tears. Deep emotion, dark and intense, flooded out of her, engulfing the small room, almost taking Philip Ye's breath away.

"Constable Ma, you must explain yourself."

"I met Old Man Gao in December," she said, the tears beginning to roll down her face. "Junjie had gone missing and Wukuaishi Station had turned Old Man Gao away. So Old Man Gao came to me. He knew I was police…that I walked the streets at night and saw many things."

"He asked you to keep an eye out for Junjie?"

"Yes – and he wanted me to speak to all the people in Aunty Li's building."

"To ask questions?"

"He thought somebody might know something…that someone might be lying to him."

It all made sense now. So this was how she knew Zhu Yi lived with the migrants. She had been down to the basement before. She had confronted them all already. No wonder they were terrified of her.

"You spoke to the migrants?"

"I did not trust them," she replied. "Some of them are pick-pockets."

"And Zhu Yi?"

"He would not look at me when I confronted him. He said he had no idea where Junjie was. I think him a liar. I think he hurt Junjie."

"Did you tell Old Man Gao of your suspicions about Zhu Yi?"

"I had no proof," she said, wiping the tears from her eyes with her sleeve, accepting a silk handkerchief from Philip Ye. "I didn't know what to do. No one likes me at Wukuaishi Station. Who would listen to me there? And then it was too late. Old Man Gao got beaten up outside the Mayor's Office. Those *Chéngguǎn* are bad people." She blew her nose in his handkerchief. "They really hurt him. I took him to a doctor. I paid for some medicine for him…to help with the pain."

"He had no money of his own?"

"It was all gone. His savings had been spent on travelling around the city looking for Junjie. He'd lost his job as janitor at the elementary school. I took him home from the doctor's and then Zhu Yi turned up, pretending he wanted to help, bringing food and a couple of bottles of beer. I did not trust him. I did not like him. All those false smiles. All that Willow Woman talk! Anyway, Old Man Gao was not the same after the beating. He stayed in his room and would not come out. I think his brain was damaged. He would not eat. He began to shout bad things out of the window. He told me he was going to hurt someone…really hurt someone."

"So the authorities would finally pay attention to him?"

"Yes."

"And you believed him?"

"Yes – he swore it to me."

"Is that why you kept your pistol on the safety against regulations?"

"Yes."

"Is this why you shot him when he took the knife to that girl on the street?"

"I could not let him hurt that poor little girl," she said, her eyes full of pain.

"Why didn't you tell the Procuratorate all this?"

"It is difficult for me to speak when I am frightened."

"Constable Ma, I must ask you, did you have anything to do with Zhu Yi's death?"

Her face reddened, her grief replaced by anger. "I am no murderer!"

"I am glad to hear it. Now get some rest. I will return soon."

He closed the door behind him and found the two boys waiting for him.

"What's wrong with her?" asked Qu Peng.

"Why is she crying?" asked Qu Gang.

"A friend of hers has died," Philip Ye replied, leading the boys away from the door. "So leave her be."

"She is as big as an ogre."

"A real big ogre!"

"Boys, remember what I told you. Be respectful. She is police... like me. Now get on with your homework."

Outside, he sat in the car for a while, breathing deeply, waiting for his head to clear, for the effect of Constable Ma's powerful emotions to leave him. He couldn't understand how he'd been so mistaken about her. At the scene of the shooting of Old Man Gao, he had thought her callous, unfeeling. In reality he had been witnessing someone suffering from profound shock, someone who had just killed a friend – perhaps the only friend she had made in Chengdu.

Had it dawned on her afterward that Old Man Gao had betrayed that friendship, had never intended to harm that little girl, had actually manipulated her into killing him? He hoped not. She had a burden enough to carry for the rest of her life.

Philip Ye started the engine. "You should have appeared to her and not to me, old man," he said out loud, hoping the ghost of Old Man Gao was lingering nearby. "You owe her an apology."

CHAPTER TWENTY-FOUR

Back at PSB HQ, Philip Ye found Superintendent Zuo long gone. Scorpion girl was safely tucked away in the custody suite, her interrogation delayed until Superintendent Zuo's return for his next shift later that evening. Philip Ye considered briefly going down to take a peek at her, to satisfy his curiosity, to see what sort of creature was happy to stick a knife in the neck of her own boyfriend. But he dismissed the idea. There were better things he could be doing.

He phoned the Media Team and briefed them on Zhu Yi's murder, providing very few details, telling them to stick to the story that it was a robbery gone wrong. Best the murderer think their aim had been achieved for now. He was asked about the migrants detained at Wukuaishi Station. Just routine questioning, he said – no news there. It remained to be seen what the local journalists made up later in the day.

That done, he took the stairs up to Chief Di's office. The door was open. Chief Di was sitting at his desk, a pile of financial documents in front of him. He was speaking to his secretary Ms. Miao. She was assisting him prepare for the crucial budget meeting Sunday morning. The only item on the agenda that mattered was the potential release of extra funds from the city for the recruitment of a new mass intake of police cadets – a subject very dear to Chief Di's heart. He didn't want to lose the argument this time.

Ms. Miao stood by with her pen and notebook as Philip Ye

briefed Chief Di on the events of the morning, omitting none of the detail this time – excepting the fact that he was working with Constable Ma. Philip Ye had brought the painting of The Willow Woman with him and unfurled it for both Chief Di and Ms. Miao to see.

"So, is this a religious killing?" asked Chief Di.

"I honestly don't know, sir."

"Have we ever heard of this Willow Woman cult before?"

"Not that I know of, sir."

Chief Di looked to Ms. Miao for confirmation of this. Not yet thirty, highly educated, her personal life a mystery to everyone at the PSB, Ms. Miao shook her head. She saw every document that crossed Chief Di's desk, memorising every one of them, so it was said. She had arrived after the earthquake with the rest of the Shanghai Clique and had been foisted upon Chief Di as one of the conditions of him staying in post. At first distrustful of her, Chief Di now depended on her for almost everything. No one truly knew where her loyalties lay.

"Do you need more human resource, Philip?"

"Not as yet, sir – I'm still making preliminary enquiries."

"Good, good – let me know if you do," said Chief Di, his attention already drifting back to his financial projections.

Ms. Miao gave Philip Ye an opaque smile and he left the office wondering if the trek up a few floors had been worth it. Chief Di would soon forget the conversation. Philip Ye resented having to report directly to Chief Di, who had never really understood homicide investigations anyway. Chengdu PSB needed Commissioner Wei to recover from his cancer, to get back behind his desk, to provide some real leadership, purpose and direction. Not that that was going to happen anytime soon. If at all.

Next order of business was the body.

Back in his office, Philip Ye phoned the morgue. The clerk who answered said that Doctor Kong was still in the middle of the autopsy. She would send him her report when she was good and ready and not before. Philip Ye then had the joy of the phone being hung up on him.

Unimpressed with the new discourteous attitude down at the morgue – Doctor Wang had been happy to take a call with a corpse lying open before him – Philip Ye felt his body sag, exhaustion catching up with him. He closed his eyes and leaned back in his chair, drained by another night with little sleep and by the problem of Constable Ma. She was due to be transferred back to Pujiang County. Maybe waiting for her there were people ready to put a bullet in the back of her skull. Soon he had to decide what to do with her. Soon he had to get her out of town.

The door crashed open, shaking Philip Ye out of his meditation.

"You asleep?" asked Supervisor Long, throwing himself into a chair, grinning like a monkey.

"No…but I'd like to be."

"Pick up your pen."

Philip Ye did as he was told. Supervisor Long reeled off what followed from memory.

"The Singing Moon bar in Wukuaishi…owned and managed by a Mister Bao Ling…not a Party member…no known criminal associations…which as you know means very little but that's the best intelligence we have…has a couple of other bars across the city…caters mainly for students…in fact, likes university girls so much he regularly dates them though he's pushing forty…and pays his taxes. So he seems to be a remarkably stand-up guy despite his propensity for impressionable young women."

"Thanks Clever, I'm hoping to speak to him before the end of the day."

"This to do with the killing in Wukuaishi?"

"Yes."

"How did you get landed with that? It's not on your patch."

"The only local guys with any talent were either off with flu or still drunk from my father's party. There's also a connection to that shooting of the old man the other day that I'm interested in pursuing."

"I'd heard over the radio that you've been running around with the big girl again," said Supervisor Long. "You're playing with fire there, Mister Ye. And I am not just talking about our nit-picking colleagues at the Procuratorate. The big girl's got a dark cloud hanging over her. Probably born with it…cursed at birth. Everyone can see it. You should ditch her as soon as you can."

"You'd probably tell her the same about me."

"I would, I would…but, like you, would she listen to wise old Uncle Long?" He chuckled to himself, his eyes moving all over the office, full of nervous energy.

Philip Ye knew the signs. "What is it? What else have you discovered?"

"Not me – Strike Hard found it out. We know why the big girl was armed."

"Tell me."

"Back in Shanghai, before he and the rest of his buddies arrived here to make our lives more interesting, Commissioner Ho was a very naughty boy. He had an affair with the wife of a low-level cadre employed by the Shanghai Municipal Water Authority. This cadre found out about the affair. But, before he could do anything about it, Commissioner Ho had him arrested on some trumped up charge and sent to some pestilential labour camp. That was maybe ten years ago or more. Anyway, last summer, our cadre was let out. The rumour is that he has armed himself with a machete and has promised to come south to Chengdu and wreak bloody hell. Commissioner Ho got to hear about this – we think he is still seeing that poor cadre's wife whenever he goes back to Shanghai for a visit – and decided he needed round the clock personal protection here in Chengdu.

"So he diverted some of the new recruits from last summer's beautification campaign into Robbery, armed them, and detailed them to guard him and his house. His reasoning was, I suppose, that if he was to have round the clock protection he wanted guards easy on the eye. Needless to say, when the big girl turned up at his house, he realised that she was not quite as advertised and sent her packing to Wukuaishi Station…where she was conveniently forgotten until she put two bullets into that crazy old man. It's like the old man's ghost is taking his revenge. Commissioner Ho's little empire in Robbery is crumbling. It seems he lied about the big girl to Internal Discipline and the Procuratorate, saying he knew nothing about her, how she came to be at Wukuaishi Station or how she came to be armed. By all accounts, Commissioner Ji is raging. Commissioner Ji was seen out with Party Chief Li and Mayor Cang last night. Commissioner Ho must have been the subject of their discussion. I think, for the first time, we are about to see the Shanghai Clique eat one of their own."

"Who's going to get bumped up to run Robbery?" asked Philip Ye, running through a list of likely candidates in his mind.

"Don't know…maybe Commissioner Ji will do it himself for a while. It won't be a Chengdu native. Too many Shanghai Clique secrets locked away in those offices. So don't hold your breath looking for that elusive promotion."

"Robbery's not my style."

"That's not what I've heard about the family Ye," said Supervisor Long, with a mischievous wink.

CHAPTER TWENTY-FIVE

Saturday

Fatty Deng felt sick to the stomach as Prosecutor Xu drove them both across the city to Chengdu National University. And not just because of Prosecutor Xu's impetuous and, frankly, dangerous driving. He couldn't shake the sinking feeling that no trace of Junjie would never be found. That brief meeting of minds achieved with Prosecutor Xu in Starbucks was gone, her enthusiasm for finding out what happened to Junjie evaporated, as well as any thought of embarrassing the police of Wukuaishi Station. Something had been said to Prosecutor Xu in Secretary Wu's house. Fatty Deng didn't know what, but he could guess. No doubt the Procuratorate had more important things to do than search for a missing idiot boy. It was a view Fatty Deng understood, but a tragedy nonetheless.

Prosecutor Xu hadn't been silent, though. She had explained how important Professor Ou was, how both of them had to be properly respectful. Not only was he the Director of Teaching at the university but he had a permanent seat on the Chengdu Science and Technology Committee *and* was also a senior local Party cadre.

She had then started talking about the audit proposal, how excited Chief Prosecutor Gong was by the idea, how they each had their work cut out if they were going to turn that proposal into a workable and effective product. They had to sell it not only to the other sections of the Procuratorate but also to PSB Internal Discipline as well. If they were going to succeed then both she and he had to find a way to function properly together, to communicate, to trust each other. She even hinted at some special, highly confidential work to come.

She did not mention Junjie.

Not once.

When she started babbling on about big fish and minnows, Fatty Deng found that he had lost all interest in listening to her. He turned his face away from her and stared out of window instead at the grey, mist-covered city passing by.

Chengdu National University is a most prestigious learning establishment. Not as big or as famous at the other universities located in the city – Chengdu University to the east, Sichuan University to the south – it nevertheless attracted a rigorously selected, precociously talented and highly ambitious set of students.

Or so Professor Ou maintained.

"It is almost unheard of," he said, "for one of our students to fail to get a good job upon graduation."

And so the drivel went on.

By the time Professor Ou and Prosecutor Xu began chatting about their personal experiences at universities in the West as if they were already the best of friends, Fatty Deng was beginning to feel nostalgic about collecting debts for Freddie Yun.

They were sitting in Professor Ou's luxurious office. Professor Ou, an absurdly thin man with wire-rimmed spectacles wedged on the end of his nose, could, it seemed, talk the hind legs off a donkey. However, Prosecutor Xu appeared to be in her element, the most relaxed Fatty Deng had ever seen her.

"We are truly an international university," said Professor Ou, "but fully grounded in socialist principles."

Whatever the fuck that meant, thought Fatty Deng.

Thankfully, he was saved from more of this mindless nonsense by the return of Madame Xiong Lan, the university's senior administrator. She had come into the office on a Saturday morning at Professor Ou's request to conduct a thorough search of the university records for any student named Poppy. She had the worst news though.

"Professor Ou, I am sorry to say no girl of that name is currently studying at the university – or has done as long as our computerised records go back."

A stern-faced woman in her mid-fifties with tightly curled hair, Madame Xiong exuded an air of cold efficiency. If anyone had been able to track Poppy down, Fatty Deng had trusted it would be her.

Dismayed, he studied the titles of the books on the shelving nearest him to avoid Prosecutor Xu's fierce glare.

"Oh well, you should not look upon this as a wasted visit," said Professor Ou, cheerfully. "It has been very pleasant to—"

"Professor, if you don't mind," interrupted Madame Xiong. "We should not waste this golden opportunity. Girls these days are not what they used to be. Many are strangers to common decency. Just because no trace of this Poppy has been found doesn't mean some of the girls are not having immoral pictures drawn of themselves."

"Madame Xiong, what do you have in mind?" asked Professor Ou, somewhat surprised.

"I wouldn't dare to presume to waste the Prosecutor's time. But perhaps Investigator Deng might spare a few moments and speak to some of the girls, throw a few questions at them…frighten them a bit. It wouldn't take me long to round a few of them up. Word would soon percolate around campus that the Procuratorate has been here."

"I see…I see," said Professor Ou, looking to Prosecutor Xu for her opinion.

"Investigator Deng would be delighted," said Prosecutor Xu, without hesitation.

"Excellent, excellent…and you, my dear, can keep me company," said Professor Ou. "You must tell me all about your upbringing in Chongqing. I have many friends in Chongqing. Only last month…."

Madame Xiong took Fatty Deng to a far less sumptuously appointed office. An old metal filing cabinet stood in one corner, a table and a few stools in the centre of the room. A narrow window let in a stingy amount of daylight. The office could easily have served as a police interrogation room. Which might have been Madame Xiong's intention.

Not that Fatty Deng was about to play tough policeman. Prosecutor Xu had been quite clear with her instructions prior to their meeting with Professor Ou and Madame Xiong.

"We are to consider ourselves guests of the university until there is clear, irrefutable proof of criminality," she had said. "No threats are to be issued, no groundless allegations made."

Madame Xiong had been quick to point out on meeting her that sweeps of the university accommodation were often made and no immoral pictures had ever been discovered. And, now, as there was no record of a Poppy at the university, Fatty Deng wasn't sure where this left him. He had also always assumed if any of the students were to be interviewed, Prosecutor Xu would be sitting at his side, smart as a tack, throwing out incisive questions, determined to catch them out in their lies. In the police he had interviewed many street thugs and lowlifes. But they had either sat mute or made up stupid stories to cover their wrongdoing. Alone, how was he going to outfox students far better educated and far cleverer than he? And what was Prosecutor Xu doing ignoring standard interview protocol: two investigators present at all times. It was as if she wanted to wash her hands of this investigation as quickly as possible.

"I am sorry if this inconveniences you, Investigator Deng," said Madame Xiong.

"No, no…I am happy to oblige," he replied. "But I don't want to come across too strong with these girls. Will you stay for the interviews?"

A smile graced her otherwise impassive face. "That was always my intention, Investigator Deng. I just don't want you to mince your words. I am convinced some of these girls are already dating gangsters and hoodlums. Don't let a few alluring smiles fool you."

As she left the office to gather up some prospective candidates, Fatty Deng sat down on one of the hard stools and prepared his notebook and pen, doing his best to suppress his nerves. He tried to imagine himself as Philip Ye. But, try as he might, he found it too difficult to pull off Philip Ye's relaxed air of confidence and arrogance, that: 'I'm half-English, impossibly handsome, incredibly rich, impeccably dressed and therefore I don't give a fuck' look that Philip Ye managed whatever the hour of the day or night. Fatty Deng had to content himself with adjusting his suit jacket so that it didn't pull at his shoulders so much and running through the few questions in his mind he'd like some answers to. Which led him to a sudden and shocking thought: 'Poppy' might be an alias. Why this hadn't occurred to him before? These interviews with these girls might not be a waste of time after all. And, with Prosecutor Xu happily chatting to Professor Ou, who was there to stop him asking questions about Junjie?

In the car, Prosecutor Xu had said, "At the university, we are to enquire only about Poppy. It is too early to make any connection between the university and the disappearance of Junjie."

Well, fuck that, thought Fatty Deng.

"Name?"

Barely a whisper.

"Speak up!" snapped Madame Xiong.

"Zhang Lin."

Fatty Deng made a note of the name. The first girl Madame Xiong had returned with was slim and pretty, but with a mass of hair which, when she sat down, completely obscured her face. It made it impossible for Fatty Deng to see her eyes, to get any indication of what she was thinking.

Fatty Deng took the photograph of Junjie given him by Head-mistress Han and pushed it across the table to Zhang Lin. "Do you recognise this youth?"

A brief glance from beneath the hair, a brief shake of the head.

More surprised by the question was Madame Xiong. Having taken a seat next to Fatty Deng making it clear she was not there to support the girls in any way, she leaned forward and snatched up the photograph, asking, "Investigator Deng, who is this?"

"Just a person of interest. We think he may be the artist respon-sible for the immoral pictures."

"What a strange-looking young man," said Madame Xiong, placing the photograph back down on the table. "Ms. Zhang, are you sure you haven't taken your clothes off for this man?"

Another brief shake of the head.

"Then get out," said Madame Xiong, "and stop wasting Investi-gator Deng's time. And send the next in!"

Zhang Lin was up off her chair and out of the door before Fatty Deng could think to stop her. He glanced down at his notebook. All he had recorded was her name.

The second girl entered, very different from the first. She wore a skirt far too short, heels so high she could hardly walk, and had so much make-up slathered over her face Fatty Deng had seen chickens in some down-market brothels show more restraint.

"Name?"

"Pan Mei," she replied, giving him the once-over with her eyes. "What's wrong with your suit? Can't you afford one that fits?"

"Ms. Pan!" Madame Xiong raised a finger in warning. She apolo-gised to Fatty Deng on Pan Mei's behalf.

Feeling a headache coming on, Fatty Deng pointed to the photo-graph of Junjie. "Do you know him, Ms. Pan?"

Pan Mei laughed derisively. "You think I'd be friends with an idiot like that?"

"How about a girl named Poppy?"

"What a stupid name!"

Madame Xiong ordered Pan Mei from the room, apologising to Fatty Deng again. "I don't know how any of these girls will find a decent husband," she said.

Fatty Deng looked down at his notebook again. He had added a second name to the first and that was it. So much for giving these girls a shock. It was he who was suffering, not they.

The pattern was repeated with the following five girls, though mercifully none were as brazen as Pan Mei. Junjie wasn't recognised, Poppy hadn't been heard of and nothing was known of immoral drawings. Fatty Deng had a list of names and not much more than that. Then the last girl entered. Not only wouldn't she look at him, she kept her mouth firmly shut. Madame Xiong sent her packing without Fatty Deng ever learning her name. He didn't bother asking Madame Xiong. What would be the point?

Madame Xiong was very satisfied with the interviews, however. "Between you and me, Investigator Deng, Professor Ou is a soft touch. I'm glad you came. Those girls won't forget this day in a hurry."

Neither will I, thought Fatty Deng, grimly.

"What happens next in your investigation?" asked Madame Xiong. "I'm so envious. You have such an exciting job."

"That's up to Prosecutor Xu," he replied, truthfully. "Some investigations come to a natural end."

"Don't be disheartened, Investigator Deng," she said. "I'll keep an eye on those silly girls. Give me your business card. If I discover anything amiss I will call you."

Fatty Deng thanked her for her assistance, placing the photograph of Junjie securely back in his pocket, dreading what was to come. But, in the car, Prosecutor Xu made no critical comments. Her mood was good, if not joyous. She actually began to sing to herself as she drove. It seemed Professor Ou had flattered her by inviting her to speak at the graduation ceremony at the end of the academic year, asking her to speak about what it took to succeed in the new, ruthlessly competitive – but, strangely, still socialist – China.

When she dropped him off outside the Starbucks near her apartment building, she could not resist saying, however, "Let this be a lesson to you about the reliability of evidence provided by children. I'll see you bright and early Monday morning."

Then, with a screech of tyres, she was gone.

Good-looking as she was, and intelligent too, Fatty Deng felt he was fast falling out of love with Prosecutor Xu.

He considered drowning his sorrows at a nearby bar. But, feeling wrung out and in need of a good lie down, he decided to go home. In hindsight, he should have followed Prosecutor Xu to the university in his own car. The university was barely a two-minute drive from his home. Now he had to cross the city all over again.

And yet, tired and depressed as he was, when he arrived back in Wukuaishi, he couldn't resist a short detour. He parked up outside of Aunty Li's building. He walked around the back, ducked under some pointless police tape, switched on his torch, and took the stairs down to the basement. It was a mess of scattered bedding and belongings, the chaos more likely caused by the forensic teams doing a sweep of the room rather than by the migrants themselves. There was no sign of anyone. The air was cold and damp and smelled of mildew. As his own breath clouded about him he wondered how anyone could live like this. He expected the migrants were still being detained, probably being questioned by Philip Ye – the questioning done properly as well. Which troubled Fatty Deng. For all of his faults, Philip Ye was no fool. His green eyes missed very little. He was shaping up to be, so the rumour went, one of the best homicide detectives Chengdu had ever had, regardless of the relative lowliness of his rank. Philip Ye would not have detained the migrants on a whim. Fatty Deng knew he was missing something here, but what? Apart from the mildew, something did not smell right.

He switched his torch off, letting the dark envelop him

Junjie goes missing.

Old Man Gao gets shot.

A barman living in the same building is robbed and murdered two nights later on his way home from work.

A bunch of migrants, room-mates of the barman, are detained by Philip Ye.

What was the connection apart from the fact that they would have all known each other?

And what was a barman with a steady income doing living with poor migrants?

Fatty Deng shook his head, the problem too much for him. He needed more information, especially about this murdered barman.

Up the stairs and out into the light of day again, Fatty Deng found the young girl Tingting waiting for him. She was wearing a large floppy hat and boots too big for her against the rain that had just begun to fall again.

"Well?" she asked, hands on hips.

"Waste of time," he replied, sadly. He told her of the visit to the university, the failed trawl of the university records, the pointless interviews with the girls there.

"Those bitches are lying!" exclaimed Tingting, furious.

Deep in his gut, if he were honest with himself, Fatty Deng thought so too.

CHAPTER TWENTY-SIX

Philip Ye couldn't get the painting of The Willow Woman out of his mind. While completing his preliminary notes on the murder of Zhu Yi, despite it being evidence, he had taped the painting to the office wall, hoping that its constant presence in his eye-line might provide some necessary illumination. So far nothing. Both the painting and Zhu Yi remained an enigma.

However, his was not the puzzlement of those Party diehards, militant atheists all, still committed to Marxist-Leninist dialectical materialism, unable to comprehend the resurgence in religious belief and practice since the beginning of the Reform Era. Philip Ye fully understood it. The people, no longer subject to a barrage of Party propaganda, no longer required to give themselves over wholesale to the cult of personality that had surrounded – and had been propagated by – Mao Zedong, able to breathe freely again, had returned to the old traditions. Solace was now sought from the trials of life in the temples and the churches again, at the graves of their ancestors, at the family and village shrines. All of this made sense to Philip Ye. It was highly likely, after Isobel's death, he might have embraced religion himself, had it not been for that sense of direction given him by that first ghostly visitation, and the personal enquiry he had begun in earnest into the barrier between life and death.

It was Zhu Yi he didn't understand. Zhu Yi didn't fit the profile of a religious preacher. A clever young man, accepted as a student at university, technically able, and from Mianyang – not exactly a rural backwater – Philip Ye couldn't think of anyone less likely to be caught up in spreading the faith of a hitherto unknown cult. Unless dropping out of university and losing his girlfriend had provoked some religious mania in him – which in itself would be odd. Young men with broken hearts more often than not (he considered himself a rare exception to this rule) consoled themselves with alcohol, chasing other women, or staying at home playing computer games. They didn't actively seek out a group of poor migrants with whom to set up house and then begin preaching about a goddess nobody had ever heard of; which brought Philip Ye back to the puzzle that was The Willow Woman, dressed as she was in the Sun Yat-sen suit, her figure a peculiar mixture of the religious *and* the revolutionary.

He had placed a call to the local office of the State Administration for Religious Affairs, hoping somebody there might have heard of The Willow Woman cult, and be able to give him some information on cult numbers and where it might have originated. But the phone just rang and rang. Either the office was empty on Saturdays or no one was interested in taking his call. It was a long shot anyway. Most of that office's time was spent monitoring the activities of the five major religions in China, not only ensuring that the right candidates were selected for the leadership of each movement, but also in assisting each movement *with the interpretation of its own doctrine*. A small religious cult such as that of The Willow Woman might not yet have attracted its attention; or if it had, not warranted the creation of a file.

With luck, Yao Lin, Zhu Yi's former girlfriend, would provide the key to both puzzles. Though he had already mentioned to Constable Ma the possibility that Yao Lin might be involved in Zhu Yi's murder, even if indirectly through a new and violently jealous boyfriend, Philip Ye felt it much more likely that Zhu Yi's proselytizing on behalf of The Willow Woman had for some reason got him killed; or, even more intriguing, because of something that had happened in Aunty Li's building. Constable Ma had revealed that Zhu Yi knew Old Man Gao well. False smiles, she had said; Zhu Yi a liar, she thought. Had Zhu Yi known more about the disappearance of Junjie than he had revealed? Had he been responsible for that disappearance? And had someone, after Old Man Gao's suicide, taken revenge? Much depended on Yao Lin. Philip Ye needed her to be in a talkative mood.

But he couldn't be everywhere. Somebody had to go visit The Singing Moon bar sooner rather than later to get a feel for the place, speak to the owner Mister Bao Ling, inform him formally of Zhu Yi's violent demise and then take a few simple statements from the staff.

He would get there later, as soon as he could, to give the bar a really close look. He phoned Boxer Tan and asked for the favour. Boxer Tan reluctantly agreed, but he wanted a favour in return.

"Mister Ye, I don't want to end up losing my nerve like Supervisor Meng. I'm very tired. I want out of uniform. Maybe Homicide is the place for me."

"There are going to be vacancies in Robbery in a day or two."

"I'd sooner drown myself."

"Do you want me to speak to Commissioner Wei? I'll be visiting him at hospital again in a day or two."

"Would you?"

"Sure."

Boxer Tan promised to call later if The Singing Moon gave up any dark secrets. By then, Philip Ye felt certain, Boxer Tan would have changed his mind about leaving Wukuaishi Station. He had applied to join specialist units before, only to pull out on the eve of a positive selection. He would never say so but Boxer Tan enjoyed the rough and tumble of the streets too much. And if he left Wukuaishi Station, who would take care of his people? Who would keep a watch over Baby Wu?

Not wanting to bother Chief Di directly, and suspecting he might refer the decision downwards anyway, Philip Ye placed a call to the PSB Legal Affairs Section. The weekend duty advisor, Supervisor Han Fei, answered the phone. Philip Ye quickly ran through the details of Zhu Yi's murder with him, how Zhu Yi was a former student at Chengdu National University, how Zhu Yi's student records would be immediately useful to the investigation, and how he didn't want to walk onto campus without a properly authorised search warrant in his hand.

"Ah, the university will be tricky," said Han Fei, feeble as ever. "There are important people who sit on the board. And my boss, Commissioner Wang is away for the weekend visiting his mistress back in Shanghai." Han Fei let out a little laugh. "Let me speak to him Monday morning. First thing, Superintendent, I promise."

Philip Ye thanked him for his help, disappointed but unsurprised. Han Fei wasn't a bad policeman. He just preferred to remain as invisible as possible.

Philip Ye closed his eyes, feeling sleep beckoning him again. Maybe ten minutes in the chair—

His phone rang. He picked it up immediately, thinking Supervisor Han was calling back, having tripped over some courage by mistake.

"Yes?"

It was Ye Lan. "Handsome Boy, I cannot stand it. You must come. You must take her away. You have brought a sickness into my house. She is possessed by a demon. She just cries and cries. I cannot think...I cannot cook. This restaurant is all I have."

He said the right things. He told Ye Lan not to worry, that he would be there very soon. He put on his raincoat. Sleep would have to wait. And the sooner he tracked Yao Lin down the better. But, before he could get out of the office, his phone rang again. He considered ignoring it but then decided it might be important.

"Superintendent Ye."

"Superintendent, this is Doctor Kong. I have just completed the autopsy of the man identified to me as Zhu Yi. He died of massive blood loss. Of the twenty-five puncture wounds to his chest and abdomen, one sliced through his aorta. Death was very quick. The blades used were of approximately twenty-five centimetres in length and—"

"Forgive me, Doctor, did you say blades?"

"Yes, Superintendent, one of the blades was curved. It is my opinion, though of course I cannot be certain, that you are looking for at least two assailants."

"Any defensive wounds?"

"None, though some material was recovered from underneath the fingernails. However, I have my doubts whether this will prove useful and yield any DNA. We shall have to wait and see. As for the toxicology results, you may have to wait weeks or months, if not longer, due to the state of the facilities here. They are rudimentary at best and—"

"Thank you, Doctor...I look forward to receiving your full written report."

"Before you go, Superintendent Ye, I have been struggling to remember where I have seen you before. It has now been brought to my attention that it was you I saw fighting on TV with the PAP officer a few days ago. May I say that I think you are a disgrace to Chengdu PSB and I hope never to have to work with you again."

Philip Ye sighed. Doctor Wang might not have known one end of a dead body from the other but at least he had always been civil.

When he finally reached The Silver Tree after negotiating the appalling lunchtime traffic, he was disturbed to find the restaurant closed, the lights off, and a queue of angry people outside, some of whom were banging on the door wanting to get out of the cold and wet. Philip Ye hurried around to the kitchen entrance and found that locked as well. He thumped on the door with his fist. The lock turned and the door opened barely a crack. The pale, anxious face of one of the young cooks stared out. When the cook saw who it was, tears welled up in his eyes with relief. He opened the door up wide and pulled Philip Ye inside.

Instead of the usual frenetic activity, the kitchen was in silence, each of the cooks at their stations, standing as statues, their faces showing signs of terrible strain. Ye Lan was sitting on a stool, her hands over her ears. Her husband, Qu Fang, was doing his best to comfort her. From the floor above, Philip Ye could hear a dreadful keening, reminiscent of a distant eerie siren.

"It is like the end of the world," said Qu Fang.

Philip Ye did not linger in the kitchen. There was nothing to be said. Upstairs, he found the boys safe in the lounge at their studies, otherwise untroubled, insulated from the noise by earphones run from the mobile phones. He knocked on the door of the spare room. The keening stopped instantly. Not waiting for an invite, he pushed the door open. Constable Ma was sitting on the bed, as if she hadn't moved from where he had left her hours ago. Her big, round face was streaked with tears.

"Dry your eyes," he said. "And leave your luggage here. We have work to do."

She did not argue. She followed him downstairs and through the kitchen. The kitchen silently watched her passing. In the car, with her safely in her seat next to him, he saw the restaurant lights flicker on, The Silver Tree return to life, the queue outside begin to cheer.

"Constable Ma, never make that awful noise again," he said, starting the engine.

She kept her face away from him, refusing to speak. The atmosphere in the car felt heavy and oppressive – a thunderstorm about to burst.

"And think only good thoughts," he advised her.

"There are no good thoughts to think," she replied.

CHAPTER TWENTY-SEVEN

I n her kitchen, Xu Ya made herself of a cup of Silver Needle white tea, hoping it would soothe her heart and mind. So far nothing about the day had gone right. From the moment she'd misinterpreted Investigator Deng's reason for wanting to meet, there hadn't been a single moment she hadn't been made to feel like a fool.

In Starbucks, once she'd got over the shock that Investigator Deng was not about to resign, she had allowed herself to be talked into accepting a child's oral evidence without question. This crucial mistake had taken her to Secretary Wu's house where he had not only lectured her on how many children go missing every year – a fact she should have known! – but he'd also had to remind her why he had recruited her in the first place: to catch the big fish. And so, with that gentle admonishment ringing in her ears, she'd had to suffer through the meeting with Professor Ou thoroughly ashamed of herself, the search for Poppy proving – as she should have guessed – fruitless.

Professor Ou, kind as he was, had tried to sweeten the bitter pill by – to her horror – inviting her to speak at the university's graduation ceremony. He wanted her to educate the final year students on what it took to succeed in China in these modern, complicated days. She had agreed. How could she refuse? But what did she know about success, she who had made an absolute disaster of her life? It wouldn't take her long on that speaker's dais to make a fool of herself. Outside of the law, her chosen field of expertise, she hadn't much to say about anything. She was bound to stutter, lose her place, and reveal to the world what an utter mess she was inside.

She had realised there was something very wrong with her soon after starting school. An only child, used to the isolation and comfort provided by her parents' home, the environment of the classroom had come as a terrible shock. Always a giggling chatterbox with her parents, she found the discipline and enforced silence of the classroom difficult to bear. The break periods were a different kind of hell. The other children pinched her and pulled at her long hair, the noise of their games and their fights as they chased each other around so great that Xu Ya often resorted to sitting on the ground with her hands over her ears. Her misery was such that she found it impossible to learn. And when, one day, her temper had boiled over with a particularly obnoxious boy and she had punched him directly on the nose, the teacher had kept her back after class, beaten her, and spoken to her in a manner she'd never been spoken to before.

"Ms. Xu, spoiled little girls with bad tempers will achieve nothing in life. Don't you realise you are lagging behind with your studies? You are not as bright as the other children. You must work harder to succeed, not less!"

Her parents moved her immediately from that school.

However, a similar pattern emerged in the next school she was enrolled in, and the next. And it was not just her inability to study in the group environment. She found it impossible to make the other children like her. When she opened her mouth, she was just as likely to offend as to befriend.

Her parents took her to a therapist who specialised in the problems of children.

"She is borderline stupid," concluded the therapist, speaking to Xu Ya's parents in her presence. "She is also a hypersensitive and deeply troubled child. Have you considered home tutoring?"

Her parents had money.

Xu Ya did not set foot in school again.

One of her home tutors – a Mister Qin Qiang – actually saved her life. She was by then fifteen years old. Wheelchair bound, crippled Xu Ya first thought by some painful illness, Mister Qin proved himself a thoughtful, patient and insightful man. Hired to teach her history, he put up with her complaining and her day-dreaming for three weeks. When she failed the first simple test he set her, spectacularly so, he did not scold her as many of her other tutors had done in the past. Instead, he spoke to her with genuine concern.

"Ms. Xu, what is troubling you?"

"Nothing – except that I am borderline stupid."

He considered this for a few moments and replied, "You are not stupid, Ms. Xu. Your mind is, in fact, overly active. At present you bore easily and tire easily. You are also highly impressionable. None of these traits is serious or life-threatening. With proper effort, with commitment to your studies, these traits will become less troublesome to you."

Then, for reasons she did not understand to this very day, she began to sob uncontrollably in his presence. When she managed to bring herself under some semblance of self-control, she said, "I cannot make friends. I do not understand people. I can never tell what they are thinking. I am utterly useless as a human being."

Again, Mister Qin did not reply immediately. When he did, he surprised her. "Ms. Xu, it is not what people think or say that is important – it is what they do. Have you ever considered the study of law?"

She shook her head, wiping her tears away. She thought he was teasing her to cheer her up.

"Law is important, Ms. Xu. Law is a body of rules crafted not only to regulate the behaviour of people, but also to regulate the role and power of the government of those people. Without law, we are no more than animals. Without law, our society cannot be described as civilized. Without law, there will be no future for China. The study of law will give you insight into the best and worst of human behaviour. The study of law will anchor your mind in the world. And the practice of law will enable you to contribute fully to society – for the good of all. I cannot promise that the law will bring you friends, romance or happiness, but it will give you a meaningful life. Through the law, you will understand what it is to be human. And such knowledge, Ms. Xu, cannot be underestimated."

So said Mister Qin.

Beloved Mister Qin.

History had never really been Mister Qin's subject. Formerly a lawyer in private practice – a relative uncommon creature in those days – his aggressive and passionate defence of a client, as well as his vociferous criticism of the corrupt and violent investigative practices of Chongqing PSB, had led to his professional demise. Unknown assailants had kidnapped him from his office, transported him to a patch of waste ground on the bank of the Yangzi, and smashed the bones in his legs with metal rods. On leaving hospital, he found his law licence had been revoked and every teaching establishment in the city refusing to employ him. This she learned years later when working at Chongqing People's Procuratorate from an all-too-thin case file she had come across by accident. The case file detailed the assault on Mister Qin but little else. It appeared that hardly any work had been done on identifying his assailants except a little note stating that serving police officers were probably to blame. When she had tracked down the prosecutor in charge of the case, now conveniently retired, he told her, "Prosecutor Xu, there are some cases that are healthy to pursue and others that are not – only experience will tell you which are which."

At the age of fifteen, still innocent of such concerns, she soon learned what it meant to be a protégé. When Mister Qin spoke, she listened. Very soon she began to understand the importance of words. "In law, Ms. Xu," he told her, "vagueness will not do."

Her grades began to improve in her other subjects also. Her parents did not notice at first. Not for months, in fact. They were quite preoccupied with their careers. But when they did find out they were not pleased. Law had not been on their desired curriculum. They dismissed Mister Qin in her presence.

Xu Ya cried through the night.

In her temper, she also broke ornaments and damaged expensive furniture.

Mister Qin was rehired the very next day.

Beloved Mister Qin.

He was dead now; not from his old injuries but from lung cancer. A cigarette had never been far from his lips. She had received a last letter from him while studying at Wuhan. Not a single word of self-pity. That had never been his style. He had used all his ink and all that had remained of his life-force to urge her on.

Beloved Mister Qin *had* saved her life. He had given her a purpose and a profession. And the law had given her a framework within which she could speak and express her ideas – be creative even. Outside of the law, however, outside of the office, she still found it difficult to communicate, to know how to say the right thing. It was for this very reason she couldn't walk up to Philip Ye at Wuhan and say hello. She had been so afraid of upsetting him or making a fool of herself she had waited four long years for *him to speak to her*; which, perhaps, was proof of her foolishness anyway.

But in her professional life, up to this day anyhow, she had never once been proved foolish. Today, however, stupidly, she had let herself be persuaded by Investigator Deng that the search for Junjie was important.

Intellectually she knew the problem was that she had never worked with an investigator before – not directly, that is. At the Procuratorate in Chongqing, she had reviewed and prepared cases from her office, only emerging when needed to speak as the prosecuting authority before the panel of judges in court. If further investigative work was needed it was done on her written order by the police. Or the procuratorate police had brought witnesses or suspects to the Procuratorate for her to re-interview, again on her written order. She had never needed to work in concert with an investigator before, had never needed to know what made them tick.

She had hired an investigator on Secretary Wu's insistence. She had tried to refuse after her successful presentation to the Political and Legal Committee.

"Secretary Wu, I work best alone."

"In the past, Ms. Xu, but not here in Chengdu. You will require someone with investigative experience, someone you can trust. Feel free to use the authority of the Procuratorate to search through relevant personnel files. Many gems were discarded by the PSB after the earthquake. Go find one of these gems, Ms. Xu. Find someone to rely on."

And so Mouse had found her Investigator Deng.

The problem was that Investigator Deng was not a lawyer. Like most police, he had never had any proper legal training. It was obvious that his instincts and perspective were going to be so different to hers. But his interview had been so successful, and she had found him so personable, that she had been left with the hope that she could bridge that gap, that she and he might learn to communicate effectively with one another. Now, it seemed it was not meant to be. From the first day he had started working with her, from that first hour when they had viewed the footage of the shooting of Old Man Gao together, she had found his reactions quite unfathomable.

She thought she had made it very clear that the object of their investigation was Constable Ma. Why then was he so suddenly enthusiastic about finding Junjie?

She knew the dead-end at the university had been a great disappointment to him. In the car, she had tried to cheer him up, thinking that was what a friend should do. She had spoken of the graduation ceremony, concealing her misery at being invited to speak, hoping that he might have some advice for her, some input he could give so that she didn't make a complete idiot of herself. But he had appeared uninterested. She had begun to sing. A music teacher had told her once that she had a good voice. But her effort was in vain. He turned his face from her as if he blamed her for their failure. Dropping him off, she had tried to remind him of the perils of relying on evidence provided by children. But all he had given her was a look of complete contempt – a look that had shaken her to the core.

She considered phoning Mouse to ask for her opinion, for a different perspective on Investigator Deng's character. But she quickly dropped the idea, not wanting to compound the agony of the day by losing face in front of Mouse as well.

She had to review the evidence.

This was what Beloved Mister Qin would have advised.

She had to start at the beginning, from when she had first noticed Investigator Deng's odd behaviour, when they had watched the killing of Old Man Gao.

From her study she retrieved the DVD copy of the footage she had made. She played it on her laptop. As before, it made unpleasant viewing. Old Man Gao snatching the screaming child, Constable Ma emerging from the crowd to shoot Old Man Gao twice in the head without uttering a word.

She stopped the footage before Philip Ye's fight with the drunken PAP officer, not wanting thoughts of *him* to cloud her mind. She considered what she had just seen.

Nothing.

Not a clue to Investigator Deng's odd reaction when he had reviewed the footage with her.

What had he noticed that she had not?

She viewed the footage again.

And again.

Soon she felt so sick from watching the shooting of Old Man Gao she had to retire to the kitchen to prepare some more tea. She had to be careful. She did not want to make herself ill before the Mayor's reception that evening. She promised herself one more viewing and that would be that. Let Investigator Deng's reaction, his enthusiasm for finding Junjie, remain a mystery if need be.

She started the footage again. She put her face as close to the screen as she could and watched Old Man Gao snatch the schoolgirl to him, wave his knife in the air and begin shouting and then—

"Āiyā!" she exclaimed like a common housewife, dropping her cup of tea to the floor.

She had been so focused on Constable Ma she had missed what must have been so obvious to Investigator Deng. At no time had Old Man Gao's knife come anywhere near to the schoolgirl. And, more importantly, at no time had he tried to hide behind the schoolgirl when Constable Ma had raised her gun to him.

"Āiyā!" she repeated.

Not a crazy man after all – a suicide!

She began to shake all over. What a caring father he had been. Old Man Gao had loved his son so much he'd given his life to draw attention to his son's plight.

CHAPTER TWENTY-EIGHT

Saturday

"I have a new life now."

These were the first words uttered by Yao Lin when Philip Ye informed her, as gently as he could, of Zhu Yi's violent death. There was no sign of regret, of any emotion whatsoever. The only clue as to her interior life was her clasping her hands tightly with her mother as they sat close together on the sofa.

It was the mother who had opened the door to Philip Ye and Constable Ma. To prevent needless anxiety, Philip Ye had explained swiftly that his visit concerned Zhu Yi, a young man her daughter had once known. The mother, having already recognised Philip Ye, and freed from fears she might have for her own family, welcomed him and Constable Ma in wonderment into her home and inquired after the health of his father. Chengdu was not the same without Mayor Ye, she had said. It wasn't right for a man in the prime of his life to be confined to his home and charged with no crime, she had said.

She sat Philip Ye in the best armchair in the lounge, left Constable Ma to her own devices – Constable Ma stood by the window blocking out most of the light – and went into the kitchen to prepare tea and some snacks. She did this even though Philip Ye told her she should not bother. This done, she phoned her daughter, who was out shopping, and ordered her to come home straight away. While they waited, which was not long, the mother explained that her husband worked every Saturday at the factory, as he had done for the last twenty years. He would not be home for some hours yet. When Yao Lin walked through the door, she sat down on the sofa next to her mother. Yao Lin's face was devoid of any expression as Philip Ye explained how Zhu Yi's body had been discovered earlier that morning. With a subtle shake of her head, Constable Ma indicated to Philip Ye that she'd never seen Yao Lin before.

"Ms. Yao, what do you mean you have a new life now?" asked Philip Ye, taking a silver pen from his pocket and opening up his notebook.

"I have a new boyfriend," said Yao Lin, proudly. "He works in an office."

"My daughter is taking a secretarial course at college," said her mother. "She is also going to work in an office."

Philip Ye kept his attention on Yao Lin. "When did you last see Zhu Yi?"

"I don't know," replied Yao Lin.

"It was August last year," said her mother, wanting to be helpful.

"How did you meet him?"

The question woke Yao Lin from her assumed indifference. Her eyes began to burn with intensity. "Two years ago I got a job in a tea shop near to the university. I'd been told it was a good place to meet intelligent boys. Zhu Yi came in one day with some of his friends. He was good-looking…funny as well. He asked me out. He told me when he finished university he was going to be an electrical engineer with a good salary. I thought we would have a happy life together. I did not see him much. He was always studying. Sacrifices have to be made at first. But then he began to have problems and—"

"What kind of problems?"

"I don't know," said Yao Lin, with a shrug.

"I need you to be more helpful, Ms. Yao."

"He said that he kept getting headaches…that his tutors were putting too much pressure on him. I should have realised then he was weak and wouldn't amount to much. Two years I wasted on him and he just drops out of university. He came here and cried like a baby in front of my mother and my father. I was so ashamed. He wouldn't go home to his family. He wouldn't tell them what he'd done. I shouted at him. It did no good. I offered to go with him to the university…to go speak to his tutors. But he wasn't interested. Father offered to get him a job at the factory. But I said no. I did not want to end up like my mother married to a factory worker all my life. Anyway, I have a new boyfriend now. There's no point in dredging up the past."

Philip Ye watched Yao Lin carefully, refusing to judge her – not yet anyway. "Did you ever meet his family?"

"No, they lived in Mianyang. When we first started dating he wanted to take me there at New Year. I wasn't interested. My life is in Chengdu. He sulked but he got over it."

"Do you have contact details for them?"

"No – why should I?"

"He must have had a nice family," said the mother. "Zhu Yi was always very polite."

"He was a loser," said Yao Lin.

"Where did he live when he dropped out of university?" asked Philip Ye.

"He stayed with his student friends for a while," replied Yao Lin. "They were all losers like him. We argued a lot. I asked him what he was going to do with his life but he wouldn't answer me."

"How did he end up working at The Singing Moon bar in Wukuaishi?"

"It was one of his old tutors…just phoned him one day and told him about the job."

"So Zhu Yi had a phone?"

Yao Lin stared at Philip Ye as if he were stupid. "Everyone has a phone."

"Have you his number, Ms. Yao?"

"Not any more…why would I?"

"Ms. Yao, do not lie to me."

"Okay, okay…but it will do no good." Yao Lin pulled her phone from her pocket, played with it for a few moments and then reeled off the number from the screen. "I think he threw his phone away or stopped paying the bill. He doesn't answer anymore."

"So you've phoned him since you broke up?"

Yao Lin appeared shaken by the question. "No," she said, defensively.

"I told you not to lie to me, Ms. Yao."

Her mother slapped Yao Lin hard on the thigh, making her hiss with anger.

"Okay, okay…I called him once or twice," said Yao Lin. "But he never answered so what does it matter?"

Philip Ye saw the truth in her eyes, the hurt that she was trying so hard to conceal. She was a complex character, nothing like her serenely affable mother. He wondered if the office worker Yao Lin was supposedly dating actually existed; and, if he did, if he knew quite what he was letting himself in for.

He thought then of The Singing Moon bar, wondering how Boxer

Tan was getting on there. He considered it strange a tutor could, or would, find a drop-out student a job as a barman.

"Tell me about this tutor who got Zhu Yi a job at the bar."

"What is there to tell?" said Yao Lin, with a wearisome exhalation of breath, making clear that she was tiring of all the questioning.

"It was Professor Xiong Yu," said the mother. "Zhu Yi was always speaking of him. Professor Xiong was his favourite. When he dropped out of university, Zhu Yi said he had really let Professor Xiong down. Professor Xiong is a very important man. My daughter met him once." She turned to Yao Lin. "You went to his house last summer with Zhu Yi, didn't you?"

"It wasn't Professor Xiong's house," snapped Yao Lin, irritated by her mother's openness, feeling she had no option now but to continue. "Professor Xiong lives in Chongqing. But he teaches one day a week at the university in Chengdu...Thursdays...and stays overnight with his sister, Madame Xiong. She is a senior administrator at the university. She has an apartment on campus. I went there once with Zhu Yi to some kind of student party. I only went because I thought it might help Zhu Yi get back into the university."

"When was this...before or after Professor Xiong had helped Zhu Yi get the job at the bar?" asked Philip Ye.

"About the same time, I think," said Yao Lin. "But the party was horrible. And Professor Xiong was a creep, always smiling at me, always sneaking looks. And Madame Xiong – what a bitch! She pulled me into the kitchen and said my skirt was too short. She called me a whore. I should have slapped her! But I didn't because I wanted to help Zhu Yi. But then the Professor started telling everyone about his dead wife and then he began to cry like a baby. It made me sick. Who wants to hear about how much he misses his dead wife? But all the students there...you should have seen their faces. It was like they all worshipped the old fool. And then he started saying that his wife had just come to visit him...as a ghost! I started laughing. Only children believe in ghosts. Then Madame Xiong grabbed me by the hair and started hitting me. She threw me out of the apartment. Zhu Yi did nothing...didn't say a word. So I came home on the bus on my own. I was done with Zhu Yi. I didn't want to see him again."

"But you did see him again, didn't you, Ms. Yao?"

"Yes, it is important you tell Superintendent Ye what happened next," said her mother.

"It's nothing," said Yao Lin. "I went to The Singing Moon bar to try to speak to Zhu Yi...one last time...to see if I could talk sense to him. But I found out he was now living with some stinking migrants…in a basement. I went there and we argued again. It was no use. I think he'd gone mad. He started talking to me about The Willow Woman—"

"Who's that?"

Yao Lin grew angry, almost shouting her response. "I don't know. Some woman he'd seen in some comic, I think. Some woman he'd made up. I tried to drag him out of the basement, to go see a doctor, to get some pills for his brain. But he wouldn't come. He started crying again and I walked out of there. I wasn't going to waste my life on that loser."

Philip Ye held up his phone, showing them the photograph he had taken of the painting of The Willow Woman. "Have either of you seen this picture before?"

They shook their heads in unison. Philip Ye instructed Constable Ma to show them her photograph of Old Man Gao and Junjie. Mother and daughter looked at the photograph for some time before shaking their heads again.

"Who are they?" asked the mother.

Not bothering to explain, Philip Ye asked, "What did you mean by saying that Professor Xiong is a very important man?"

Yao Lin looked to her mother. They were holding hands again. The mother answered after searching her memory.

"Zhu Yi had come to dinner one evening…before he became depressed. He told us all about Professor Xiong. He said that apart from teaching one day a week in Chengdu, Professor Xiong has a company in Chongqing – a company doing secret work. Zhu Yi told us he hoped to get a job there when he graduated. He was very excited about the prospect. But he said only the best of the best get to work there. We were very pleased for him…very impressed."

"But it doesn't matter anymore," said Yao Lin. "I have a new life now."

"Yes, that's true – she has a new life now," confirmed her mother.

CHAPTER TWENTY-NINE

Saturday

Philip Ye missed his isolation, the time he could take sitting alone in his car, reflecting on all he had heard, all he had learned. It was difficult to meditate with Constable Ma sitting next to him. Her mind was unquiet, her massive physical presence stifling. The rhythms of her breathing had even begun to intrude on him, shallow and rapid most of the time, but raspy and irregular when especially stressed – which was whenever anybody took notice of her. He closed his eyes, trying to ignore her. He tried to concentrate on his own breathing – in for eight beats, hold for four, out for eight – searching for that still, silent place within.

"I do not like her."

Philip Ye was forced to open his eyes. Constable Ma was absently fiddling with the catch to the car glove-box. She was bored, impatient to be away. They remained parked up outside of Yao Lin's apartment building, awaiting his decision on where to head next.

"Whom don't you like?"

"Superintendent, do you think it's true that Yao Lin went to work at a teashop just to catch a husband?"

"I do."

"I do not like her."

Despite being pulled from his meditation, Constable Ma's reaction to Yao Lin made him smile. Yao Lin had offended some deep-seated morality within her.

"You shouldn't condemn Yao Lin for wanting to better herself," he said.

"She's a liar too."

"Why do you say that?"

"That Professor she spoke of…the one who supposedly sees ghosts and talks to his dead wife…she made all that up. A professor is a clever man. A clever man wouldn't say such a thing. No one sees ghosts. They don't exist. Dead is dead."

"You know this for a fact, Constable Ma?"

"Dead is dead," she replied, as if to think otherwise would be crazy.

His phone rang. It was Boxer Tan.

"How did you get on at The Singing Moon?" asked Philip Ye.

"Ah, Mister Ye…the owner…Bao Ling…what a sleaze-ball! He was wearing sunglasses inside the bar like he was some sort of movie star. A real ladies' man too – or so he thinks. He's surrounded himself with them. The majority of the staff are dopey young girls – students working part-time. I'm surprised Zhu Yi got a job there. Some of the girls looked a bit odd and unhealthy though, nothing much behind the eyes. Might be worth giving Narcotics a call. I wouldn't be surprised if something is being shifted through that place. There was a strange atmosphere too…not anti-police…it was just like nobody cared whether I was there or not."

"And Zhu Yi?"

"None of them seemed too upset. Bao Ling was pleasant enough. He offered me tea…spoke to me like I was his best friend. He told me Zhu Yi was a good kid, a hard-worker, no fights with customers or with any of the other staff. No girlfriend either that he knew of. He whispered to me that he thought Zhu Yi was gay."

"How confident was he?"

"I don't know, Mister Ye. It was hard to see what was going on behind those sunglasses. But he did tell me Zhu Yi had just been paid and had a fair bit of cash on him that night. Are you and Superintendent Zuo certain it wasn't a robbery?"

"Zhu Yi had twenty-five stab wounds to chest and abdomen from two different blades."

Boxer Tan whistled. "Two assailants then?"

"It looks that way. This wasn't about money. They wanted Zhu Yi dead. Anybody offer anything up about Zhu Yi's religious convictions?"

"Bao Ling said he didn't know Zhu Yi that well and it was difficult getting a single word out of any of the girls. I got a list of who was working that night. Maybe they'll all perk up a bit when you walk through the door later. They seemed a superficial lot, too easily impressed with good looks...though I suppose now that yours are fading fast you might not do much better than me."

"Boxer Tan, what's put you in such a bad mood?"

"I'm sorry, Mister Ye – it's those fucking migrants. When I got back to the station they were making a hell of a racket. I want rid of them."

"What were they fighting about?"

"Food - what else? You'd spoiled them at breakfast."

"Give me a day or two. I should know by then whether I've got any more questions for them."

Boxer Tan rang off, muttering to himself before Philip Ye could properly thank him.

What had been learned from The Singing Moon?

Philip Ye thought very little. He was glad he had prioritized the interview with Yao Lin. Zhu Yi's possible homosexuality was an interesting angle but one to be filed away for consideration later. It was time to find out a bit more about him and simultaneously deal with another issue nagging at the back of his mind. Constable Ma was still fiddling with the catch to the glove-box, her mind elsewhere, annoying him with her restlessness.

"Let me make one more phone call and then we'll be off," he told her, their next destination as yet unclear to him.

Startled by him talking to her directly, Constable Ma's hand slipped and caught the catch too firmly. The glove-box fell open, spilling some of its contents onto her lap. She mumbled an apology as she tried to put a torch back inside as well as the exercise book given Philip Ye by Aunty Li. He'd forgotten he still had it.

"That belonged to Junjie," said Philip Ye. "He used to practice his sketches in it. Just put it back where you found it." He dialled Chongqing PSB.

"Supervisor Lang, Homicide."

"Wolf, are you well?" asked Philip Ye.

First silence, then, "It is a cold wind that blows when the family Ye come calling."

"You don't know what I'm going to ask for yet."

"My wife, my daughter, my life's savings – what'll it be?"

"Information – in two parts."

"Why am I feeling I'm going to regret this?"

"Wolf, I need some background on a Chongqing resident, name of Professor Xiong Yu."

"Address?"

"Don't know."

"Where does he work?"

"Don't know."

"What's he done?"

"Maybe nothing?"

"Philip, what are you doing to me?"

"Wolf, he's important...probably high up in the local Party in Chongqing, teaches part-time at Chengdu National University. I believe his field is electrical engineering. He manages a company in Chongqing, possibly fulfilling government defence contracts...but that's just a guess on my part."

"Fine...fine...what else?"

"Chengdu People's Procuratorate have recently employed a new prosecutor, full name Xu Ya, who—"

"No, Philip...I've got nothing to say about *her*," said Wolf, brusquely. "Those waters are far too cold and murky for me. Give me a few hours and I'll come back to you with some background on this professor of yours."

"Wolf?"

"I'll call you, Philip – give my best to your father."

Philip Ye put down his phone, disconcerted by Wolf's reaction. Wolf was not the nervous type. The anxious did not last long in Chongqing PSB. But one mention of Prosecutor Xu and Wolf was rattled. Philip Ye wondered just what Commissioner Wei had got him mixed up in. Constable Ma stirred next to him.

"Superintendent?"

"Not now, Constable Ma – I'm trying to think."

Constable Ma reached out and touched his hand, surprising him. "You must see," she insisted, holding open Junjie's exercise book.

Philip Ye found himself looking at a very rough sketch in black charcoal – a practice run, he presumed, for what was to come. A willow tree. A river rushing by. A woman dressed in the uniform of a more revolutionary past. He forgot to breathe.

"Junjie must have painted Zhu Yi's picture of The Willow Woman," said Constable Ma, stating the obvious, misinterpreting his shock for stupidity.

CHAPTER THIRTY

Saturday

Lunch, for Fatty Deng, was a depressing affair. His mother's nerves were such that she nagged and nagged at him until he spilled the whole sorry story of the morning's misadventures. He did not cast Prosecutor Xu in a bad light. Nor did he mention the big fish and the minnows. The failure, he told his mother, was his and his alone.

"You let those university girls run rings around you," she said.

"I know."

"Philip Ye wouldn't have allowed it."

"I know that also."

She put her hands to her face. "It's my fault for not teaching you how easily some girls lie."

"No, Mother – I just wasn't strong enough. It's not like being in the police, interviewing someone down at the station with all my colleagues around. I don't know what I'm doing."

"Well, you'd better learn fast. Prosecutor Xu has put her trust in you. I did not raise you to give up."

Fatty Deng let that pass. Even during the worst of times, he had never given up. He had always gone out, sometimes doing questionable things, just to put food on the table and pay the rent.

After lunch, in his room, he shrugged off his suit and hung it in the cupboard, next to his old police uniforms. He had never had the courage to get rid of them. They were preserved in plastic covers, as fresh and starched as if he were about to wear them, his superintendent third class insignia – one bar and one flower – proudly displayed on the shoulder-boards. He had just been promoted, about to be selected to go to detective school, when The Purge had taken his future away. His ten years hard work, the arrests he'd made, the injuries he'd suffered, the fears he'd had to conquer, all rendered meaningless by the posting of a simple list of names.

To cheer himself up, he put on his favourite new shirt – a gift of a few weeks before from a clothing store owner. The trader had owed protection money to Freddie Yun. The trader had paid as much as he could, and then given the shirt to Fatty Deng as a gift, hoping he'd put in a good word for him, buy him enough time to find the rest of the cash. The shirt, genuine and direct from Hawaii so the trader said – though, obviously made in some local sweat-shop – was of a lurid, floral design, full of bright colours. But it had made Fatty Deng laugh. Brother Wang thought him mad for accepting it. But Fatty Deng persuaded Brother Wang to give the trader those few extra days needed to raise the remainder of the cash.

Fatty Deng admired himself in the mirror, letting the shirt hang loose over his belt. It did make him look thinner. And it was defi-nitely *him*, or at least how he would like to be seen – a casual and fun-loving guy. Not some stuffy investigator in a suit. Somebody people would warm to, open up to.

His mother knocked on the door, worried still. "What are you going to do?"

"I'm going out again."

"To find the truth about Junjie…that poor murdered boy?"

"Yes, Mother."

"Oh, I am so pleased. Prosecutor Xu will be so impressed when you break the case wide open. You'll be the talk of the Procuratorate."

I'll probably be no longer employed by the Procuratorate, he thought.

His mother made no comment on the shirt. She wished him luck, though, when he headed back out the door. She meant well. And she was right. He had given up too easily. It would do him some good to find Junjie, to make a difference again.

It was fine for Prosecutor Xu to speak about big fish and minnows. In the meantime, what happened to the minnows: the little people, the poor, the migrants, the retarded, the mentally ill, the lonely, the sick, the old and frail? Catching the big fish might get the big headlines, might restore some confidence in the system, but in Chengdu the big fish seemed to breed faster than the minnows –

catch one and there were another five evil fuckers lurking in the shadows.

He didn't have a proper argument, certainly nothing that could convince Prosecutor Xu that Junjie was worth searching for. It wasn't because of Old Man Gao's suicide, or because the police at Wukuaishi Station should have done more than they did. If this had happened five years ago and he'd been manning the desk at Wukuaishi Station, Fatty Deng had no doubt he would have sent Old Man Gao packing also. But the bitter struggle of the last five years to make ends meet had changed him – for the better, he hoped. He understood now what it was to struggle every day. His time as a fridge salesman, household-waste collector, fake watch dealer, road-sweeper, private investigator, club doorman, waiter, pot-washer – the list went on and on – had taught him something that was hard to put into words. But it went something like this: if justice didn't reach down into the lives of the little people, people like Old Man Gao and Junjie, then what the fuck was it for?

Fatty Deng drove his old Japanese relic the short distance to the university and parked near to the main entrance. Unfortunately, he didn't have a plan. As he stared through the deepening gloom of the afternoon at the lights of the girls' dorm, he had to wonder what he was doing. He couldn't very well march in and start throwing his weight around without bringing a great deal of trouble down on his head.

So what would Philip Ye do?

He was still mulling this over when three security guards converged on his car, shining bright torches into his face though it was daylight still. He wound down the window, furious.

"Hey, pervert – we know what you're up to," said one of the guards. "Get out of here!"

Fatty Deng flashed his badge. "People's Procuratorate, leave me alone!"

The guards leaned closer to him, staring at the badge as if it were something he had just bought from a dodgy stall in Wukuaishi Market.

Enraged, he threw open the door and slapped the nearest guard, almost knocking him off his feet. "What's the matter with you? Are you blind, you goofy fuckers?"

The guards backed away quickly, muttering to themselves. They retreated to the gatehouse but continued to watch him from the window. Fatty Deng got back into the car, feeling a little guilty. He'd been a security guard too for a short time. He knew how little those guys earned, the long hours they worked. He was also aware his temper was a product of him not having any sensible plan. If he was going to talk to some of the girls without getting into trouble he had to get creative.

However, apart from hanging out at some of the local clubs frequented by students and where he'd stand out a mile, no great solution came to mind. The rain that had slowed to a steady drizzle began to pour again, pounding on the roof of the car, dulling his senses. His eyes began to droop, and soon he was dreaming of lying on the white sands of a tropical beach, a hot sun beating down on him, warm water lapping at his toes. At his side was a nice cool glass of beer. There was a woman too. Not Prosecutor Xu, but someone else, someone he couldn't quite make out…

Raucous laughter woke him from the dream. A gaggle of girls, on their way into the city, passed him by, gossiping and laughing. He shielded his face, not that he recognised any of them. He looked at his watch. He had lost over an hour. The sky was darker than before, the lights of the girls' dorm seeming brighter. He yawned. The day had already been far too long.

Not wanting to be caught napping again, he spotted a convenient teashop across the road. A hot drink and a bite to eat should refresh him. He made his way across the road, and ordered tea and a bowl of noodles. The teashop was full, every table occupied. Not wanting to return to his car with the bowl of noodles in his hand, or stand outside in the rain getting soaked, he slid into the nearest empty seat opposite a young woman reading a paperback, apologising as he did so.

The book did not waver. He thought her rude for not acknowledging him. But he tucked into the noodles with gusto and sipped at his tea, trying to put a brave face on the day. But tasty as the noodles were, it was the book that soon took his attention. It wasn't the subject matter. The title meant nothing to him. He could count on the fingers of one hand the number of books he'd read. It was that the book was being held by trembling hands. He looked over the book. The young woman's face was covered by a mop of unruly hair.

He opened his notebook.

He couldn't believe that the wheel of fortune was continuing to turn in his favour.

Zhang Lin.

The first of the interviewees from the university that morning.

She must have spotted him as soon as he walked in and prayed he would not sit down opposite her. Too frightened to run, she had held the book up as a shield against him.

He reached out and took the book from her. She did not resist. He laid the book down on the table and took her trembling hands in his. He spoke softly so as no one would overhear, so that the other people in the teashop would think them boyfriend and girlfriend, no matter how unlikely that might seem.

"Ms. Zhang, I think you lied to me this morning," he said. "Who is Poppy?"

A whisper, inaudible.

He leaned toward her, smiling, insistent. "I don't want to formally detain you, Ms. Zhang. You must speak up."

"He Dan," she said.

"He Dan is her real name?"

"Yes."

"Why 'Poppy'?"

"It was her nickname – she preferred it."

"She is a student at the university?"

"No...not anymore."

"Ms. Zhang, tell me where she is and I'll leave you alone."

"She is gone."

"Gone where?"

She lifted her head to him, the mop of hair parting slightly, enough for him to see two shining eyes. He thought them lovely though they were as afraid as any he had ever seen. He hated himself for creating that fear.

"Poppy disappeared in October," she said. "It is a great scandal. We are not to talk about it."

"The law says, that if I ask you a question then you must answer me truthfully. If you do not, you are committing a crime."

She bit her lip. Through her hands he could feel the tension in her body, the conflict in her mind. He waited, letting her come to the right decision.

"Poppy went out one day and never came back," Zhang Lin said. "I didn't know her well. She shared a room with Pan Mei. You should ask Pan Mei."

"I'm asking you, Ms. Zhang."

"They say she ran off with an older man...just abandoned her studies, her family, everything. It's a big scandal. No one must know. Madame Xiong said it could ruin the university, damage all of our prospects."

"Madame Xiong said this?"

Zhang Lin nodded, tears forming in her eyes. "She said if we spoke to anyone about it we would be expelled. She said it again this morning. She said we must lie to you for the good of the university."

Fuck.

He had trusted Madame Xiong.

He had actually warmed to the woman, agreeing with her rather negative assessment of the morals of the youth of today. Not only had she lied about Poppy, she had also orchestrated a series of pointless interviews. Why, he didn't know.

"I must go," said Zhang Lin. But she made no effort to pull her hands from his.

He let go of her hands anyway, fishing in his pocket for the photograph of Junjie. "Tell me the truth this time. Do you know this youth?"

"I saw him once or twice."

"When and where?"

"I think it was September. Poppy brought him up to her room in the dorm. It was against the rules but she did it anyway. I still have a photograph of Poppy and Pan Mei and him on my phone."

"Ms. Zhang, I need to see that photograph and you are going to speak to me of everything you know and everything you suspect. I am going to write as you talk. Then, when we are done, I will let you read my notes. If you are happy that I haven't put words in your mouth, I will ask you to sign the page and then you will be free to go. Is that okay?"

And so it was that Zhang Lin began to talk. And, as she talked, she began to grow in confidence, to not tremble so much, as if a great weight was being lifted from her heart. But, the more Fatty Deng wrote down, the more burdened he began to feel. And when the gangster Freddie Yun was mentioned, he almost lost the few noodles he had just eaten.

When she was finished, she said, "I like your shirt. It's much better than that suit you were wearing."

Under different circumstances, and if he'd been a different person, he would have asked her out. He told her not to worry but not to speak to anybody of her meeting with him. She promised. She glanced back once as she hurried out of the teashop, forgetfully leaving her book behind. He left it on the table. There was no point trying to return it to her.

An hour later he returned home, more depressed than ever. Chengdu was a fetid swamp. There was no denying it. The story she had told had not opened up a shining path before him. Maybe, as Prosecutor Xu had wanted, he should have left well enough alone. Zhang Lin had left him with more questions than answers. Instead of one missing person, he now had two.

He opened the door and found the apartment not as he had left it. His mother sat at the table, playing *májiàng* with Aunty Ho and

Uncle Ho, more content than he'd seen her in years. The fourth player he had last seen trudging away from the Procuratorate, her big peasant face smarting from the slap Chief Prosecutor Gong had given her.

And, in the comfy chair, Fatty Deng's favourite chair, in his perfect suit, his hair slickly cut, his nails precisely manicured, his eyes gleaming, a magazine open before him, sat an impossibly handsome man.

"I hear you're still looking for Junjie," said Philip Ye.

CHAPTER THIRTY-ONE

Saturday

The best Fatty Deng could say of the apartment is that it was clean and tidy. Bad cook his mother might be, and always in a near state of nervous collapse, but she didn't skimp on the housework. Even so, with Philip Ye in the apartment – a man used to the finest things in life – Fatty Deng couldn't help but feel a deep sense of shame. A good son would have provided better for his mother – a more spacious apartment, for instance.

Philip Ye stood to shake hands but Fatty Deng's mother was having none of that formality. She wanted to pretend to Uncle and Aunty Ho that with her son now working for the Procuratorate, a visit from Philip Ye was going to be – in modern parlance – the 'new normal'. She ushered them both into the kitchen before either could utter a word.

"I am sure you men have important business to discuss in private," she said, shutting the door on them.

"Nice shirt," said Philip Ye.

Fatty Deng ignored the comment, unsure if he was being mocked. He opened the fridge and took out a bottle of beer. He offered it to Philip Ye who declined with a curt shake of the head. Fatty Deng kept the beer for himself, his mouth dry, nervous, not knowing what to expect. The cardboard box came to mind. Had Philip Ye come to collect on the favour?

They took seats opposite each other at the kitchen table. Philip Ye placed a school exercise book down between them. Fatty Deng pointedly ignored it.

"Ever been to Hawaii?" asked Philip Ye.

"The shirt's fake, Mister Ye. I've never been out of Chengdu."

"Ah."

"Please excuse me, Mister Ye, but what are you doing here? And why bring the big girl with you? She's supposed to be on suspension. By the end of the week she's to be shipped back to whatever flea-infested village she came from."

"It suits me to keep her nearby," replied Philip Ye, unruffled by Fatty Deng's displeasure.

"Aunty Ho cheats at *májiàng*. If the big girl notices, then…"

"Constable Ma's been told to be on her best behaviour. *Májiàng* was your mother's idea. And I am grateful for it. I have found Constable Ma is best kept occupied or else her mood deteriorates rapidly."

"Has she figured out yet that Old Man Gao used her to commit suicide?"

"No, and that's for the best. She's upset enough as it is. Old Man Gao was her friend."

Fatty Deng was amazed. "Her friend?"

"After getting no help from Wukuaishi Station, Old Man Gao approached Constable Ma. She agreed to help search for Junjie with him. I think they became quite close. When Old Man Gao decided he'd run out of options he betrayed that friendship. He persuaded her that he was going to do something dreadful. She assumed he was a man of his word and had no choice but to use lethal force to stop him."

"That was wrong of him," said Fatty Deng, taking a swig of his beer.

"Maybe, but I doubt if the beating he suffered at the hands of the *Chéngguǎn* left him in his right mind. And I am sure, wherever Old Man Gao is now, he regrets his action. But, for those of us who remain in the land of the living, life must go on. I have a murder to solve. And I hear you've been pounding the streets looking for Junjie."

"My mother has a big mouth."

"I remembered you speaking to me the other night about the missing pictures from Old Man Gao's walls. I should have listened to you then. I came over because I was hoping you were still considering that puzzle. Your mother merely confirmed this for me."

"Mister Ye, what I'm doing is off the books. The Procuratorate does not waste its time looking for missing people."

"Then why are you doing it?"

"Because no one else seems to give a fuck."

"Were you already acquainted with Old Man Gao and Junjie? Aunty Li's building is only a few minutes' walk from here."

"I would have told you the other evening if that was the case. This isn't about friendship or family, Mister Ye – it's about a boy wrongly taken from his father."

"Have you ever heard of The Willow Woman?"

"Who's that?"

"A goddess – in the religious sense."

"Don't think so."

"Neither had I." Philip Ye took out his phone and brought up the photograph of the painting of The Willow Woman. He showed it to Fatty Deng. "This is her."

Fatty Deng took the phone from him and examined the photograph closely. "Why is she wearing the Party uniform?"

"Good question."

"You're going to tell me Junjie painted this, aren't you?"

"I am."

"This is not charcoal."

"It's painted in pen and inks, not a medium Junjie could afford, I think. I have the painting back at the office. I seized it from the basement of Aunty Li's building."

"When you lifted all those migrants this morning?"

"So you heard about that?"

"The news is all over the neighbourhood," replied Fatty Deng.

Philip Ye opened up the exercise book so Fatty Deng could see the practice sketch of The Willow Woman done in black charcoal. "It is possible that the pictures taken from Old Man Gao's walls before you got there could be similar practice sketches. Somebody didn't want the suicide of Old Man Gao, or the disappearance of Junjie, connected to the worship of The Willow Woman. That someone could be my murder victim from this morning."

"The barman from The Singing Moon?"

Philip Ye nodded. "His name was Zhu Yi, a drop-out from Chengdu National University."

"I was there this morning."

"At the university?"

"Yes."

Philip Ye laughed in astonishment. "Fatty, I think we should pool our resources."

"Mister Ye, I'm not police anymore, remember?"

Philip Ye considered this for a time, breathing deeply. Then he said, "If I explain where I am in my murder investigation, any comments you might have will be appreciated."

"Mister Ye, you should not—"

"Fatty, all I ask is that you listen."

Fatty Deng shrugged and took a swig of his beer. Listening could not hurt. He wasn't doing anything else this evening.

So Philip Ye began to describe the events of the day from the time he arrived in the alley off the Yusai Road and viewed Zhu Yi's body, to the interviews with the migrants and the verbal autopsy report given by Doctor Kong over the phone.

"Two assailants and twenty-five stab wounds is not a street robbery," said Fatty Deng, unable to help himself.

"Zhu Yi knew both Old Man Gao and Junjie very well," added Philip Ye. "My working theory – and it is just a theory – is that after Zhu Yi arrived in Aunty Li's building last summer to spread the word of The Willow Woman among the migrants, he met both Old Man Gao and Junjie and noticed Junjie's artistic talent – as well as his susceptibility to suggestion or coercion."

"And in October delivered Junjie into the hands of other members of the cult to paint pictures for them?"

"Yes, I believe so," said Philip Ye.

"In Chengdu?"

"The practice sketches indicate Junjie was either taken to see the original or instructed on how the painting should be composed beforehand, in the hours his father was at work. I would lay odds Junjie is still alive and is being held somewhere nearby."

"Evil bastards," said Fatty Deng, draining his beer bottle and opening the fridge for another. "You sure you don't want one?"

"I have found I don't get on well with alcohol."

"Mister Ye, I have found I don't get on well *without* it."

"Shall I continue?"

Fatty Deng settled back down into his seat, more intrigued by Philip Ye's investigation than he wanted to admit, but equally puzzled by how it diverged so much from his own findings.

Philip Ye continued by relating his interview with Zhu Yi's former girlfriend Yao Lin, explaining how Zhu Yi came to drop out of university, his weakness of character, his shame at not being able to inform his family in Mianyang of his decision, and how it took a former tutor of his to find him a job at The Singing Moon.

"So this tutor's name is Professor Xiong Yu?"

"Yes, and I can tell you a little more about him." Philip Ye described the party at Professor Xiong's sister's apartment on campus, where Yao Lin had been verbally abused and eventually physically thrown out, and where Professor Xiong had spoken emotionally not only about his dead wife but also about his conversing with his dead wife's ghost.

Fatty Deng nearly choked on his beer. "Do you believe this Yao Lin?"

"Many people believe in spirits and ghosts."

"I don't deny that, Mister Ye. After a few night patrols, show me a police officer who doesn't believe in spooky stuff. But for a professor to speak so openly at the university…"

"Yes, I know…very strange. But these are strange, chaotic days. He only teaches one day a week at the university so he might consider that he hasn't much to lose. His real job is running a company in Chongqing. I have a contact there doing some background on him as we speak."

"The Professor's sister…her name isn't Xiong as well is it?" asked Fatty Deng.

Philip Ye checked his notebook. "Yes, Yao Lin referred to her as Madame Xiong – an administrator at the university. Why do you ask?"

"I met her this morning at the university."

"In connection with Junjie's disappearance?"

"Not exactly, Mister Ye – it's slightly more complicated than that. But you haven't said how Zhu Yi joined up with this Willow Woman cult. Did Yao Lin know about that?"

"No, it's a complete mystery. Yao Lin didn't see much of Zhu Yi last summer. I don't think she knew what he was up to. I believe her when she said she'd never heard of The Willow Woman cult. There is no explanation as yet where Zhu Yi's sudden religiousness came from."

"Professor Xiong?"

"Unlikely, but, as I said, we are living in strange days. I've come to the tentative conclusion that Zhu Yi was killed as a direct result of Old Man Gao's suicide. The migrants told me Zhu Yi had been suffering from depressions since Junjie's disappearance and was in a very bad way the day after Old Man Gao's death. I believe The Willow Woman cult, to keep its activities secret, murdered one of their own."

"You think Zhu Yi was about to confess what he'd done?"

"I do, but this is all supposition. I don't want to travel too far down that path until I have something more to go on…or a pointer or two from you. I would like to know how you came to be at the university this morning. I need access to Zhu Yi's old student records but I've been told by PSB Legal Affairs I will have to wait for a formal search warrant – Monday at the earliest. So how about telling me what you've been up to?"

Fatty Deng was in a quandary. Nothing he'd uncovered himself seemed to connect to Philip Ye's investigation. And, by telling all, he might not only betray the confidence of the Procuratorate but he also might make himself look a fool. Philip Ye waited patiently in silence. And it was that intense silence that finally broke Fatty Deng. But first he went into the lounge to check on his mother, to make sure the game was progressing peacefully. Uncle Ho gave him a wink, letting him know there was nothing to worry about. In his bedroom, he collected together all of Junjie's drawings and returned to the kitchen and shut the door. He put them down on the table, the portrait of Tingting on the top.

"What do you think of evidence given by children, Mister Ye?"

"Depends on the child."

"This girl is Tingting," said Fatty Deng, tapping the portrait. "She was good friends with Junjie. She told me Junjie had got into the habit of drawing some of the girls at the university. The girls wanted pictures of themselves without many clothes on. The day Junjie went missing he told Tingting he was going to the university to meet up with a student named Poppy. He never came back."

"So you went looking for Poppy?"

"Not at first, Mister Ye. Like you, I didn't want to mess with the university without the proper authority. I met with Prosecutor Xu and told her what I'd uncovered. You should understand, Mister Ye, that Prosecutor Xu has never been interested in finding Junjie. Her interest was only in dealing with the big girl Constable Ma…getting her off the streets. But when I told her about Junjie meeting up with this Poppy – information that Old Man Gao never had – she suddenly became enthusiastic. I guess she thought if we found out what happened to Junjie she could write a fancy report and rub Wukuaishi Station's nose in it. I told you she hates police, didn't I?"

"Do you know why?"

"She's probably been pulled over by some traffic police in Chongqing and given a fine. She drives like a crazy woman."

Philip Ye raised his eyebrows.

"It's true, Mister Ye – she scared the shit out of me this morning. Anyway, she decided she needed authority to approach the university. Because Chief Prosecutor Gong was away, she phoned Secretary Wu – the Chair of the Political and Legal Committee. I started shaking when I realised who she was talking to. I mean, have you ever heard of a prosecutor bypassing the chain of command and phoning Secretary Wu directly? I couldn't believe it."

Fatty Deng waited for Philip Ye to comment. But when none was forthcoming, he continued. "So we went to Secretary Wu's house. I wasn't allowed inside but something happened in there. Prosecutor Xu wasn't so keen on finding Junjie afterward."

"So Secretary Wu gave her a sharp reminder of her proper duties at the Procuratorate?"

"Big fish and minnows."

"Excuse me?"

"I wasn't really listening, Mister Ye, but I think the argument goes that if we focus on the big fish...the major players...it's safer for the minnows...the common people...to swim in the sea."

"But you did get to the university?"

"Yes, and it was a bust. That's where I met Madame Xiong. She's the Head of Administration there. I actually took a liking to her for a while. While Prosecutor Xu made friends with Professor Ou...he's the boss of the university...Madame Xiong did a trawl for Poppy in the student records and came up empty. Madame Xiong then invites me to interview a few of the girls."

Fatty Deng tried to put himself in the best light as possible, that he already knew something wasn't right. But, in narrating the sorry story of the interviews, it was hard to conceal that he'd fucked the whole thing up.

"It's very difficult to interview people in their own environment, especially with Madame Xiong breathing down your neck," said Philip Ye, sympathetically.

"You would have got more out of the girls, Mister Ye."

"Sure, but that comes from experience. And Prosecutor Xu should have been there with you. Sometimes, outside of a police station, you only get one chance. That ought to be explained to her. I take it she was trying to distance herself after she had been spoken to by Secretary Wu. What happened next?"

"Prosecutor Xu and I went our separate ways. I came home, had lunch, and went back to the university again. Not on the campus. I'm not that stupid. I need this job. But I had a stroke of luck. I bumped into one of the girls I'd interviewed earlier. After a little persuasion she tells me that Poppy does in fact exist. It's a nickname. Her real name is He Dan. This girl, Zhang Lin, confirmed that Poppy had been friends with Junjie and that she had invited Junjie into the dorm to draw portraits of some of the girls, with or without their clothes. Unfortunately, she couldn't tell me how Poppy had met Junjie. But she did say that Poppy had vanished from the university sometime in October and Junjie hadn't been seen there since."

"The same day Junjie vanished?"

"That's the question, Mister Ye. I cannot be sure. Zhang Lin told me Poppy left her books, her clothes and her phone behind."

"Her phone as well?"

"Odd, isn't it, Mister Ye. There's some talk among the girls about a romance with an older man. But, if he exists, none of them know his name. So the university get worried about a scandal. They clear Poppy's stuff out of her room as if erasing her existence, and Madame Xiong orders the girls never to speak about Poppy ever again or else they will be thrown out of the university."

"Could this older man be a tutor at the university?"

"I asked the question but Zhang Lin didn't know. No tutors have gone missing as far as she knows. But the girls are all doing different courses. They don't know each other's tutors. Poppy was studying electrical engineering."

"So was Zhu Yi."

"Really?"

"According to his old student ID."

"Zhang Lin tells me the only girl who might know the truth is Pan Mei, Poppy's old room-mate," said Fatty Deng.

Fatty Deng took his phone and showed Philip Ye the photograph that Zhang Lin had provided him: Junjie smiling, standing between a laughing Poppy and Pan Mei. He pointed out Pan Mei.

"Are you going to pick her up?" asked Philip Ye.

"Getting to talk to her on the quiet might be a problem." Fatty Deng felt his face redden. "Pan Mei is one of Freddie Yun's girl-friends. If she's not on campus, she's at his place, The Rainbow Karaoke TV Club."

"Who's Freddie Yun?"

"Local gangster...small time...protection and extortion...runs girls out of the club. Rumour is he's moving small quantities of meth and coke too."

"So why is that a problem?"

Fatty Deng took a deep breath. "Before I got this job at the Procuratorate I used to collect debts for Freddie Yun. Prosecutor Xu doesn't know. If she did, I'd be out of a job. I'm not proud of this, Mister Ye. But I had to provide for my mother. If I go anywhere near that club and get recognised, then..."

"Have you severed all links with Freddie Yun?"

"Yes."

"Any other criminal associations?"

Fatty Deng thought that question a bit rich coming from Philip Ye, heir to the shady business empire of the family Ye. It was also a difficult question to answer in Chengdu at the best of times.

Everyone was either related to, or friendly with, somebody up to no good.

"I'm clean, Mister Ye. I was clean in the police...as much as I could be...and I'm clean now."

"Good, send that picture of Junjie with the two girls to my phone. I'll pick Pan Mei up and save you the worry."

"What's the point, Mister Ye? If this Poppy is just laughing her knickers off every night being spoiled by some rich old guy, how does finding her take your murder investigation forward? Zhang Lin made no mention of any religious cult. Poppy may know nothing about what happened to Junjie."

"Or she may...and I don't like the coincidence of her going missing at about the same time as Junjie. We also need to speak to Madame Xiong. She's the link between your line of enquiry and mine. You've already proved her an able liar. And she played you, Fatty. Those interviews with the girls at the university were for her benefit not yours. She has some nerve. She wanted to know what you knew. She's worried about more than just a simple sex scandal."

"Do you think Poppy got involved with her brother, the bereaved Professor Xiong?"

"That makes more sense...gives Madame Xiong some personal motivation to cover up what's happened. We need to act now, Fatty. You and I have stirred up enough trouble as it is. I don't want any more evidence going missing or any other bodies turning up."

"Mister Ye, I've done all I can."

"Fatty, you know how short-staffed Homicide is at the moment. I could do with another set of eyes and ears. Just for this weekend. What Prosecutor Xu doesn't know won't hurt her."

"Mister Ye, she's really smart. She'll have my neck if she finds out I'm moonlighting with the police. I can't take the risk."

"Don't you want to find out what happened to Junjie...or Poppy for that matter?"

"That's not fair, Mister Ye. And how are you going to get to speak to Madame Xiong without prior approval from PSB Legal Affairs? You'll lose your job if you step foot on campus without good reason. It isn't worth the risk."

"Prosecutor Xu, speaking on behalf of the Procuratorate, could give me authority."

Fatty Deng laughed out loud until he realised Philip Ye was serious. "Mister Ye, you cannot—"

"Madame Xiong lied to her about Poppy too. That's an offence. If Prosecutor Xu is serious about the law she won't appreciate that. And don't forget this is all part of a murder enquiry now. It's not just about some missing idiot youth. There might really be a big fish behind all this...big enough to please even Secretary Wu. Let me have her number."

Fatty Deng began to panic. "I'll lose my job, Mister Ye."

"Leave Prosecutor Xu to me."

"Mister Ye, I don't have a rich father to fall back on," Fatty Deng said, in exasperation.

Fatty Deng saw Philip Ye's eyes harden, his lips compress into a thin line. Then Philip Ye nodded and those lips curled up into a slight smile, the anger fading as quickly as it had come.

"Forgive me," Philip Ye said. "I lost perspective for a moment. But Fatty, appearances are often deceptive. I drive a nice car and I wear good clothes, but that is as far as my playboy lifestyle goes. I may have money but if I lost my job – which, with the Shanghai Clique in charge, is always a daily possibility – then I do not know what I would do. You of all people should understand this. And I have to live every day with the fear that if I make a wrong step in any of my investigations, tread on the wrong person's toes, I might unwittingly bring down formal charges on my father's head and see him led out into the execution yard. But, because it is my job, because I am police, I am going to pursue Zhu Yi's killers as far as I am able. And, if I also manage to bring Junjie home, then I will think of that as a good day's work."

Fatty Deng felt his resistance crumbling, that old Ye family black magic washing all his good sense away. "Prosecutor Xu is at the Mayor's reception this evening," he blurted out. "It should be in full swing by now."

Philip Ye took out his gold pocket-watch and checked the time. "Women in Law Enforcement?"

"That's the one," replied Fatty Deng. "I have her number if you—"

"No need," said Philip Ye, already dialling a contact of his own.

CHAPTER THIRTY-TWO

Saturday

Xu Ya arrived at the Mayor's reception in no mood for a party. For reasons she found difficult to understand, she had spent most of the afternoon crying, the suicide of Old Man Gao weighing heavily on her mind. He had loved his son Junjie so much he had given his life to draw attention to his disappearance. She could think of no greater sacrifice. When she, on the other hand, had made the only great mistake of her life and entered into a loveless marriage, her parents had responded by promptly disowning her.

Above the entrance to the banquet hall a large red and gold banner had been hung. It read:

Women Hold Up Half The Sky

Predictable, thought Xu Ya, unimpressed.

Not an ancient Chinese proverb as many idealistic feminists in the West liked to believe – had there ever been a Golden Age for women in Chinese history where such a proverb would have had meaning? – it was, in fact, a quote from the Great Helmsman himself, Mao Zedong, made in 1968, at the height of the social disaster that was the Cultural Revolution. It was considered acceptable now – within limits – to discuss Mao Zedong's political and economic legacy, to even offer a little criticism. But any discussion of his personal life, any hint that his supposed respect and support for women in the public arena may not have been replicated in his private life, remained taboo. Xu Ya did not know the truth behind the constant rumours. But there had always been a level of hypocrisy running through the Party. In the same year as Mao Zedong made his famous quote, at a time when the viewing of Western films was forbidden to the people, it was no secret that senior Party cadres were enjoying those very same films for the purposes of doing 'research'. And this sort of hypocrisy, not necessarily as blatant or as conscious, was very much alive and well today. When she walked into the banquet hall she was unsurprised to see a throng of grey-suited middle-aged men with hardly a smattering of women among them – and this a reception to celebrate the achievements of women in law enforcement.

This was not to say that progress had not been made. Prior to 1911, dynastic law had hardly protected the rights of women. But since the revolution of that year and especially so after the end of the War of Liberation in 1949, many laws had been passed which endorsed, if not necessarily guaranteed, gender equality: equal rights in marriage, education for all, equal pay for equal work and so on. The Party had to be applauded for this. However, by the time of the Cultural Revolution, when all law was rendered meaningless and when men and women were encouraged to dress the same – in those awful Sun Yat-sen suits – one had to wonder if gender equality had been the Party's intention or rather gender elimination instead.

Had the Reform Era brought any further improvement to the lives of women?

Women were dressing as they saw fit now, which was something. Xu Ya was especially pleased with the black silk dress she had bought for this very occasion. But, in her view, this new world, 'the socialist market economy with Chinese characteristics', was as difficult for women as it had always been. And though she detested them for it, it came as no surprise to discover that some of the most talented girls at Chengdu National University preferred to catch a rich boyfriend rather than attempt to carve out a career of their own.

Five percent was the national average of women in law enforcement. During her interview with Secretary Wu, on the bench in Chongqing Zoo, he had told her he was trying to improve this figure for Chengdu.

"Talent and potential is what Chengdu is about," he had said. "Not old-thinking and old-values."

She had no reason to dismiss Secretary Wu's words as mere fluff. He had recruited her, hadn't he? But the PSB 'beautification' campaign – a subject about which Secretary Wu had been noticeably mute – was a reminder of how little progress had been made. A woman's value in China depended more on her youth and attractiveness than on any positive contribution to the country she could make.

Feeling terribly nervous – she hated all big social occasions – and not wanting to be cornered by any of the grey-suited vultures – her entrance had already been noted by some – she swiftly made her way over to the drinks table, waved away the sparkling rubbish the boy-waiter tried to offer her, and asked for a red wine instead. Credit to him, he didn't blink. He asked her to wait a moment, disappeared into a backroom and returned with a bottle, his hand unfortunately masking the label.

"Thank you," she said.

"From the Mayor's private stock," the waiter explained as he poured.

"It's nice to meet a woman who knows what she wants," said a voice from behind her. Xu Ya detected the sing-song lilt of a Cantonese accent beneath the badly pronounced Mandarin.

She turned to find herself face to face with a boyish-looking woman of indeterminate age, with short spiky hair sticking out in all directions. She was wearing a grim chocolate-brown trouser suit bearing one or two visible tears in the material. But it was the woman's ears that held Xu Ya's attention. From the left ear dangled a cheap gold earring, from the right nothing at all. In fact, the whole lobe of the right ear was missing. It took Xu Ya some long moments to realise she was staring.

"Forgive me," she said.

"There's nothing to forgive, Prosecutor Xu. I wear my scars with pride. First day on the job I was walking my beat in Kowloon when some muppet with a grudge against the police jumped me and bit off a chunk of my ear. Then he just stands and laughs at me, with my blood dribbling from his mouth. So I jumped him in return, bit his nose off and spat it back in his face. From that day I really knew policing was for me." She shook Xu Ya's hand, her grip strong, like a man's. "Supervisor Maggie Loh – I work homicide out of Wangjiang Station."

"You know who I am?" asked Xu Ya, disturbed by the story she'd just been told, and by the force and exuberance of Maggie Loh's personality.

"Everybody knows you, Prosecutor. Copies of your photograph from a Procuratorate memo are making the rounds of all the stations in the city. The boys are so impressed they're calling you the 'The Flower of the Procuratorate.' So you've made quite an impression.

And it's not just your pretty face. Not only have you suspended one of our finest – that big girl from Wukuaishi Station is a real delight, isn't she? – but you've also decapitated the Robbery Section. That drunken bastard Commissioner Ho has been placed on administrative leave pending further enquiries. Not bad for your first week. I'm almost in love with you myself. Come with me and I'll introduce you to our new pathologist, Doctor Kong. She's not a bundle of laughs… staring at dead bodies does that to you…but if we three ladies stick together none of the suits will dare lay a finger on us."

So Xu Ya, her psyche reeling in shock, not only from her first encounter with Maggie Loh but also from the unsettling news that her photograph was being passed about the police, dutifully followed her to a table well away from the crowd. There she was introduced to Doctor Kong. The pathologist, clothed in a slate grey trouser-suit almost as poorly cut and unfashionable as Maggie Loh's, briefly stood to greet Xu Ya, before sitting back down again and clutching at her stomach.

"It's the local food," Maggie Loh explained for the benefit of Xu Ya. "Far too hot and spicy. I've told her not to worry. Her stomach will adjust eventually. Mine did."

"I will die if I stay in this city much longer," said Doctor Kong. "But it is very nice to meet you, Prosecutor Xu."

"Doctor Kong assumed she was coming here for a few weeks study under the affable but grossly incompetent Doctor Wang," said Maggie Loh. "But the old fool has caught some grief down in Macao and won't be returning in a hurry. Doctor Kong's just been told by the Mayor that she is expected to sign a three year contract next week – a contract the Ministry of Public Security back in Beijing heartily approves of. So like it or not, Doctor Kong won't be going back there anytime soon."

"I'm stuck here," said Doctor Kong, her misery evident to all. "I am the victim of some sort of conspiracy."

Maggie Loh put her hands over her face and sneezed. "Don't worry, Doc – I'll look after you. I might even find you a husband. Not for nothing am I known throughout the PSB as 'The Queen of Romance'."

Worried that Maggie Loh was going to enquire after her own marital status, Xu Ya was relieved to be asked instead where she had set up home.

"Tranquil Mountain Pavilions."

"I know it well, Prosecutor," said Maggie Loh. "You're actually on my patch. I remember when they were building it last year and I thought to myself then that…"

Maggie Loh then paused. Xu Ya saw her expression harden, her eyes grow dark and suspicious.

"What is it?" asked Xu Ya. "Is it not a good place to live?"

"I'm sorry, Prosecutor, I just remembered a conversation I was having with a colleague about Tranquil Mountain Pavilions earlier today. Nothing sinister, I assure you. I'd love for a dead body to turn up there just so I could take a good look around. And speaking of bodies found in posh buildings, only the other month I was called out to..."

As Maggie Loh talked and talked – a font of inexhaustible energy, stories and good humour – Xu Ya allowed the wine to take effect. She let the cares of the day drift away. She felt safe in the presence of these ladies, more confident somehow. She began to look around the hall, watching the people congregate in groups, sticking together with those they knew, she guessed – always a problem with these networking events, never quite as successful as advertised. It had been Secretary Wu who had told her to attend. Mayor Cang was apparently looking forward to meeting her. But when Xu Ya did spot the Mayor, he was surrounded by an attentive pack of young women, hardly more than schoolgirls, all dressed in their pretty blue police cadet uniforms – almost certainly some of the harvest from the beautification campaign. Mayor Cang looked to be revelling in their attention.

But it was Lucy Fu who stole the show.

Not even expecting her to attend – why should she? – Xu Ya's mouth dropped open when Lucy Fu walked into the hall, already surrounded by a gaggle of grey-suited admirers, dressed in a stunning red and gold *qípáo* – a full length, silk evening gown that clung to every curve and just kissed the floor. That the colours of her dress and that of the welcoming banner were identical could be no coincidence. Laughing at one of her male admirer's jokes, Lucy Fu quickly surveyed the room, passing over Xu Ya without a smile, without acknowledging even that Xu Ya was known to her.

"Makes you wonder why we bother putting on any clothes at all," said Maggie Loh. "That's Lucy Fu – the family Fu are sponsoring this sad event."

"Why?" asked Xu Ya.

"To get her photograph in all the magazines and across the internet again, I suppose," replied Maggie Loh, knocking back her drink. "I doubt she woke up one morning and thought to herself that there ought to be more women in law enforcement. I met her once. Cold eyes, even colder heart. Real man-eater though. Years ago she dated the former mayor's son, Philip Ye. He's a homicide detective…friend of mine. I've pleaded with him but he won't kiss and tell."

"I met Philip Ye this morning," said Doctor Kong.

"What do you think, Doc?" asked Maggie Loh.

Doctor Kong wrinkled her nose in displeasure.

"He's not to everyone's taste, I'll grant you," said Maggie Loh. "A year ago I sat with him for a whole afternoon drinking tea. I think I told him my whole life story. I'm sure he must have spoken but if he did I remember none of it. He's as much a mystery to me as the first day I met him. This is the reason I so wanted to meet Prosecutor Xu."

"Oh, why?" asked Xu Ya, suddenly feeling hot and flustered.

"Wuhan," said Maggie Loh. "The rumour is that you were at university with him."

Xu Ya was saved by the ringtone of Maggie Loh's phone.

"Excuse me, ladies, but I'm still on call," said Maggie Loh, standing up to answer her phone.

Xu Ya looked down into her glass and found all her wine gone. She glanced across at the drinks table, trying to decide whether or not to have another glass. It might not hurt. There was plenty of food to come. Or she could make her excuses and leave.

Xu Ya looked up and found Maggie Loh offering the phone to her.

"It's for you, Prosecutor."

Xu Ya was confused. "For me?"

"Just don't let him walk all over you."

Not understanding this advice, or who could be calling her at this hour, she spoke tentatively into the phone. "Hello, this is Prosecutor Xu."

CHAPTER THIRTY-THREE

Saturday

The death of Beloved Mister Qin had affected Xu Ya deeply. Her grades at Wuhan did not suffer. Out of respect for his memory she had worked harder than ever. But it seemed to her, before he came into her life and then after he left it, that she had no independent will of her own, that she was like a person thrown overboard from a ship, tossed this way and that by a vast, unfeeling ocean. Beloved Mister Qin had given her confidence. Beloved Mister Qin had taught her to believe in herself. Beloved Mister Qin had lectured her again and again that she was the mistress of her own destiny, that her life was something to be embraced, that her work was to be for the good of all, that the law would anchor her in this world. Unfortunately for her, without his presence in her life and his wise counsel, she discovered – in regard to that anchoring – that the law was not quite enough on its own.

In reviewing a multitude of criminal cases at the Procuratorate in Chongqing, and in her interviewing of many victims and witnesses and defendants in the offices there, she had come to the remarkable conclusion that the thinking of these people governed their general life's trajectories, that their very often tragic and violent lives could have been predicted – in the most general terms – from the start. This was not about simple economics and family background – though, those naturally had a part to play – but she saw it was the mentality of the people themselves that appeared to govern their life's experience, regardless of the decisions they made or attempted to make.

And so it was with her.

There was a flaw in her mentality, a deep need within her for a man of mystery, of inner strength and of charisma to provide security and certainty and yet also be a source of endless fascination. Where this flaw originated she did not know. She assumed she had been born with it. As some babies were born with deformities, she had been born with a gaping hole within her that was constantly crying out to be filled.

For a while – honourable as he was – Beloved Mister Qin had satisfied this need. Not that she'd been aware of the flaw in her character then. Such self-knowledge would have to wait. It would be hard won through the years of hungering after Philip Ye at Wuhan, the wasted hours she had spent wandering the corridors and offices of the Procuratorate in Chongqing looking for a similar man and failing, only to stumble into a man she thought to be filled with the qualities she both desired and needed while volunteering her time to help the stricken victims of the earthquake. She had found herself swept up into his arms, with no conscious decision on her part made. She had luxuriated for a short time in all those qualities that she felt she desperately needed, only to discover that her husband was nothing at all like Beloved Mister Qin or indeed like the dreamy Melancholy Ye. She had literally taken a monster into her bed.

It was during the painful five years that followed that a gradual illumination came, that after much meditation and bitter reflection she saw within herself the flaw that had always plagued her and now was the ruin of her life. It was a weakness she could not control.

"Ms. Xu, self-knowledge is freedom," her psychiatrist had said after the ending of her marriage.

She knew different.

Just because one was self-aware did not mean one was cured. It was in her nature to be a moth to the flame. It was in her nature that when Philip Ye asked her over the phone to meet with him all she could say was, "Yes."

She knew she was being stupid. She knew she should have asked him to contact her office on Monday morning and make an appointment. Or, more properly, contact the duty prosecutor in the Criminal Procuracy Section, who would, in turn, invite her to contribute to whatever discussion was needed. And there was also Secretary Wu's instruction for her to introduce herself to Mayor Cang at this evening's reception. But as she spoke to Philip Ye all good sense flew out of the window.

"Prosecutor, forgive this intrusion," he said over the phone, "but I have discovered a correlation between your investigation of the shooting of Old Man Gao by Constable Ma of PSB Robbery and a homicide I am currently working. I would like your advice."

"Of course," she replied, her heart hammering in her chest.

"Are you available this evening?"

"I am."

"Could we meet?"

"Yes – where do you suggest?"

She handed the phone back to Maggie Loh. She told Maggie Loh and Doctor Kong that she had to go, that she hoped to meet them both again soon. She asked the nearest waiter to go find her coat and summon a taxi. She found the nearest mirror to make herself look as presentable as possible, frowning at the face that stared back at her, the psychological ravages of the last five years very evident about her mouth and eyes, and stepped out onto the street, the chill of the foggy air taking her breath away. At least the rain had stopped again.

"Where to?" asked the taxi-driver, a genial man with a cigarette hanging out of his mouth.

She told him.

The taxi lurched forward, throwing her back into her seat. She shivered and gathered her fur coat around her. The heating in the car had apparently failed. It felt colder inside than out.

"Do you know who owns The Silver Tree restaurant?" asked the driver, glancing back at her.

"I do," she said.

"You can get into trouble these days for saying so," he said, "but things have never been the same in Chengdu since Mayor Ye was forced out of office. But I don't mind trouble. I've been married three times, each wife worse than the last. How do you explain that? I don't know. I guess a bad wife alleviates the boredom. Or maybe because I'm a nice guy these bad women think I'm an easy mark. That's what my friends say. And who am I to disagree but…"

Fortunately the journey was short. She paid the driver generously, took his business card from him, and accepted his best wishes for the evening. With the taxi gone, she stared through the window of the restaurant. Every table was full. She had never seen so many people crammed into such a relatively small space.

Why had he wanted to meet her here?

Why not at PSB HQ or at the Procuratorate?

She pushed open the door and the clamour of a hundred or so people talking, laughing and eating hit her like a tidal wave, as did the pungent aroma of wonderful food. She put her hands to her ears. She usually avoided such places. As a child, her parents had learned very early that the press of too many people disturbed her unduly.

She looked for him but could not see him. She started to panic, wondering if someone had played some terrible trick on her, that the voice at the other end of the phone had not been his at all. But then a pretty young waitress appeared before her, took her hand without a word and led her through the mêlée, through the swinging doorway into the kitchens at the back, past grinning cooks and a squat and scowling middle-aged woman with a cleaver in her hand, and up a narrow flight of stairs to a short landing at the top. There Xu Ya was confronted by a number of closed doors.

"Are these the private dining rooms?" she asked.

"Oh no, Prosecutor, my boss and her family live up here," replied the waitress. "Would you like something to drink? Food will be served soon."

"Red wine," said Xu Ya, confused by what was happening to her, forgetting she had already drunk her allowance for the evening. "But it must be good quality."

"Do not worry, Prosecutor, I am sure we will have something acceptable hidden away."

The waitress ran back down the stairs. It was a few moments before Xu Ya realised she had been left with a conundrum. The idiot girl had failed to tell her through which door she would find Philip Ye. She did not want to knock on every door. And if the waitress returned to find her still standing there it would make her appear a simpleton. Xu Ya put her hand to her brow, feeling very hot in her fur coat, and trapped by her own stupidity.

What was she doing here?

What disastrous experience lay in wait for her now?

A door to her right opened a crack and she saw a pair of young faces, one above the other, staring at her, giggling as they did so.

"Hello," she said, having no expertise with children and thinking of nothing else sensible to say.

The door opened wider and the boys approached her, the smaller of the two reaching out to touch the fur of her coat.

"I'm looking for Philip Ye," she said. "Do you know where I can find him?"

The elder boy thumped the next door along with his fist, shouting, "Uncle! Uncle!" Then he grabbed the younger boy by the arm and they scampered back inside their own room, stuck their tongues out at her and slammed the door shut while laughing uproariously.

And to think I once wanted children of my own, she mused.

Before she could contemplate her fortunate escape from motherhood more deeply, the door in front of her opened and a man she had not seen in the flesh for ten years stood before her, taking her breath away. He was not the smiling boy with the hawk on his arm from Secretary Wu's photograph. Nor was he Melancholy Ye either. Before her stood the latest incarnation of Philip Ye, the policeman who, in front of a crowd on a busy street, thought nothing of knocking a PAP officer to the ground. She looked up into his face. It was more Western than she recalled, as if he'd grown more English with the passing years. She saw no recognition in his vivid green eyes, only puzzlement. She didn't need to be a detective to realise he had no memory of her at all.

"Prosecutor Xu?"

"Yes," she replied, hiding her intense disappointment.

"Thank you for meeting me."

He was taller than she remembered, and his figure had filled out though he could still be described as slim. She marvelled at the expensive fine woollen weave of his dark blue suit, the gold watch chain – such an English affectation! – dangling from his waistcoat. He had never dressed like this at Wuhan. But it was his presence that most affected her. It was so different to how he'd been before: more confident, more confrontational, she thought, and more magnetic too – much more dangerous to her than ever before. Her mother had been right. She should not have come to Chengdu.

"Please come in, Prosecutor."

As he turned aside to welcome her into the room, she caught sight, not only of Investigator Deng, smoking a cigarette, a sickly grin on his face, wearing the most hideous floral shirt imaginable, but also of Constable Ma, big eyes balefully returning her stare.

"What is this?" Xu Ya asked of Philip Ye, the spell cast by him abruptly broken.

CHAPTER THIRTY-FOUR

There was a demon inside of Philip Ye.

This was the only explanation that made sense to Fatty Deng. The encounter with Prosecutor Xu could have been handled very differently. A difficult situation need never have arisen at all.

For all her sneering during her watching of the footage of Philip Ye's punching the PAP officer, it came as no surprise to Fatty Deng that she had agreed to meet with Philip Ye without argument. As far as Fatty Deng was concerned, the woman who would refuse to sit down with Philip Ye had yet to be born. Even some of the daughters of high-ranking Shanghai Clique, people who supposedly loathed the family Ye, had gone out of their way to throw themselves in Philip Ye's path. But it was Philip Ye's *expectation* that Prosecutor Xu would meet with him which had disquieted Fatty Deng. No other policeman of his rank would have had the nerve to phone a prosecutor on a Saturday evening, pull them away from a civic reception and – though it was done politely – demand a case conference.

Was it all an act?

A simple display of bravado to demonstrate his power over women?

Fatty Deng didn't think so.

Making that phone call had seemed very natural to Philip Ye. He was heir to a self-confidence that was passed down from generation to generation. Fatty Deng had never met Philip Ye's father, but he had heard it said, that while in office, Mayor Ye had only to open his mouth for people to queue up to do his bidding. And this was nothing to do with *guānxì*, favours done to get a favour in return. This was more about Mayor Ye himself, about the spirit – or demon – that animated him, as it animated his half-English son. Fatty Deng had always hated this sense of privilege, the arrogance that others would always come running to serve. But he was also forced to admire it too. It was a mystical thing, a Heaven-sent gift – granted only to the precious few.

Fatty Deng was conscious he was also feeling somewhat protective toward Prosecutor Xu when he had no right to be. Prosecutor Xu wasn't his baby sister. And he certainly would never ever have any romantic claim upon her. He wasn't even sure he still liked her after the morning's debacle at the university. And yet this did not mean he would see her hurt, picked up and dumped by Philip Ye as so many women had been in the last few years (according to the society magazines), to become just more temporary grist for the Chengdu rumour mill.

"What are you going to do with the big girl?" he asked Philip Ye earlier, wanting to at least avoid any fireworks with Prosecutor Xu.

"She's coming with us."

"Mister Ye, she's on suspension and…."

Fatty Deng did not bother wasting any more of his breath. He could see that Philip Ye was not prepared to listen. Constable Ma wasn't going to be hidden away. It was as if Philip Ye was intent on deliberately provoking a confrontation.

The sense that this was exactly what Philip Ye had in mind was reinforced for Fatty Deng when they had reached The Silver Tree after a hair-raising and gut-wrenching journey in the Mercedes, Philip Ye racing his car so nothing would be left to chance. Fatty Deng and Constable Ma had been taken around the side of the restaurant and in through the kitchens. They had watched on as Philip Ye had calmed and persuaded his protesting half-sister Ye Lan to allow the meeting to take place in the living accommodation above the restaurant. He had then taken a waitress to one side to give her very detailed instructions which no one else could hear, and then they had followed him up the stairs to wait.

This is not going to go well, had thought Fatty Deng. No prosecutor under Heaven liked surprises. But as he glanced over at Philip Ye who was staring intently at the closed door, Fatty Deng wondered why he would provoke Prosecutor Xu in this way if he needed her help?

"May I smoke?" Fatty Deng asked, taking his cheap packet of

cigarettes out of his shirt pocket, frankly terrified of what was to come.

"You may," said Philip Ye.

"Smoking is bad for you," muttered Constable Ma, the first words she had ever spoken to him.

"Are you a doctor?" Fatty Deng said in return, lighting up, drawing heavily on the cigarette, feeling all the better for it.

Fatty Deng took the full force of Constable Ma's intense glare. But he ignored her. At this moment the cigarette was more important than his life.

They did not have long to wait. First footsteps on the stairs, then muffled voices. Fatty Deng looked again at Philip Ye but the homicide detective chose not to move. He waited, wanting to play games with Prosecutor Xu's mind, wanting to see what she was made of, perhaps. There was a sudden sharp knock on the door followed by the laughter of children. Only then did Philip Ye rise from the table and stride across to the door.

It was now that Fatty Deng saw the full extent of Philip Ye's perverse choreography. In the doorway, Philip Ye spoke to Prosecutor Xu, thanking her for coming, making her wait a few more seconds before turning his body to reveal just who awaited her in the lounge: her terrified investigator resplendent in a fake Hawaiian shirt (Philip Ye had allowed him no time to change back into his suit) and Constable Ma, whom she hated with a passion.

Fatty Deng died a thousand deaths when he saw the horror and betrayal in Prosecutor Xu's eyes. It was a great pity. In her long black fur coat, open to reveal a long black silk dress underneath, he had never seen her look so glamorous. He knew his job was gone, that all his hopes for the future had become nothing but dust.

However, he had not counted on Philip Ye's mastery of the situation. Philip Ye was soon at her side, taking her fur coat from her and showing her to her seat at the table. The waitress placed the tray of drinks down and smiled conspiratorially with a second waitress who entered with a single glass of red wine for Prosecutor Xu.

Fatty Deng took a couple of swift gulps of the Snow beer he'd ordered to take the dryness from his throat, only to find Prosecutor Xu's eyes upon him, the colour high in her cheeks.

"Investigator Deng, you are not to smoke in my presence," she said.

He stubbed his cigarette out.

She then spoke to Philip Ye. "Superintendent, I hope you are not going to waste my time."

Had Philip Ye seen all it needed to see? Fatty Deng certainly hoped so. He himself had just learned something about his new boss. When cornered, she could maintain her self-control and bide her time like a tigress, her claws bared, ready to strike. He was proud of her for not going to pieces or for fawning like a silly schoolgirl in Philip Ye's presence.

"I assure you I will not waste your time, Prosecutor," said Philip Ye, retaking his seat.

"And what is she doing here?" asked Prosecutor Xu, pointing at Constable Ma.

"She is an integral part of the story I am going to tell – a story which I am sure you will find fascinating and disturbing in equal measure. Did you manage to eat at the Mayor's reception?"

"No, I—"

Before she could complete her reply, a line of waitresses brought trays of food into the room. The Silver Tree's reputation for fine dining was well known in Chengdu. But what was laid down on the table before Fatty Deng was nothing short of a small banquet. There was so much food, and of such high quality, he didn't know where to begin. He wished his mother could be here. He had always wanted to take her to The Silver Tree but had never had the money.

"Please, eat – and then we'll speak," said Philip Ye,

Constable Ma needed no second invitation. She reached for the beef slices with tangerine peel, her face almost childish with joy. Trying to recapture some of Prosecutor Xu's good opinion, Fatty Deng waited for her nod of permission before opting for the rabbit cooked with rock sugar. He then watched Prosecutor Xu hesitate before being seduced herself, the duck with caterpillar fungus her first bowl of choice.

Only Philip Ye refused the food, preferring to sip at a tall glass of mineral water, content to watch them all eat, seemingly the perfect host. And then, before the appetizers were done, he began to speak to Prosecutor Xu in even, measured and unemotional tones. He spoke of both his and Fatty Deng's separate investigations, sticking to the known facts, refusing to speculate as he had done back at Fatty Deng's apartment. Using his phone, he showed Prosecutor Xu the photographs not only of the painting of The Willow Woman, but also of Junjie on the campus of the university, standing arm in arm with both Pan Mei and the missing Poppy. He spoke of everything, including Constable Ma's long-standing friendship with Old Man Gao, how she had helped him look for Junjie until Old Man Gao's hope had deserted him after his beating outside the Mayor's Office. All Philip Ye omitted was Old Man Gao's final decision to commit suicide, saving Constable Ma from that uncomfortable truth. When

Philip Ye was done, Prosecutor Xu, in between mouthfuls, fired off a series of questions.

"Superintendent, what is your assessment of the witness Yao Lin?"

"Evasive – but essentially truthful."

"So you believe she did attend a gathering at Madame Xiong's apartment on campus?"

"I do."

"And that the Madame Xiong she described is the same woman Investigator Deng and I met this morning?"

"Yes – the description given is almost identical."

"And you believe that Zhu Yi, Poppy and Junjie were all known to each other?"

"I do."

"And so finding Poppy as well as Junjie has become a priority for you in regard to solving Zhu Yi's murder and for understanding the activities of a hitherto unknown religious cult?"

"Indeed."

Prosecutor Xu placed her chopsticks on the table and interlocked her fingers, her eyes down, as if she were struggling with some inner conflict. Fatty Deng watched her intently, waiting for what was going to happen – as did Philip Ye. The room fell silent for a while, except for Constable Ma's chewing and slurping, interspersed with her unashamed sighs of pleasure.

When Prosecutor Xu did raise her eyes, Fatty Deng saw something pass between her and Philip Ye. If was a brief but very telling moment, an arrangement made between them, some mutual understanding arrived at that Fatty Deng was not party to. He felt a pang of jealousy in his heart.

"I don't like being lied to," said Prosecutor Xu.

"I am glad," replied Philip Ye.

"Are you intent on detaining Pan Mei?"

"Yes."

"In theory neither of us should need to seek higher authority to pursue a criminal investigation at the university," said Prosecutor Xu. "But the politics are delicate. That being said, problems can be avoided in the short term if you pick Pan Mei up at the gangster Freddie Yun's club, if she is to be found there. Madame Xiong is much more difficult. You may have been made aware by Investigator Deng that I sought authority myself from Secretary Wu before approaching the university this morning due to the absence of Chief Prosecutor Gong. For you or any other police to enter the grounds of the university and detain Madame Xiong for questioning will have repercussions, especially if the witness Yao Lin is lying or exaggerating.

"Furthermore, as yet, there is no proven link between the disappearance of Poppy and Junjie, or between either of them and the murder of Zhu Yi. So you have a choice: either you wait until Pan Mei gives you a more substantial reason to investigate the university or you allow me to question Madame Xiong for you. Investigator Deng has discovered that she lied to me this morning and deliberately obstructed a Procuratorate investigation. Though the scope of that investigation has been severely narrowed by Secretary Wu – and with good reason at the time – it is my view that he would now accept, due to Madame Xiong's deceit, that my own investigation is not yet closed. In normal circumstances, I would seek further advice from Chief Prosecutor Gong. But at this moment it is likely that evidence pertaining to both of our investigations is being deliberately destroyed or obscured. We cannot wait. So I am willing to return to the university this evening with Investigator Deng and question Madame Xiong again. I will also request access to Zhu Yi's old student records, not only to aid your investigation but also so that his family in Mianyang can be properly informed of his death. If I am not satisfied with Madame Xiong's responses, or if she otherwise gives me cause, I will order Investigator Deng to detain her. Is that acceptable to you?"

"More than acceptable, Prosecutor," replied Philip Ye. "However, I do not want you to get into trouble for—"

"Superintendent, I will not be lied to by anybody…and certainly not by a university administrator."

Fatty Deng watched Prosecutor Xu and Philip Ye lock eyes. Again they shared some silent understanding he could not quite grasp. And again he felt the stab of jealousy to his heart. Not that it mattered. He was satisfied. The investigation into Junjie's disappearance was to continue, which was good enough for him.

"May I also offer you some advice, Superintendent," continued Prosecutor Xu. "If in future you require assistance from the Legal and Disciplinary Procuracy Section, you should speak to me first before you speak to my investigator. Moreover, if I see you fighting again on TV, whether I have the support of PSB Internal Discipline or not, and regardless of who your father is, I will charge you with an infringement of Article 22 of the Police Law 1995. Is that understood?"

"Perfectly," said Philip Ye.

"Additionally – though you don't have to take this advice as I am not officially overseeing your investigation – you should consider releasing the migrants from Wukuaishi Station. If I am asked to review the legality of your investigation in the coming months, I may be very critical of any extended detention without cause."

Philip Ye stood, and then said, "Thank you for your advice and assistance, Prosecutor. Please take you time and finish your meal." He touched Constable Ma on the arm, and she, taking a few last bites, rose and followed him out of the room.

The threat from Prosecutor Xu toward Philip Ye had been unexpected, but enjoyable for Fatty Deng just the same. He couldn't help but grin. But then he saw the toll that it had taken on Prosecutor Xu, the trembling of her hand as she tried to pick up her chopsticks again. She caught him studying her.

"What?"

"I'm sorry, Prosecutor."

"So you should be – I am yet to decide whether in hiring you I have recruited an imbecile or a man with a special talent for uncovering the truth...or maybe both." She put a morsel of food in her mouth. "Ah, this is so good. Come, eat up, we have work to do!"

CHAPTER THIRTY-FIVE

Saturday

"**S**uperintendent, I do not like her," said Constable Ma.

"Whom don't you like?"

Philip Ye was driving them back to Wukuaishi to visit The Rainbow Karaoke TV Club, with the intention of picking up Poppy's old roommate Pan Mei.

"I don't like Prosecutor Xu."

"She was only doing her job when she suspended you."

Constable Ma refused to budge. "She is not a nice person. And I don't agree with fur coats. Fur should be on animals not rich people. I'm not sure about Fatty Deng yet. But his mother is a good person. And Uncle Ho was nice. But Aunty Ho…I don't like her. She cheats at *májiàng*. Cheating is wrong."

"Do you want me to arrest Aunty Ho?"

Constable Ma looked askance at him, her brow furrowed. He failed to keep the smile from his face, amused as he was again by her stark morality.

"You should not tease people," she said.

"Is that wrong too?"

"Yes."

"I do not mean anything by it, Constable Ma. It is just my way. Tell me more about what you think about Prosecutor Xu."

"I do not like her."

"So you said."

"She thinks the common people are beneath her."

"People have also said the same about me, Constable Ma."

"But you care about what's right and wrong, about catching murderers and finding Junjie. She only cares about being clever. Article 22 of the Police Law. Who cares about that? I am glad you punched that PAP captain. He was drunk. He said bad things to me. I do not like Prosecutor Xu. I could not tell what she was thinking. She hides her true self. I would sooner trust a snake. And Fatty Deng is frightened of her."

"He ought to be. She holds his new career in her hands."

"Prosecutor Xu is frightened of you, though."

"What makes you say that?"

"I have eyes. It is probably because she is evil. Evil people are always frightened of those who are good."

"Constable Ma, that's quite enough!"

She fell silent and began to brood. Soon the atmosphere in the car became close and oppressive. Philip Ye dropped the driver's window a crack, to allow fresh air into the car, hoping it would blow away some of Constable Ma's emotional miasma. Unlike Constable Ma, he had yet to form a solid opinion of Prosecutor Xu. She was undeniably clever. During his narration of the events of his and Fatty Deng's investigations, he had sensed her mind leaping ahead, searching out as yet unmade connections, looking for other avenues of enquiry, needing nothing to be repeated, nothing to be explained. Her cleverness had awed him. He thought of himself as no slouch in terms of intelligence but she was of a much superior league. There was none of the stuffiness of the other prosecutors he had met, their intellects addled by numbing bureaucracy. Her mind had been like quicksilver, incredibly pliable and – he would lay odds on this – highly sensitive and very, very psychic. If he had learned anything through his long-standing investigation into the barrier that separates the worlds of the living and the dead, it was that there were people – how many, he did not know – born with a special gift, able to receive and/or transmit across that barrier. He thought she might be one such if she ever chose to turn her mind in that direction. This made him envious of her. He had been born with no such natural ability. It had taken Isobel's death, and the despair and near madness that had followed, to open such a pathway in his mind. And then this pathway flowed only in one direction. He had no control over the visitations. He had no ability to communicate back to the spirits in return. He wondered if she had ever had experiences she could not explain. Maybe he would find a way to ask her one day. It could be significant, he thought, that when he had spoken of Professor Xiong's supposed conversations with his late wife, Prosecutor Xu had not even flinched. But whether this meant that she believed in such things, or considered the story ludicrous and not worthy of comment, he couldn't say.

Philip Ye had sensed about Prosecutor Xu, beneath her cleverness, an almost childish vulnerability (was this the vulnerability Commissioner Wei had been referring to, the reason she needed protection?), her character a complex mixture of fear and courage, spitefulness and warmth, cynicism and innocence. He had found it a beguiling mixture. He suspected her moods would be ever-changing and endlessly fascinating, somewhat like watching clouds race across the sky on a windy day.

He had seen something else too. As Constable Ma had implied, Prosecutor Xu was a wearer of camouflage. Above her left breast she had worn a silver brooch, fabricated in the form of a butterfly, studded with sapphires and diamonds. The brooch had sat elegantly enough on her dress but, despite the rapid motions of her mind, and sometimes her hands too, there was nothing else of the butterfly about her. Maybe it had been his imagination, but deep within her eyes her soul had taken an altogether different form, a form that reminded him of the distant past, of a highly-strung hunting-bird, of a precious little hawk....

"Superintendent, I am sorry."

"For what?"

"For being disrespectful about Prosecutor Xu."

"She has treated you badly, Constable Ma. I understand your bad feelings toward her."

"There is something else you should know, Superintendent."

"What is that?"

"She will spend all of your money if you marry her," said Constable Ma, bluntly.

"Why would you say that?"

"I have seen women like her before on TV."

"No, Constable Ma, I mean why would you think I would want to marry her?"

"She is in love with you."

"I thought you said she was afraid of me."

"I see what I see," muttered Constable Ma, the subject now closed as far as she was concerned.

There was no more time to think on Prosecutor Xu as Philip Ye stopped the car on the Sayuntai West 2nd Road not far from The Rainbow KTV Club. Constable Ma pointed to a group of girls entering the club.

"Look, that's Pan Mei!" she exclaimed.

Philip Ye had to take her word for it. He didn't get a good look at any of their faces. He got out of the car and one of the doormen approached, waving his arm at him, telling him to move his car, that the space was reserved for important guests of the club yet to arrive. Philip Ye didn't need to show his badge. Another doorman, older and wiser, took the first by the arm and spoke quickly to him, explaining to him the error of his ways, and then pushed him out of the way.

"Welcome, Mister Ye," he said. "How is your father?"

"He's fine, thank you. Is this Freddie Yun's club?"

The doorman nodded. "Do you want to make an appointment to meet with him?"

"I'm not here to cause a problem. I just want to speak with a young woman." Philip Ye showed him the photograph of Pan Mei.

The doorman pulled a face. "That's his girl."

"Is she inside?"

"She'll be back at the university tomorrow, Mister Ye."

"I need to speak to her now."

"I cannot help you, Mister Ye."

"But you won't get in my way?"

"Of course not, Mister Ye."

Inside, the air was thick with cigarette smoke and stale perfume. Raucous music blared out from a massive TV on the wall. Scantily clad bargirls converged on Philip Ye, only for him to send them away with a single flash of his badge. He looked around the dimly-lit main bar area, seeing no sign of Pan Mei. She could be in any of the many private rooms, upstairs or downstairs. The Rainbow KTV Club was a maze. He wasn't sure where to start.

He turned to Constable Ma. "Have you been in here before?"

The look of horror on her face told him everything he needed to know. Karaoke was not her thing.

A woman appeared before him, older than the other bargirls, but hardly less provocatively dressed. He assumed her to be the manageress.

"What do you want, Policeman?" she asked, her attention more on Constable Ma, uncomfortable with what she saw.

"Pan Mei," he replied, struggling against the noise from the TV.

"There's no girl of that name here."

"She's Freddie Yun's girlfriend."

"Freddie Yun has lots of girlfriends."

"Then take me to him. He can tell me where she is."

"Freddie Yun is busy tonight, Policeman."

Tired of this, he asked, "Would you risk everything over one stupid girl?"

He saw the flash of intelligence behind the otherwise opaque eyes, the sudden dawning that this was not a battle worth fighting.

"Okay! Okay! But only you, *lǎowài* – not that monster you've brought with you."

She strutted off toward the stairs, her short skirt barely covering her behind. Philip Ye moved to follow, then saw Constable Ma hang back, having heard every word.

Annoyed, he said, "Constable Ma, you're police – you go where I go. Is that understood?"

"Yes, Superintendent, I go where you go," she repeated, very pleased.

Satisfied Constable Ma was now behind him, Philip Ye ran up the stairs after the manageress. The music was not so loud on the first floor. The manageress pushed bargirls carrying trays of drinks out of the way, snapping at them with her tongue if they didn't move quickly enough. Philip Ye lost count of all the doors he saw, how many men he glimpsed in the private rooms, dressed in suits or casual attire, at the club for business or for pleasure, or for both. The manageress took them up another flight of stairs, narrower this time. At the top she told him to wait. She pushed open a door and closed it behind her. Having no patience for that, he followed her in, finding himself in a room with almost every seat taken by middle-aged men, all in various stages of drunkenness, some with bargirls sitting on their laps, the men plying them with drinks and expensive cigarettes; others, in spite of the early evening hour, fast asleep, able to do so because the TV was turned down low.

Philip Ye noted two court assessors deep in conversation, and the elderly Judge Wang, of the Family Court, seated nearby with a particularly attractive bargirl on his lap. Philip Ye also briefly locked eyes with Supervisor Ran from Jinhua Police Station. He was Shanghai Clique, and worse than useless. Philip Ye didn't know the man he was conversing with, but he had the smell of organised crime. The manageress was leaning over and speaking in the ear of a slim man in his early thirties, white suit, black tie, with pretentious blue spectacles perched on his nose. So this was Freddie Yun. Philip Ye was singularly unimpressed. Freddie Yun had a weak chin and, by the slowness of his responses to the manageress, was either drunk or high. He glanced over at Philip Ye and then turned away, not looking for a confrontation. So, a frontman only – not the serious gangster he had expected. Someone else, someone happy to stay back in the shadows, owned The Rainbow KTV Club. Pan Mei was nowhere in sight.

Feeling a tug on his raincoat, he turned around. Constable Ma was pointing at a young woman just emerging from the toilets, as yet unaware of them, rearranging her skimpy clothes about her.

"Take her," said Philip Ye, glad, for once, he was not working alone. Pan Mei, though not big, looked a handful.

He took out his handcuffs, expecting Constable Ma to hold her still. But Constable Ma picked up the shocked girl and threw her over her shoulder, proceeding then to hurry back down the stairs with Pan Mei screeching every step of the way. The commotion meant nothing to the men in the private room. And, with the manageress still trying to get through to Freddie Yun, Philip Ye left them to it. Outside, in the cold and foggy air, glad he was away from all the cigarette smoke and the noise – it was said there were more than a few thousand such karaoke bars in Chengdu – he found Constable Ma. She was standing next to the Mercedes, the doormen keeping their distance, her one massive hand securing Pan Mei's body, the other clamped over Pan Mei's mouth. Constable Ma was breathing hard, but she was exultant, her eyes as large as moons.

Philip Ye phoned Boxer Tan. "How's your evening?"

"It's Saturday night, Mister Ye, what do you think?"

"Kick the migrants loose and put some fresh tea on. I'll be with you in a few minutes."

CHAPTER THIRTY-SIX

Saturday

"Is he a good detective?" asked Prosecutor Xu.

Fatty Deng gave himself time to consider the question. They were sitting in a taxi on their way to Chengdu National University. Unsure of the proper etiquette, whether he should have occupied the front passenger seat next to the driver, he had clambered instead into the back of the taxi and now sat next to her. She hadn't protested. She was distant, sad even. He did not know what to make of her mood.

"I believe so," he replied.

"Do you know why he joined the police? As the son of Mayor Ye, he could have been so much more."

Fatty Deng resented the implication that there was a better job than being police, but he supposed she was implying he could have added to the Ye family fortune by going into business. "No one knows for certain, Prosecutor. He doesn't volunteer anything about himself. At the time, when he joined the police, we all thought it was a joke, a publicity stunt. But then he stayed, and he got promoted again and again."

"Deservedly?"

"Some say so, others not. His promotions came faster than most. Until the earthquake and the arrival of the Shanghai Clique he was on track to be the youngest ever commissioner."

"Why didn't he resign?"

Fatty Deng thought back to what Philip Ye had told him only a few hours before. "Because he's police and wouldn't know what else to do."

She stared at him quizzically.

"Prosecutor, if you weren't a lawyer, what would you be?"

"Yes, but—"

"Prosecutor, the job gets under your skin. Trust me, I know. Mister Ye is police. It doesn't matter how much money he's got. He can't imagine being anything else."

He saw she wanted to continue the argument but decided against it, biting her lip, staring out of the window instead. They were stuck in heavy traffic, the taxi slowed to a crawl. He felt the need to smoke but daren't in her company.

"Why do you refer to him as 'Mister Ye'?" she asked, suddenly.

"I guess because when he joined the police it seemed disrespectful to call the son of Mayor Ye by a lowly rank such as cadet or constable. So we were told to refer to him as 'Mister Ye'. It suited him. You've seen how he is."

She considered this, then asked, "Why do you think he is keeping her by his side?"

"Constable Ma?"

"Yes, that thick peasant! Did you see how protective he was of her? Loyalty is commendable, but misplaced loyalty is dangerous. She does not belong on the streets of this city."

"I agree, Prosecutor."

"He has her following him around like a lovesick puppy. I should report him for breaching my suspension order. Perhaps he feels sorry for her. Perhaps it's an English thing."

"Maybe, Prosecutor."

She fell silent for a while. Fatty Deng thought he saw tears in her eyes. In the dark of the taxi it was hard to tell. Anyway, what had she to cry about?

They had ended their meal at The Silver Tree, just the two of them, in convivial spirits. With Philip Ye and Constable Ma gone from the room Prosecutor Xu had relaxed. She had even seemed enthusiastic about being given licence – in her own mind, at least – to retrace their steps to the university and confront Madame Xiong. She had praised Fatty Deng, saying he had done good work re-interviewing Zhang Lin. She had also told him about the Mayor's reception, how relieved she was to have been pulled away. Very dull, more men than women, she said. She had even teased him about his fake Hawaiian shirt, saying it suited him more than a jacket and tie.

"But if you need money to buy some new clothes I would be happy to lend it to you," she had said.

The offer had moved him. But he had declined it. Better to borrow from one's family or even from Brother Wang than from one's boss.

When the meal was done, however, her mood had changed for the worse. After walking through the kitchens and thanking the cooks personally, she told Fatty Deng that Ye Lan had given her an evil look. And then she would not wait in the main body of the restaurant because of all the 'noise'. Instead they had stood together for ten minutes in the cold and the light rain that was now falling again for the taxi to arrive, Fatty Deng unable to cheer her up.

"Investigator Deng, may I ask you a personal question?" she said, the university now not more than ten minutes away, the taxi making good progress.

"Of course, Prosecutor."

"From a man's perspective...do you think...when you see me... what I mean to say is...if I returned to Chongqing...and a few months had passed by...would you remember me?"

Fatty Deng was shaken. "Are you leaving, Prosecutor?"

"No, just ignore me, Investigator Deng. I am babbling like a little girl. Too much wine. Neither of us should be working this evening after drinking alcohol."

Nothing more was said until they reached the university. Prosecutor Xu got out of the taxi lost in her own thoughts, leaving Fatty Deng to search his pockets for the cash to pay the driver. The driver winked at him when he handed over the money in the mistaken belief that Fatty Deng had struck lucky.

"Don't be stupid," said Fatty Deng.

After the taxi had sped away into the night, Fatty Deng ran to catch up with Prosecutor Xu. He found her surrounded by the very same three security guards who had accosted him that afternoon. However, this time one guard was holding an umbrella for Prosecutor Xu to shield her from the rain while the others were kowtowing to her as if she were the Empress Wu Zetian risen from the grave.

Fucking marvellous, thought Fatty Deng.

The security guards not only told Prosecutor Xu where Madame Xiong's apartment could be found, but they chose to escort her all the way, each of them competing for her attention, jabbering away as they did so, telling her everything they could about the university, its history, its most famous alumni. Fatty Deng had no umbrella with him. Nor did he have a coat. Philip Ye had forced him to leave home so quickly all he had with him was his cigarettes, notebook and pen. He was frozen and soaked to the skin by the time one of the guards punched in the key code for the lock on the door of the staff accommodation block. Prosecutor Xu thanked each of the guards for their kind assistance before going inside.

"Imbeciles!" Fatty Deng muttered to them as he pushed past after Prosecutor Xu. He heard them mutter something similar in return.

He caught up with Prosecutor Xu on the first floor landing. She was already thumping on a door, much to Fatty Deng's dismay. He had hoped for a brief discussion about tactics. She was showing her headstrong side again, not thinking. Music and singing could be heard from the apartment: Saturday night TV, some stupid talent show.

"Prosecutor, could we talk—?"

She thumped the door again, shaking the rainwater off her fur coat as she did so. The TV fell silent. A lock turned. The door opened slightly.

"Who is it?"

"Madame Xiong, it's Prosecutor Xu – you lied to me this morning."

Fatty Deng couldn't believe his ears. She could have at least waited until they'd got safely into the apartment.

He put his weight against the door, fearing it was about to be slammed in their faces. The door flew open and Madame Xiong staggered backwards. She was dressed in pink flannel pyjamas. There were pink plastic rollers in her hair. Her expression was a combination of shock, amazement and anger, her eyes narrowed to tiny slits, viewing them with the greatest suspicion. And then, as if suddenly remembering who they were, a smile opened like a vast crooked crack across her face.

"Prosecutor Xu, Investigator Deng – please come in. Forgive my state of dress. This is so unexpected. I am not a social person. Not at all. If you'd phoned ahead I could have dressed and received you properly at the administration building. Would you like some tea? Oh, poor Investigator Deng is drenched. Of course he'll have tea. What unusual weather we are having for this time of year."

She scurried off to the kitchen. Fatty Deng shut the door behind them, unamused. It was not ideal. Madame Xiong was giving herself time to prepare a story. But Prosecutor Xu appeared unperturbed. She was too busy staring at the photographs mounted on the walls. They reminded Fatty Deng of Junjie's drawings covering the walls of Old Man Gao's room. There must have been fifty or more of these photographs, some blown up to an impressive size. Mostly they were of Madame Xiong herself, standing alone and beaming at the camera, taken at what he took to be various tourist destinations around the world. Some appeared to be of family, groups of people standing together, but there were no portraits of a husband or children, not that this came as a surprise to him.

"This apartment is indeed big enough for the gathering described by the witness Yao Lin," whispered Prosecutor Xu.

Fatty Deng agreed. It was heated too, lovely and warm. He and his mother could be very happy here. His mother wouldn't have to wear a coat inside all day during the winter.

Madame Xiong returned from the kitchen with a tray of tea. "Oh, please sit down. It is so nice to have guests for once. Let me take your coat, Prosecutor Xu. It's so lovely. Real fur. What is it? Mink? Rabbit?"

"Rabbit," replied Prosecutor Xu.

"There are some women whose coats wear them rather than the other way around. But you are so naturally stylish, Prosecutor. I am sure you can wear anything and look good."

Fatty Deng sighed. This was more like a get-together between old friends than an interrogation.

"Oh, and that butterfly brooch! I have never seen anything so lovely," continued Madame Xiong. "You are such a beauty, Prosecutor. Your husband must be very proud."

"I am not married," replied Prosecutor Xu.

"Oh, that can't be," protested Madame Xiong.

"I was married…but he died."

Madame Xiong put her hands to her face in shock. This was also news to Fatty Deng. He watched on in disbelief as Madame Xiong, her eyes now full of tears, reached over and took Prosecutor Xu's hands and guided her to a chair, uttering all manner of sympathies and condolences.

"A woman such as you will not be alone for long," she said.

"I shall never marry again," said Prosecutor Xu, whose eyes had also welled up with tears.

"Ah, my dear, such loyalty to the dead is commendable. But the shade of your husband will not begrudge you marrying again if it is for the purpose of having a child. And a child of yours would be especially talented, would it not?"

"Thank you, Madame Xiong."

"Now what was it you've come to speak to me about? Was I not helpful enough this morning?"

"You concealed the truth," said Prosecutor Xu.

"But I would never—"

"Poppy exists," said Prosecutor Xu. "It is a nickname. Her real name is He Dan. She was a student here until October when she vanished. It is an offence to obstruct a Procuratorate investigation, Madame Xiong. You also instructed some of the girls to lie to Investigator Deng. This is unacceptable behaviour, Madame Xiong…quite unacceptable."

Unfortunately, the flattery and attention from Madame Xiong had done its work. Prosecutor Xu had said all the right words but, to Fatty Deng's ears, her tone had lacked bite. Even so, Madame Xiong reached for a tissue and dabbed at her eyes.

"Madame Xiong, you must tell me the truth," said Prosecutor Xu, her voice weakening further.

"Oh, Prosecutor – promise me you will keep this from Professor Ou. He doesn't know. I alone am to blame. I wanted to avoid a dreadful scandal. Young women these days…they have no self-respect. Instead of concentrating on their studies, instead of making their families proud, they run around with all manner of unsuitable men. This is nothing to do with immoral pictures. The young artist that Investigator Deng told me about…."

"Junjie?"

"Yes, I have no knowledge of him. I have never come across any immoral pictures at the university. But I admit I did tell the girls to lie about He Dan. I was beside myself with grief. He Dan was so smart, so innocent. And yet she has now absconded with a man. When I had to explain to her distraught parents what had happened I had never been so ashamed in my life. He Dan was top of her class. She has thrown her whole life away."

"Who is the man?"

"None of the girls can tell me, Prosecutor. And don't think I didn't threaten them. Some of the girls thought that He Dan had met someone from the city but none of them ever saw him or learned his name. All this new money swilling around has corrupted the girls. There was no warning, Prosecutor…no sign He Dan would give up everything just to catch a rich husband."

"So he is rich?"

"He must be," replied Madame Xiong. "Why else would He Dan run away to be with him and leave all her belongings behind? All girls want these days is to be looked after."

"Does the name Zhu Yi mean anything to you?"

"Should it? Is this the man you think He Dan ran away with?"

"No, Zhu Yi was a former student of the university. He was murdered early this morning, not far from here."

Madame Xiong threw her hands up in shock. "Oh, my goodness!"

"He attended a gathering in this very apartment last summer."

Fatty Deng could have jumped for joy. At last Prosecutor Xu had put Madame Xiong on the spot. Madame Xiong sat as still as a stone Buddha, the crooked smile swept from her face.

Prosecutor Xu tried to get her attention. "Madame Xiong?"

The words then uttered by Madame Xiong came slowly, haltingly, as if she was speaking in a trance.

"This is about my brother…a great man…a famous man. He lives and works in Chongqing most of the time. You may have heard of him. He is very senior in the Party there. He owns a company that does important work…secret work…so secret that even if you torture me, Prosecutor Xu, I am not allowed to tell you what they do. Yet he has never forgotten me…his baby sister. He found me this job. He and Professor Ou are lifelong friends. Because of the man my brother is…because he cares so much about the youth of today…he gives freely of his time. He teaches here one day a week for no salary. He shares all of my concerns about the direction our society is heading in. You should hear him speak, Prosecutor. There is no more eloquent or passionate man alive. He will tell you how the people have been seduced by the false lure of individualism and by the making of money, how China has been ruined by the capitalist roaders…our great revolution betrayed. Thursday evenings he stays here with me. I have a spare bedroom. Sometimes, when he is not so tired…he is an old man now, you understand…he invites some of the students back here on the evening. He speaks to them about the old days, gives them some much-needed moral guidance. I do not know the names of all of these students. So it is quite possible that this Zhu Yi came here. But what I can tell you is that He Dan came here regularly. She was one of his favourites. Everyone will tell you so. Her running away hit him very hard. He took the loss personally, you see. It is always those we are most fond of who stick a knife in our hearts."

"Wasn't your brother bereaved recently?" asked Prosecutor Xu.

Madame Xiong expressed no surprise that Prosecutor Xu knew this. "These last two years have been a difficult time for him. But my parents never liked her. His wife, Yi Li, always had a cruel mouth. She was never as supportive of my brother's work as she should have been. He is much better off without her. They never had children, which tells you a lot, I think. He still has me. I am fifteen years younger. I will look after him as he gets older. A loyal sister can do no less."

"Would he remember Zhu Yi?"

"I am sure of it, Prosecutor. You must go speak to him. Clever that you are, you and he will get on famously. There is no finer mind in all of China. Did you know he was the first recipient of the State Preeminent Supreme Technology Award? I was so proud. He gave most of the prize money to me. I have travelled the world because of it. He is such a good brother. Yi Li protested about him giving me the money…but what could she do?" Madame Xiong's laughter dripped with malice. "It's better now she's dead. He has more time for his work…for his students…for me. Come, Prosecutor, take a look at my photographs. My brother is in some of them. I will point him out to you."

Prosecutor Xu rose and walked the perimeter of the room with Madame Xiong, listening as Madame Xiong spoke about each photograph in turn, the missing Poppy apparently forgotten.

Evil bitch, thought Fatty Deng. As far as he was concerned the Procuratorate ought to begin an investigation into the death of Yi Li as soon as possible. It wouldn't surprise him if Madame Xiong had murdered her. Not interested in viewing any photographs, he stood his ground, preferring to complete his notes. It troubled him when he read them through. Nothing useful had been uncovered.

Fuck.

His phone rang.

Philip Ye spoke rapidly, almost breathlessly, communicating the latest troubling news. He wanted to know if they had detained Madame Xiong.

"Not exactly," said Fatty Deng, promising that he and Prosecutor Xu would get downtown as soon as possible where Prosecutor Xu could explain all.

He put his phone back in his pocket. "Prosecutor, we have to go."

Engrossed in her discussion with Madame Xiong about the photographs, she made no sign she had heard him. He picked up her fur coat, finding it surprisingly heavy, and headed over to her.

"Prosecutor, we must go," he announced, louder this time.

She turned to him then. But her eyes had a dull, sleepy quality about them he had not seen before. Had the wine she had drunk this evening suddenly taken effect? He helped her with her coat, ignoring the baleful look Madame Xiong was giving him.

"You must come back and visit again," said Madame Xiong as Fatty Deng ushered Prosecutor Xu out the door.

The door was slammed shut behind them. Fatty Deng took Prosecutor Xu's arm and helped her down the stairs. She was slightly unsteady on her feet. Neither of them had had time to taste the tea so she couldn't have been poisoned, he reasoned.

Outside, in the rain, she recovered somewhat, though she was still not her bright-eyed self. "What is it, Investigator Deng? What has happened? Has Junjie been found? I fear the worst now. I really fear the worst."

Confused, he replied, "No, Prosecutor, it's Poppy. Mister Ye has found her."

She read his eyes. "Oh no!"

"Prosecutor, we have to go see."

"Yes, we must go," she agreed.

As they walked across the campus, Fatty Deng realised with some regret that they had forgotten to request Zhu Yi's student records. Nor had they questioned Madame Xiong about The Willow Woman cult. Philip Ye was not going to be impressed.

CHAPTER THIRTY-SEVEN

I n an interrogation room within Wukuaishi Station, Pan Mei demonstrated that she had lost none of her attitude.

"You cannot hold me! I have done nothing wrong. My father is an important man – an official in the Ministry of Agriculture. He will get me a lawyer!"

"The law is very clear, Ms. Pan," said Philip Ye. "You are entitled to legal advice only after you have answered all my questions."

"My father will—"

"Your father doesn't interest me. This morning you lied to a Procuratorate investigator. You will not lie to me. Is that understood?"

Pan Mei glared at him, proud, defiant. But at least she closed her mouth. Constable Ma, sitting next to Philip Ye, stared across the table at Pan Mei as if she had descended from another world. Wearing the shortest skirt imaginable and a crop-top that barely covered the top half of her body, and with cosmetics liberally and carelessly plastered all over her face, Philip Ye had to admit Pan Mei looked quite a sight. She desperately needed expert tuition from a beauty parlour. Fatty Deng had been correct in his assessment that it would be hard for Pan Mei to disappear, day or night.

Philip Ye placed his phone down on the table. He pointed at the photograph on the screen: Junjie standing between two women, his arms interlinked with theirs.

Philip Ye tapped one of the figures on the screen with his index finger. "This is you, Ms. Pan. The youth next to you is Gao Junjie. He has been missing since last October. On the other side of him is your good friend Poppy, real name He Dan. She has also been missing since October. I am a detective with the Homicide Section. Tell me everything you know, Ms. Pan, or it will not go well for you."

Pan Mei's reaction after all her insolence was quite unexpected. She put her hands to her mouth. Philip Ye made a grab for his phone. Constable Ma, her reflexes even quicker, almost cat-like, picked up the bin from the corner of the room and put in in front of Pan Mei just in time to catch her vomit. The stench was bitter, rank. Philip Ye had no idea what she had been eating or drinking. He walked out the room. Constable Ma took her to the toilets to clean her up.

"Why my station?" asked Boxer Tan, sitting behind the desk in his office. Constable Ma's cat, Yoyo, was curled up next to him on a pile of case files. "We've still got lots of cleaning up to do after those filthy migrants."

"I like it here," said Philip Ye.

"And I see you're still dragging that big lump of a woman around with you."

"I'm beginning to like her too."

"This will not end well, Mister Ye. Nor will working too closely with the Procuratorate. Fatty Deng's a good guy. You can trust him. He's former police. But prosecutors are self-serving at the best of times – even the pretty ones."

"Your advice is well noted," said Philip Ye.

Boxer Tan shook his head, feeling his words, as expected, had fallen upon deaf ears. "Are you making progress on that murder of yours?"

"Maybe – and on finding out what happened to Old Man Gao's kid."

"Seriously?"

"He may still be alive."

Boxer Tan grunted and returned to the mountain of paperwork he needed to get through before he could say his shift was done. Philip Ye wandered into the kitchen and prepared himself a cup of tea. Then, remembering he was not working alone, he made a cup for Constable Ma as well. He found her in a better smelling interrogation room with Pan Mei. The young woman's face had a greenish hue but she was able to talk. Philip Ye had no need to throw questions at her.

"I feared this would happen," said Pan Mei. "Poppy was my best friend, not that I thought so at first. We were so different. I liked to party and she lived with her head in her textbooks. She was not from a rich family like me either. All their savings had gone into sending her to university. She was going to become an electrical engineer. I'm only studying English. For me, university is three years holiday until I have to find a job or a husband. When she wasn't working she was either reading a book or writing in her diary. But me, no one can shut me up. I just talk and talk. But, in sharing a room, you either fall out badly or you get to like a person. Poppy was nice, really honest. She never spoke about me behind my back. She even bought me presents when I felt low though she didn't have much money. So, after the first year I asked her to be roommates again with me and she agreed. But over the summer…last summer…she changed. Not so much other people noticed…just little things. She became secretive, like locking her diary in her desk…not that I ever read it…and not telling me where she was going on weekends or evenings. I asked her if she was in love. She just cried. She made me promise not to tell anyone. She said it was an older man…a famous man. She wouldn't tell me his name. I found out that instead of going home every other weekend to Deyang to visit her family she was taking the train in the opposite direction. There was a ticket stub in her bin which—"

"Chongqing?"

"Yes, that's right. Is that where you found her body? I told her to be careful. Some men are vile, nothing more than monsters. But she always saw the best in people. She was very innocent. She had never had a boyfriend before."

"Tell me about Junjie."

"Poppy brought him to the dorm one day…not long after the start of the autumn term, maybe late September. He was funny but an idiot, you understand…soft in the head. He could really draw though. Poppy wanted to impress this man of hers in Chongqing. She wanted Junjie to draw her portrait so she could give it as a gift to her man."

"Did she undress for this portrait?"

"Not completely," said Pan Mei, defensively. "But, as I said, she was desperate to impress him. And Junjie was good at drawing, so good that when the other girls saw Poppy's picture they all wanted one."

"Including you?"

Pan Mei nodded. "What a waste of time that was. Freddie Yun is a pig. He laughed at it and threw it away. I should leave him. He is no good for me."

"What happened after Junjie had drawn these pictures?"

"Not much, not until late October. I went to some party in the city with Freddie. Not a club. It was at someone's apartment in Chenghua District…for the whole weekend. On Monday morning, when I got back to campus, I found Poppy had gone...all her stuff too. I couldn't understand it. I asked the other girls what had happened. They said Madame Xiong had gathered them all together late on Saturday night and explained that Poppy had run off with a man. Madame Xiong had gone into our room with a couple of security guards and taken all Poppy's stuff away so it could be sent back to her family. I went to see Madame Xiong to find out for myself what had happened. But she's a vindictive bitch. She asked me if I knew the man's name. I said no. Then she told me to keep my mouth shut for the good of the university or else she would call my father and tell him I'd been doing drugs. She said I couldn't even contact Poppy's family and—"

"Ms. Pan, are you saying that Madame Xiong told the girls on your corridor that Poppy had run off with a man, not the other way around?"

"Yes, somehow she knew," replied Poppy. "She has spies everywhere."

"Did you try to phone Poppy?"

"There was no point. Poppy had left her phone behind. Madame Xiong showed it to me."

"And it was definitely Poppy's?"

"Yes – I recognised the scratch on the side."

"Where's the phone now?"

Pan Mei shrugged. "Back with her family, I suppose...with the rest of her stuff."

"And Poppy's diary?"

"I don't know. I never saw it again."

"Have you got the family's address in Deyang?"

Philip Ye assumed Pan Mei would ask for her phone to be returned to her so she could call up the relevant information. But she proved not to be as scatter-brained as she appeared, giving him not only the address and phone number in Deyang, but Poppy's mobile phone number also from memory. The phone log, when he could get hold of it, might prove interesting reading.

"Did Madame Xiong ask you about Poppy's man?"

"No," replied Pan Mei. "I tried to tell Madame Xiong about Chongqing but she told me to shut my mouth, that the matter was now closed."

"Have you ever visited Madame Xiong's apartment on campus?"

"Why would I do that?"

"Did you ever see Junjie again after that weekend?"

"I don't think so."

"Ms. Pan, why do you think Poppy is dead?"

"You said you were Homicide and—"

"Ms. Pan, tell me the truth. You saw Poppy again after that weekend, didn't you? She gave you cause to worry."

Pan Mei held a tissue close to her mouth. "Yes."

"Where did you meet her? Chongqing?"

"No, here in Chengdu – just after the New Year. I'd given up all hope of seeing her again. Then I got a phone call. She had borrowed a phone from some man on the street. She wanted to talk with me. She sounded frightened."

"Where did you meet?"

"At a teashop, near the river, just off the Siguan Road. She had to give me directions. When I got there she was sitting at a table. She didn't look well…far too thin. She said she'd had the flu."

"Was Junjie with her?"

"No."

"Did she mention Junjie?"

"No, why should she? She was worried about her family… wanted to know if they were alright. I didn't know what to tell her. I think she was missing them terribly. I asked her what she was doing in Chengdu…what had happened to the man from Chongqing. I was hoping she had dumped him. But when she talked she made no sense. She said he had wanted a painting of his dead wife, not her. She said that it was all her fault…that she was too weak…too easily influenced by demons."

"Demons?"

"She said they were everywhere," continued Pan Mei. "I thought she was suffering from some mental illness. I wanted to take her to a doctor. But she got really scared then and said she had to go. I tried to stop her but she ran off. I followed her as best I could. But she ran into a building overlooking the Siguan Road, near to the river. I went in after her but she had vanished. I didn't know what to do. I should have gone to the police but I didn't know what to say. And I was frightened of Madame Xiong. You will protect me from her, won't you?" Pan Mei began to cry. "No one has spoken to me about Poppy until this morning when the fat man with the bad suit and the kind eyes asked me about her. Madame Xiong ordered us to lie. I wished I'd been brave enough to tell the fat man the truth. I wish I was a better person."

"Did Poppy or Junjie ever mention The Willow Woman to you?"

"Who is The Willow Woman?"

"Have you ever heard of a man called Zhu Yi?"

"I don't think so."

"Ever been to The Singing Moon bar?"

"No, that place is rubbish!"

"Ms. Pan, the teashop where you met Poppy…could you point to it on the map?"

Forty minutes later, Philip Ye was sitting in his car outside the teashop. It was open for business but had few customers. It was situated on a narrow street, slightly off the beaten track. Not that there were many potential customers around. The fog was thicker here by the river and Philip Ye could not blame people for just wanting to get home for the evening.

"How far is the building you followed her to?" he asked.

Pan Mei, sitting on the back seat with Constable Ma, was doing her best to be helpful. It had slowly dawned on her that Poppy had not been found murdered after all and that all Philip Ye wanted to do was find her and keep her safe. Pan Mei had become pliant then, almost pleasant.

"It's like I said…it's just around the corner, overlooking the Siguan Road and the river. It's not a nice place to live. It's like a rabbit warren and freezing cold. I started asking some of the people there if they knew Poppy but they wouldn't talk to me. I got scared in there on my own. I don't know why I didn't go to the police."

Philip Ye guided the car slowly around the street until Pan Mei pointed the building out to him.

"That's it! That's it!"

Philip Ye stared up at it. It was at least six stories high, the roof lost in the fog. It was an old building, very different to the many new constructions being thrown up nearby, luxury apartments like Tranquil Mountain Pavilions where Prosecutor Xu had made her home, not more than fifteen minutes' walk away.

"Wait in the car with Constable Ma," he told Pan Mei.

He wasn't sure he was going to have better luck than her. There was no guarantee anyone in the building would want to talk to him or even if Poppy was still there. His real hope for the future of the investigation lay with Prosecutor Xu's handling of Madame Xiong. But the building was worth a quick look. Getting in was easy. The front door was ajar, the lobby deserted. It was freezing inside, as Pan Mei had said. He ignored the ground floor, hearing footsteps on stairs. Halfway up the second flight he caught up with an old man struggling with a bag of groceries.

"Grandpa, let me help you," he offered.

The old man, both surprised and grateful, his eyes aglow when he realised just who his new helper was, started speaking about the old days, about when Chengdu had been a poorer but friendlier place.

"Now it has become a cess-pit," he said. "This building is set for demolition. I don't know where I shall live then. It is like we have all lost our minds."

"Progress is progress, Grandpa."

"How is your father?"

"He does not complain."

"There are many who pray for his return every day."

"So I am told."

The old man held onto Philip Ye's arm as he was struck by a fit of coughing. His breath reeked of tobacco, his worn teeth stained dark yellow. When he was done, the old man asked, wheezing, "Do you think your father could have prevented all of this madness?" He waved his gnarled hands in every direction, indicating the building, the city around him.

"Who can say?" replied Philip Ye.

When they arrived at the old man's door on the second floor, he thanked Philip Ye and asked, "Would you like to come in for a cup of tea? My wife is three years dead. And my son and daughter-in-law do not visit me as often as they should."

"I am sorry but I cannot, Grandpa. But you could help me find this young woman."

Philip Ye showed him the photograph of Poppy standing with Junjie and Pan Mei on his phone.

"All these girls look the same to me now," replied the old man. "And my eyes are not what they once were. But my neighbour, Mister Mu, has made a complaint to the building supervisor about some students living together on the fifth floor. I haven't seen them but Mister Mu says they are a strange lot. They all live together, maybe fifteen of them. And they keep themselves to themselves. Mister Mu says fifteen in one apartment isn't hygienic. He is very frightened of disease. They might be able to help you."

"Thank you, Grandpa."

"You will give your father my best."

"I will."

Up more flights of stairs, Philip Ye encountered no one else. On the fifth floor he found himself on a long empty corridor. A fluorescent ceiling light was broken, another flickered intermittently. A TV was blaring away from one of the apartments. Somewhere, maybe on the floor above, a dog was barking. He stood still, suddenly feeling uncomfortable. Something wasn't quite right. He could smell violence in the air, the metallic scent of blood reaching his nostrils.

He listened and heard nothing. Was it just an echo of the past? Only a short distance away, on the Zhimin East Road, he and Superintendent Zuo had nearly died five years before in a hail of bullets.

He began to walk down the corridor slowly. A door in front of him opened unexpectedly. A middle-aged woman emerged carrying a bag full of trash. She started when she saw him.

"Aunty, the students – where do they live?"

She pointed to the last door on the right and ran back inside, not wanting anything to do with him. Philip Ye put his hand in his raincoat pocket and pulled out his expandable metal baton. It wasn't the past he was reliving. He could sense recent violence imprinted on the fabric of the building. At the door he waited and listened. Silence. There was a smudge half-way up the slate grey surface of the door glistening in the light of the overhead fluorescent. When he touched it, his finger came away bright red, the blood not yet dried. He put his shoulder to the door and the lock gave way with ease. Inside, the light was on but the apartment was empty, the furniture in disarray, sleeping bags strewn across the floor. On the wall of the lounge was a painting of The Willow Woman, exact in every respect to that which he had seized from the basement of Aunty Li's building. There was one bedroom, both beds empty. The kitchen was a mess, some evidence of a group meal being prepared and hastily abandoned. There was a small shower room and toilet. Blood pooled in the corners of the base of the shower. Whoever had tried to rinse it away had been careless in their work. He cursed. Not more than an hour or two earlier and he might have arrived in time.

He phoned the nearest station, Wangjiang Road, for assistance. No more than ten minutes and some uniforms would be with him, he was told. Feeling defeated, he stared out of the murky window, looking down across the road to the river, trying to figure out his next move. Then, between the trees, by the bank of the river, in the cool yellow light cast by the streetlamps, fog swirling around them, he saw two figures struggling with a heavy load. He ran out from the apartment without thinking, taking the stairs three steps at a time. He flew out of the front door, raced around the side of the building, heard the squeal of brakes as he thoughtlessly crossed the road without looking, and finally caught up with them just as they were about to heave their cargo into the water.

"Police!"

His surprise of them was total. They turned toward him, each carrying one end of a heavy sleeping bag. He had been expecting young men of student age, easily intimidated by authority. But they were tough, lean men of similar years to himself, unimpressed by who and what he was. They unceremoniously dumped the sleeping bag on the ground, knives instantly appearing in their hands. Philip Ye was good with his hands but by no means a skilled fighter. He was no Boxer Tan. He recalled Ye Lan's bad dream of seeing knives in the dark and as they rushed him he knew he was a dead man. His baton caught the closest in the face as a wickedly curved knife ripped through his raincoat. But there was nothing he could do to stop the other assailant. He felt the impact of the knife thudding into his lower ribs, winding him. And then he was down on the ground. Desperately, he tried to squirm away from the blade that now reached for his neck. Then he heard a bellow, an explosion of air from something less than human, and one by one his assailants were pulled off him. Then they were gone, running, soon to be swallowed up by the fog. Constable Ma, breathing hard, her face white with concern, peered down at him. With incredible strength she pulled him to his feet. The curved blade lay on the ground not far away. He put his hand to his ribs, searching for blood and finding none. He pulled out the pocket-watch given him by Isobel. The casing was dented, evidence of where it had deflected the blade. He did not deserve such luck this night.

"Should I chase them?" asked Constable Ma, her big eyes gleaming.

"I told you to stay in the car," he gasped.

"Forgive me," she said, hanging her head in shame. "I saw them sneak out of a side entrance after you went in. They did not look right to me. I was worried. Then I saw you—"

"Well, Ma Meili...Sister...I thank you for disobeying me...and for saving my life. I shall never forget."

A sharp cry of horror shattered the moment between then. Pan Mei was bending over the sleeping bag. It had split open upon being dropped. Constable Ma was soon at Pan Mei's side, holding her as she emptied the little that remained in her stomach into the river.

CHAPTER THIRTY-EIGHT

Police cars had blocked off the Siguan Road. The resulting traffic jams made it necessary for Fatty Deng to explain to Prosecutor Xu the need to abandon their taxi and make their way to the scene on foot. Withdrawn and silent since their visit with Madame Xiong, she did not argue. She got out and started walking, leaving an exasperated Fatty Deng to pay the driver again. He put the receipt safely inside his notebook. He had yet to read the Procuratorate's expenses policy. He hoped it was generous where Prosecutor Xu was concerned.

She had set off at quite a pace, her high heels clicking down the road. Fatty Deng had to hurry to catch up with her. At the police cordon he was disheartened to find little discipline. They were admitted through without comment, no one bothering to make a note of their names or even the official capacity in which they were in attendance. The uniforms were distracted, listening intently to their radios. A manhunt was in progress, much more exciting than enforcing the security of a crime scene. Sadly, he saw few of the old faces. Many of the uniforms would have come from Wangjiang Road, his old station, not far away.

The body was near to the river. It was illuminated by a single floodlight powered by a portable generator someone had rustled up. Figures moving about in front of the light cast eerie shadows against the fog. The victim, hardly recognisable as the young woman in the photograph standing arm-in-arm with Junjie and Pan Mei, had been stabbed to death. Poppy's blood had soaked through the sleeping bag used to carry her. Small jagged concrete blocks, probably lifted from some nearby building-site, had also tumbled out of the sleeping bag. Presumably they were to be used to help take the body below the water.

"This is awful," said Prosecutor Xu. She was watching Doctor Kong examining the body.

No, this is amateur hour, thought Fatty Deng.

It didn't make sense. Who would carry a body out of a building in the middle of a Saturday evening when there were people out and about – the Siguan Road had its fair share of bars and restaurants, many lit by harsh but colourful neon lights and blasting out raucous music – lug it over the road in an old and ragged sleeping bag, and then attempt to throw it in the river in the hope that it would never be seen again? The murderers had either been in a real hurry to dispose of the body, or over-confident that the fog would obscure what they were up to, or complete morons – or maybe all of the above.

"This cannot go unpunished," said Prosecutor Xu.

"Don't worry, Prosecutor, we'll catch them – you, me and Mister Ye."

He had tried to sound positive and cheery but it did no good. It seemed nothing could lift Prosecutor Xu out of that dark place she had entered into. Something had happened to her in Madame Xiong's apartment, something Fatty Deng had missed when Madame Xiong had been giving her a tour of the photographs on the walls.

"A few moments more and Poppy would have been lost forever," said Prosecutor Xu.

Fatty Deng was relieved when Doctor Kong rose from the body and came over to speak to them. Back at The Silver Tree, after Philip Ye and the big girl had left, Prosecutor Xu had told Fatty Deng all about the new forensic pathologist with a delicate stomach. Fatty Deng liked the look of Doctor Kong – a vast improvement on that old fuck-wit Doctor Wang.

"Prosecutor Xu, this is unexpected," said Doctor Kong.

"I have an interest in this case."

"Well then, my preliminary findings are death from massive blood loss due to multiple stab wounds to the face, neck and chest. There are many defensive wounds to the hands, wrists, and upper arms. Time of death is within the last two hours. She was not killed here. Supervisor Loh can be found on the fifth floor of that building."

She pointed across the road to the nearest apartment block. "She will give you more details."

"May I have a copy of your full report when it is done?" asked Prosecutor Xu.

"Yes, of course. Prosecutor, are you alright? You don't look well. There is a lot of flu going around. Despite what Supervisor Loh says, by tomorrow morning she will be bed-ridden. You might be too."

"No, I'm fine, Doctor. It has been a long, challenging day, that's all. We had hoped to find this young woman alive."

Doctor Kong nodded, looking unconvinced. She moved off then to supervise the loading of the body into the ambulance. Fatty Deng was slightly put out. He knew a procuratorate investigator was not a person of great importance but he would have liked to have been introduced to Doctor Kong. But Prosecutor Xu had already walked the few steps to the river and was staring morosely down at the black water. Fatty Deng felt weary. He preferred the angry or over-talkative Prosecutor Xu to this. Even her singing in the car hadn't been so bad.

"Prosecutor, we should go see where she was killed," he said. He wanted to keep up with the investigation. He needed to keep up with Philip Ye.

"A few moments later and no one would ever have known what had happened to her. The water would have swallowed her up and—"

"Prosecutor, please!"

He touched her elbow but she shrugged him off. He apologised but she acted as if she hadn't heard him. He decided to go view the murder room alone. But, as he walked out across the Siguan Road, he was relieved to hear her heels behind him. He slowed so she could catch up with him and then take the lead.

There was a uniform posted as security on the door of the apartment block. Fatty Deng remembered him from the old days: Squint-Eye Yong from Gonghe Road Station. When Fatty Deng had been in the job, Squint-Eye Yong had had the reputation for taking home more in bribes every month than his salary. Honesty wasn't always the best policy in China – too much could get you killed – but Squint-Eye Yong, with twenty years in the job, had always been unable to comprehend the difference between right and wrong, both morally and legally. It was the reason he remained a constable first class.

Squint-Eye Yong opened the door for Prosecutor Xu, saluted her for some reason, and then ogled her as she went past him. Then, when Fatty Deng got close, Squint-Eye Yong muttered out of the corner of his mouth, "Fatty, you look like a fucking clown in that shirt."

Fatty Deng shoved him hard against the side of the building. "Maybe so...but look at my boss like that again and I'll drop you where you stand."

Feeling better, Fatty Deng caught up with Prosecutor Xu as she made her way up the stairs. On the fifth floor, a constable, unknown to Fatty Deng but pleasant enough, pointed the way. The door to the apartment was wide open. A couple of forensic guys were down on their hands and knees. The place was a mess, sleeping-bags strewn across the floor, furniture in disarray, to Fatty Deng signs of a hasty and panicked exit. Prosecutor Xu stood for a long time staring up at a painting of The Willow Woman upon the wall. There was no TV, no computer games left lying around. Whoever had been living here had not been any kind of students that Fatty Deng had ever heard of.

Two more forensic technicians were sampling blood from the base of the shower. So this was where Poppy had fought for her life and lost, Fatty Deng thought, grimly. He hadn't needed Doctor Kong to tell him about the defensive wounds on Poppy's arms. He had seen them for himself from ten paces away. Poppy had fought like a tigress. Not that it counted for much in the end. Facing one knifeman was bad enough but two was impossible. Philip Ye had spoken on the phone of his own close encounter with death, how the big girl had unexpectedly and fortuitously saved his life, and how the two murderers had fled leaving behind a curved dagger – almost certainly one of the weapons that had done for Zhu Yi. Fatty Deng had repeated all this to Prosecutor Xu in the taxi.

"See, Prosecutor, this is the proof we needed that the disappearance of Junjie and Poppy and the murder of Zhu Yi are all connected."

She had not replied.

She had actually turned her face from him.

Fatty Deng found Philip Ye in the kitchen, speaking to a woman in plain-clothes he hadn't met before. Philip Ye didn't seem himself. His raincoat was stained and torn and, for once, his hair was not quite perfection. But, for someone who had nearly died, he looked remarkably in control of himself. As for the woman, she looked much worse. Her face was filmy with sweat and she could hardly speak without coughing. Fatty Deng guessed who she was. Back at The Silver Tree, Prosecutor Xu had described to him the one-eared detective from Hong Kong: Supervisor Maggie Loh. Prosecutor Xu had told him how Maggie Loh had lost most of her ear, how impressed she was with Maggie Loh's bravery and fortitude. Fatty Deng had thought the story typical Hong Kong bullshit – not that he'd said so.

"Who are you?" asked Maggie Loh, contemptuously, as if he were some civilian who'd walked in out of curiosity or by mistake.

"He's with me," said Prosecutor Xu, appearing at his side.

"Prosecutor, good to see you again so soon," said Maggie Loh. "The Mayor's reception took a dive after you left."

Philip Ye wasn't so welcoming. "Have you detained Madame Xiong?" he asked, brusquely.

Prosecutor Xu lowered her eyes. "She gave me no cause."

What happened next appalled Fatty Deng. He thought Philip Ye was going to explode. Philip Ye's face reddened and he verbally tore into Prosecutor Xu, speaking rapidly in a language Fatty Deng couldn't understand – English? – jabbing an accusing finger toward her face. It got so bad, so quickly, and Prosecutor Xu's responses were so feeble – spoken in that same incomprehensible language – that Fatty Deng was forced to step between them.

"That's enough, Mister Ye!" he yelled.

He thought Philip Ye was going to strike him. But Maggie Loh had also seen and heard enough. She dragged Philip Ye away, berating him in Cantonese. At least Fatty Deng had some knowledge of that, mainly the curse words she was using.

"Prosecutor, what was all that about?" he asked.

She wouldn't look at him, trying to hide her face.

Maggie Loh soon reappeared and, speaking in Mandarin now, apologised. "Prosecutor, he had no right to speak to you like that. He will be disciplined. I will make sure of it. A brush with death is no excuse. Would you like me to arrange for a car to take you home?"

"No, Supervisor Loh, it's not far. The walk will do me good," replied Prosecutor Xu, weakly.

"Are you sure?"

"Quite sure – Investigator Deng will be with me."

While retracing their steps down the stairs, Fatty Deng didn't know what to say. He could not understand it. All the fight had gone out of Prosecutor Xu. Where had the prosecutor with the volatile temper and sharp tongue gone, the prosecutor who had frightened him so?

Outside, he found that Squint-Eye Yong had slunk off somewhere. Across the street Philip Ye was sitting in his car staring at them. His expression was impossible to discern. In the back of the car Fatty Deng could see Constable Ma. She had a consoling arm around a young woman very familiar to him.

Pan Mei.

If you hadn't lied to me this morning we might have recovered your friend alive, Fatty Deng thought, sadly.

He pushed the regret aside.

What was done was done.

As Prosecutor Xu had told Maggie Loh, it was not a long walk to Tranquil Mountain Pavilions. They made the short journey in silence.

In front of the ornate entrance, Prosecutor Xu said, "Thank you for your assistance today, Investigator Deng. I am sure you realise by now that I am not a very good judge of character. But I do not have to be told by any that you are a better man than most. You must never lose that inner drive you have to unearth the truth. I hope soon you will think as well of me as I do of you."

"Prosecutor?"

But she was already pushing open the door, her face turned away from him, visibly upset.

"Tomorrow morning, Starbucks, at nine…let's meet and discuss the case!" he shouted after her.

She threw a hand up in acknowledgement. But that was all she did. He stood and watched her march across the lobby, her fur coat flowing about her. She stepped into the lift, wiping her eyes as she did so. He stood staring for some time after the lift doors closed; until, that is, the concierge began to eye him suspiciously through the window. He ambled off down the street, lighting a cigarette as he did so, not knowing what to make of her parting words. He decided to take the bus home to save some money. Then, when the rain began to fall again, and he realised all his energy was spent, he slumped into the first taxi he could find.

CHAPTER THIRTY-NINE

Pan Mei was booked into the cells at Wangjiang Road Station. Distraught over the murder of her friend Poppy, unshakable in her belief that if she had only acted sooner she could have saved her friend, Philip Ye had decided confinement was best for her state of mind. Moreover, until he better understood Madame Xiong's involvement in the disappearance of Poppy, he wanted Pan Mei kept away from the university. The custody officer promised he would take good care of her but only after Philip Ye had persuaded him she was an important witness and not a hysterical suspect. That done, Philip Ye had been drawn into a bruising argument with Maggie Loh. She had laid into him for his rudeness toward Prosecutor Xu, for stupidly confronting knife-wielding maniacs without the proper back-up, and – much, much worse in her opinion – concealing the truth about why he needed an informant inside Tranquil Mountain Pavilions.

"What were you doing?" she asked. "Trying to get some background on a prospective girlfriend?"

"I was following orders."

"Whose orders?"

"I don't answer to you, Maggie."

"I am your senior officer."

"This has nothing to do with normal police operations."

"Then at least explain why you're dragging around that monster

Constable Ma with you. She's suspended and about to be trans-ferred. Are you deliberately trying to provoke the Procuratorate?"

"She's been badly treated."

"She's a thick peasant! Anyone can see she doesn't belong on the streets of a city."

"Go home, Maggie – you're sick and you don't know what you're saying."

"This is my station – you go home!"

So Philip Ye turned his back on her and left. Ma Meili was waiting patiently for him in the Mercedes. He drove her back to The Silver Tree. She had admitted to him that she had nowhere to stay that night, that her old landlord would have already let the apart-ment she had vacated Friday afternoon. At the restaurant she made to get out of the car, but he stopped her by touching her arm.

"Sister…before we go inside…you must tell me what happened to you in Pujiang County."

"There's nothing to tell, Superintendent."

"Why can't you return home?"

She brushed a lock of hair from her face. "I am not wanted there."

"What do you mean by that?"

"My brother is to inherit my parents' farm. His new wife isn't nice. She says that I eat too much…that I am a burden on the family…that she will cut my throat in my sleep if I come back."

"Is this the truth?"

"Yes, Superintendent."

"What about the drug dealers?"

"What drug dealers?"

He searched her eyes and could find no lie. So much for the story told by Supervisor Cai's informant about corrupt police, a meth lab in the hills, and an honest policewoman banished for her own good.

"Sister, why did you come to Chengdu? You could have found another place to live in Pujiang County."

"I am afraid to say."

"Why?"

"You will think me a bad person."

"If I am to help you find a job somewhere, I need to know what happened in Pujiang County."

He saw the uncertainty in her eyes. He waited patiently for her to find the courage to trust him.

"When I was little," she began, "I saw a TV programme. It was about a brave policeman. I knew then that I was born to be police. I told my father but he said no. I pleaded with him but he beat me. I had two cousins who were police and my father said they were worse than criminals. When my older sister left home to get married I asked him again if I could be police. He said no. He also said I mustn't marry as I had to stay and work the farm with my brother. Not that I wanted to get married. A man asked me when I was eighteen…but he was like Junjie, not right in the head. So I told him to go away. When I was twenty-one…on my birthday…I disobeyed my father. I walked the twenty miles to the police station. One of my cousins was senior there. I said I wanted to be police. But my cousin told me that the police didn't have any money for new recruits and anyway he didn't want to cross my father. When I got home my father beat me again. Every year after that, on my birthday, I would walk to the police station and ask my cousin if the police had enough money now to recruit me. They never did. Last year I was thirty. In the spring, my younger brother got married unexpectedly. His new wife came to live with us. She said because my brother is to inherit the farm I must obey her. She said she would murder me if I didn't leave. My parents also said I should go. They said she is a better daughter than me. So I walked to the police station and pleaded with my cousin. He said I could sleep in one of the cells for a short time."

So, this explained the informant's story. There had actually been some truth to it. The informant had indeed seen Ma Meili asleep in one of the cells.

"What happened next?"

"My cousin went to visit with my father…to try to reason with him, to get him to accept me back into the family. But it was no good. I didn't want to go back anyway. My cousin – who is a good man – said I could stay for a time at the station. He said I could earn my meals by cooking and cleaning and running errands until I found a job on another farm. He said he would ask around for me. But then in the early summer he heard that Chengdu was recruiting police… women especially."

"The beautification campaign?"

"I don't know what that is…but he said there was a way for me to become police without an interview. He made me sign lots of forms. He wrote a letter for me. Two weeks later he got a phone call and said that I was now police in Chengdu…in the Robbery Section. I was so happy. He was so happy for me. He said it was the best joke ever. I don't know what he meant by that. He is to retire soon. He says he doesn't really care anymore."

"Are you telling me that you were never in the police in Pujiang County?"

"No, Superintendent."

"And you've never been to Police College?"

"No, Superintendent."

"Jesus Christ!" he exclaimed, in English.

She hung her head. Big round tears began to roll down her cheeks. He could guess what her cousin had done. He had forged a police personnel file, lodged a transfer request for her, probably given her a glowing recommendation, and affixed a photograph of some unknown attractive woman. As long as the woman in the photograph looked the part for the beautification campaign, none of the proper background checks would have been done. The Personnel Section at PSB HQ would have welcomed her application and assumed she needed no training so she could start immediately because of all her 'experience'. It was no surprise the drunken and lecherous Commissioner Ho had snapped her up for his personal protection detail, only to discover her appearance was not as advertised, whereupon he had then dispatched her to Wukuaishi Station. The story was so bizarre, so elegant in its simplicity, so very Chinese, it just had to be true. He couldn't wait to tell Superintendent Zuo. His friend had always maintained that the Chinese people were so incredibly literal, that if something was written down, particularly in an official file, it was to be believed.

So this was why she had decided to run. As soon as the transfer order reached the Personnel Section in Pujiang County, they would consult their files, discover Ma Meili didn't exist, and contact the Procuratorate and PSB in Chengdu saying there must be some mistake. It wouldn't take long for a sharp operator like Prosecutor Xu to uncover the truth and charge Ma Meili not only with impersonating a police officer but also something a lot more serious in regard to the shooting of Old Man Gao – no matter how well-intentioned Ma Meili had been.

He passed her his silk handkerchief so she could dry her eyes. "How did you learn to shoot?"

"My cousin taught me…in a few days. It wasn't hard. He made me shoot at trees in the forest. And he gave me a police manual to read. He showed me how to speak and how to behave. Are you going to arrest me?"

"No, but I need time to think about what to do with you."

"I just wanted to be police, Superintendent. I just wanted to serve the people…to bring bad people to justice."

She put her hands to her face and her whole body began to shake. Philip Ye stepped out of the car so he could breathe, so he could distance himself from the powerful emotional currents that flowed in and about her. She had saved his life. He owed her. And he now finally understood why the ghost of Old Man Gao had asked him to find her, to help her out of this predicament – a predicament caused by Old Man Gao himself. If Ma Meili had not thought herself forced to shoot Old Man Gao, she could have been patrolling Wukuaishi for the next twenty years as a policewoman and no one been any the wiser.

He walked around the car and opened the passenger door. She got out wiping her eyes, standing before him, almost a head taller than he.

"Sister, tomorrow you will accompany me to Deyang. We will meet with Poppy's family. We need to inform them of her death. I also want to see if we can get hold of her phone or her diary."

"Superintendent, you want me with you even though you know I am not really police?"

"Is there somewhere else you would rather be?"

She shook her head, putting on a brave smile. "I would still like to find Junjie for my friend Old Man Gao."

In the kitchens of The Silver Tree, Ye Lan could not understand why Ma Meili had to stay the night. But, as Ma Meili stood to one side trying not to obstruct the cooks in their hectic motions, Philip Ye explained to Ye Lan that not only had her bad dream of knives in the dark come true, it was Ma Meili who had saved his life. To Ma Meili's surprise and embarrassment, Ye Lan ran over to her and embraced her. Philip Ye left them to get to know each other, both difficult women in their own right.

He drove home depressed in spirit though. His argument with Maggie Loh and, more importantly, losing self-control before Prosecutor Xu, had left him deeply ashamed. He appreciated Maggie Loh. Like him, she was an outsider. Like him, she had developed a strategy to cope. She never stopped moving, never stopped talking; he, almost the opposite, preferred to keep as still as possible, preferred hardly to speak at all. As for Prosecutor Xu, in the apartment where Poppy had been murdered, she had not been the same woman he'd met at The Silver Tree. Not only had she been unable to meet his eyes, her responses to his questions had been so ridiculously inadequate – and therefore so maddening – that it was as if she had been replaced by her stupid twin. It was a mystery he would have to sleep on.

Back home, he found his father sitting at the kitchen table reading a newspaper, his pipe merrily alight, his phone silent for once. Both Day Na and Night Na were out running errands.

"Philip, what happened to you?"

"Nothing, Father," he replied, taking off his ruined raincoat, finding his suit damaged underneath as well, a jagged tear on his waistcoat pocket where his pocket-watch had miraculously deflected the knife.

"Philip, I do not understand why you have to live such a violent life. If you got hurt...."

"Father, I am fine."

"Have you eaten?"

"No, there wasn't time."

"Then I will cook and you and I will eat together. We rarely get a chance to talk...to properly talk."

"Father, you remember the shooting of Old Man Gao?"

"How could I forget? The callousness of Mayor Cang, the monstrous assassin he had employed—"

"She is no assassin, Father. And Old Man Gao himself chose the time and manner of his passing into the afterlife. Her name is Ma Meili. This evening she saved my life at some risk to herself. I would ask you to think of her as family."

Ye Zihao weighed his son's words carefully. "Is this your considered decision?"

"It is, Father," Philip Ye replied, seriously.

"Then she is family."

CHAPTER FORTY

Earlier that evening, because she was a moth to the flame, she had decided to meet Philip Ye at The Silver Tree. And, though it had been a shock to find her very own investigator and Constable Ma also waiting for her, soon enough her coat had been taken from her, a glass of a gorgeous velvety red wine placed before her – as well as trays of the most aromatic and inviting food imaginable – and Philip Ye had begun to tell of his investigation into the circumstances of Zhu Yi's murder. He had also – speaking for the abashed Investigator Deng who had apparently lost his tongue – detailed the continued investigation by Investigator Deng into the disappearance of Junjie, conducted against her direct orders.

It had never occurred to Xu Ya to interrupt. She had never heard Philip Ye's voice before, except for a few hastily mumbled apologies when he had bumped into someone by accident at Wuhan. His head always elsewhere, Melancholy Ye had been adorably clumsy. However, this incarnation of Philip Ye was anything but. He moved with feline grace and did not mumble. He spoke clearly, choosing his words with care. She found the rhythm of his phrasing and timbre of his voice hypnotic and utterly beguiling. His voice made her feel safe. She could have closed her eyes and listened to him all night.

Philip Ye was not her Beloved Mister Qin whose words had reached right inside her, instructing her, building within her a moral and intellectual foundation by which she could live her life. He was not her hated husband either, whose words, in the beginning, had smothered her with false emotion, and later, had served only to undermine and abuse her. Instead, Philip Ye had allowed his words to hang in the air between them, placing no pressure upon her, giving her space for her own thoughts and feelings, asking of her but one unspoken question: Would you be willing to work with me in the interest of justice?

Yes, had been her unspoken reply.

It had been hard to contain her excitement. Disappearances, murder and the emergence of a new religious cult of unknown origin was much more suited to her talents than the development of a boring audit tool for the inspection of police stations.

By the time Philip Ye had finished speaking, Xu Ya had made three important decisions. Firstly, she would re-interview Madame Xiong without seeking further authorisation from Secretary Wu. Madame Xiong had lied. Madame Xiong had obstructed a Procuratorate investigation. Secretary Wu would understand she had no choice but to confront Madame Xiong again.

Secondly, she would request Zhu Yi's old student records from Madame Xiong. After all her lies, Madame Xiong would not be in a position to make a fuss.

And finally, Xu Ya, feeling somewhat empowered – it may have been the wine – had decided to put Philip Ye in his place, giving him notice that she would not tolerate his speaking to Investigator Deng again without her prior permission, or his fighting again on TV, or any illegality in regard to the conduct of his investigation.

It had been a joyous moment for her.

Had any woman ever had the nerve to speak to Philip Ye so?

She thought not.

It had been sweet revenge – admittedly, petty – for his lack of remembrance of her.

She had also afforded herself the pleasure of withholding information from him. He had been chasing a false lead. She could tell he had been very taken with the oral testimony provided by Yao Lin, particularly that in regard to Professor Xiong conversing with the ghost of his dead wife. Xu Ya had thought it would be fun to let Philip Ye discover his mistake for himself.

Yao Lin's story of what had happened in Madame Xiong's apartment had been highly personal, emotive and surely false. Philip Ye, an experienced detective, should have known better than to trust the word of a wronged girlfriend. It was clear to Xu Ya that Zhu Yi had tired of Yao Lin's nagging, and that matters had come to a head in Madame Xiong's apartment. Out of frustration and jealousy, Yao Lin had concocted a hurtful story about Zhu Yu's favourite tutor,

Professor Xiong. It was all very clear to Xu Ya. She had given Philip Ye an opportunity to rethink Yao Lin's testimony. But he had not taken it. His gullibility had amazed her.

However, travelling in the taxi with Investigator Deng to re-interview Madame Xiong, Xu Ya had had a change of heart. She had begun to consider her concealing of information as both petulant and unethical. She had the advantage of Philip Ye. It was true he should have seen through Yao Lin's lies, but he lacked her personal knowledge of Professor Xiong. She knew she had no choice but to phone Philip Ye and apologise to him. If he had a sense of humour – and she hoped he had – he might even see the funny side of being deceived by Yao Lin and for believing in ghosts.

"Men are so blind in respect of women," she would tell him, meaning Yao Lin, but hoping he would also pick up on the extra layer of meaning underneath.

She would confess to Philip Ye that she was well acquainted with Professor Xiong, that she had been friends with the Professor for years, that he was famous in Chongqing for all of his achievements, that there was no more rational or sceptical man in all of China, no one less likely to be conversing with the ghost of his dead wife or, indeed, to have anything to do with a murderous religious cult. Professor Xiong was a scientist and electrical engineer through and through.

She had not known it then, but this imagined conversation, would never come to pass.

In her apartment on campus, Madame Xiong had provided not only the most logical explanation for her wrongdoing – a none-too-subtle attempt to cover up a scandal – but the *only* explanation. Xu Ya had felt sorry for her. Madame Xiong's obstruction of a Procuratorate investigation was a serious matter. A report would have to be compiled. Professor Ou and the Board of Directors of the university would have to be informed. Madame Xiong could very well find herself out of a job. The pressure she had applied to the students to get them to lie could not be overlooked. It was a gross abuse of her authority. So, when Madame Xiong had offered to show off all of her photographs mounted on her walls, Xu Ya was moved, out of compassion, to humour her.

The photographs were, for the most part, dreadfully dull – blatant evidence of a narcissistic streak running through Madame Xiong's personality. Madame Xiong was at the centre of each photograph, having cajoled some unsuspecting bystander or fellow tourist to allow her to pose for her own camera. She grew very animated telling how each photograph had come to be, describing in great detail what she thought of the country in which the photograph had been taken, and, more especially, what she thought of the people – as if Xu Ya had never travelled herself. There were a few photographs that featured her brother. She spoke of Professor Xiong in such terms of adoration that Xu Ya was left wondering if narcissism wasn't her only personality disorder. In those that featured Professor Xiong, Madame Xiong was always standing beside him, staring up at him admiringly – so much so that an uninformed observer might have mistaken her for a loyal wife rather than a sister. Xu Ya found these photographs the most disconcerting. She struggled to quickly find a reason to close the tour of the photographs down and to leave the apartment, never to return.

But then Madame Xiong directed Xu Ya to one of the larger photographs, the most recent of her collection.

"Prosecutor, this was taken at my brother's magnificent house in Chongqing during the evening of the recent New Year's celebrations. It was taken in the inner courtyard. So this gives you some idea of my brother's great success and his wealth. That's me standing next to him, as you can see. The other people gathered round us are some of his colleagues from his company. They are all quite devoted to him. They would rather celebrate the New Year with him rather than with their own families."

Xu Ya, exhausted by this constant self-promotion, was of a mind to prick Madame Xiong's bubble and tell her that not only was she herself known to Professor Xiong, she had also visited that very same house pictured in the photograph on many an occasion in years gone by. Xu Ya would explain away the fact she hadn't mentioned this earlier in the day by stating, quite truthfully, that not only hadn't she seen any family resemblance between Madame Xiong and Professor Xiong, but Professor Xiong had never once mentioned that he had a sister. Let Madame Xiong, unsettling creature that she was, make of that what she will.

But Xu Ya said nothing. The breath was taken from her. Her head gone light, her legs grown weak, she had put her hand against the wall to steady herself. Thankfully, Madame Xiong had not noticed her distress. Madame Xiong had been too absorbed in describing in nauseating detail how her brother had been on such fine form the evening the photograph was taken, how he had entertained everyone with his witty jokes and fascinating anecdotes. Xu Ya had nodded and smiled, desperate to regain her composure, to keep from her face the devastating truth that had just been revealed to her.

It was she who was the fool, not Philip Ye. All of his suspicions had proved correct, his detective's instincts right on the money.

It was all she could do to keep herself from plunging her long fingernails into Madame Xiong's wrinkled neck and throttling the very life out of her.

In the photograph, behind the celebrating group with Professor Xiong and Madame Xiong at its centre, the camera flash had caught the image of a face at a window looking on. It was a minor detail at the very edge of the photograph. Xu Ya doubted Madame Xiong had ever seen it, caught up as she was in always admiring herself and her brother. The face was also indistinct and would be, to many an observer, proof of nothing at all. But Xu Ya's eyes were sharp, her memory even sharper. Never in her life had she ever forgotten a face. And never, except for what had transpired after her wedding, had she ever been so shocked. Inside the house and staring out through that window into the inner courtyard had been Junjie.

Her mind in overdrive, Xu Ya looked for every possible excuse for Professor Xiong. But try as she might, she found none that made sense. Professor Xiong was the sort of man to know exactly what was happening in his house, the sort of man whose household staff would be attentive to their duties or else they would find themselves out of a job. It was a strict house. If Junjie was in that house, it was because Professor Xiong had decided it should be so.

Which begged the question, why?

At first, Xu Ya wove an overly complicated scenario in her mind, where Professor Xiong had discovered that the residents of Aunty Li's house had all been seduced by The Willow Woman cult, including Old Man Gao. Professor Xiong had rescued Junjie and had been keeping him safe. But the logic of this scenario broke down so quickly – why hadn't Professor Xiong informed the authorities, for instance? – that Xu Ya soon discarded it. She was forced to consider the impossible: Professor Xiong was guilty of a terrible crime.

Maybe Professor Xiong had gone insane. This had to be the explanation. Back in The Silver Tree, Xu Ya had considered Yao Lin's testimony ludicrous and vindictive, her tale of Professor Xiong detailing conversations with the ghost of his dead wife quite ridiculous. However, now she had found Junjie in the one place he should not be, Xu Ya was not so sure.

The death of Professor Xiong's wife, Yi Li, had passed Xu Ya by. No TV had been allowed by her husband in their marriage house – no phone, no newspapers, and no radio either. No invitation to the funeral had been delivered either. Trapped in the house, Xu Ya had been quite forgotten by the world. But, at least in regard to Yi Li's passing, Xu Ya had no regret. Though she had met Yi Li only once, Xu Ya had taken an instant dislike to her. Yi Li had been much as Madame Xiong had described: a woman with a cruel mouth and little charm, unable to exhibit the least semblance of human warmth. Yi Li had also not been shy about expressing her political views. She had been especially critical of the direction of the Party – and, therefore, of China – since the advent of the Reform Era.

"We have squandered the revolution," Yi Li had said out loud to a room full of people, shocking everybody, causing much embarrassment to her husband.

Though Xu Ya was not sad Yi Li was gone, the same might not be said for Professor Xiong. It had to be remembered that Yi Li and Professor Xiong had been married for almost fifty years. There had always been rumours about the marriage, about Professor Xiong's supposed proclivity for extramarital affairs, but Yi Li's death must have affected him.

Had his grief caused him to hallucinate and to see her ghost?

Had he given up on a life of scientific enquiry and taken up with a religious cult?

Or was his insanity – and it had to be insanity – been caused by something more physical, the early onset of dementia for instance, or perhaps the growth of a tumour in the brain? Xu Ya had heard of such cancers causing serious personality changes.

As Madame Xiong had continued to drone on about her other photographs, totally unaware of Xu Ya's discomfort, Xu Ya had eventually realised that all of these questions could wait. For the time being they were irrelevant. Of primary importance was Junjie's life. Xu Ya could only hope he was still at Professor Xiong's house, that he hadn't been moved elsewhere. The New Year was almost two months gone. Anything could have happened since then.

Xu Ya let her mind wander freely to examine all of the risks and potentials. She soon came to the momentous and terrifying conclusion that she – and only she! – could rescue Junjie; that is, if she could keep her mouth shut and play the incompetent fool.

The problem was that there was no one she could trust with her plan.

Investigator Deng, keen as he was, would insist on travelling to Chongqing with her. There he would prove to be a hindrance, his presence awkward, hard to easily explain away to Professor Xiong. Or, if made to stay behind, Investigator Deng might just open his mouth, social person that he was, and blab of what she was up to. Xu

Ya understood cults. It was quite possible that The Willow Woman cult had already infiltrated the police and the Procuratorate in both Chengdu and Chongqing. A word in the wrong ear and an insane Professor Xiong could make Junjie vanish forever.

It was only now that she properly comprehended Philip Ye's caution, his decision to hold their meeting out of sight at The Silver Tree. *He had understood the need for secrecy.* It was a great pity she could not speak to him now and confide in him her plan. Cautious though Philip Ye might be, he was still police. And the police had a chain of command. Philip Ye would be duty bound to report up to his senior officers that Junjie had been found – or at least sighted – at Professor Xiong's house and that Professor Xiong must therefore be involved with the cult. Those senior officers would then have to consider what should be done. Contact would have to be made with Chongqing PSB. It could take days for the order to be given to search Professor Xiong's house, and then, in all probability, even if by some miracle word had not leaked out thereby forewarning Professor Xiong, the police would descend as a mob upon the house with guns drawn. Junjie would be just as likely to be shot as to be rescued.

So Xu Ya had decided to keep her mouth shut.

So Xu Ya had decided not to trust anyone.

Let both Philip Ye and Investigator Deng be amazed and impressed when she returned from Chongqing with Junjie at her side. Such a rescue would not be bad for her new career either.

However, for Xu Ya, playing the dumb fool proved more easily imagined than done. When Investigator Deng finally extricated her from Madame Xiong's apartment she found his solid presence suddenly so comforting, and the concern for her in his eyes so moving, that she nearly spilled out her plan. And then, at the shocking scene of Poppy's murder – the cult obviously trying to cover its tracks – she had felt so ill, so frightened, so fearful that someone could be watching her, could read her thoughts, that it took all of her strength not to run for home.

And then she had had to withstand a blistering attack from Philip Ye. But Xu Ya forgave him this unseemly show of emotion as soon as he was done. Not only had she withheld the truth from him, avoided the gaze of his piercing eyes, and given the most pathetic and mumbling answers to his questions – her performance, though necessary, had infuriated even her – he had also had a close brush with death. According to Investigator Deng, Philip Ye had chased Poppy's murderers and nearly paid for his bravery with his life. The resultant shock on his face was evident to see, as were the tears in his raincoat and suit. She had wanted to lose *her* temper with him for being so stupid.

In her apartment, she had heaved a sigh of relief, glad she at least had got home without giving away her plan. Her appalling marriage had made an actress out of her; its only useful legacy. But this relief had soon given way to great waves of emotion and she had spent the next half hour slumped on the floor crying, feeling sorry for herself. Then, after two cups of coffee to wash the wine out of her system, and after staring at her own pale image in the mirror trying to find the courage to do what had to be done, she had phoned Professor Xiong's house.

A maid answered. Xu Ya gave her name and was told to wait. And then, quicker than expected, his voice was in her ear.

"Ms. Xu, how unexpected! Would you believe I was only thinking about you the other day? I heard the tragic news last summer about your husband. So sad…so sad. You must come and visit me. The company of a beautiful woman again would make me feel less old."

"Could I come tomorrow?"

He was surprised. "Aren't you living in Chengdu now?"

"Yes, but I have few friends and…."

"Ms. Xu, say no more. For you I would clear my schedule for the month. You must come and have lunch with me."

The arrangement made, they chatted about the health of her parents for a short while before Xu Ya made her excuses, saying she had to get a good night's sleep so she could travel first thing in the morning. Hating herself for the deception, and worse for not having the wits to offer her condolences for his own loss, she was otherwise relieved the call had gone so well – that he hadn't sensed the tension in her voice and smelled a rat, so to speak. But it worried her that she caught no taint of madness in his voice, that he had sounded as normal as he had always been.

Had she been mistaken about seeing Junjie's face in the photograph?

Had she imposed Junjie's dull-witted features upon some unsuspecting servant looking through the window?

It was possible.

Her eyes had fooled her before.

She had once thought her husband a handsome man.

However, committed now to making the journey to Chongqing, she put the matter to rest. She undressed and took herself off to bed.

After tossing and turning for an hour, unable to shake the uncomfortable feeling she was not alone in the room – strangely, she kept imagining Old Man Gao standing over her – she got up and dragged herself to her desk. With her law books open before her, she picked up a pen and began to make notes, trying to organise her thoughts. However, it was not long before her courage began to fail again. She looked over at the clock. It was already well after midnight. Unable to call Philip Ye or Investigator Deng, not wanting to give anything away, she dialled Mouse's number instead.

CHAPTER FORTY-ONE

Sunday

Philip Ye had slept some, but his dreams, colourful and chaotic as they had been, now eluded him. He had occasionally, in years gone by, kept a dream diary. He had taken to heart the theory that during sleep, the soul – or the two souls, the *pò* and the *hún* – temporarily left the body and walked the streets of the afterlife. He had certainly recorded dreams where he had met and spoken with Isobel. But there had been nothing in his written notes when perused in the light of day that led him to believe these dreams were anything other than the reprocessing of old memories. Though he was in possession of instructional texts on the subject, he had yet to master the technique of lucid dreaming. On the nights he had attempted to control his dreams and travel in search of Isobel, he had either found sleep too difficult to come by, or sleep had crept up on him unseen, the mental, physical and moral exhaustion of the job taking its toll, dragging him into unconsciousness.

He had woken this morning, however, not with Isobel on his mind but Prosecutor Xu. His loss of self-control toward her haunted him. He could explain his behaviour away partly by the provocative nature of her personality. There was an inconstancy about her, her mind ever-shifting, hard to pin down, one moment strident and opinionated, the next shy and defensive. But he had dealt before with difficult personalities. As for her lying to him, avoiding his eyes, pretending she had found no cause to detain Madame Xiong and had somehow forgotten to question her about The Willow Woman cult or even demand Zhu Yi's student records, well, Philip Ye was used to confronting liars. It was part of the job, nothing to be concerned about. But with Prosecutor Xu he had, for some reason, felt personally betrayed. He had to admit that he had liked her. Against all his expectations, he had enjoyed her company at The Silver Tree. He had thought, for once, he had found a like mind, a woman with a spiritual need to impose justice on an unjust world.

Had he then been mistaken about her?

This, he could not answer.

Not yet, that is.

He was certain something had happened to her in Madame Xiong's apartment, something that had either frightened her or caused her to lose interest in the investigation and deceive him. If he had been more in control of himself the last evening, he could have questioned her further, got to the root of her problem, or, more straightforwardly, taken Fatty Deng to one side and got the story out of him. Instead, he had probably lost all chance now of any help from Prosecutor Xu *and* he had an official reprimand coming his way from Maggie Loh. Not bad for an evening's work.

He sat up in bed and switched on the lamp. He picked up his pocket-watch from the bedside table. The case now bore a dent from the knife that had been destined for his innards. But the watch-glass was undamaged and the mechanism was functioning as smoothly as ever. It was an 18 carat gold hunter, English, hallmarked with the leopard's head for the City of London, and with the letter *k* for the year 1885/6. The pocket-watch said thirteen minutes after three. Glancing at the digital clock on the wall, Philip Ye saw that the pocket-watch had lost three minutes the previous day, the same as always. He corrected it and wound it, glad it had not been broken by the assault on him. The pocket-watch had been Isobel's last gift to him before she died. She had been unaware that in China the giving of watches as gifts was generally not practiced. It was almost a taboo, the association with the swift passing of time, with the hours of one's life running out, too strong. She had spent all of her savings on the pocket-watch, savings that had been originally reserved to be used as a deposit on their first house together. He had accepted the pocket-watch without argument, in the terrible knowledge that it was the hours, minutes and seconds of her life winding down, not his.

"Wear it and remember me," she had said.

He did and he had.

And this night it had saved his life.

His phone rang, shaking him out of the past. He put the pocket-watch down and picked up the phone. Caller ID unknown.

"Yes?"

"You sleeping?" It was Wolf.

"Are you rotating phones again?"

"Philip, this is life Chongqing style. I live and work in a crazy town. You can never tell who's listening in."

"Have you got something for me?"

"Not much…you got me into a whole heap of trouble."

"How so?"

"I started asking around about your Professor Xiong, making a few phone calls, calling in a few favours…and then lo and behold I'm dragged by my collar into Commissioner Min's office. He starts cursing me out, wanting to know what I'm up to. It seems your Professor Xiong is a real heavyweight, the Chair of the Science and Technology Committee here in Chongqing…a senior Party cadre… owner and Chairman of a defence contractor doing super-sensitive work for the military. Commissioner Min had taken a cease and desist call from State Security. They told him Professor Xiong is not to be looked at, not to be touched."

"Wolf, I'm sorry."

"No harm done. I told Commissioner Min it was an honest mistake, that as a favour to a detective over in Yunyang County I'd been looking for some fake mathematics tutor with the same name who'd murdered a kid and was possibly now in the city. I thought Commissioner Min was going to kiss me he was so relieved. Luckily he didn't ask any more questions. So I've got nothing useful for you except a warning not to go wading in shark-infested waters. That being said, what has this Professor been up to? And tell me the truth this time."

"I believe he's connected to a religious cult that's going about Chengdu eating its own."

"You serious?"

"Yes, but proof is distinctly lacking. I was hoping to get to speak to the esteemed Professor personally, to size him up. I guess I'll have to think again."

"Don't mess with State Security, Philip. Your English charm won't protect you from those fuckers."

"Your advice is noted. There's not much I can do immediately anyway. My best hope for information on the cult just got murdered last evening."

"This cult covering its tracks?"

"Maybe – it's hard to say at present. But it's more likely she was made an example of – to instil discipline in the rest of them. Another cult member had been killed the night before for a similar reason. I suspect she knew him, was disturbed by what had happened to him, and was about to make a run for it. Anyway, it's not your problem, Wolf. I'm sorry for getting you in trouble with Commissioner Min. I should have known better. I should have realised Professor Xiong was going to be someone important."

"As I said, Philip – no harm done. Now, if you have a moment, I have a scary story for you."

"You know I don't enjoy such stories."

"You'll enjoy this – it's about the latest appointment to Chengdu People's Procuratorate."

"I thought you had nothing to say about Prosecutor Xu?"

"Not on the phone in the office. As I said, I don't know who's listening in. Now promise me, Philip – you keep away from Prosecutor Xu. She's trouble of the worst kind."

"She's a prosecutor…how much harm can she do?"

"Philip, you don't know her as I do. Which procuracy section has picked her up?"

"Legal and Disciplinary."

Wolf cursed.

"What's the problem?"

"Philip, there's a rumour doing the rounds here that your Political and Legal Committee have taken her on as a hired gun."

"Who's the target?"

"Your father, maybe."

"Wolf, why didn't you warn me?"

"Philip, I'm sorry…I've got plenty of other things on my mind. And until a week ago I assumed she was out of the game for good. Let me give you some background on Ms. Xu. Her father is a serious individual. The whisper is that he's a behind-the-scenes hirer and firer for the Central Organisation Department, and takes his orders direct from Beijing. I've never met him and, if I saw him coming toward me, I think I'd run the other way. The mother is a senior cardiologist at Chongqing University Hospital. I've never met her either but I understand she is more in need of a new heart than the majority of her patients, if you get my meaning. Anyway, Ms. Xu is their only daughter. She was schooled at home by expensive tutors. A year abroad studying comparative law in the United States, and then to Wuhan to get her degree in law. After that, six months in private legal practice, passes the bar exam first time and before you know it she's not only picked up by the Procuratorate here in Chongqing but within a month she's already working as a fully-fledged prosecutor. No slumming for her as a legal clerk for a couple of years to learn her trade."

"The father has that much pull?"

"Believe it or not, Philip, for once this has nothing to do with family connections. This girl is talented. She has a razor-sharp mind, an almost photographic memory, and is absolutely fearless in her pursuit of correct legal practice. Six months go by and she's not only appointed to the Procuratorial Committee and even correcting the Chief Prosecutor for his sloppy work, she's also having stand-up arguments with some of our less-reputable judges – behind closed doors, that is."

"You mean she's stupid not fearless, don't you?"

"Well, that's the point, isn't it, Philip? Our Ms. Xu didn't seem to mind who she pissed off. She made so many people look bad…in the Procuratorate and the Courts…they began to call her Princess Poison behind her back. And she wasn't shy with us police either. She would rigorously review our case files and send them back to us if she thought them deficient in some way, attaching her personal comments, often questioning our intellects, or our sanity or our morality, or all three. She even ordered the release of some of our defendants for lack of evidence. I mean…Philip…who has the fucking nerve to do that? We're supposed to be one big happy law enforcement family: the PSBs, the procuratorates, and the courts, the three corners of the glorious 'Iron Triangle', all working in harmony to produce the perfect socialist society."

"Anyone try to reel her in?"

"No one would touch her, Philip. Perhaps her father had cast a protective shell about her. I don't know. Or maybe it was because she was never wrong. She even sent one of my cases back. She wrote on it that the file had obviously been put together by a brain-damaged cross-eyed monkey."

Philip Ye laughed.

"I kid you not, Philip. I could have strangled her. Not enough evidence, she wrote. Improper procedure. Confession obviously extracted under torture. I admit it didn't help that our forensics team had been out drinking the night before. So I took another look. An elderly mother had been beaten to death. I'd liked the son for it. He was a drinker, unstable most of the time. And he'd confessed after I'd given him a slap or two to calm him down. Anyway, after I'd released him I dug a little deeper. It turned out it was the daughter. Some dispute about money. Princess Poison had been right after all."

"We all make mistakes, Wolf."

"I know, Philip. And we all have blood on our hands because of those mistakes. But Prosecutor Xu never seemed to learn that some of us, those odd mistakes aside, actually know our trade. Some of us don't sleep much because of the cases we cannot solve. Some of us actually care so much we develop ulcers or smoke ourselves into an early grave. Prosecutor Xu thought we were all the same, mere thugs and bullies, to be treated with nothing but contempt."

"So what's the twist in her story?"

"I'm coming to it. So Princess Poison is busy strutting around Chongqing People's Procuratorate dispensing legal instruction and unlooked for advice when the Year of Calamities comes around. Not a good year for you either, if I remember right."

"Go on."

"After the earthquake she lends her face to a charity drive."

"She takes a good picture."

"So you've seen her then?"

"Yes."

"Good looks aren't everything, my friend. I've told *you* that often enough. Anyway, while courting every camera in Chongqing, she meets her match in evil…ex-army…a newly appointed judge to the Intermediate People's Court here: Yu Jianguo. Within a week she'd moved out of her parents' house and in with him. A month later they were married. Her parents disowned her."

"Seriously?"

"Would you want your twenty-six year old daughter to marry a forty-five year old former colonel in the army with a shadowy past and extremely dubious family and social connections? Before he'd even sat his first case we were already hearing whispers at the PSB that he was taking bribes and associating with gangsters. It was fucking outrageous. The irony was, the only person with the intelligence and fearlessness to potentially take him down had just become his brand new wife."

"Did he plan it that way?"

"Who can say? Anyway, a couple of weeks after the wedding she's presenting a homicide case in court. Not one of mine, thank Heaven. It was a simple enough case. No mystery, just a stabbing in the street caught for once on camera. But would you believe that the judge sitting on the case is her husband? That's Chongqing for you… rotten to the core. Anyway, as you would expect, the Procuratorate and the Courts – by which I mean husband and wife – have had the usual meetings, have run through the evidence, and a date is set for the court to sit, to listen to what everyone has to say and then give the guilty verdict. So on the day, our Ms. Xu stands up to present the evidence and begin cross-examining the few witnesses that there are, when out of the blue Judge Yu Jianguo begins shouting at her, berating her in front of the whole court for not doing her job properly. There's uproar in the public gallery. Ms. Xu tries to stand up for herself but her husband just shouts her down. Honestly, it was a fucking disgrace. Her delivery had been as perfect as usual. But those watching, those who knew Ms. Xu well, laughed themselves silly."

"He was putting her in her place?"

"More like destroying her in public. He even let the defendant go. Told him, in spite of the camera evidence and the witnesses who had seen him stab the victim twenty times, that he had no case to answer. When I learned what had happened, I didn't know whether to laugh or cry. I was happy to see Princess Poison humiliated, brought down a peg or two, but to let a guilty man go in the process…."

"Did the Procuratorate protest?"

"Philip, you're missing the point. It wasn't about the case; it was about her. She didn't turn up for work the next day, nor the day after that. We later heard she crept into the office one weekend and cleared her desk. She quit the Procuratorate. She wasn't seen again for five years."

"Where was she?"

"At home brooding, I guess."

"Didn't anyone try to get her to change her mind?"

"Philip, she had made so many enemies, most considered her a menace. Good riddance, they thought. And I…for my sins…was one of them. Once she'd gone we all started to relax again. We were able to return to our usual comfortingly familiar mixture of incompetence, corruption and the occasional good result."

"So how has she ended up here in Chengdu?"

"This is when my story turns really murky. Last summer, late one night, I was on call…the only homicide detective in Chongqing not drunk, sleeping, out gambling or whoring, or at home waiting for the results of a disciplinary committee. So I get a call from the 110 despatcher. There's a dead man at a house, she says. No other information, just gives me the address. I drive off in my car thinking it's going to be a night like any other. But when I get there I recognise the house. Not that that does me any good. I don't even make it through the gate. There were men in suits everywhere…real hard bastards. One of them puts a gun in my face and tells me to fuck off. So I phone Commissioner Min. He lives nearby, can't quite believe what I'm telling him and comes out to help. They put a gun in his face too. By the time our SWAT team arrived it was all too late. Me and Commissioner Min had to just stand there like a couple of turnips watching on as they brought a body out of the house in a black bag and threw it in the back of a limousine – untraceable government plates, if you're interested – like a bag of rubbish. Then her parents arrived and they took their long lost daughter away, her head covered with a blanket. By the time they'd all gone and we'd finally got access to the house all we found was a pool of drying blood on the floor."

"Autopsy?"

"Philip, the body has never been seen again. Our forensic pathologist never even got to see it. I tried to open a case, make a few calls, but all I got was a wall of silence. Not even our esteemed judge's family wanted to speak to me. I reckon they'd already been paid off by someone. I tried to get an interview with the newly single Ms. Xu but I got nowhere. When I started getting threatening phone calls late at night I dropped the case. Commissioner Min didn't argue. He said nobody was going to mourn Judge Yu Jianguo's passing anyway."

"So what's your thinking?"

"After five years of misery she puts a knife in his guts. She then made the mistake of calling the 110 despatcher before telling her parents."

"Wolf, she doesn't look like a killer."

"You've made that mistake before."

"That's true."

"Philip, just stay away from her. I don't know why your Political and Legal Committee has decided to resurrect her career. But keep your head down and tell your father to prepare for the worst."

"Wolf, she was at Wuhan with me."

"What?"

"And before you ask, I didn't date her. I don't even remember her."

Wolf laughed. "I keep forgetting you used to be an intellectual. Did any of her tutors end up dead?"

"None, that I recall."

"Just keep your distance, Philip. And think on this: some years ago, your target, Professor Xiong, won some scientific prize. I don't know what. But he was feted by all of Chongqing high society for a while...*including the family Xu*. I expect Ms. Xu knows him very well."

Philip Ye felt a chill in his heart. "I appreciate the warning."

"Look, I've got to go. I've got divers dredging a pond for a little girl."

"You stay safe, Wolf."

"And you keep away from beautiful women bearing law books."

CHAPTER FORTY-TWO

Sunday

At the time of the Year of Calamities, at the time of the earthquake, Xu Ya had as yet no awareness of the flaw in her character that made her vulnerable to a certain type of man. Until then she had believed, despite having no religious foundation to her thinking, that bad things did not happen to good people; and therefore, as she was 'good people', nothing untoward would ever befall her. It was a salutary lesson in life for her to learn that this was not so.

Seeing the devastation caused by the earthquake, upset by the images of those who had lost everything through no fault of their own, Xu Ya had decided she must do whatever she could to help. Her motivation was more complex than simple altruism, however. She was sensitive to the animosity directed at her by her colleagues at the Procuratorate for her calling them to task for their shoddy work. So a break from that tense environment was sure to do her soul some good. Also, she had recently been captivated by photographs in the society magazines of Lucy Fu out on the town in Chengdu with Philip Ye. Readers of the magazines were left in no doubt that not only was Lucy Fu glamorous at 'any hour day or night', she was also heir to the Fu family fortune – set to make her one of the richest women in China – and was already renowned as a great philanthropist, lauded for her support of many charities, both domestic and international. It would surely help her own image, Xu Ya thought, if she practiced some philanthropy of her own.

So, after steeling herself to give blood for the very first time – it was odd how affected she had been by old superstitions about losing one's vital fluid – she had asked for, and being granted, a brief leave of absence from the Procuratorate so she could assist in the drive to raise money and gather relief supplies for those most affected by the disaster. To her great surprise she had found herself not only exhilarated by the experience of working alongside similarly motivated and enthusiastic people – such a change to the Procuratorate! – but also to be pushed to the fore. You are so pretty, she was told. The cameras will love you. And you are so confident. You can speak for us all. With a face and voice like yours, how could the people not be moved to make donations?

This proved to be true.

She was wheeled out in front of the media at every possible occasion. The journalists always mobbed her. They wanted to know everything about the talented young prosecutor who was not only fearless in the pursuit of criminals but also tireless in her support of the less fortunate. They called her a heroine. The Party gave her a special commendation. She took many congratulatory calls.

The donations flooded in.

Xu Ya could not have been happier.

Philanthropy, she had discovered, was almost as fulfilling as the practice of law.

It was in the midst of this whirlwind of charitable activity, exhausted by the many long days, that she was found by her nemesis, Yu Jianguo. She had just concluded an interview with a Western TV crew – they had praised her for her command of English – when, while drinking a restorative cup of her preferred white tea, Yu Jianguo had appeared at her side. Dressed in the new pine-green uniform of the People's Liberation Army with the three stars of a full colonel on the shoulder-boards, he grinned at her and made a shallow mock bow.

"Ms. Xu, you are a wonder."

"Thank you," she replied, thinking him quite handsome, if not dashing, in his uniform.

"There has never been a brighter moon in the sky."

"Oh, now you're just being silly," she said, flushing, putting her hand to her mouth to suppress an embarrassed giggle.

During the following days where he shed his uniform and pitched in to help with the charity drive, similar words trotted off his tongue. He made her laugh every day, made her feel good to be alive. And he not only brought energy and added impetus to the work but also his military flair for organisation and discipline. They were soon being spoken of as one – a partnership made in Heaven.

One stifling afternoon while sitting together in the relative cool of a distribution warehouse, he confessed to her that his army career had come to a natural end – as had his marriage. He went on to explain that he had already chosen a new career. Because of his experience as a judge for a military court, he had been appointed – by a process he chose to leave vague – as a judge for Chongqing People's Intermediate Court.

It seemed to Xu Ya quite perfect, the stars in the sky aligning just for her.

I will not miss you, Philip Ye, she told herself.

I will not miss you at all.

On any other occasion, Xu Ya would have spat blood after hearing of yet another judge appointed from the army because of the antiquated belief that only former military personnel had the necessary backbone to make the tough decisions to enforce civil order. In her view, such men and women had very little comprehension of society's ills; and, as for their military legal training, Xu Ya had nothing but contempt. But sitting next to Yu Jianguo, she knew him to be different, special – a rare honest man in a dishonest world. She could not wait to be working alongside him for the good of the people.

What had Yu Jianguo seen in her?

Why, out of all of the desirable women in Chongqing, had he picked her?

The same way, she would later surmise, that a wolf selects its prey: a weakness had been perceived in her, the fatal flaw in her character.

Before she could understand what was happening to her, before she could think to defend herself, his fangs had been sunk deep into her veins, infecting her blood with such a debilitating toxin that even now, almost a year after his death, she was by no means cured.

The day before her marriage to Yu Jianguo, Xu Ya wrote a long and rambling letter to Philip Ye. She outlined her reasoning for getting married. She described Yu Jianguo as the perfect man, how she and he now shared a common purpose in bringing justice to the people, how she wanted a child before she was too old, how she – at last! – understood why a romance between them (meaning she and Philip Ye) was never meant to be. The universe had been waiting for her to meet Yu Jianguo all along.

She did not post the letter. But she had got slightly drunk on wine and had burned it as one would burn a piece of parchment on which had been written a magical incantation with a view to exorcising an evil or unwanted spirit.

Her parents refused to attend the wedding. Her father had raged at her rash decision. He had asked her, derisively, "Who is this Yu Jianguo?" Her mother had tried cold logic. Neither had prevailed. Xu Ya had discovered she had been born stubborn, wilful and impetuous. More to the point, her parents did not know Yu Jianguo as she knew him. Having no interest in the machinery of justice, her parents could not comprehend what a partnership between her and Yu Jianguo could mean for the Rule of Law in Chongqing. They were also, as she told them to their faces, born of an older, more emotionally constipated generation. They had little idea about romance or true love.

She did not speak to her parents again for five years.

The wedding was paid for out of her own savings. For complicated reasons – his divorce from his first wife, problems with back pay from the army – Yu Jianguo had no available funds of his own. Not that this bothered Xu Ya. The wedding was a simple affair, attended only by a few of his immediate family, whom Xu Ya thought rather common and vulgar, and some of his old army buddies, who were worse. More of her savings were used to rent a luxury apartment for them both in the city.

In the years that followed, boredom was a greater enemy than her husband. He had done his worst in court, humiliating her before her colleagues, before the laughing people in the public gallery. Her shame total, her ruin complete, her life as she had known it was over. Unable now to work, she wiled away most of the hours of the day staring out of the window at the streets down below. I am like a lost bird, she thought, looking down on all of humanity. Every few days she went out to buy food and other necessities. But, no matter what the weather, frightened of being recognised and being subjected to further ridicule, she always wrapped a scarf around her head. Given the choice, she would rather have fled abroad. However, in the unsuspecting days after the wedding, her husband yet to reveal his true nature, he had persuaded her to hand control of all her finances to him. He had also taken her passport from her; for safekeeping, he said, citing security concerns. Being former military, she assumed he understood such stuff. So, though she was not chained up, he had made it impossible for her to leave.

After the wedding she had received an extraordinary letter from her parents, legally disowning her. As for friends, she had none. Her remarkable ability to rub people up the wrong way had seen to that. Mei-Mei and Ju from Wuhan would not have been sympathetic anyway. More likely they would have laughed at her predicament. As for Mouse, the witty and talkative legal clerk from the Procuratorate in Chengdu, Xu Ya had not spoken to her since before the charity drive. Nor had she invited her to the wedding. Never having met Mouse in person, she had been afraid that a lowly legal clerk would show her up before her new husband. It was an awful, regrettable decision. And one she could not undo.

The only visitors to the house were her husband's old army buddies – whom she was forced to wait upon while withstanding a constant stream of obscene observation and verbal abuse – and her husband's mother and two sisters. The mother, a vicious old hag, was free and easy with her hands if she saw something in the house she didn't like. As for the sisters, they had foul mouths and even fouler manners. Thankfully, these familial visitations occurred only a few times a year. Most of the time, Xu Ya had the house to herself, her husband either out at work pretending to be the honourable judge, or out on the town, trawling the clubs and bars with his ever-expanding network of cronies, staying out late, drinking, gambling and whoring. With no TV, or telephone, or radio, or newspapers allowed in the house, she was forced to sit and read novels or her law books. Sometimes she would don her headscarf and go out and walk the streets, to flick through magazines in the shops, or to stare in through the windows of restaurants, or just look out over the river and imagine herself living a better life – a life where her husband (he was twenty years older than she) was dead.

In the fourth year of this twilight existence, she became very ill. Feverish, her husband out, she stumbled out of the house and made her way to the nearest payphone. She dialled a number she had memorised years before, the number for Chengdu PSB.

The receptionist asked her which department.

"Please, I don't know…I am not thinking straight…I just need to speak to Philip Ye."

The receptionist laughed at her. "We have a hundred calls a day for Philip Ye from desperate women such as you."

Then the line went dead.

Back in the house, dizzy and disorientated, Xu Ya took to her bed. She did not stir for three days. Furious at her continued idleness, her husband cursed and punched her – the first time he had ever felt he needed to lay a hand on her. When this didn't get the desired result, he summoned a doctor, one of his drinking friends. This doctor prescribed for her a fistful of coloured pills even though he maintained he could find nothing really wrong with her. She took none of this medicine, only pretending to do so that her husband would not abuse her anymore. She was content to stay in bed forever, to die.

One evening, after a week of inactivity, her husband out with a new mistress, Xu Ya had fallen into a strange dream. In this dream-world, the colours of her room had become more vivid than in reality and she had not felt as burdened as before with the heaviness of her life. A bearded man appeared before her, old and careworn, but still with the light of vitality burning in his dark, intelligent eyes. He wore the robes of an official of the Qing dynasty. In the dream, Xu Ya sat up in bed and pulled her quilt up to her chin, worried for her modesty. She knew she should be properly dressed for an audience with such a man.

"Ms. Xu," he said, "my name is Huang Liu-Hong. In your brief time in post, you chose to conduct the administration of justice from the safety of your office. Never once did you go out among the people. Never once did you go see how they lived. Never once did you visit a scene of violence, or extend your condolences to the bereaved, or lend counsel to victims assuring them that justice would be done. Is that what Mister Qin taught you? Is the law nothing but a dispassionate process, nothing but words written down on paper? I think not. In my time as a magistrate, as the voice of the emperor, it was expected of me to be as a 'father and mother' to the people. As a prosecutor, in this modern age, how can you not be the same? It is not enough, Ms. Xu, that you are clever, able to correct others in their work, and willing to write caustic letters of reproach to wayward or floundering constables. You are a prosecutor. You are to lead by example. You are to take the law – which is a living, breathing thing – out onto the streets among the people. You are to dispense justice, compassion and wisdom. You will not succeed every day. I, myself, was far from a perfect man. But you must try. In ancient times it was understood that wrong-doings left unchallenged would upset the cosmic order, disturb the balance of Heaven and Earth, and all manner of natural disasters would result. Now I do not expect your sceptical modern mind to accept this notion as fact. But I do ask you to pursue justice *as if it were true*. Surely, that is not too much to ask."

She woke in the morning a different woman, the dream very clear in her mind. The fever and the pains in her body were gone. When her husband returned, smelling of perfume and alcohol, she pronounced herself able to serve him as a proper wife should. She could do this because her heart had been put at ease. She did not know how or when, but one day soon her marriage would be over and she would be a prosecutor again.

The clock on her desk said a little after five. It was morning. Xu Ya had fallen asleep in her chair in the study of her apartment. She shivered, not from cold but from fear. A difficult day lay ahead of her. She was to travel alone back to Chongqing, the city of her birth, the city of her great humiliation, to correct a great wrong. The shade of Huang Liu-Hong would expect no less of her.

In his great instructional work for fellow magistrates, *A Complete Book Concerning Happiness and Benevolence*, Huang Liu-Hong had railed against meaningless suicides, those committed for petty reasons. But Huang Liu-Hong had always been careful to make the distinction between those who took their own lives over 'insignificant grudges' and those poor people who had been pushed to the brink of despair by dire circumstances or the vicious ill-treatment of others. The latter deserved, Huang Liu-Hong wrote, 'compassionate consideration'. And in those latter instances, he would not have rested until he had discovered those responsible for pushing the person to suicide and would not have hesitated to mete out harsh punishments and fines.

What had Xu Ya done for Old Man Gao?

Nothing much, as yet.

But this day, once she'd found her courage, she was going to go off in search of Junjie, to right a terrible wrong; to preserve the balance of Heaven and Earth, she thought, smiling to herself. And then, when Junjie was safe in her custody, let Professor Xiong – if he was guilty – and all those who made up The Willow Woman cult tremble, for she could dispense harsh justice too.

CHAPTER FORTY-THREE

Sunday

Fatty Deng was raised from a deep sleep by his mother's singing. At first he thought it was the TV from next door, the sound bleeding through the thin walls again. His mother had lost her voice years ago, the sadness of life taking away her natural gift. But as he got up and opened the blinds – the sky was low and leaden but at least it was no longer raining – he realised it was indeed his mother doing the singing, that she had rediscovered her musical spirit. One visit from Philip Ye and suddenly all was right with the world. Such was the magic of the family Ye.

Glad at least his mother was happy, that she had something to crow about to the neighbours for the next month at least, Fatty Deng showered, found a clean shirt – plain, this time – and put on his suit. He didn't want Prosecutor Xu looking down her nose at him again. He skipped breakfast. He would order something off the Starbucks' menu and eat with Prosecutor Xu.

"Will Philip Ye visit again today?" asked his mother, taking a break from her cleaning regime as he was about to run out of the door.

Not wanting to ruin his mother's happiness, he replied, "It all depends on how the case progresses."

Only if Philip Ye wanted something, is what he actually meant. Which, at the moment, seemed highly unlikely.

When Fatty Deng got down to his car on the street, he glanced up and saw his mother in the window. She was smiling, waving. He returned the wave. It was nice to see her like this. And, putting all his resentments about Philip Ye to one side, if he was honest with himself, and despite all the tribulations of the last few days, he too was feeling good. Fourth day in and he still had his job. He had done some fine work, made a few mistakes along the way – but nothing to lose sleep over – rubbed shoulders with the great and the good – and not suffered too badly for it – and, though he was unable to predict or understand Prosecutor Xu's ever-changing moods, he had to admit that life was better than it had been in years. He felt like he was growing a new skin, a happier skin – like a snake. He was busy sloughing off the past. He had a procuratorate badge and ID in his pocket, a notebook full of details about a fascinating case, and a stable financial future to look forward to. All he needed now was a couple of new suits that fitted him properly and to find a sweet and loyal girlfriend.

Not Prosecutor Xu.

That had always been a fantasy.

And she'd be too much hard work – for any man, he suspected.

No, he wanted someone who didn't expect too much of him or life, who didn't complain that he still lived with his mother or about the long hours he had to work, and someone who – please Heaven, make it so! – could cook. He thought about Zhang Lin, the student with the mop of hair. He wondered, when the case was over, whether it was worth giving her a call. He was only thirty-four, the age difference not that great.

Fifty minutes later he had found an ideal parking space outside of the Starbucks not far from where Prosecutor Xu lived. By ten to nine, he was settled in his favoured seat, able to watch the pretty girls walking by the window – they were out in force now the rain had gone – and, at the same time, keep an eye on the door. He had a steaming cup of green tea before him and couldn't wait to discover if Prosecutor Xu was a creature of habit, whether she would opt for that raspberry and lychee mooncake again.

However, Prosecutor Xu did not arrive at nine. By twenty past nine Fatty Deng began to grow worried. Hard work she might be, but unpunctuality was not one of her sins. He thought back to the last evening, the change that had come over her in Madame Xiong's apartment, how distant she had seemed at the scene of Poppy's murder, how little she had done to defend herself in front of Philip Ye. She had been distant still when they had parted after he had walked her home to Tranquil Mountain Pavilions. Had she not heard him properly when he had suggested the time that they should meet?

He waited until nine-thirty. With no sign of her, he took his phone out of his pocket. His call went straight to her messaging service. He left no message. He waited another ten minutes and called again, with the same result. Had she fallen ill? It wouldn't be the first time someone had become sick after viewing a dead body. Poppy had been a bloody mess. When he had encountered death for the first time, a traffic accident, him barely a month out of Police College, he had puked up all night.

He phoned the Procuratorate.

No, he was told by the snappy receptionist. Prosecutor Xu had not called in sick. She didn't have to. Didn't he realise it was Sunday morning and only the duty staff were in?

At ten, he decided to go see for himself what was up. He walked the short distance to Tranquil Mountain Pavilions. Inside, the concierge – a different man to last evening but a similar hard-nosed type – glared at him when he showed his Procuratorate badge.

"I'm here to see Prosecutor Xu," he said.

"She's out," replied the unsmiling concierge.

"Out where?"

"How should I know?"

"Has she left a message for me?"

"Do I look like her secretary?"

"Would you at least call her apartment for me then?" asked Fatty Deng, exasperated.

"Why would I do that?" The concierge tapped the side of his skull. "She's gone out – are you deaf or daft?"

Fatty Deng retreated from the building. He had wanted to give the concierge a smack. However, not only did the concierge look like he could handle himself, such behaviour was unlikely to impress Prosecutor Xu. He phoned her again. Again the messaging service. He lit a cigarette, his anxiety turning to fear. She had chastised him only the day before for not keeping in touch. She would always answer her phone, she had said.

He was loath to do it but, out of ideas, he phoned Philip Ye – which turned out to be a complete waste of time. Philip Ye was up in Deyang, about to speak to Poppy's family, in no mood to discuss a missing prosecutor. Not that Fatty Deng could blame him. Speaking to the bereaved was never easy. He slowly walked back to Starbucks, bought himself another cup of tea, and was about to take the first sip when his phone began to vibrate on the table. His hopes lifted, only to be dashed when he didn't recognise the Caller ID.

"This is Investigator Deng," he said.

"Hi, this is Superintendent Cao from Wangjiang Road Station. I work homicide with Maggie Loh."

Fatty Deng's heart skipped a beat. He imagined Prosecutor Xu lying in the middle of the road, a knife sticking out of her chest, blood gushing out of her.

"What can I do for you, Superintendent?" he asked, nervously.

"Investigator, we have a young woman detained for her own protection – a Ms. Pan. Superintendent Ye dropped her off here last evening. Trouble is, she's screaming the place down, refusing to eat unless she speaks to you. She says she knows you. I've tried threatening her with a slap but she's an important witness and Superintendent Ye wanted us to treat her carefully. Superintendent Ye is up in Deyang this morning and Maggie Loh is off with the flu. I don't want to trouble you but—"

"I'm on my way."

"You mean that?"

"I'm only around the corner so I'll be with you in a few minutes."

Superintendent Cao terminated the call, very grateful, saying he would tell the custody officer to expect him. Fatty Deng hadn't bothered to tell him that until Prosecutor Xu turned up, he had nothing better to do. Fatty Deng also thought it wise to cultivate Superintendent Cao. He'd never heard of Cao before, which probably meant he was Shanghai Clique. But who knew when a friendly contact in Homicide could prove useful in the future?

Fatty Deng left a hurried note with a waitress in case Prosecutor Xu finally made it to Starbucks and wanted to know where he was, and then he was off around the corner to Wangjiang Road Station.

It was a home-coming of sorts. Wangjiang Road Station had been his one and only police station, his home from home for ten years, his favourite place under Heaven – until The Purge, that is. Never once had he returned. Now, he stood outside for a short while, all those memories, good and bad – but mostly good – flooding back to him. If he hadn't been thrown off the force perhaps he might have been a homicide detective by now, wearing a flashy suit like Philip Ye and making a name for himself. That future had been taken away from him by an arbitrary stroke of the pen. To overcome his sadness, he had to remind himself that he was a new man now, a procuratorate investigator, a man reborn. There was no longer any need for regret, no longer any need to linger in the past. He stepped through the doorway.

He held his badge up to the officer manning the reception desk and looked around him to see what had changed. Nothing! It was like he'd never been away, as if the last five years had been nothing but a bad dream.

"I'm here to interview the prisoner Pan Mei," he announced.

"Fatty, you dopey fuck – it's me!"

And so it was.

Big-Mouth Wang, constable first class – a friend going back as far as Fatty Deng's first day at Police College.

"Big-Mouth, what are you doing here? I thought you still worked out of Sanwayao Station."

Big-Mouth Wang came running from behind the desk and enthusiastically pumped Fatty Deng's hand. "I got fed up at Sanwayao," he said. "Too many Shanghai Clique, the politics got me down. It's better here. Commissioner Xia's in charge, but Supervisor Maggie Loh really runs the show. She's Homicide and from Hong Kong, so she's not quite right in the head. But she makes this station a happy place. Nobody fucks with Crazy Maggie Loh. It's a shame you're not still around. But then again, you've done well for yourself with the Procuratorate. All the old crowd are talking about you."

"They are?"

"Sure, last time we heard you were selling fake watches at Wukuaishi Market. Now look at you, a new job, a new badge, an awful suit *and* you're working for the Flower of the Procuratorate."

Fatty Deng laughed, more than pleased. "Ah, is that what you're calling her?"

"No one's ever seen a prosecutor like her. She's a real beauty. What's she like? Come on, you can tell me."

Suddenly feeling uncomfortable, reminded of Squint-Eye's leering of the evening before, Fatty Deng merely shook his head and smiled, as if he didn't want to give away too much too soon.

Big-Mouth Wang cursed and playfully punched him in the chest. "I always knew you'd land on your feet. You must come out for a drink with the lads one evening this week. You shouldn't have hidden yourself away for so long."

And at least one of you could have given me a call in the last five years, thought Fatty Deng.

But he kept this bitterness to himself. After all, it was indeed good to meet up again with Big-Mouth Wang. And it would be nice to see some of the others. Still talking about the old times, Big-Mouth Wang personally escorted him to the cells. Fatty Deng was then handed over to the care of a taciturn custody officer he had never met before but who'd been expecting him. He opened up Pan Mei's cell door and left Fatty Deng to it.

Pan Mei was slumped face down on the bunk, a blanket pulled

over her, her breakfast tray on the floor, the food untouched. But, as soon as she saw who it was, she sparked into life, jumped up with a squeal and threw her arms around his neck.

"Oh, I knew you would come," she said. "You have such kind eyes. A bad suit and kind eyes – that's how I will always remember you. Not like that evil *lǎowài* with his fancy suit and his cruel green eyes…like a cat. He blames me for Poppy's death. He wants me to rot in prison for the rest of my life."

Not wanting any scandal – just as the day before, Pan Mei seemed hardly dressed – Fatty Deng extricated himself from her arms and sat her back down on the bunk. He then took a seat beside her.

"No one blames you, Ms. Pan. You weren't to know Poppy would be murdered. But it was wrong of you to lie to me yesterday."

"But, Investigator Deng, it *was* my fault. I've been thinking about it all night. I should have gone to the police when I saw Poppy that day. I knew she was in trouble. She looked so thin and ill. And she was speaking of demons. Only the mentally ill do that. I just thought her lover had abandoned her and she was having a hard time coping. I thought she would get her head back together and come back to university. She told me she was living with some people and was working at a bar. I thought she'd be okay and—"

"Working at a bar? Which bar?"

"The Singing Moon…that's what she told me before she ran off."

"In Wukuaishi?"

"No, no, The Singing Moon not far from here. It's a chain of bars. They opened up last summer. They're all over Chengdu. I should have checked up on her. But I hate student bars. And my boyfriend, Freddie Yun, doesn't like leaving his club. He doesn't like doing anything much." She batted her eyes at Fatty Deng. "Do you think I should dump him?"

"Did you tell all this to Superintendent Ye – about the bar?" he asked with some urgency.

Pan Mei looked vague, a little frightened. "I think so."

"Are you sure?"

"Oh, I don't know. He was so horrible to me…kept staring at me. He made me ill. I thought he was going to hurt me. If it wasn't for the big policewoman I think he would have done. I thought she was a brute at first but she turned out to be really nice and—"

Fatty Deng stood up. "I'll be back in a short while."

"No!" Pan Mei squealed. "Don't leave me! Take me with you! If I stay in this cell much longer I'll die."

She grabbed hold of his arm and wouldn't let him go. It took all of his strength, and some timely help from the custody officer, to free himself and slam the cell door shut. He could still hear her screams as he made his way back to reception.

When he'd found Big-Mouth Wang again, he asked, "The Singing Moon bar…is it close?"

"Sure, Fatty, it's where The Golden Pheasant used to be – up on the Siguan Road."

"The Golden Pheasant has gone?"

"Last spring – Mister Fang vanished, taking a suitcase of cash with him. He hasn't been seen since."

Fatty Deng was horrified. He'd always liked The Golden Pheasant. It had been a great place to go drinking with the lads. And Mister Fang, the owner, had really liked the police. Fatty Deng had thought there was no more honest man alive. What was happening to Chengdu? What was happening to China?

"Last summer The Singing Moon opened up in its place," continued Big-Mouth Wang. "It's not the same though…caters mainly for young people. Lots of girls…but the music's far too loud for me."

Big-Mouth Wang started speaking about more suitable bars in the area for a good night out. But Fatty Deng made his excuses and left, saying he'd be back in an hour or so. Outside, he phoned Prosecutor Xu. All he got was her messaging service again. He left a message this time, telling her he had gone to the Siguan Road to check out a promising lead. It could not be a coincidence that both Zhu Yi and Poppy had worked for The Singing Moon bar chain. The Willow Woman cult had to be active in those bars, maybe even recruiting new cult members from the patrons. He strolled off toward the Siguan Road to go see for himself.

CHAPTER FORTY-FOUR

Sunday

Mouse did not go out of her way to eschew human contact. But she was much happier chatting to people on the phone. Over the phone she had friends all over Chengdu: in all sections of the Procuratorate, in the PSB, in the courts, and in every municipal and provincial government department. She also had friends beyond Chengdu, contacts in almost every major town and city in Sichuan – and some in Beijing too. But only a few of these friends had she ever met face-to-face. Most had busy social lives or extensive families to be concerned with. And, though Mouse got many invitations to attend weddings, funerals and birthday parties all through the year, she declined them all. Her attendance would not only have bankrupted her because of all the money she'd be obliged to give as gifts, but she would also have been put in crowded and chaotic social situations at which she was not very good. She preferred her solitude. She enjoyed working alone down in the archive of the Procuratorate. This meant she got lonely from time to time. But life was much easier this way.

She lived in a small, damp apartment above a flower shop. The apartment had been left to her by her parents when they, fed up of city life, had decided to return to their home village. They had asked her to go with them. But Mouse, seeing no future in the country, had refused.

When not at work, she spoke to very few people. She would laugh at the TV, immerse herself in books – some good literature, some bad – and take English language classes in the evening so she could better herself one day. She was currently top of her class. One day, if she could save up enough money, she hoped to travel to the United Kingdom and practise this skill and visit Shakespeare's house in Stratford-upon-Avon.

So, Saturday evening, after cooking herself a simple meal of rice and meatballs, she had laughed at a stupid singing competition on TV, and had then taken herself off to bed with the latest novel she was reading – a comic romance – and tried to get warm under the quilt. However, the gist of the story continued to elude her. It was not the sound of the rain hammering on the cracked windows, or the screeching of the elderly neighbours next door too deaf to under-stand each other's speech, that served to undermine her concentra-tion. Rather it was the constant replaying in her mind of the day Deng Shiru had arrived at the Procuratorate for his interview with Prosecutor Xu.

Aware of the date – after all, it was she who had arranged the interview – Mouse had gone out specially and spent a lot of money on some new clothes and tried out many different scents in the shop before selecting one that was not so outrageously expensive. But Deng Shiru – she hated him being called Fatty, because in truth he had never been *that* fat – was not the same jolly and outgoing youth she remembered from her past. It wasn't the ten years in the police that had done this to him. This she knew for a fact. It was the last five years spent in the wilderness that had taken its toll. He continued to exude a great deal of human warmth – his best quality – but he seemed to have become much more guarded. And he hadn't joked and laughed as he had always done. Lines had also appeared on his face about his eyes and lips; they spoke more about the enduring of great stress than the natural passing of the years. As for the suit he had worn, she didn't know what he'd been thinking. Did he not have the money to hire something that came even close to fitting him?

Mouse had told Huiling on reception that she would personally escort Deng Shiru to Prosecutor Xu's office. Huiling had made no comment. But she said she liked the way Mouse had done her hair. Mouse had told a lie, saying she was meeting a man for a first date after work, not wanting to give the impression that she knew Deng Shiru. Huiling had told her to be careful. Find out where he works and if he is married before you accept a second date. Mouse assured Huiling she would. When Deng Shiru arrived, Mouse led him the longest path she could think of through the Procuratorate to Prose-cutor Xu's office, hoping he would remember her, that he would broach the subject of their shared past. But he had said nothing and there hadn't been any recognition in his eyes. Maybe she too had aged. All she could manage to say to him was a breathless 'Good Luck' when she had delivered him to Prosecutor Xu's door. She had then returned to the archive to bite her nails, hoping Prosecutor Xu would see Deng Shiru for the decent and hard-working man he was.

Mouse had had two marriage proposals since leaving school: at age twenty-one and again at twenty-five. She had turned both men down flat. Not that there had been much wrong with them. They had both been good candidates in different ways. But she had been hoping for something more. Now, at the age of thirty-four, after Deng Shiru's failure of memory, these rejections seemed a little rash. Mouse knew, after many years of staring at herself in the mirror, that she did not have a memorable face. She was certainly no Prosecutor Xu! And Deng Shiru had only ever spoken to her once before, when they had been fifteen, back at school. Already intent even then on becoming a policeman, Deng Shiru had rescued her from a marauding gang of bullies, and, in the process, had named her.

"Hey, little mouse, you've got to learn to stand up for yourself," he had told her before walking her home.

He had been accepted by the police a few years later. She, too shy to ever approach or speak to him again, had tried to follow in his footsteps. She had sat before the policeman at the recruiting office while he had listened in disbelief to the prepared speech that she read from a piece of paper. Boiled down to its essentials, she wanted to promote justice and serve the people. That was all she wanted to do.

The policeman had stood up, leaned toward her, and suddenly clapped his hands together in front of her face. She had cringed in her seat, fighting back the shock and the tears.

"You are not police material," he observed.

She did cry then. He found her some tissues so she could dry her eyes and blow her nose, and then, perhaps feeling sorry for her – maybe the speech had impressed him after all – he had made a phone call on her behalf. Then he gave her directions, told her what bus to catch, and soon enough she found herself standing outside of the Procuratorate. In the foyer she was met by Madame Ko Yi-ying, the senior legal clerk, but always referred to as Madame Ko by all the staff rather than by her job title. Madame Ko was as imposing as the building she worked in.

Madame Ko made her take some tests, in basic numeracy and verbal reasoning. Mouse passed both with ease. Madame Ko then picked up a legal file from her desk and threw it to the floor, displacing all the papers from it, leaving quite a mess, shocking Mouse.

"Sort that file out!" Madame Ko commanded.

Mouse got down on her hands and knees, unsure of the order the papers should be placed in, trying to work out in her head a logical sequence though she knew nothing of the law. She got flustered. She changed her mind a few times. But she didn't give up. She finally settled on a sequence she thought should be right. She handed the file back to Madame Ko and retook her seat.

Madame Kong did not bother to check the file. Instead, she asked, "Ms. Hong, why don't you apply to college? You are bright enough."

Too ashamed to say she didn't have the money, that her parents had, to all intents and purposes, abandoned her, Mouse could only shake her head. Madame Ko sent her away for a few days while background checks were done and then, before she knew it, she was a trainee legal clerk at Chengdu People's Procuratorate – and very proud of the fact. She didn't have a uniform, but at least she could do her bit to promote justice and serve the people. And she was ideally placed to keep track of Deng Shiru's police career. This had meant, through the years, sharing his successes from a distance, fearing for him out on the streets night and day – his incredible run *toward* the gun-battle on the Zhimin East Road had been seared into her mind for all of time – and then crying all night for him when he had been unlucky enough to be caught up in The Purge, knowing what this would do to him. It had taken her five long years to make that injustice right, to repay the debt from school that she owed him.

Before taking up her new post at Chengdu People's Procuratorate, Prosecutor Xu had contacted Mouse from Chongqing. After an emotional catch-up (tears were shed by both of them), Prosecutor Xu had said, "Mouse, I have to employ a special investigator. I need your help finding suitable candidates."

Mouse told her not to worry.

Mouse broke a few rules.

Mouse left the archive for once.

She took the bus and met up with her friend, Jiayi, who worked in the Personnel Department at PSB HQ. Jiayi allowed her access to the old files, including the files of those purged. Prosecutor Xu had given her a long list of requirements: non-smoker, former police but with no current attachments to the PSB, no criminal record, a Party member, a stable family life, a stable financial situation, no known sexual deviancy, and so on, and so on. Mouse didn't waste her breath telling Prosecutor Xu that she was being silly with her list of requirements. Mouse knew exactly whose file she was looking for. And, after she'd found it, she had let Jiayi have some fun and pick the most useless candidates under Heaven. Reading their thick files full of disciplinary citations made the two of them almost split their sides with laughter.

Mouse had also advertised the post as instructed. But she had made unfortunate mistakes with the contact phone numbers and with the application cut-off date. She also completed Deng Shiru's application for him – she couldn't trust him to do it right – and sent it to his home so he could just attach his signature. And then, when Prosecutor Xu had arrived at the Procuratorate to do some preliminary work before taking up her post proper, Mouse had put the pile of candidate files on her desk with Deng Shiru's at the very top. Wanting to leave nothing to chance, Mouse had brazenly pointed at the file and said, "Prosecutor, he's the one."

"How do you know?"

"He is a safe pair of hands."

Prosecutor Xu had protested. "Mouse, I want talent not a safe pair of hands."

But Mouse refused to budge. "No, Prosecutor, *you* are the talent. Believe me, in Chengdu, you will need a safe pair of hands and also someone who will always watch your back."

Prosecutor Xu had been persuaded.

And then Investigator Deng, in his interview with Prosecutor Xu, had done his bit – as Mouse prayed he would. Mouse personally arranged to have his shiny new procuratorate badge sent to his home by special courier.

It was the least she could do.

At last, her debt of honour had been repaid.

After midnight, having finally given up on her novel, Mouse was curled up under the quilt trying to get to sleep when her phone unexpectedly rang. This was unusual. No one called her at night. Anxious that something had happened to her parents back in the village, Mouse picked up the phone with some trepidation.

"H-Hello," she stammered.

"Mouse, forgive me…did I wake you?"

Mouse sat up in bed. "Prosecutor Xu! Is everything alright? Is Investigator Deng alright?"

"Fine, fine…Mouse, I have a favour to ask. I know you don't work for me directly, and I should first get permission from Madame Ko, but I need you to do some research for me."

"What kind of research?"

"On a family…but it must be done quietly. No one must know. You cannot trust anyone. Do you understand?"

"Yes, Prosecutor," replied Mouse, secretly thrilled.

"So will you do it?"

"I'd love to."

Mouse switched on the light, grabbed a pen and some paper, and made copious notes as Prosecutor Xu talked. By the time Prosecutor Xu was finished, Mouse was trembling with excitement and fear.

"Mouse, you must be careful," warned Prosecutor Xu. "Tomorrow my phone will be switched off. I can't explain why. I just don't want anyone to know where I am. Perhaps you and I could meet up on the evening, have a bite to eat, and speak in private. Do you agree?"

"Oh yes, Prosecutor."

"And I'll buy you a gift."

"There's no need to—"

But Prosecutor Xu was already gone.

Mouse giggled. Prosecutor Xu was a fireball. She only worked at one speed – fast! Chengdu People's Procuratorate had yet to fully comprehend just whom it had taken on.

Mouse went back to bed. But, try as she might, she could not sleep. And it wasn't just because she was still thinking about Deng Shiru. Prosecutor Xu had set Mouse's spirit alight. Having worked on important projects through the night before, Mouse decided to start Prosecutor Xu's research immediately. She dressed for the weather, completing her spring ensemble with a warm hat and sturdy boots. She picked up her trusty laptop, locked the door behind her, and ran down the stairs. Usually she would walk or take the bus. But the lateness of the hour, and the continuing heavy rain, precluded such choices. She hopped in a taxi instead. Ten minutes later she was signing in at the Procuratorate. A few minutes after that, a cup of tea in hand, she was descending in a lift to the archive.

By dawn she was done; in terms, that is, of what she could discover in the paper and computer files. She broke off from the work, left the Procuratorate for a while to grab some breakfast at her favourite local noodle bar, and then on her return slept for an hour or two in her chair with her coat wrapped around her. After nine she began to make calls – very discreet calls – to those contacts of hers unlucky enough to be working Sunday morning, contacts with good memories, contacts happy to share those memories in return for a chat and a gossip, and a favour done sometime soon in return. These calls filled a few gaps in Mouse's knowledge. But they also served to frighten her.

Her work complete, ready to brief Prosecutor Xu when she returned from Chongqing, Mouse decided to have her lunch in the park. By all accounts the weather was now set to be dry for the coming days, and the temperature due to rise a few degrees or so. Summer was just around the corner. That was when the rains would really begin.

When the lift opened out onto the ground floor, and Mouse popped her head into the main administration office to say goodbye to the girls, she found them in a state of mild hysteria. Huiling separated herself from the arguing group and ran toward her.

"Mouse! Mouse! I forgot you were here. The police are looking for Prosecutor Xu. That snooty cow has forgotten to put her personal number on the system. You're bound to have it. You know everything."

"What do the police want with her?" asked Mouse, fishing about in her bag for her phone, fearing one of her own 'discreet' calls had somehow backfired. She saw tears in the eyes of some of the girls and wondered what that was all about.

"It's that investigator of hers...the fat man," said Huiling.

Mouse felt her blood drain into her boots. "Investigator Deng – what about him?"

"Oh, he's dead...murdered," said Huiling, bluntly. "I had a feeling he wouldn't be any good."

The office went dark and Mouse tumbled to the floor.

CHAPTER FORTY-FIVE

On the way into the city, Philip Ye called Maggie Loh. She was in bed, complaining of aches and pains, a persistent cough, and a temperature not what it should be.

"Babe, I think I've got the flu."

"Maggie, I'm sorry for last evening."

"It's not me you should be apologising to."

"I know."

She sneezed and blew her nose. "The reprimand still stands."

"Fair enough - anything from the canvass?"

"Nothing of value. The neighbours can't decide how many were living in that apartment with Poppy. We can't find the landlord either. That may be nothing. He appears to be out of the city on business. Lots of forensics from the apartment...fingerprints, hair samples, you name it...but it's going to take a while to process it all. As for the bastards who attacked you, they're long gone. We couldn't get a print off the knife they dropped. None of the local informers have heard of them, or The Willow Woman cult for that matter."

Philip Ye wasn't surprised. As far as he knew – and he wasn't an expert – cult members usually kept themselves to themselves, trapping themselves in a world of their leader's making, only ever venturing forth from the bosom of the cult to recruit new members. If the leader's agenda was insane enough cult members would take violent action against the wider world – which did not appear to be the case, as yet, with The Willow Woman cult. In most cults, the violence – physical, emotional, intellectual and spiritual – was directed against cult members themselves to keep them under the leader's control. He could guess what had happened to Zhu Yi, that some experiment to send him out to preach to, and convert, struggling migrants had proved a failure. Zhu Yi had also found his conscience after the suicide of Old Man Gao. Rather than let him run to the authorities, or infect other cult members with a dose of his rediscovered sanity, Zhu Yi had been butchered.

But what about Poppy?

If his working theory was correct, that Zhu Yi had introduced Junjie to Poppy, then it stood to reason that Zhu Yi and Poppy had been friends – or maybe more than friends. It was also possible Zhu Yi's flash of conscience had infected her, and so she had also been put down like a dog, not only to stop the spread of the infection throughout the cult, but to serve as a warning to other cult members about what could happen if the leader's patience was tested. From the defensive wounds on her hands and wrists Poppy had seen her death coming. It was possible the other cult members in the apartment had been forced to watch before being ordered to scatter.

But scatter where?

Before he would sit down and try to answer that question he needed more insight into Poppy's life at the university. He wanted her diary and her phone.

"Where are you off to this morning?" asked Maggie Loh.

"Deyang."

"Poppy's family?"

"Yes – I've already been in touch with the local boys. They offered to do the dirty work. I wanted the family over the initial shock of her death so when I get there they'll be more responsive to my questions."

Maggie Loh began to cough violently. "I'll be in the office shortly. Maybe one hour, maybe two. My darling husband's just making me some tea with honey."

"Sure, Maggie – I'll talk to you soon."

Philip Ye ended the call with a smile. Maggie Loh would be out of action for a week at least. He phoned Chief Di to update him on the progress of the investigation but only reached his secretary, Ms. Miao. The long-awaited budget meeting had already begun, she explained.

Just before nine, Philip Ye found Ma Meili waiting for him out on the street in front of The Silver Tree, dressed in her usual smock and shapeless jeans. Something would have to be done about her clothes.

"How did you sleep?" he asked, as she got into the car.

"Ye Lan gave me some more food before I went to bed," she replied, brightly. "I like her. She is very nice. The restaurant was very noisy until late but I did not mind. I helped out in the kitchen."

"That was kind of you."

"Ye Lan says that Prosecutor Xu is trouble."

"Is that so?"

"Yes – and I am in full agreement with her."

Deyang was not more than an hour's fast drive from Chengdu. An industrial city of about four million souls, it was most famous for the production of Jian Nan Chun liquor and relics from the Shu civilisation. Philip Ye had visited Deyang before, just the once, with Lucy Fu. He had taken her to a museum – a romantic date of sorts – to view some of the Shu artefacts on display there. But she had grown bored very quickly, and of him soon after.

The car satnav guided them into the city and the excellent directions Philip Ye received from the local detective had got them to the correct apartment door.

Before he knocked, Philip Ye said to Ma Meili, "This is a family taken in grief. Be respectful but observant also – a minor detail, easily missed, could prove important."

She nodded, her expression grave.

The Deyang detective who, as well as offering directions, had visited with the family to pass on the bad news had not hung around. But he had left a policewoman behind, hardly more than a cadet, seemingly younger than Baby Wu, to act as liaison. It was she, with a shy smile, who opened the door to them. The family, the little there was of it, was seated together on the sofa: the father and mother, holding hands; the paternal grandmother, as Philip Ye soon learned she was, seated next to them. The policewoman made the necessary introductions and then went into the kitchen to prepare tea. Philip Ye took a seat but Ma Meili remained standing, trying to hide herself in the corner of the room. It occurred to Philip Ye that he had hardly given any thought to Ma Meili's confession from the last evening, that she had never been police and had arrived in Chengdu with a fabricated past. Why was he then taking the risk of continuing to drag her around with him? He owed her his life for sure. But he also had to admit that what he had told Boxer Tan was true: he actually liked Ma Meili.

He turned his attention to the family, opening his notebook. The father and mother were looking anywhere but at him. The grandmother, made of sterner stuff, never let her eyes leave his face. He felt uncomfortable sitting before her, guilty that he had been unable to prevent Poppy's murder. He accepted tea from the policewoman, as did Ma Meili, and waited until she had sat down on a stool, demurely smoothing her trousers underneath her, letting the room settle before he posed his first question.

But, before he could do so, his phone rang. "Please excuse me," he said, annoyed at his lapse. He had been so busy telling Ma Meili how to behave properly he'd forgotten to switch it off.

It was Fatty Deng, sounding anxious. "Mister Ye, I—"

"Investigator Deng, I can't speak right now. I am in Deyang with Ms. He's family."

"I understand, Mister Ye, but I can't find Prosecutor Xu. I was supposed to meet with her this morning but—"

"I'm sure she'll turn up."

"Yes, but—"

"I'll speak to you later."

Philip Ye switched off the phone. He apologised again to the family for the interruption. He then offered condolences for the loss of their daughter.

"Is it truly Poppy...the body you have found?" asked the grandmother.

"I believe so," replied Philip Ye. "But a formal identification will have to be made."

"When?"

"Soon – in a day or two. But first I have some questions."

The grandmother stood, startling him. "Come with me," she said.

With a nod to Ma Meili to remain where she was, Philip Ye followed the grandmother from the room. He was taken to a small bedroom. The walls were bare, the bed stripped of linen. On the bed sat a large box. The freight stamps declared it had been sent from Chengdu. There was a small school-desk against a wall. The atmosphere of the room was heavy, laden with sadness.

"I sit in here often," said the grandmother. "I knew months ago she wasn't coming back. I don't know how I knew but I did." She pointed at the box. "Her clothes are in there and some books too. That is all the university sent us back of Poppy. That is what remains of her life. I do not think my son and his wife will survive this. My son is not strong and his wife has started drinking. She hides it but I know. Poppy was the future of this family. She was clever. She was set to become an engineer. Soon I will be dead and my son and his wife will follow me quickly enough. That is how it is, *lǎowài*."

"I understand."

"You will catch the person who did this to Poppy?"

"That is my intention."

"Will he be executed?"

"That is not my decision to make."

She clicked her tongue, dissatisfied with his response. She ran a hand through her long grey-streaked hair. "I like you, *lǎowài*. You understand loss. You know what it means."

"When did you last see Poppy?"

"Early in September – the day she caught the train to Chengdu. But she was not the same girl even then. She'd had a job through the summer in Chengdu. When she came home for a week before term began she was different."

"How so?"

"Secretive."

"Where had she been working?"

"She said a bookshop. But I think that a lie. I tried to talk to her. I told her that some girls do bad things for money. But it was like talking to someone asleep. She had been the sweetest child."

"You raised her while her parents had been out working?"

"Yes, she was no trouble."

"What happened after she went back to university?"

"She used to come home every two weeks. This term she did not. She phoned a few times but that was all. She said she was too busy with her studies. Then at the end of October the university phoned us."

"Who called you?"

"My son took the call but he got so distraught I had to take the phone off him. She said her name was Madame Xiong. She said Poppy had run away with a man. I called her a liar. She said it was our fault for raising a whore. I then tried to call Poppy but her phone wouldn't answer. My son travelled to Chengdu to look for her. But the university security men wouldn't let him speak to her friends. They roughed him up and threw him off the campus. Then this box arrived."

"I need to examine her diary and her phone."

"I have looked – they are not in the box."

Philip Ye tried to hide his disappointment. "What happened next?"

"My son stayed on in Chengdu looking for her. He went to the police but they told him there was nothing that could be done. Young women run off with men all the time, they told him. Then he ran out of money and had to come home. He had to go back to work. All our savings had been used up sending Poppy to university. I phoned the university. I asked for our money back and for Poppy's diary and phone. Madame Xiong told me that if I made trouble for her then she would make trouble for me."

"What did she mean by that?"

"I don't know."

Philip Ye sensed there was something more. "Tell me," he said, gently.

The grandmother shut the door fearing they would be overheard. "It was soon after the New Year. There was a phone call. My son and his wife were out. It was Poppy. She called me a demon."

"A demon?"

"Yes – then she started to cry and was gone."

"Did you take a note of the number?"

"There was no number. It was very odd. I did not tell my son and his wife this. They are not strong people."

"And you're certain it was Poppy?"

"Her voice was strange but it was her. Then yesterday, there was another call. It was Poppy again. She seemed more like herself. She told me she was coming home. She cried and cried. She said a friend of hers had died. She said the man she had loved was not the man she thought he was. It was gibberish mostly and then she said she had to go. I did not tell my son and his wife. I did not want to give them false hope. In my heart I still believed I would never see her again. And so it proved."

"I am very sorry."

"*Lǎowài*, do you believe in the afterlife?"

"I do."

"What do you think it is like there?"

"I do not know," he replied, honestly.

She sat down on the bed and began to sob. "I stayed awake all night praying my premonition was wrong, that she would come through the door this morning. Then, when the police came, I knew."

Philip Ye took her hand. He put more questions about Poppy's friends at the university, whether Poppy had any interest in religion, whether she had ever spoken about The Willow Woman. But the grandmother shook her head to them all.

"Grandmother, you must be strong," he told her.

"This family will wither and die now," she replied. "It doesn't matter anymore. Nothing matters anymore."

· · ·

He completed his notes in the car. The grandmother had allowed him to search through the box. All it contained, as she said, were clothes and a few academic textbooks – nothing of any evidential value. Philip Ye supposed Madame Xiong had destroyed the diary and the phone, if Poppy had indeed left them behind. Whatever the case, he doubted if anyone would ever see them again. At least he'd be able to get hold of the phone's call log from the provider sometime in the near future. He looked across at Ma Meili. She was silent, thoughtful.

"Sister, what's on your mind?"

"Constable Chu."

"Who's that?"

Ma Meili raised her eyebrows and pointed back in the direction of the family He's apartment.

"Ah, the young policewoman."

"I spoke to her in the kitchen when she was cleaning the teacups," said Ma Meili. "She went to university before she joined the police."

"So?"

"She said that the police in Deyang want all their cadets to have had a good education."

He saw the problem. The sum of Ma Meili's education was probably a few years in her local village school.

"Sister, a way will be found for you," he told her.

She gave him a faint smile, wanting to believe him. He checked his watch. It was already after eleven. He began the drive back to Chengdu. He allowed Ma Meili to play with the radio. She tried to cheer herself by humming along to the tunes. At the outskirts of Chengdu, he remembered to turn his phone back on. He was minded to return Fatty Deng's call, to see if he had calmed down yet. But, before he could do so, another call came in.

"Mister Ye, it's Constable Wu." The young constable's voice sounded strained.

"What's troubling you, Baby Wu?"

"Superintendent Tan said you should be informed."

"Informed about what?"

Philip Ye pulled the car over as Baby Wu explained in as much detail as he could about what had happened. When he was done, Philip Ye said he would be there as soon as possible. He put down the phone, closed his eyes, breathed, and looked for the quiet space within.

In breath, there is life; in breath, there is serenity; in breath, there is clarity.

"What is wrong? What has happened?" asked Ma Meili, not content to let him disappear from her.

For a while he could not speak. Guilt ate at him again. He searched for the right words. "It's Fatty Deng...he's dead...murdered."

Ma Meili's mouth opened and closed like a fish.

CHAPTER FORTY-SIX

Sunday

The Golden Pheasant had indeed gone. On the Siguan Road, in its place, was a replica of The Singing Moon bar in Wukuaishi, complete with tacky notices in the window advertising cut-price alcohol on Monday nights. It was dark inside, the doors locked. The bar was not due to open until noon. Fatty Deng checked his watch. It was not yet eleven. Determined not to waste the morning, he wandered down a side-alley to the rear and was pleasantly surprised to find the trade door propped open and a delivery being made. One man was standing in the back of a red truck passing out crates of spirits, wine and beer, and two others were stacking the crates on the ground. Fatty Deng didn't like the look of them. They were rough types, unshaven with bad haircuts, lean but well-muscled, used to heavy lifting; to fighting also it seemed, as the man standing in the back of the truck had a blackened eye and a cut across his nose.

"Hey, is the boss in?" asked Fatty Deng, jerking his thumb toward the open door.

"Who wants to know?" It was the injured man in the back of the truck who spoke.

Fatty Deng showed his badge. "Procuratorate – just a routine inspection for illegal foreign workers."

It was as plausible an explanation as any.

"On a Sunday?"

"I'm behind on my work," replied Fatty Deng, annoyed at being questioned.

"There aren't any foreign workers at this bar."

"I still have to check for myself."

Fatty Deng smelt trouble. The three of them stopped working to stare at him. They were not as frightened by his badge as they should have been. He suspected that they were tough guys who'd had a few clashes with the law in the past. Either that or they were stupid – a distinct possibility. He memorised the truck registration plate and the name of the delivery company to run checks on them later.

"I'll go find the boss for myself," he told them, entering the bar, squeezing past the crates that had already been stacked in the passageway, and making his way up the rickety wooden stairs to the upper floors. Mister Fang, the previous owner, had always had his office on the second floor. Fatty Deng doubted much had changed since he'd run off with a big heap of cash.

On the first floor landing he heard the murmur of voices. But all the doors leading to the private function rooms were shut. He carried on up to the second floor and was pleased to find the office right where it had always been, with the door wide open and someone sitting at the old desk. It was a pity it was not the kindly and world-weary Mister Fang, whom Fatty Deng had greatly liked. He had shared a drink with him over five years ago in this very same office. Instead, at the desk now sat a man hardly twenty years old, with a wisp of a moustache and a bad case of acne. He was smoking a cigarette and was arguing with someone over the phone. It sounded personal, some bust-up with a friend over a girl. The office was a mess. Mister Fang had always been an orderly man. Now piles of papers littered the office and an old computer was perched precariously on the edge of the desk. The ashtray was filled to the brim with cigarette butts and a layer of grey dust covered everything. The young man didn't notice Fatty Deng until a procuratorate badge was pushed in his face. Pale and frightened, he put the phone down quickly.

"Are you the boss?" asked Fatty Deng.

A rapid shake of the head.

"Then where is he?"

"Mister Bao is at the bar in Wukuaishi and—"

"Hey, there's no need to worry," said Fatty Deng. "This is just a routine inspection. I'm looking for illegal foreign workers."

"I don't think there are any."

"That's good to hear – but I need proof. What's your name?"

"Fan Yao – I just help out Mister Bao from time to time. I should call him—"

"There's no need. I'm pressed for time today. I'm trying to visit as many bars as I can. Just give me a list of all the people you have working here, together with their ID numbers, home addresses and copies of their household registrations and I'll get out of your hair. If your bar staff are students and from out of town, don't worry – copies of their temporary household registrations will do."

"I should call Mister Bao," said Fan Yao.

"You're wasting my time," said Fatty Deng, sharply.

Fan Yao stubbed his cigarette out and nervously lit another, offering the pack to Fatty Deng who declined.

"All that stuff's on the computer," said Fan Yao.

"So turn it on."

"But bar staff come and go and—"

"Listen," said Fatty Deng, putting his fists on the desk and leaning toward Fan Yao, "I'm not here to give you a hard time, or to check whether your business records are fully up to date, or even whether Mister Bao is making all the proper social security payments for you all – I'm just looking for illegal foreign workers today. So turn on your computer and give me a printout. What could be easier than that?"

Fan Yao sucked on his cigarette some more and then, reluctantly, switched on the computer. It took some time to boot up.

"I've been telling Mister Bao he should invest in some new hardware," said Fan Yao, by way of explanation.

"I've a cousin who runs a computer shop in Wukuaishi," said Fatty Deng, truthfully. "I could get Mister Bao a good deal."

"Really?"

"Sure kid, no problem. I'll tell my cousin to drop by and speak to Mister Bao if you like."

"Mister Bao doesn't understand computers. He was running a carpet-fitting business before he came into some money and set up The Singing Moon bars. Maybe your cousin could talk to me and then I could talk to Mister Bao."

Fatty Deng shrugged. "Sure – now let's have that printout."

Soon Fan Yao was tapping away on the keys and the little printer next to the computer was spewing out pages of information. When done, Fan Yao put them in some sort of order and passed them over to Fatty Deng for approval. Fatty Deng scanned down the pages quickly. It was hardly what he had asked for, just a list of names – sometimes with home addresses and contact phone numbers, sometimes not. The names weren't even in any sort of order. There was not even a record of when each employee had commenced work at the bar. But what pleased Fatty Deng immensely was that there were far more names on the list than could possibly work at any one bar – even allowing for staff moving on. Fan Yao had just given him the list of employees for the whole chain of Singing Moon bars. Many of the home addresses recorded were repeated down the list, indicating to Fatty Deng that a number of staff were living together. On the fourth page, he found Poppy. She was recorded on the list by her real name, He Dan. As for the apartment where she'd died, that had been recorded as the address for at least ten other employees. Fatty Deng almost laughed out loud. He'd got what he wanted. Those ten were probably implicated in Poppy's murder.

"Is it okay?" asked Fan Yao.

"No foreign workers," said Fatty Ye, pretending to be satisfied, folding the papers up and sliding them into his jacket pocket. "You've been a great help, kid."

"And you'll tell your cousin with the computer shop to give me a call here?"

"It's as good as done," said Fatty Deng, giving him a cheery wave and retreating back down the stairs. He was moving so quickly he almost collided with a young woman emerging from one of the private rooms off the first floor landing.

"Please excuse me," he said, taken aback. At first glance he thought it was Poppy standing in front of him, returned from the afterlife. Her skin was as pale as Poppy's had been in death, her face thin and drawn, with the same unfocused glassy-eyed stare. But Fatty Deng lost interest in her as she mumbled something and moved past him. It was the room she had come from which took his attention.

She had left the door slightly ajar. The room was filled with people, the majority of student age, some seated, some standing. There was a painting of The Willow Woman mounted on the wall. Addressing the group, in hushed and urgent tones, as if she was trying to instil something important in them all, was a woman he knew very well. His heart skipped a beat. Their eyes met briefly; her shock, he saw, akin to his own.

And then Fatty Deng hurried down the stairs, trying not to lose his footing. He ripped a couple of buttons from his shirt as he squeezed past the stacked up crates in the passageway and then he was at last out into the fresh air.

The delivery men had finished unloading the crates and were securing the tailgate of the truck.

"Hey, what's up with you?" one of them asked him. "You look like you've seen a ghost."

"I nearly fell down those fucking wooden stairs," Fatty Deng replied, laughing, trying to hide his true emotions. "And you were right – no foreign workers."

He marched off, not looking back. He felt better when he was on the main Siguan Road, able to merge with the mass of other pedestrians out and about. He forgot about Wangjiang Road Station and Pan Mei. When he reached Starbucks he looked inside. Prosecutor Xu still hadn't arrived. The waitress he'd left the note with shook her head at him. He sat in the car, tried calling Prosecutor Xu – her messaging service yet again – and then wrote up his notes. He could guess what was happening now. He had read of it somewhere before. A cult would set up a business, all the employees being cult members, working as little more than slaves, their wages not paid to them but ploughed back into the cult instead. The list he had in his pocket was more valuable than he had first thought. Every name on the list was probably a cult member and every address recorded a safe-house for the cult.

But Madame Xiong?

If he hadn't seen her with his own eyes speaking to all those youngsters in that room in The Singing Moon he would not have believed it. She had known where Poppy was all along. And, more importantly, Madame Xiong had probably ordered Poppy's murder after his and Prosecutor Xu's visit to the university Saturday morning. He felt a stab of regret. If he'd pushed Zhang Lin and Pan Mei harder during those interviews, if he'd acted more professionally and kicked Madame Xiong out of the room, Poppy might well have been saved. As it was, Madame Xiong had thought the Procuratorate getting too close and decided Poppy had to go.

The question was: what would Madame Xiong do now?

Madame Xiong had surely recognised him as he had recognised her. Would she run? Would she tell the cult members to scatter? But with the list of employees with all their addresses in his pocket where would they all run to? Madame Xiong had a passport. Would she try to escape abroad? It was a pity he hadn't arrested her on the spot. But with the number of people in the room he doubted he would have got out alive. He thought about requesting police support now but quickly discounted it. Without Prosecutor Xu's authorisation he could land himself in a lot of trouble. It would be best to go home, grab some lunch, speak to Philip Ye as soon as he got back to Chengdu, and find Prosecutor Xu first.

Maybe it would be fitting to first share the good news with his mother anyway, explain to her how he had cracked the case wide open. He started the engine and pulled out into the slow-moving traffic. He lit a celebratory cigarette as he drove, smiling to himself at how easy it had been getting the information he needed out of Fan Yao. It was a pity Fan Yao was now a marked man, the cult sure to dispose of him for his mistake. It was also a pity he had as yet no clue as to Junjie's whereabouts. As Fatty Deng was pondering all this, he did not notice the red delivery truck take up position a few car lengths behind him.

By noon he had parked in his usual space on the opposite side of the road from his apartment building. He had phoned ahead, telling his mother to forget the expense and order some good food in for lunch. When he got out of the car and looked up at his window, not only was his mother waving down at him but Uncle Ho and Aunty Ho as well. It was going to be a small party. The weather was even clearing. Up above, a pale sun was poking through the clouds.

His mind still on Junjie, he stepped out into the road, forgetting to look. The screech of brakes brought him back to his senses. He waved an apology to the driver. There was no time for him to register than he'd seen both the red truck and the driver before. The passenger had already jumped out and was upon him, punching and kicking him, winding him, knocking him to the ground. He tried to fight back but all his strength had suddenly departed him. He couldn't prevent the printout he'd obtained from Fan Yao being pulled from his pocket. Then the truck was gone in a cloud of diesel fumes. He tried and failed to sit up, struggling to breathe. He reached for his phone but it slipped from his bloody hands. He tried again to sit up and saw more blood staining his shirt and jacket. He hadn't just been punched and kicked, he had been stabbed also. Too tired to do anything else he laid his head back on the ground. He looked up at the window and saw his mother was gone, as were Uncle Ho and Aunty Ho. He was grateful for this at least. He didn't want his mother to see him this way. In the distance he could hear sirens. The police. He'd been police once, he remembered, with some regret. Clouds drifted across the face of the sun as he faded away.

CHAPTER FORTY-SEVEN

Aboard the fast train to Chongqing, Xu Ya fiddled with her phone. Much as she would like to, she dared not turn it on – not yet anyhow. Technology was not her speciality but she had heard that the police, if they wanted to, could track a person's location from the signal emitted from a mobile phone. Of course, whoever had told her this could have been preying on her general naivety in regard to many things outside of the law. But she couldn't take the risk. She put her phone back in her handbag and opened up her journal instead. Beloved Mister Qin had told her, in times of personal crisis, that she could bring order to her thoughts by writing them down. So, as she was carried at speed across the verdant Sichuan countryside, she settled back in her seat to consider religion in China and the problem of subversive cults.

She was well aware that she did not possess a single religious bone in her body. She did not believe in gods, spirits or the afterlife. Not once was she tempted during the five years of the hell that was her marriage to offer up a prayer to any supernatural agency to gain her release. As far as she was concerned, religion was nothing but fearful superstition, wishful thinking, and self-delusion.

This did not mean, however, that she was a militant atheist. On the contrary, though a lifelong Party member, and raised in a highly rational household, she did not begrudge the common people their beliefs, their need to pray, to light incense, to make offerings to the spirits of the dead. In China, for many, life was hard. If such religious practices helped people get through the day, then so be it. Though it had never deviated from the Marxist position that all religion is 'the opium of the people' and as such the need the people had for religion would eventually wither and die, the Party in its wisdom had become much more tolerant of religion due to China's social complexities. Not only had the Party realised that in spite of all its efforts religion remained very popular in China, it had been forced to conclude that religion would indeed linger in China for many years to come *and* was inextricably linked to very delicate ethnic relations. The Party also had to consider the 'knock on' effect its treatment of domestic religious groups had in regard to its diplomatic exchanges with foreign powers.

Xu Ya accepted the Party position in its entirety – as she did the drafting of Article 36 of the Constitution, in which the people's right to exercise their religious belief was upheld.

With important safeguards, however.

No one had the right to '*make use of religion to engage in activities that disrupt public order, impair the health of citizens or interfere with the educational system of the state.*'

To Xu Ya, these safeguards were key.

And they were very Chinese.

Throughout the history of China, the belief in gods, spirits and all manner of prognostication had been rife among the people. The effective governance of the Empire had been ensured by the emperor making offerings in the form of sacrifices to Heaven and Earth, as well as to the spirits of past legitimate rulers. These rituals – and only the emperor was allowed to perform them – had granted the emperor the right to rule, the right otherwise known as the Mandate of Heaven. Any communication by the common people with gods or spirits *outside* of the 'approved' imperial pantheon had therefore been considered a threat to the emperor and, by extension, to the stability of the Empire. The state had had no choice but to define such errant behaviour – loosely but all-inclusively – as sorcery. And, as such, it had been proscribed by law. The fear had been – and this fear was borne out many times in Chinese history – that the common people could become deluded by 'heterodox teachings' and their passions inflamed, so much so that civil disorder would result. If caught quickly, such disturbances could always be quelled by the ruthless use of force.

But in Imperial China, as in the China of the 21st Century, perception had been everything. If heterodox teachings had taken root among the people and mass social unrest had been the result, then it could have been argued that the Mandate of Heaven was already slipping from the emperor; which, in turn, could have led to outbreaks of panic and greater instances of social unrest, thereby creating an unstoppable, revolutionary dynamic. So, by political necessity, all heterodox teachings – unapproved religions and cults, that is – had had to be suppressed, and their leaders decapitated, figuratively and literally. The Party of the 21st Century was not foolish in regard to its own legitimacy and longevity – its own Mandate of Heaven, if you will. It had absorbed the lessons of history. If the Party could not maintain order and stability in China, what right did it have to govern?

Xu Ya had travelled extensively in Europe and the United States. She had seen the best and worst of what the liberal democracies had to offer. There was much that she had admired. And she had met a number of people – some knowledgeable, some not – who had been very critical of the Party in China, a few even of Chinese descent. She understood these criticisms, how they had arisen. But for Xu Ya, for now, the Party remained the only sound choice of governance for China – with the provisos that the Party was as benevolent as it was firm, that the Party did not slide back into committing the mistakes of the past (primarily factionalism and excessive deification of the leader), and as long as a fair and just society was created, with the Rule of Law applying to all.

Xu Ya really believed in the Party; as she did the *very* gradual liberalization of society. As with many people, she feared chaos. Allow a child to run free and it would get up to all kinds of mischief, including all manner of ways to injure itself.

And so it was, quite sensibly, that though the freedom of religious belief was protected by the constitution, there had to be limits placed on that freedom. Even in the most liberal of Western democracies, a religious group advocating the sacrifice of young children would soon be stamped upon. The Party had the right, therefore, to choose which religions were acceptable in China and which were not. But the conditions of acceptability were very easy to fulfil: the religion must be a force for moral good; the religion must not incite civil disobedience; and the religion must always recognise the authority of the Party.

Five religions were sanctioned by the Party: the Buddhist Association of China, the Islamic Association of China, the Chinese Daoist Organisation, the Three-Self Patriotic Movement (Protestantism), and the Chinese Patriotic Catholic Association. The State Administration for Religious Affairs continuously monitored the behaviour of these religions so all remained as it should be; which, for Xu Ya, was a proportionate and sensible approach. However, cults, secret societies, and criminal fraternities were a different matter entirely.

In her year studying at Harvard, Xu Ya had become fascinated by how much the liberal democracies tolerated cults of every persuasion – religious, political, psychological, prosperity, New Age, and so on – and how such cults were allowed to proliferate, to prey on individuals who were weak by nature, or just weakened by circumstance, or those merely seeking a greater sense of community and love.

Academics in the West, more often than not, chose not to differentiate between such cults and the more usual expressions of organised religion – a perspective with which Xu Ya had to admit she had some sympathy. After all, self-delusion was self-delusion. However, many psychiatrists had taken a different view, identifying that cults (as opposed to mainstream religions) were led by highly persuasive people who sought always to be the focus of the cult members' lives, to dominate them wholly, to reduce and ultimately destroy their sense of self, to isolate them from society and turn them against their families, to separate them from their savings, and to mentally and sometimes physically and sexually abuse them at will. But unless a cult seriously crossed the line, the governments of these liberal democracies would turn a blind eye to such practices, believing every adult had the right to choose their own path in life, ignoring the fact that these cults used every indoctrination technique under the sun to gather prospective members into their folds. It was a sad truth, well known to Xu Ya through her researches (mainly in the West), that these indoctrination or 'thought reform' techniques were similar to those learned by the Party from the Soviet Union in the early days of the revolution, and adapted and perfected for use in China in the years afterward to ensure loyalty and unquestioning obedience to the needs of that revolution.

But what shocked Xu Ya, however, was not the proliferation of cults in the liberal democracies – about three thousand or so at any one time – or the numbers attracted to their siren calls – a few million – but how some of these cults controlled not only media outlets but had spread their webs of influence into all areas of government as well. And many of them now had the financial capacity to defend themselves against proper scrutiny, using the very freedoms enshrined in the laws of those democracies to hide from those who would subject them to proper investigation, fair criticism and publicity. It was no coincidence that the leaders of some of the cults suppressed in China had fled to the West, free now to continue to direct and influence and abuse the lives of cult members in China from a safe distance.

As far as Xu Ya was concerned the liberal democracies could do as they wished in regard to their own people. And, though it riled her, if the liberal democracies wanted to lecture other countries on religious freedoms, certain of their own moral superiority, then they were also free to do so. But the Party in China had to take a much more responsible approach. It had initially puzzled her why so relatively few Westerners were actually caught up in cults despite the aggressive recruiting techniques the cults used. She had eventually come to the conclusion that it was something to do with Western culture, the concentration on the individual – individualism being the liberal democracies' saving grace; in respect of cults, that is. The majority wanted to live their lives as they wished and chose not to subsume themselves completely to the will of others.

But the culture of China was different. A person's identity was perceived mainly in relation to others. The family, or the group, was of paramount importance. Authority had always to be respected, as is the Confucian way. Moreover, it did not take much historical analysis to note that cults always proliferated at times of great social stress and upheaval. The many changes wrought by the Reform Era (the movement of over 200 million people from the country to the cities, for example – the biggest migration in human history!), including the break-up of many family units as people searched all over the country to find work, and the disbandment of most of the old communist work units, had left many of the people lost and bewildered. These people were especially vulnerable to charismatic and persuasive men (or, less often, women), promising them utopia if only they would follow and devote their lives to them.

Xu Ya could not condemn such people. After all, such a charismatic and persuasive man had found her.

Xu Ya chewed her pen. This was not the time to think on her husband or the wasted years of her marriage. She put her journal away and stared out of the window. She slept for a time. When she alighted at Chongqing North Station, she reminded herself that only she could do this, that only she could rescue Junjie.

But then a sudden dread gripped her heart. An image of Investigator Deng filled her mind, lying in a pool of blood as her husband had done the night he had died. The image was so powerful that she almost tripped over her heels and fell. A kindly old gentleman asked her if she was alright. She assured him she was, pushed all thought of Investigator Deng and her dead husband from her mind, told herself not to be so silly and hurried toward the taxi rank.

CHAPTER FORTY-EIGHT

Sunday

There was a time, before the Reform Era, when the murder of a policeman – or a Procuratorate investigator, for that matter – was almost unheard of. But, since Deng Xiaoping's momentous decision to embrace capitalism, albeit with Chinese characteristics, the whole social fabric of China had changed, not necessarily for the better. The people had become more individualistic, more selfish, more unruly, and prone to emotional outbursts, sometimes violently so. And although this violence was not on a par with other developing countries, it was always the police who had to bear the brunt of it. This was only natural and to be expected. But, with four hundred police officers or more dying in China every year in the line of duty, Philip Ye thought the sacrifice far too great.

Like the majority of people, he did not want to see a return to the old days. Too many mistakes had been made, the resultant suffering of the people unforgivable. But he did see the need for the recruitment of not only many more police, but also for the development of a substantially different approach to policing – albeit with Chinese characteristics. No longer just an instrument of state political power, the police as an evolving professional law enforcement body had to become more embedded within the community – of the people, for the people! – more sensitive to the heartbeat of that community, and able to respond firmly, proportionately and compassionately to wanton criminality and the flames of discontent whenever they arose.

Unfortunately, as Philip Ye entered the crowded foyer of Wukuaishi Hospital with Ma Meili at his side, he knew this policing ideal to be a forlorn hope – in the short term, at least. There was too much to be done and not enough available money with which to do it. He had no great hopes for today's budget meeting. So, in the meantime, good officers would continue to be lost to violent death, or injury, or premature retirement through depression and disillusionment, or ridiculous and wasteful purges. Even those officers with a surfeit of optimism and energy, officers such as Maggie Loh, were being ground down to the bone. It should be a surprise to no one that the current flu epidemic across Chengdu had hit the PSB harder than any other organisation.

"Mister Ye! Mister Ye!" cried Baby Wu, from across the other side of the foyer.

Ma Meili, undeterred by the press of people, forced a path for her and Philip Ye so that they could reach the young constable, and was none too gentle with some who stood in her way.

"I'm so glad you are here, Mister Ye," said Baby Wu, standing to attention and saluting, smiling despite the day's traumatic events. Though he had already phoned Philip Ye twice to apologise for his error in misreporting Fatty Deng's death, he apologised yet again, bowing solemnly as he did so.

Philip Ye waved the apology away. "Is he still alive?"

"Yes, Mister Ye – I think so. He is in surgery. But the doctors have told us they have little hope."

"And Boxer Tan?"

"He is quite distraught, Mister Ye. If you follow me I'll take you to him."

Philip Ye had never visited Wukuaishi Hospital before. It was a labyrinth of similar-looking corridors, wards and rooms, all equally as crowded as the foyer. But Baby Wu was up to the task. He seemed to know his way about. "My mother is a nurse here," he explained, while leading them up the stairs to a surgical wing.

They found Boxer Tan sitting in an otherwise empty waiting-room. The blue shirt of his uniform was ruined, soaked with Fatty Deng's blood. He looked exhausted, defeated, older than his forty or so years. He was sipping water from a plastic cup. Philip Ye noticed Boxer Tan's hands were bloody also, that he had not yet had thought to wash. Baby Wu excused himself to go find some tea.

"What have you heard?" Philip Ye asked Boxer Tan.

Boxer Tan lifted his head. His eyes were dull, lifeless. "The surgeons threw me out of the theatre, Mister Ye. They said, even if they were able to save him, it would be hours yet before they knew for sure. I'm sorry about Baby Wu phoning you…telling you Fatty Deng was dead. That was my fault. I honestly thought it was true. When we got here, the first doctor…she was young and inexperienced and—"

"Tell me the story from the beginning," said Philip Ye, taking the seat next to Boxer Tan.

"Mister Ye, the 110 system worked flawlessly for once. I was driving Baby Wu home with me to have lunch. My wife was cooking. Then the call came through to us. We were only a few streets away… got there in a couple of minutes. Didn't see them though. A dark red truck, the witnesses said. Two attackers, maybe three – no one was sure. His neighbour, Uncle Ho, told me he saw one of the attackers take a document out of Fatty Deng's pocket. No cameras in the area, so we may never know for sure."

"Unless Fatty Deng pulls through."

"Sure, Mister Ye, but—"

"What happened next?"

"When we got to him, he was lying on the ground. There was so much blood I thought he was already dead. His mother was out on the street, screaming and screaming. She'd seen everything from her window." Boxer Tan took another sip of his water. "They've found a bed for her on a ward here. They had to sedate her. Fatty Deng was her life. The neighbours, Uncle Ho and Aunty Ho, are sitting with her. Good people. If it wasn't for Uncle Ho – he was a medic, years ago, in the army – Fatty Deng would have bled out. He kept pressure on Fatty Deng's wounds. He told me there was no time to wait for an ambulance. He and I threw Fatty Deng in the back of the car as Baby Wu drove us to the hospital. We tried to staunch the blood but it was just running out of him like a river. When he got here that young doctor shook her head. She couldn't find a pulse. I went crazy, Mister Ye. Uncle Ho was still pounding Fatty Deng's chest and I was shouting and cursing, saying I would arrest her if she didn't do something. I told her Fatty Deng was police…had been police…and you don't just give up. Baby Wu had to drag me out of there. That's when I told him to call you and the Procuratorate. That's when the mistake was made. I'm not sure what happened next. Maybe that young doctor was right and Fatty Deng was dead. But other doctors heard me shouting and came running and started a transfusion, pumping him full of blood, with Uncle Ho still with his hands stuck in Fatty Deng's wounds. Then they ran him off to surgery. I know I did wrong. I shouldn't have shouted at that young doctor. But what I said was right. Fatty Deng was one of us…a good guy. Forget about The Purge and the Procuratorate and all that crap;

deep down, underneath that rubbish suit he was wearing, Fatty Deng was still police. Did you know he came out to make an inspection of Wukuaishi Station the other day? We had such a laugh. Didn't cause me any trouble. And he promised to give me fair warning when another inspection was due. I thought to myself then, in hiring Fatty Deng, the Procuratorate has finally done something right. Do you remember him from the old days? Wangjiang Road Station. He was just a constable but he was the glue that held that place together well before Crazy Maggie Loh arrived. If you wanted something done at Wangjiang Road, or just to speak to someone with an ounce of sense, you spoke to Fatty Deng. Remember the Zhimin East Road shoot-out? Fatty Deng was first on the scene. He heard your distress call on the radio. He came running out of the station...unarmed. That was the sort of guy he was."

Philip Ye shook his head. He couldn't recall. All he remembered of that day was that it had been cold, that he had thought both he and Superintendent Zuo were going to die.

"He took down the fourth of those bastards," continued Boxer Tan. "After you shot the three dead, the last tried to run away. He ran straight into Fatty Deng. Fatty Deng knocked the pistol out of his hands with his baton and then had him on the ground and cuffed before he knew what was happening to him. Fatty Deng didn't even get a commendation. No one took his photograph that day, Mister Ye. There were no queues of women out on the streets of Chengdu that evening hoping to buy a newspaper with his picture on the front page. I don't mean anything by that, Mister Ye. You did the business that day. And you didn't get to choose your father, or your looks, or the money you were born into. That's just karma. But Fatty Deng should have been treated better. And then he gets taken by The Purge. Maybe that was karma too. Who the fuck knows? But it was a fucking disgrace. Chief Di just stood by and did nothing when the Shanghai Clique decimated us, getting rid of some of our best."

"Have you informed the Procuratorate?"

"As I said, Baby Wu called them, but what a waste of time that was. They haven't sent anyone out to see what's happened. It's a fucking Sunday so they're short-staffed. And Chief Prosecutor Gong is playing fucking golf somewhere, so there's no one there to make a decision about anything. Spineless bastards. As for Prosecutor Xu, not even the Procuratorate knows where she is. The receptionist told Baby Wu to try the Chunxi Road. She thought Prosecutor Xu might be out shopping. I thought Baby Wu was joking when he told me. Fatty Deng, her guy, lying in a pool of his own blood, and she's spending all her parents' money on shopping and having a good time. It's a fucking scandal and—"

"She's not shopping," said Philip Ye. "Fatty Deng called me this morning to tell me she was missing. He was nervous in his new job but, as you said, he was police. His instincts are sound."

Boxer Tan sat up. "What should we do?"

"You – nothing. You sit tight. And keep this to yourself until I've had a look for her. It might help if you get back to Wukuaishi Station, have a shower, put a fresh uniform on, organise an armed guard for Fatty Deng for when he gets out of surgery and go find me that red truck. And tell your boys I want at least one of those bastards alive."

"We'll see," said Boxer Tan, unwilling to commit himself

Baby Wu reappeared with a tray of tea. Philip Ye drained his cup quickly, wanting to be off. There was nothing further to be done or learned at the hospital. As for Fatty Deng, his fate was in the hands of the surgeons – or Heaven, depending on your point of view. Philip Ye was half-way down the corridor with Ma Meili trotting after him, when Baby Wu came running to catch them up, a small plastic bag in his hands.

"Good boy," said Philip Ye, taking the bag off him, seeing Fatty Deng's badge and ID, and, more importantly, his notebook inside.

In the car, Philip Ye quickly read through Fatty Deng's notes with a mixture of amazement and profound regret. Fatty Deng had been well-named, his full name Deng Shiru, for the famous Qing Dynasty calligrapher. Fatty Deng's notes were clear, concise, methodical, and detailed. Philip Ye read all about Fatty Deng's frustrated search for Prosecutor Xu, his interview with Pan Mei, his visit to The Singing Moon bar on the Siguan Road, and his sighting not only of another of Junjie's paintings of The Willow Woman but of Madame Xiong too. Fatty Deng had also written down a description of a red delivery truck together with its registration. Philip Ye made the connection with the assault on Fatty Deng. He phoned the registration number through to Boxer Tan to aid him with the search. He had the urge to go look for that red truck himself but Prosecutor Xu had to be his priority for now. As for his own failure to visit The Singing Moon bar in Wukuaishi and sending Boxer Tan in his place, there was nothing he could do about that now. He may or may not have sensed something was amiss, may or may not have prevented Fatty Deng having to fight for his life now. He put down the notebook, feeling Ma Meili's eyes upon him.

"What?"

"You…you were in a shoot-out?" she asked, hesitantly.

"It was years ago."

"You killed people?"

"I did – now stay in the car."

He got out and opened up the boot. Inside, he unlocked a metal box and took out the contents. Back in the car he held out the pistol in its holster to Ma Meili, her eyes widening in surprise.

"Sister, I have a lot on my mind," he told her. "I am very distracted at the moment. You must be my eyes and ears. You must keep both of us safe. This pistol is not standard police issue rubbish. It's a military QSZ-92, double-action, 9mm with fifteen rounds in the magazine."

"But I am not real police," she said.

"That's the least of my problems today," he replied, dropping the pistol in her lap. "Familiarise yourself with it while I drive. And don't shoot me in the process."

CHAPTER FORTY-NINE

Sunday

Mister Gan, the day concierge of Tranquil Mountain Pavilions, did not easily get flustered. Nor was he a stupid man. After twenty years honourable service in the People's Liberation Army, having risen to the rank of a senior NCO, he had been recruited by FUBI International Industries – the owner of the apartment building – for those very same qualities. He was employed to keep a close watch over the building and to respond to the needs of the tenants. He was also required to observe and report on the activities of some of those tenants – the foreigners, in the main – under the terms of a secret understanding reached between Mister Fu Bi, Chairman of FUBI International Industries, and State Security. There were similar secret agreements in place between FUBI International Industries and the other organs of law enforcement. These agreements, made at the very highest levels, guaranteed that no police officer would visit Tranquil Mountain Pavilions without first making a prior appointment with the legal team at FUBI International Industries – an arrangement that, until today, had proved very effective.

Of course, the primary drawback with such secret agreements is that very few knew of them, including the rank and file officers supposedly bound by them. So, on occasion, Mister Gan – and Mister Ni, the night concierge – had had to get tough, as he had done that very morning with the fat man from the Procuratorate. However, after attempting this approach with two more unwelcome visitors,

Mister Gan now, quite unexpectedly, had a pistol pointing at his chest. Though never one to panic, Mister Gan had to admit to himself he was quite disconcerted.

"Superintendent Ye," said Mister Gan, fixing his attention on the *lǎowài* rather on the giantess with the gun, "if you wish to gain access to Prosecutor Xu's apartment while she is out, you must either get her prior written permission, or you must be in possession of a properly authorised search warrant – which I assure you, you will not get."

"I do not have time for this," replied Superintendent Ye.

"Then I suggest—"

"It is you, Mister Gan, who have no choices here."

Naturally, Mister Gan knew who Philip Ye was. As part of his employment training, he had been required to memorise the faces of a hundred of Chengdu's most notable personages. And though, he had to admit, being in Philip Ye's presence had increased his heart rate somewhat – the family Ye might not be the power they once were in Chengdu, but one could not be too careful – it was the big woman with the pistol who was really making him sweat. Mister Gan remembered her from the TV, shooting that crazy old man twice in the head. Today, she had reacted with improbable speed to a slight nod from Philip Ye after he had been refused access to Prosecutor Xu's apartment. The pistol had left her holster so fast the movement had been nothing but a blur. Mister Gan was an expert in unarmed combat. There was also a concealed cache of weapons nearby for his use if the situation ever demanded it. But Mister Gan had to be realistic. Another nod from Philip Ye and the big woman might indeed shoot. He also had to admit that, if so many were looking for her then Prosecutor Xu might indeed be in some trouble. He was beginning to worry for her himself. So, for safety's sake, he picked up his electronic master key, took them both up in the lift to the tenth floor, opened up the door to apartment 1021, and then went off in search of advice and assistance.

At his first sight of the apartment, Philip Ye thought the concierge had deceived him. Apartment 1021 was hardly more than a shell, the walls of the living-room painted in an off-white undercoat, the floor devoid of any carpet or rugs, and with hardly any furniture to speak of at all. But, as he stepped over the threshold, he caught a faint trace of her scent, the expensive and subtle perfume Prosecutor Xu had been wearing the previous evening. As Ma Meili closed the door behind them, it then occurred to Philip Ye that the Fu family's affluent tenants might often prefer a blank canvas on which to create their own personal ideal of a private living-space. Either Prosecutor Xu had yet to make up her mind, or else she had moved in at speed, wanting to take up her post at the Procuratorate before any decoration could be done.

"Superintendent, what are we looking for?" asked Ma Meili.

"Some clue as to Prosecutor Xu's whereabouts."

Philip Ye had believed the concierge when told Prosecutor Xu was out for the day. But, he was still relieved not to find Prosecutor Xu sprawled across the floor, her body cold, her spirit long departed. There was no cloying smell of death in the air, no imprint of violence. If anything, the psychic atmosphere was uncannily clear, as if no one was living, or had ever lived, at the apartment. Had she not lived here long enough to make her mark? Or was she one of those people who left no lasting impression anywhere? Back at The Silver Tree, Philip Ye had indeed sensed something bird-like about her, that she was a creature of constant movement, of the air, not one to let her feet touch the ground for too long.

"How much does it cost to live here?" asked Ma Meili, disturbing his train of thought. She was standing at the window, admiring the skyline of the city, the pale sunlight reflecting off the surface of the river below.

"Upwards of forty thousand *yuán* per month, I should think," he replied.

Ma Meili hissed at the astronomical figure, more than a constable's basic *annual* salary.

"I expect her family has money," Philip Ye added. "A prosecutor's salary is not much greater than mine."

In the kitchen, they discovered the remains of a half-eaten breakfast of congee and bitter melon. A carton of pineapple juice had been left out on the counter. Philip Ye returned it to the fridge so it would not spoil.

The master bedroom was a mess, the bed left unmade, clothes discarded carelessly on the floor. Not the result of a struggle or even of a burglary, it was indicative, Philip Ye thought, of Prosecutor Xu's natural state, her speed of motion – her inability to focus on what she would consider to be the inessentials. He quickly made the bed and then picked up the clothes, folding them neatly, laying them down in a tidy pile on the bed. He caught Ma Meili staring at him, frowning.

"A disordered room disturbs my thinking," he explained.

"She will know we have been here."

"Sister, people usually sense when a stranger has been in their home. Furthermore, we are not spies. We are police. We go where we will. We do not, and should not, hide our presence."

"I would not like you folding my clothes."

"Then, Sister, if you ever invite me to your home I suggest you do not leave clothes on the floor."

Ma Meili hissed again and shook her head, making him smile.

The second bedroom was in the process of being converted into a study. A desk had been set up near the window. Philip Ye fell in love with it at first sight. It was an antique, probably 19th Century, constructed of pear wood. He would have bought it himself if he had seen it first.

"Whatever you think of Prosecutor Xu, she has taste," he said, laying his hand upon the desk lovingly.

Ma Meili scowled and peered closely at a large photograph mounted on the wall. Philip Ye bent over the desk. Law books were piled up upon it and Prosecutor Xu had been making notes on a legal pad. He reached for the uppermost book on the pile and found himself holding an old favourite: *A Complete Book Concerning Happiness and Benevolence* – written by the former magistrate Huang Liu-Hong in the final years of the 17th Century when the Qing Dynasty had been barely fifty years old. China had then been still trying to come to terms with its new masters, the Manchus, the invaders from the north. The book, an instruction manual for magistrates, had been written to counter a perennial problem. Since the Sui and Tang dynasties, the civil service examinations – the only sure key to career advancement for officials – required of the candidates the ability to write essays in a prescribed format on the classic texts. Successful candidates became therefore very learned in the 'four books and five classics' and other Confucian works as well; but, as for legal theory and the application of the law – a magistracy could well be an official's first posting – not so much. Philip Ye wondered what Huang Liu-Hong would think of present-day China, whether he would consider there had been much improvement in the education of officials.

"Superintendent, you are in this photograph," announced Ma Meili.

He walked over to her. She pointed to a much younger version of himself, standing at the edge of a group, looking away into the distance. He had initially ignored the photograph, believing it to be memorabilia from Prosecutor Xu's old school. He had forgotten for a time that Prosecutor Xu, according to Wolf, had been home tutored. The photograph was in fact of his graduating law class from Wuhan.

"And there is Prosecutor Xu," said Ma Meili, pointing at the young woman sitting front and centre, beaming proudly at the camera.

"Sister, you have very good eyes," he said.

Prosecutor Xu had hardly changed, he thought, still beautiful if more guarded. And she continued to take a good photograph.

"I did not know you were friends with her," Ma Meili muttered, reprovingly.

"I honestly don't remember her." He ran his eyes over all the other faces and found some consolation in recognising none of them. They were all strangers to him. "Sister, it was a difficult time for me. My fiancée had just died. I was not sure myself if I still wanted to live."

Ma Meili's mouth dropped open, as he now realised it was prone to do when she was surprised.

He turned his back on the photograph and brought his attention back to the book he was holding, Huang Liu-Hong's masterpiece. There was a piece of paper sticking out from between the pages. He pulled it free and unfolded it.

He read:

THE WILLOW WOMAN CULT

PROFESSOR XIONG YU
Charismatic leader?

MADAME XIONG
Abuses her position at the university to identify those students most vulnerable to approach?

MUST SET MOUSE LOOSE ON THE FAMILY XIONG!!

He refolded the paper and replaced it between the pages, putting the book back down on the desk.

Who was Mouse?

Looking down at her legal pad, he saw Prosecutor Xu had been making notes from a modern law book, the pages kept apart by a heavy glass paperweight moulded in the form of a butterfly. There, that lie again; she was no butterfly.

She had been researching Article 300 of the Criminal Law, which made it an offence for anyone to organise or utilise a superstitious sect or religious cult, or to utilise superstition, with a view to hindering the laws and administrative regulations of the State, or to deceive others and cause the death of a person, or to have sexual intercourse with a woman, or to defraud someone of their property.

Philip Ye knew the vaguely worded article very well. It, and the more clearly defined interpretation (which some academics argued actually created new law) written by the Supreme People's Procuratorate in the autumn of 1999, which in turn led to the *Standing Committee Decision Regarding Outlawing Cult Organisations and Punishing Cult Activities*, had been used to great effect in the suppression of the *Fǎlún Gōng* movement – a cult of practitioners of a form of *qigōng*. A mixture of physical exercises, traditional Chinese medicine and spiritual cultivation, *qigōng* had been popular with, and even promoted by, the Party since the 1950s, until charismatic exponents of *qigōng* had begun to appear out of the woodwork in the 1980s and 1990s, claiming miraculous healing powers and gathering thousands of enthusiastic, excitable and very loyal followers to themselves. Only slowly did the Party realise that it had itself spawned a threat to its legitimacy and authority. In April 1999, followers of *Fǎlún Gōng*, unhappy with perceived criticism and discrimination of the movement by the media, had demonstrated in Tiananmen Square in Beijing outside the Party offices. Unsettled by the threat, the Party's response had been severe. *Fǎlún Gōng* followers had been imprisoned, a few thousand had died from mistreatment, and Li Hongzhi, its leader, had sought refuge in the West.

"Superintendent, someone is coming!" Ma Meili's hand was on the pistol at her belt. She hurried from the bedroom.

Philip Ye followed her, listening, hearing nothing. But he should not have doubted the acuity of her hearing. The lock of the door clicked and the door was suddenly thrown open, imperiously so.

She was a vision, her figure-hugging white silk dress cut just above the knee, diamond rings on her fingers, diamond studs in the lobes of her ears. Gleaming, impenetrable eyes and a short pixie cut topped off the image of a successful and glamorous businesswoman. Her intense fragrance filled the room, drowning out Prosecutor Xu's light floral scent with exotic, oriental spices. The concierge stood behind her.

"Well, well, Mister Gan, you were quite right," she said. "It is the strangest of pairings: a green-eyed *lǎowài* and an ogre come down from the mountains. Though to be fair, Mister Gan, *lǎowài* is a misnomer. To us pure bloods, Philip Ye may look mostly English, but I assure you his heart is very Chinese – quite unfathomable."

"How are you, Lucy?" Philip Ye asked.

Her tone hardened. "Philip Ye, I haven't heard from you in years and then you barge into my father's building, point a gun at Mister

Gan, and force your way into an apartment that is not yours. I am very disappointed in you. My father will be extremely disappointed in you. He will be speaking to Party Chief Li, I am sure."

"I am looking for Prosecutor Xu."

"Mister Gan has already told you she is not here. Was that not clear?"

"Do you know where she is?"

"Why should I? We may be friends but we do not live in each other's pockets. I keep an apartment here for those rare occasions when I am in Chengdu. Tonight I am heading out to New York. But, let me make a deal with you Philip," she said, sashaying up to him, touching his silk tie with a finely, manicured fingernail, whispering in his ear. "You're looking older Philip…tired, in fact. You should give up this policing nonsense. Come work for my father. Do this, and we shall forget about this nasty little incident."

"I am only here for Prosecutor Xu."

Lucy Fu pouted, shrugged and laughed. "I should have known a lame duck like Xu Ya would fascinate you. You always did have a thing for the weak and the damaged – that dead girlfriend of yours, for instance. Did you know Xu Ya's husband died last summer in the most mysterious of circumstances? And that she has been seeing a psychiatrist ever since? Why the Procuratorate hired her I do not know. It was only a matter of time before she ran back to her parents. Both my father and I told Secretary Wu he was being unwise. Not that that insufferable and pompous little man ever takes advice. He quite tests Party Chief Li's patience some times."

"Lucy, I have to go."

Her eyes glittered. "Come see me again, Philip – and leave the ogre behind next time. You will be quite safe, I assure you."

"Goodbye, Lucy."

Mister Gan stepped out of his way and Philip Ye walked out of the apartment. He heard Lucy Fu's laughter following him down the corridor, as did Ma Meili's heavy footfalls.

In the lift, Ma Meili, said, "I am no ogre."

Philip Ye sighed, rattled by the encounter with Lucy Fu. "I know."

"Is that bad woman your friend?"

"Years ago, I used to date her."

Ma Meili's mouth opened and closed again. As the lift doors opened into the lobby, she said, "I do not like her."

"I don't like her either," he replied.

In the car, Philip Ye phoned Ms. Miao. "I need you to disturb the budget meeting…to pull the Chief out. A procuratorate investigator has been attacked and critically injured and a prosecutor has gone missing. The Willow Woman cult is responsible."

"Superintendent, I will do what I can," she replied.

Philip Ye then called Superintendent Zuo, waking him. "I need you to come in early."

Philip Ye heard giggling in the background.

"My wife says no," said Superintendent Zuo.

"Tell her I will buy her a new summer dress."

Philip Ye heard a brief whispered exchange followed by more laughter.

"My wife has suddenly changed her mind," said Superintendent Zuo. "She says she can do without me."

"Can you be in the office in under an hour?"

"Philip, is everything alright?"

Philip Ye found it hard to keep the emotion from his voice. "Remember Friday night...the body in the alley in Wukuaishi?"

"Sure."

"I've lost control of the investigation."

Superintendent Zuo asked no more questions. He promised to get to the office as soon as he could.

Philip Ye sat for a few moments to catch his breath.

"Prosecutor Xu has gone to meet with Professor Xiong, hasn't she?" said Ma Meili.

Philip Ye stared at her. "What makes you say that?"

She shrugged. "Because Professor Xiong is at the heart of this and because she already knows of him. I saw her face change when you mentioned his name back at The Silver Tree."

Philip Ye was both astonished and pleased. Her awareness was extraordinary. It was a pity she had not mentioned this last evening. It was a pity he had not noticed this himself.

"Sister, you will make an excellent detective one day," he said, meaning it.

She flushed, her face, for the first time since the death of Old Man Gao, lit with pleasure. She turned away from him, not wanting him to see the depth of her feeling.

CHAPTER FIFTY

Mouse came round slowly. The office girls were leaning over her, concerned, rubbing her hands and putting cold compresses on her head.

"Poor little Mouse."

"Poor sensitive little Mouse."

They asked her if she needed an ambulance. She said no. They asked her if she was related somehow to the fat man or knew the family. She said no – on both counts. They lifted her up, sat her in a chair and brought her a cup of tea. Then they squabbled among themselves, unable to decide what to do next. Chief Prosecutor Gong was away and Madame Ko had unusually taken some leave to help care for an elderly aunt forty minutes away in Pixian. None of the duty prosecutors were worth consulting – they would form a committee and after many hours come to no conclusion – so it was up to Mouse to track Prosecutor Xu down and tell her the bad news.

They pushed her phone into her hands and Mouse, despite feeling woozy, made a big show of being both relieved and surprised to find Prosecutor Xu's number. She let them all listen in, as expected, to the call being routed straight to the messaging service. Mouse left Prosecutor Xu a message, to call the Procuratorate as soon as possible. Not that she would ever collect that message. If Deng Shiru was dead, Mouse was certain that Prosecutor Xu was dead also. Deng Shiru would have defended her to his last breath. Her body just hadn't been found yet.

The girls started arguing among themselves again, trying to decide where Prosecutor Xu could possibly be. They eventually discounted her being out shopping along the Chunxi Road, adding – the girls had noticed – more designer items to her already extensive wardrobe. No modern woman would leave her phone off while out shopping. The only alternative that made sense to them was that Prosecutor Xu was with a man.

Did Mouse know who he was?

Was he from Chongqing?

Was he rich?

Was he handsome?

Was he married?

Mouse shook her head, feigning ignorance of Prosecutor Xu's personal life, already planning her escape.

"You cannot trust anyone." Those had been Prosecutor Xu's exact words. Prosecutor Xu and Deng Shiru might have been betrayed by someone inside the Procuratorate, someone who might have already learned what Mouse herself had been up to all night in the archive. Mouse knew, if she didn't want to end up in the afterlife with them, she needed to escape the Procuratorate and find a safe place to go.

Deng Shiru dead.

Prosecutor Xu dead.

It was almost too awful to believe.

All her hopes for the future – vain hopes, to be sure – had been destroyed. And it was her fault. In regard to Deng Shiru, that is. She had made certain Prosecutor Xu would hire him. If it hadn't been for her, he would have been working elsewhere – unhappily, perhaps, but alive.

The room spun about her as she got to her feet. She held onto the back of the chair to steady herself, waiting for the sickening motion to slow, her legs like jelly. Huiling had returned to reception, and most of the other girls were back in their chairs, speaking to their boyfriends or families on their phones, passing on the dreadful but fascinating news of Deng Shiru's murder. Mouse liked some of the girls. But outside of the Procuratorate she knew very little about them. Suspicious of them all now – any one of them could have been recruited by The Willow Woman cult – it was time to escape the Procuratorate. Mouse bent over with some difficulty and picked up her laptop bag, feeling she was going to retch. She told the girls she was going home, that she would feel better after a few hours in bed. She staggered out of the office and down the corridor, willing her knees not to buckle. She waved weakly as she passed Huiling.

"I told everyone that fat man would be no good," Huiling shouted after her.

Her heart in her mouth, fearing she might be stopped and her laptop taken from her, Mouse avoided all eye contact with the security guards manning the doors. She slipped past them without a word and soon found herself out on the street, a cool sun on her face, with no idea where to go.

Deng Shiru dead.

Prosecutor Xu dead.

Only Mouse – anxious little Mouse – left alive, for now.

She started walking, heedless of her direction, her mind only on the hole in her life left by Prosecutor Xu's and Deng Shiru's deaths as well as the important information she had gathered on her laptop. She needed to pass the information to someone she could trust, someone who could use it to do what needed to be done.

No such person came to mind. She needed time to think, a safe place to hide. She could not go home. She had lied to the girls about her destination. Her apartment would surely be the first place The Willow Woman cult would come looking for her. They would cut her throat and smash her laptop. If a big, strong man such as Deng Shiru could not fight them off, what hope would a little mouse have against their sharp knives?

Her parents came to mind. If she could get to her parents' village she would be safe. An hour's journey by slow train and then a meandering bus ride up into the hills, the village was secluded, surrounded by forest, forgotten by most, the villagers suspicious of strangers. It would be ideal. The Willow Woman cult would never find her there.

Mouse stopped to take her bearings, to figure out the best route – and mode of transport – to East Train Station. But, when she looked about her, she found herself on an unfamiliar street. She recognised no shops, no office buildings, no nearby landmarks. How long had she been walking aimlessly?

She pulled up her sleeve to check her watch but it was gone, perhaps fallen from her wrist when she had fainted back at the Procuratorate. She put her hand in her coat pocket for her phone to find her location on the map, but that was gone too, forgotten she realised, left lying on a desk after she had tried to call Prosecutor Xu. Panic began to claw at her. She tried to calm herself, reminding herself that she had at least a purse with money and credit cards, and the all-important laptop. She could buy a new phone anywhere. She had a good head for phone numbers, her parents' number she had never forgotten. She started walking again, hoping that if she pressed on she would suddenly figure out where she was. But when she came to the next road junction and then the junction after that, she may as well have been walking on the moon than in Chengdu. The city had become suddenly alien, threatening, the people walking by her, some jostling her rudely, all converts to The Willow Woman cult. Every face to her – man, woman or child – seemed murderous. She walked and walked. Soon there were blisters on her feet, and her breath was rasping in her throat. Her arms burned from having to carry the laptop.

She found a bench to sit upon, to rest awhile, to gather her thoughts and her courage. A youth threw himself down next to her, leering at her, egged on by a group of his friends. She turned her back to him, clutching her laptop bag to her chest.

"Go away!" she screamed.

None of the many passers-by ran to help her. This was the new China; people cared only for themselves. The youth began to laugh and, emboldened by her fear, began to touch her and stroke her hair. Mouse jumped up and ran off, glancing back from time to time, not seeing the youth but certain she was seeing others following her. It would not be long now. She was weakening. They would catch her and she would be stabbed in the street like Deng Shiru.

Oh, Deng Shiru, how will your spirit ever forgive me for what I have done to you? I should never have interfered with your life and helped you get that job.

She turned corner after corner, stumbling forward, her breath coming in gasps, still no closer to figuring out where she was. Then she almost stumbled into a payphone kiosk. All she could think of was her parents. She wanted to hear their voices one last time. She fumbled in her pocket for coins, spilling some of them to the ground. She put the phone to her ear but, before she could dial their number, a face flew into her mind, half-English, green eyes, more handsome than any man had a right to be – the kind of man that would never be seduced by the promises and lies of a cult. She punched in a number from memory.

"Homicide."

The voice was gruff, unknown to her.

"Please…please…I need to speak to Superintendent Ye."

"Who wants him?"

"It's Mouse…Mouse from the Procuratorate."

"Mouse?"

"Yes, I must speak to him…I am so frightened…there is this cult—"

"He is unavailable right now. This is Superintendent Zuo – may I help you?"

She nearly dropped the phone. It took her precious seconds to register the name, and put a face to that name. A car honked its horn nearby, startling her, four men inside staring out at her. She turned away from them, cringing, thinking they were going to jump out and seize her, make her disappear for ever.

Superintendent Zuo...yes, she knew of Superintendent Zuo. He was Philip Ye's colleague, wasn't he? Badly hurt at the Zhimin East Road shoot-out, he now walked with a limp. Hadn't she heard it said of him that he was a decent if rather morose man who went home to his family after every shift?

"Mouse, are you still there?"

"Please...please...you must help me, Superintendent Zuo. They are coming to kill me. Deng Shiru is dead. Prosecutor Xu is dead. I have worked all night and on my laptop—"

"Where are you, Mouse?"

Mouse looked about her, Chengdu closing in on her, threatening her, about to murder her. "I don't know," she said, tears rolling down her face.

CHAPTER FIFTY-ONE

Sunday

The PSB budget meeting was still in session. Down the corridor from the conference room, in a small office, Philip Ye delivered his verbal report. He stuck to the facts as he knew them, and was allowed to read from Fatty Deng's bloodstained notebook to fill in the gaps. Only Ma Meili was absent from his narrative. Philip Ye thought it best, for her protection, that her part in all this began and ended with the shooting of Old Man Gao.

Party Chief Li, Mayor Cang, Secretary Wu and Chief Di sat in judgement of him, with Ms. Miao taking notes. They heard him in silence, without interruption. When he was done, all eyes were on Party Chief Li, the real power in the room. Philip Ye had expected an explosion of temper but there was none. Instead, Party Chief Li made them all wait, taking a cigarette and carefully fixing it in the end of his ivory holder. As he lit the cigarette with a silver lighter, blowing smoke in Philip Ye's direction, he said, more to himself than to anyone else in the room, "This is a fucking disaster."

Ms. Miao made a note of these very words as Mayor Cang and Chief Di nodded sagely, in full agreement with him. They, too, lit cigarettes, filling the air of the room with blue-grey smoke. Secretary Wu, however, kept all his attention on Philip Ye, the most affected of all by his report.

"Superintendent, what is the latest news on Investigator Deng's condition?" he asked.

"He is in surgery, sir."

"Is he expected to live?"

"I cannot say."

Secretary Wu paused, frowning, unhappy with this reply. "And Prosecutor Xu – what are your thoughts on her situation?"

"Again, I cannot say."

"Will you at least speculate!" insisted Secretary Wu, exasperated.

Philip Ye chose his words carefully. "It is my belief, last evening in Madame Xiong's apartment on the university campus, Prosecutor Xu learned something of great importance – either to her personally, or to the investigation, or both. What she learned encouraged her to travel to Chongqing, probably to meet with Professor Xiong. From the notes I discovered in Prosecutor Xu's apartment, she had identified – correctly in my estimation – Professor Xiong to be the prime mover behind The Willow Woman cult. So she would have had no illusions about the danger she was putting herself in. It is highly likely, though, that Professor Xiong is known to her, and she to him. Professor Xiong is a famous personage in Chongqing, and relatively senior in the Party there. It is therefore possible she was intent on using a past social association with him to gain access to wherever he lives and gather intelligence on him. Or, she may have had another motive. I just don't know. I don't believe she intended to warn him of our investigation. From the legal research she had been doing last night, I would suggest she was determined to lead any prosecution against the cult in Chengdu."

"A glory-seeker then?" remarked Party Chief Li.

"It fits the evidence," said Philip Ye.

"So she is at Professor Xiong's residence as we speak?" asked Secretary Wu.

"At one of his residences," said Philip Ye. "He is wealthy and I have been led to believe he has a few. I have failed so far to identify them. Because of the nature of his government defence contract work, Professor Xiong is afforded State Security protection. I did not want to stir up a hornets' nest by inquiring too deeply until authorised to do so."

"Chongqing is a rats' nest, not a hornets' nest – always was, always will be," said Party Chief Li.

"What about her phone?" asked Secretary Wu.

"Switched off," replied Philip Ye.

"Is she dead, Superintendent?" asked Secretary Wu, anxiously.

"How would I know? I do not pretend to possess the gift of second sight."

Secretary Wu looked taken aback by Philip Ye's words. A faint smile crossed Ms. Miao's face as she continued making her notes.

"Enough of this," said Party Chief Li. "Who cares about Prosecutor Xu? Superintendent, please speculate on the nature of this cult. How dangerous is it?"

"I sense the cult is in an embryonic form," said Philip Ye, "not yet ready to reveal its true nature, its aims and ideals. Because of this it is dangerous to those who might betray it – Zhu Yi and Poppy, for example – and those investigating it. I have been puzzling about The Willow Woman herself. In the paintings of her, she is represented wearing a Sun Yat-sen suit – not quite a relic of the past but its wearing becoming rarer by the day. I suspect this is an important clue. At first glance this cult has every appearance of being religious in nature, but it is my suspicion – based on very little evidence, I have to admit – that its motives are political. Universities have always been hotbeds of leftist and rightist argument. But it is the leftists we should concern ourselves with here, those people who believe the reforms of the last thirty years have gone too far, that the reforms have been a betrayal of all the People's War of Liberation had achieved."

Party Chief Li turned to Chief Di, pointing a finger at him. "You will smash this Willow Woman cult in Chengdu. Set up a task force. Put Commissioner Ji in charge. He's the only one of you idiot police I trust. Don't inform State Security. If they've turned a blind eye to Professor Xiong's madness then heads will roll there anyway. I want all of those Singing Moon bars raided this evening. And don't go blundering into the university in front of all the cameras. Send in a small team on the quiet to pick up Madame Xiong – that is, if she hasn't already made a run for the airport. Leave that old fool, Professor Ou, to me. He should have been put out to pasture years ago. If he isn't one of the cultists, he has been stupid enough to let the cult flourish under his nose."

Party Chief Li then gave his full attention to Philip Ye. "And as for you, I'm sure there's no one in this room who doesn't believe this investigation hasn't been a joke from the start. Two murders, a procuratorate investigator fighting for his life, a prosecutor gone missing, and still to have no one in custody…it's a fucking disgrace. A few years ago, you only kept your job out of respect for your father's accomplishments. Mayor Ye Zihao made mistakes. But at least his heart was in the right place. When he enriched the family Ye with his business deals he always made sure he enriched Chengdu also. As for you, I just don't know. Where is your heart, Superintendent Ye? And is it even Chinese?"

Philip Ye remained impassive.

He'd heard much worse.

"Superintendent Ye," continued Party Chief Li, "I intend to review your future in the next few months."

Party Chief Li abruptly stood, the meeting as far as he was concerned, over.

"What about Prosecutor Xu?" asked Secretary Wu, anxiously.

Pink blotches appeared on Party Chief Li's face, revealing the extent of his fury for the very first time. He glared at Secretary Wu. "What about her? We have no authority over what happens in Chongqing. And none of us are going to communicate with anyone over there until we're done clearing up these cultists in our own backyard. If Prosecutor Xu returns with a story to tell, then so be it… if not, recruit someone with more fucking sense next time!"

Party Chief Li stormed out of the office, closely followed by Chief Di and Mayor Cang. Ms. Miao followed them, giving Philip Ye a concerned little wave as she went.

When they had been left alone, Secretary Wu dabbed at the sweat on his forehead with a handkerchief. "Philip, is there no hope for Ms. Xu?"

"How would I know?"

"Philip!"

Philip Ye felt his own temper rise. This was the first time he had spoken to Secretary Wu in years, not since his father's arrest and removal from office, when he had driven to Secretary Wu's house and pleaded with him to intervene on his father's behalf. Both Secretary Wu and his wife, Wang Jiyu, had said nothing and done nothing. From that day, both of them had been dead to Philip Ye. He stood up to leave.

"Philip, you cannot abandon her."

"As you abandoned my father?"

"What happened between us, Philip…between your father and me…that is nothing to do with Ms. Xu. She should not be punished for—"

"Why did you order Commissioner Wei to ask me to cast a protective net over her?"

"Does it matter?"

"It does to me."

"Because she is vulnerable."

"Why? Because she's a murderer and someone might uncover her crime? Because she's receiving psychiatric help? You have some nerve to recruit her and put her in a position of authority in the Legal and Disciplinary Procuracy Section, to hold the careers and livelihoods of hardworking officers in her grubby little hands. I have learned that the Procuratorate in Chongqing was glad to get rid of her...the PSB there also. Party Chief Li is correct: recruiting her doesn't inspire much confidence in your decision-making."

"Philip, you don't know what you're saying," said Secretary Wu, stunned by Philip Ye's vitriol.

"Don't I?"

Secretary Wu's eyes narrowed, colour returning to his face. "Years ago, before the earthquake, I was in Chongqing on business. While there, I was invited to attend a session in the Intermediate Court. I watched her present a case. Call it love, if you wish, Philip, but I was transfixed. I could not keep my eyes off her. Her clarity of expression, her grasp of detail, her confidence in her own abilities, her composure before the panel of judges – all of it took my breath away. Do not stare at me like that, Philip! I am no besotted youth. I admit that if I were thirty years younger and not content in my marriage I would pursue her to the four corners of the Empire. But on that day in court I realised that I had seen the future. She understands that if China is to take its rightful place among the leading nations of the world it must embrace the Rule of Law. When the earthquake struck and brought havoc to all our lives, I lost track of her. She married, left the Procuratorate, vanished from view. I don't know what her life was like then though there were rumours that her husband was a wicked man. I confess I was overjoyed when I heard he had died. Believe me when I tell you I know nothing of the circumstances."

"Did you ask her how he died?" asked Philip Ye.

"No."

"What were you thinking?"

"Philip, you must understand that a cloak has been thrown over the events of that summer night. It was my intention to be direct with her, to ask her straight what had happened to her husband. But something stilled my tongue. She had changed. Oh, the fires of justice still burned in her eyes, that same indomitable female spirit I'd marvelled at years before. But I saw also that her confidence had been shaken, that she had become more compassionate, more forgiving of the plight of the common people, of the difficulties people could get themselves into – not a bad thing, I think. I could not let her escape me, Philip. We need her in Chengdu."

"Is she a murderess?"

"No...in my heart I would say, no. Listen to me, Philip. Whatever happened in her marriage it left her fragile, vulnerable...damaged in some way. I spoke to my wife. She did not hesitate. She said, 'Let Philip watch over her. Philip will let no harm come to her.' It was cowardly of me to go through Commissioner Wei. I should have approached you directly. But I was frightened you would not listen to me. Regardless of your struggles of the last few years, of your lack of promotion, you inspire trust in all who know you. I hear much, Philip – much to make me proud. Perhaps it's that English blood in you that sets you apart from us...makes you able to stand firm in the midst of chaos. Forgive me for mentioning her name, but Isobel saw this quality in you. You were her rock, her security, while she danced about you like a whirlwind. Your father never understood this. He thought she had trapped you, whereas the opposite was true. It was a great pity that dreadful disease took her from you...from us all. Don't let Professor Xiong take Ms. Xu from us also. Remember the little hawk, Philip – the shikra. Remember how, when your father chose to give it its freedom, my wife and I walked the streets with you, searching for that beautiful bird. We didn't understand it then, that she hadn't been exercised properly, that she couldn't make a kill, that she was doomed because she was unfit to fly. Ms. Xu is *my* shikra, Philip...wounded, vulnerable, unable to make a kill. She is not yet fit to fly either. But there is a chance that we may yet bring Ms. Xu home. Go find my little hawk for me, Philip. I know you can do it."

Secretary Wu did not get the answer he was looking for. Philip Ye strode past him and out of the room without saying another word. When he had caught his breath, Secretary Wu phoned his wife, telling her all that had happened.

"How was Philip?" asked Wang Jiyu.

"Older...tired...lonely, I think...but impressive as always. His hatred of me...of you...has not lessened."

"Husband, you wasted your breath."

"I did?"

"I know him. He was like a son to me, remember? He was always going to Chongqing. It is who he is. He cannot help himself. He will bring Ms. Xu home."

"You really believe this?"

"I do not believe, Husband...I know."

CHAPTER FIFTY-TWO

Sunday

I t is said that, after living in Chongqing, every other city in China will seem flat. Chongqing is the 'Mountain City', nestled in the folds of gently sloping mountains, situated at the confluence of the Jialing and Yangzi rivers. But it is not just its topography that makes other cities pale in comparison, its Chongqing's personality, its drive, its energy, its 'in your face' attitude. Chongqing is gritty, pugnacious, determined, spicy and always hard to govern. Not for nothing is it described as the 'Chicago on the Yangzi'– though that particular moniker might have more to do with Chongqing's association with corruption and organised crime than its essential character. But, to say that Xu Ya was happy to be back after only a few weeks away, as she exited the North Train Station and climbed into the back of a taxi, would be a mistake. She was about to go visit an old friend and find out if he had committed a terrible crime.

"My home is now in Chengdu," she told the driver.

"Is that so?"

"It's not as boring as you might think," she added, feeling it necessary to defend her decision to leave, to begin another life elsewhere.

Chongqing is a mega-city, home to over thirty-two million souls, one of the most rapidly growing cities on the face of the earth – or so the world's media would have us believe. But Xu Ya knew this claim was false. If anything the actual number of residents of Chongqing City proper was declining, hovering at just above six million. The problem was with the Chinese method of counting. Chongqing was one of the four municipalities administered directly by the central government – along with Beijing, Tianjin and Shanghai. The Chongqing municipality took in a vast swathe of countryside with all its villages and a host of satellite cities. In fact, the official abbreviation for Chongqing is 'Yu', which harked back to the time of the Sui Dynasty when the whole area was known as Yu Prefecture. And so when the population of Chongqing is counted, it is the entirety of the municipality that is assessed, leading to that enormous number of people.

The history of the city dated back three thousand years. The city was once the capital of the ancient Ba Kingdom. Since then it had run through a succession of names. During the Song Dynasty, so the legend goes, when the city was known as Gongzhou, a prince was sent to tame the city and to rule over it. The city's rebellious nature was famous – or infamous – even then. The taming complete, the prince was rewarded by being made a duke of the region. And then, in the year 1190, when the prince ascended to the Dragon Throne as the Emperor Guangzhou, he renamed the city Chongqing – which means 'Double Happiness' – to celebrate these two successes.

Xu Ya wasn't sure about the city being a place of 'double happiness'. It had been nothing but a place of sadness for her. But the city had done much to form her character. Even in modern times the city had the reputation for being tough to govern. One glance in the mirror was all it took for Xu Ya to see that much of that trait had rubbed off.

"I hear that thousands of foreigners live in Chengdu," said the driver.

"That's true," she replied. "It thinks it's an international city."

The driver guffawed. "I also hear that the people are pretentious, think far too much of themselves, and are so lazy they would sit around drinking tea and playing *májiàng* all day if they could."

"That's also true," said Xu Ya, with a smirk.

"Then why do you live there?"

Because it's not Chongqing.

Because Chengdu has given me a chance of a new life.

Because Philip Ye is there.

"I had to move because of my job," she said.

The driver made consoling noises, then cursed and honked the horn furiously as another driver cut him up.

Before she was dropped off outside the house, the driver pointed at the sky. "There's a storm coming," he said.

The wind coming down from the mountains certainly tugged at

her long hair as she paid him. The clouds above were black and tumultuous. As the taxi roared off, she looked down at her clothes. She had not dressed for the weather. Wanting to impress Professor Xiong with her maturity and professionalism, she had opted for a thin trouser-suit in blue with matching leather handbag. No coat and no umbrella. Ten minutes in a rainstorm and the trouser-suit would be ruined. Still, there was nothing to be done about it now. She would have to make sure she didn't get caught out in the rain.

From the outside the house was much as she remembered it. She had forgotten about the surrounding high wall and the electronic gates though. Professor Xiong had a thing about physical security. The first time she had visited the house, on the occasion of the party for Professor Xiong for winning the first ever State Preeminent Supreme Technology award, those gates had been left wide open for all those who wanted to call and pay their respects – and there were many. Xu Ya's father had accompanied her then, nervous of Professor Xiong's reputation for seducing young women within sight of Yi Li, Professor Xiong's long-suffering wife. Xu Ya's mother had not attended, having met Professor Xiong and Yi Li before at some other social occasion. She had not taken to either of them. This suited Xu Ya. Her father was far from perfect but she much preferred his company over that of her mother.

That glittering evening, Xu Ya had not met Yi Li. For some reason – jealousy over her husband's success, some said – she had kept to her rooms. Nor did Xu Ya remember meeting or even hearing anyone mention the Professor's sister, Madame Xiong. Xu Ya had had no knowledge of any sister at that time. But Professor Xiong had been on wonderful form, spinning amusing scientific anecdotes for his adoring guests, drinking too much, flirting outrageously with all the young women and showing off his impressive house. It was very modern, full of the latest gadgets, and so extensive that it seemed to Xu Ya that she could wander for hours and still not see every room.

Her father had introduced her to the great man. She had been no more than eighteen or nineteen at the time. Socially awkward, she hadn't known whether to bow, curtsey or just extend her hand. She had managed an ugly mixture of all three. Professor Xiong had not seemed to mind. Taking her hand, he had looked deeply into her eyes and told her that he was glad she could attend. Then he had asked her to tell him everything about herself. So she had told him about being home-tutored, about the inspiring Beloved Mister Qin, and about the law, how it was to be her future.

Refusing to be side-lined, her father had said, "Professor, we are trying to convince her to consider other options."

But Professor Xiong would have none of this. Very publicly, he had rebuked her father. "You should be grateful that you have a daughter who knows her own mind. There is nothing more important than the law. Without the law, we are no better than pigs and dogs."

And he should know.

During the Cultural Revolution when the law had effectively ceased to be, Professor Xiong had been chased into his second floor office in Chongqing University of Technology (Chongqing Industrial College as it had been then) by a blood-thirsty mob of Red Guards. He had been thrown from the window, breaking both his legs. Those breaks had not healed properly – he had been refused medical attention for some hours – and he had relied upon a cane ever since.

Xu Ya's father had been infuriated by Professor Xiong's unlooked for interference in his daughter's future. But Xu Ya had been impressed by Professor Xiong and thought her father ridiculous for his reaction. She had even told her father so. He had responded then by leaving the party and dragging her along with him.

To repay her father for the embarrassment he had caused her, and perhaps to test those stories of Professor Xiong being the arch-seducer, Xu Ya had returned to Professor Xiong's house on a number of occasions without her parents' permission. To her dismay – was there something wrong with her? – Professor Xiong never tried to lay a finger on her. If he had done so, of course, she would have rejected him. But that had not stopped her being both confused and hurt by his lack of trying. He was, however, very fine company, always attentive, and always supportive of her future career. On one of these visits Xu Ya had even met the wife. But Xu Ya had found Yi Li sour-faced and far too extreme in her political views – Professor Xiong openly referred to her as the 'Red Harridan' – and Xu Ya gained the utmost sympathy for Professor Xiong's reputed, but unproven, need to seek female warmth and companionship elsewhere. The frequency of Xu Ya's visits had dwindled with the years, until her marriage when they had stopped altogether – but that was more her husband's fault than hers.

She pressed the entry button on the security gate. The speaker crackled into life and a woman's voice demanded to know her business and her identity.

"Prosecutor Xu – an old friend of the Professor's," she replied. "I am expected."

She waited, suddenly anxious, fearing that her mind had been read somehow, that she was there on false pretences, that she would be barred from entry. But then the gate began to creak open and she was through, slowly walking up the drive to the main entrance. She had hardly covered half the distance when, glancing up at the turbulent sky, the keen wind piercing her jacket, chilling her, when the thought hit her with tremendous force that she must be wrong. Junjie was as likely to be found in her own apartment back in Tranquil Mountain Pavilions as in Professor Xiong's house.

It was impossible.

There could be no reason for Junjie to be here, and even less of a reason for Professor Xiong to be involved in a religious cult. Professor Xiong was a scientist, an engineer – a wholly rational man. He had always made fun of religion. If a cultist had come calling he would have thrown them out on their ear.

Philip Ye had confused her with his suspicions. That, and her dislike of Madame Xiong, had made her see something that wasn't there.

Pareidolia – wasn't that what the scientists called it, a quite natural phenomenon where people saw faces in inanimate objects?

The sad face in the window in the photograph looking out at the celebrating group in the courtyard had been nothing but a trick of the light, a bizarre reflection created by the camera flash. So desperately had she wanted to find Junjie, to bring some good out of the tragedy of Old Man Gao's suicide, that she had superimposed Junjie's features onto that reflection. She now regretted her foolish behaviour of the night before, all that hiding herself from Investigator Deng and Philip Ye, staying up late reading and making notes, screwing her stomach up into knots, scaring Mouse silly. She would definitely have to buy Mouse a gift now. A hat or a scarf, Mouse cared little for trinkets.

The main door of the house opened before she could knock. Not a man as expected, but a young woman invited her in, exuding strength and health and vitality, in her mid-twenties, in a similar (but much cheaper) trouser-suit to hers, pistol very evident on her hip.

"Is this really necessary?" asked Xu Ya, as she was subjected to being patted down and the contents of her handbag emptied out onto a small table and rifled through. The Professor's security had never been this tight in the past.

"I will keep hold of your phone," the young woman replied. "You can have it back when you leave."

Wanting to protest, Xu Ya held her tongue. She did recall, from years before, Professor Xiong's dislike of mobile phones, describing them as the scourge of modern civilisation. At least she was allowed to roam the house unescorted. She was told the Professor was in his study. So she walked through the house, the past flooding back to her, the good times she had had here. There was incense in the air – sandalwood – and soft music emanating from the kitchen. That would be the household staff. A maid passed her by, bobbing and smiling as she did so. There was no sign of the droves of mindless cultists Xu Ya had feared, no paintings on any of the walls of The Willow Woman. Everything was as it should be.

In the study she found Professor Xiong sitting at his desk, engrossed in a technical journal. She tapped lightly on the door, feeling like an old student returned to call upon an adored tutor.

"Ms. Xu!" he cried.

He struggled to get out of his chair. But she would not let him. She ran to him, taking his hand, easing him back down. He had aged appreciably since she had last seen him. He was frailer, his skin tinged with grey, his face sagging at the jaw. She was surprised to find tears in her eyes.

"Forgive me, Professor – I should have visited you sooner. When I heard your wife had passed—"

"No, Ms. Xu, say no more," he said, his face stern, disapproving. "We are old friends. You have had your own difficulties these last few years. It is enough that you have come now and that my day is much brighter for it. You must tell me about your new life in Chengdu. Perhaps you don't remember but I teach at Chengdu National University once a week. I know the city well. Does it suit you? Oh, don't answer, Ms. Xu – it must! That city embraces the future as you now have to do. And my, what a beauty you've become. Have I not said it many times that a woman only blossoms after she has passed the age of thirty? I am sorry for the death of your husband. But, I confess, when I heard I shed tears of relief. For years I have been tormented by that terrible marriage you'd made. I even tried to speak to your father, to persuade him that something should be done. But he would not take my call. A proud man, a difficult man…."

"It is enough that you were concerned for me," she said, taking the seat that was offered her.

"Concerned? I couldn't get you out of my mind. Ah, but that is water under the bridge. Your husband is gone, and you are here, and it is like old times again. Except that I am now in my dotage and losing my wits."

A maid entered, carrying a tray of tea. She placed the tray on the side of Professor Xiong's desk. Xu Ya waved her away, happy to pour the tea for both of them. Professor Xiong watched her every move, his eyes red-rimmed and rheumy but full of warmth. When he had accepted a cup from her, she took her seat again, feeling so full of emotion she was about to burst.

"Ms. Xu, what is troubling you?" he asked.

"I am a foolish woman," she replied, taking a tissue from her handbag and dabbing at her own eyes.

"In what way are you foolish?"

"I look for love in places where there is none."

"Ms. Xu, it was but one marriage...a mistake any could have made."

She shook her head. "Professor, I do not learn. I am like a moth to a flame."

"You must explain."

The Willow Woman cult vanished from her mind, Junjie also, Xu Ya took Professor Xiong back to the time she had spent at Wuhan, and related how she had fallen for a melancholy *hùnxuè'ér*, how he had never once looked her way.

"It was as if I was invisible, Professor Xiong."

"Hardly," he replied. "This *hùnxuè'ér* is surely blind. But please continue. There is nothing we Chinese like better than a tragic romance."

Even to her own ears, it seemed so monstrous of her, so pathetic, to lay the blame for all of her life's misfortunes at the feet of Philip Ye. But this is indeed what she went on to do. She explained to Professor Xiong how Philip Ye's ignoring of her had forced her into a rash and disastrous marriage – a marriage that had destroyed her career, her confidence, and, for a time, her life.

"Professor Xiong, I know there is a flaw in my character that makes me desire men who are no good for me. But even this self-knowledge has not saved me. It is true that my only offer of a job has come Chengdu. But my first thought in taking the job was of him. Only last evening I had a meeting with him...a professional meeting. He is a policeman now. It was like I was a stranger to him. Four years I sat near or next to him at university and I am nothing but a stranger. Why is that, Professor Xiong? What is it about me that makes me so inconsequential? Do you think I should quit the Procuratorate in Chengdu and seek a position in another city elsewhere? I could choose a corporate life. I could go abroad. What do you think, Professor? Is there still hope for me?"

"Your distress is understandable, Ms. Xu."

"You must think me a self-pitying little thing."

"I do...but this is kindly meant, Ms. Xu. For I have suffered as you are suffering now. And I am not talking of physical suffering. The Red Guards breaking my legs did no good for me at all. After, I was as cruel and thoughtless and arrogant as ever. My dear wife nursed me through those terrible weeks and months and yet, as soon as I was up and about, I treated her with the same contempt as always. I will not go into the sordid details, Ms. Xu. I am just trying to make a point. It was only on her death two years ago when my real suffering began – the suffering of a soul in torment. It is what I see with you now, Ms. Xu. This *hùnxuè'ér* is just a symbol of your internal suffering – the hole in your soul that you think can never be filled. Your problem is, Ms. Xu, your self-centredness. Only through service to the greater good can that hole within ever be filled. You are a product of the Reform Era. I do not judge you for that, Ms. Xu. I was like you before the Reform Era had even begun. It took the death of my wife to make me think differently. I gave up smoking and drinking and, as for women…let me just say that I no longer treat them in the same way."

"Are you saying that your suffering from the loss of your wife has made you a better man?" she asked, with a sniff, unhappy to be described as self-centred even though she knew it to be true.

"Exactly, Ms. Xu."

"You must have loved her."

"No – not before her passing into the afterlife."

"Afterlife?"

"Do you believe in spirits, Ms. Xu?"

"No – superstitious nonsense."

Professor Xiong rocked back in his chair, laughing. "Yes, Ms. Xu – very good. The perfect answer. Years ago I would have given you top marks. But now…."

A cold hand touched her heart. He struggled to his feet. She helped him, putting his cane in his hand, suddenly afraid.

"Before we lunch together, Ms. Xu, I must show you something. I am going to heal your broken heart."

"But—"

"Ms. Xu, you must have faith. You have come to me today seeking solace. So let me provide it. She told me you would come."

"Who? Your sister?"

"Come, you will see."

He made her put her arm in his, and he took her from the study, his steps slow because of the pain in his legs, his cane tapping out their pace on the heavily varnished wooden floor.

CHAPTER FIFTY-THREE

Sunday

The sight of Superintendent Zuo limping toward her, surgical mask stretched over his face, would stay with Mouse until the end of her days. With great gentleness he had coaxed her off the kiosk phone. A kind policewoman had stayed on the line with her, speaking and singing to her to keep her spirits up. Mouse had hugged Superintendent Zuo tight for saving her from a brutal death at the hands of cultists, in front of a group of uniformed police who had also raced in their cars to find her, much to his great embarrassment.

"Investigator Deng is dead and Prosecutor Xu is missing, she cried into his shirt.

"Mouse, your information is incorrect," Superintendent Zuo told her, firmly. "Investigator Deng is badly hurt but not dead. As for Prosecutor Xu, we believe she has travelled to Chongqing. That is all the information we have on her."

Deng Shiru alive!

Mouse's heart soared.

But Prosecutor Xu in Chongqing? How could that be? Deng Shiru would never have left her side. He was not that sort of person. What had Prosecutor Xu gone and done?

Superintendent Zuo had driven her to PSB HQ. They had hardly travelled a hundred metres when Mouse suddenly recognised where she was. She must have been walking in circles for hours. She had been found hardly a stone's throw from the Procuratorate.

In the PSB HQ, Superintendent Zuo had taken her up to the Homicide office. He had sat her down at his desk and left her then, saying he had to run a quick errand but would return shortly with some tea.

"Do you have any hot chocolate?" she asked him, feeling she needed something more substantial.

"I'll see what I can do," he replied.

He had shut the door softly behind him leaving Mouse in the silent office. But she wasn't alone. At another desk, facing her, sat the largest woman she had ever seen. The woman was considering Mouse carefully with big, moon-eyes. Mouse's skin crawled. She knew this woman. She had seen her before, on TV, shooting a crazy old man dead. Frightened, not wanting to stir Constable Ma into further precipitate action, Mouse clamped her jaw shut.

Superintendent Zuo had hardly been gone a few minutes when in walked Philip Ye – Superintendent Ye, she corrected herself. Expecting to encounter him at some stage in the afternoon, it still came as a shock to her to find herself in the same room as someone so famous. Feeling she had somehow been dropped onto the page of a glossy society magazine, and not wanting that kind of exposure, Mouse dropped her head and hid her face, but not before seeing Constable Ma's lips curled up in an enigmatic half-smile.

Philip Ye stared at Mouse, curious. "Who are you?"

Mouse held her breath. He was in bad humour, she could tell. Dressed in a stylish dark-green suit, with gold watch-chain across his waistcoat and a silk yellow-patterned tie against a cream shirt – why didn't Deng Shiru own such clothes? – the air about him fizzled with impatience and the threat of violence. He was a homicide detective and yet it seemed as if it were he about to do murder.

"Well? Speak up!" he insisted.

"She is a little mouse," said Constable Ma.

"What?"

"From the Procuratorate," added Constable Ma.

'Procuratorate' was pronounced in such a way as to leave Mouse in little doubt that Constable Ma hated the institution. Mouse knew it was a common enough prejudice among the police – a prejudice reciprocated by many procuratorate personnel toward the PSB. Prosecutors criticised the police for having no understanding of the law, whereas police often considered prosecutors weak, more of an impediment to real justice than enforcers of it.

"Is this true?" asked Philip Ye. "Are you the Mouse who works for Prosecutor Xu?"

"I don't work for her...not directly," Mouse spluttered.

"But you have spoken to her recently, haven't you?" he said, planting himself in front of her.

The timely return of Superintendent Zuo saved her from further interrogation.

"Philip, leave her be," said Superintendent Zuo. "You're frightening her. Now tell me, do you still have a job?"

"Party Chief Li is to review my future," replied Philip Ye.

"It sounds like he's warming to you. Before you know it, you'll be invited to one of those tedious Shanghai Clique parties and your father will throw you out of the house for consorting with the enemy."

Superintendent Zuo pressed the cup of hot chocolate into Mouse's hands, giving her a reassuring wink as he did so.

Philip Ye was unamused. "He has put Commissioner Ji in charge of all operations against the cult. Madame Xiong is to be picked up at the university on the quiet – that's if she hasn't already made a run for the airport. And they're going to hit The Singing Moon bars tonight with all the manpower they can rustle up at short notice. Prosecutor Xu has been abandoned to her fate."

"So you're going after her?"

"Yes – I'm not wanted around here."

"Then I will go with you."

"No, I need you to get yourself onto the team going to the university to pick up Madame Xiong. Last evening Prosecutor Xu saw something in Madame Xiong's apartment – something important. I don't know what. But I need an experienced set of eyes in there."

"Are you sure?"

"Yes – but it would be useful if this little mouse opens her mouth and tells us everything she knows." Philip Ye's eyes flashed dangerously.

Superintendent Zuo turned toward Mouse, nudging her as he did so. "Well, how about it, Mouse?"

"Prosecutor Xu phoned me last night," she said, wanting to speak only to Superintendent Zuo.

"What did she ask you to do?"

"She wanted me to research the family Xiong."

"And is this research on this laptop you're keeping so close to you?"

Mouse nodded. "I'm meant to show it only to Prosecutor Xu. I'm not to trust anyone. We were supposed to meet tonight and have dinner."

"Did she give you any idea that she would be travelling to Chongqing?"

"No…when I heard about Investigator Deng in Wukuaishi…I thought she should have been with him. He would watch out for her. He's that sort of person. So she must have been taken, kidnapped. There's a house in Longquanyi District that—"

"Mouse, before we get to that, do you have an address for Professor Xiong?"

"He has a couple of properties in Chongqing."

"Mouse, give Philip these addresses because he has to start making plans. Then you can tell us everything you know about this house in Longquanyi District."

Not understanding why Prosecutor Xu would have travelled to Chongqing or what she would be hoping to achieve there, Mouse nevertheless opened up her laptop and switched it on. She called up the relevant information about Professor Xiong, pointed out the main Xiong residence in Chongqing, and leaned back while Philip Ye made notes off the screen. He then walked out of the office, his phone to his ear. When he returned, his manner was as intimidating as before. Superintendent Zuo encouraged her to tell the story of her night's researches. So, just for him, because he was a nice man, she began. She soon became so taken up with what she was saying, she didn't notice other officers enter the room and gather around her, including, for a time, Chief Di and Commissioner Ji. She would only learn, to her horror, about the seniority of some of her audience many hours later.

Mouse's story began and ended with the house in Longquanyi District, situated to the south-east of Chengdu. From the beginning of the 19th Century this house had been the country seat of the family Xiong, the house being the heart of a large estate on which tea, fruit – peaches, apples and loquats, to name a few – and other crops such as beets and sweet potatoes had been grown. Somehow, though much of the estate had been broken up and parcelled out to the peasants during the land reforms of the early 1950s, the house had remained in the family. And somehow, Professor Xiong's parents had not been vilified as landlords, shot as class enemies or sent away for re-education.

There had been three children: a boy and, born some years later, two girls. The boy, Xiong Yu, excelling in his studies, was sent away to school, first to Chengdu and then to Chongqing, going on to Chongqing Polytechnic College after deciding to commit himself to a future in electrical engineering. In 1960, with or without his parents' permission – the records suggest without – he married Yi Li, a prominent Party activist and fellow student at the college. This was about the same time that the college had invited him to become a member of staff and conduct secret ordnance research, the university by then having a close relationship with the People's Liberation Army. In 1965 he was made a full professor. In 1966, at the height of the chaos created by the Cultural Revolution, he was chased by a mob of rampaging Red Guards and thrown from his office window on the second floor, breaking both his legs. With the local Party committees in uproar – the older revolutionaries unable to cope with, or comprehend, the passions that had been aroused among the youth by the Cultural Revolution – Yi Li resigned her many positions and concentrated on nursing her husband back to health. When he did return to the university, a local military unit provided guards so his life, and his work, would never be endangered again.

Despite Yi Li's tender care, Professor Xiong never lost his roving eye for the ladies. There were numerous affairs, the most notable of which was with Bao Xiao, a former student of his. She gave birth to a son, Bao Ling, in 1974. But, by then, the affair had petered out and no father was registered on the birth certificate. Bao Xiao got a job in a factory, never married, and raised her son on her own. She died of a brain tumour in 2005. After a few scrapes with the law in his youth, Bao Ling had settled into a steady life as a carpet-fitter in Chongqing. He would have to wait until after Yi Li had died to be acknowledged by Professor Xiong as his son. It was about the time of that formal acknowledgement that Bao Ling came into a lot of money. Mouse made it clear that further research would have to be done to discover its source, whether the money was given him by Professor Xiong. But Bao Ling soon gave up the carpet-fitting business, came to Chengdu, and began opening up what soon proved to be a popular chain of bars, all named 'The Singing Moon.'

Mouse was forced to admit that the next part of the story depended more on local gossip, and on the long memories of some of her contacts, rather than on any documentary evidence. The younger daughter, Xiong Rong, had died suddenly in 1970. There is no record of her suffering from any type of chronic condition or that she was receiving medical treatment of any kind. Not long after, the elder daughter, Xiong Lan, was committed to a psychiatric hospital in Chengdu. Her records from the hospital are either lost or destroyed. It is not known whether the parents ever visited her. After the parents had died, the house in Longquanyi District fell into disuse and disrepair. In 1976, Xiong Lan, on the recognisance of her brother, Professor Xiong, was released from the psychiatric hospital. With his help she found work in the administration office at Chengdu

National University. She is there still, now as Head of Administration. As to the cause of death of Xiong Rong, no formal investigation ever took place. This could be because of the parent's connections or maybe just because, in those crazy days, the police had been tasked more with the investigation of the activities – real and imagined – of reactionaries, capitalist roaders, domestic subversives and agitators, and the odd foreign spy rather than with any real criminality committed by the people. Mouse said no more on this, but she left her audience in no doubt that she suspected Madame Xiong of having the death of a sister on her conscience – if she had a conscience, that is.

But Mouse left the most important information until the last. She skipped quickly over Professor Xiong's most recent history in Chongqing. She did not dwell on the international fame he had earned, how proud the Party was of him in Chongqing or the technology awards he had been presented with. Nor did she linger on how badly he had been affected by the death of his wife, Yi Li, how – according to her source within State Security – his behaviour had become depressed and erratic, that he had had to be removed from the board of his own company (on the orders of the Central Organisation Department), that his passport had been taken from him, and that, though his protective detail had been reduced considerably (as he was no longer active and considered less of a risk) a constant awareness of his activities was still required.

It was the old house in Longquanyi District that Mouse most wanted to discuss. The ancestral Xiong family home had come back to life. Mouse had been sent copies of police reports that had been filed away in the local offices of the Procuratorate in Longquanyi District that referred to suspicious activity at the house. The old estate was considered wilderness by most and police had been dispatched to investigate what, if anything, was going on. They found building contractors at work refurbishing the house and clearing some of the grounds, and were told that the family was planning to return in the near future. The contractors' permissions were all in place, building plans had been properly filed, and the workforce – though not local and to be resented for that – contained no obvious criminal element. No further police reports had been lodged and all police interest in the house seemed to have ceased. With a dramatic sigh, Mouse left her audience in no doubt that she found this very suspicious in light of what she had learned from the building inspector, and that when action was taken against the house it might well be worth leaving the local boys out of the loop.

She had spoken personally to the building inspector – a very frightened man. Building plans for the refurbishment had actually been agreed in advance with his office. But, when he had gone out to inspect the property, he, too, had been refused entry. However, he could see from the outside that the work being done was not as agreed, and that the house was now more like a fortress than the retirement home for an old university scholar he had originally understood it to be. He saw many young people milling about the house. Some of them started throwing stones at him so he left for the day. He complained to the local police but was told to mind his own business. He made a report to his superior for legal action to be taken. He then wrote a second report when his first report was ignored. This, too, was ignored. Though he was happy to talk to a prosecutor at a secure location, he preferred to forget the whole matter and wait patiently for his transfer to another office to come through. He had, though, sent her the digital photographs he had taken of the house, including some wider landscape shots of the hilly, difficult countryside and of the limited routes of access to the house. She clicked them one by one on her screen.

"This is where the cult must have its base," said Mouse. "Professor Xiong needed somewhere out of sight of State Security. This is why I was so frightened. If the cult knew I had uncovered this information they would certainly try to kill me."

Mouse looked around, but only Superintendent Zuo remained with her. Other officers stood around the office in groups, speaking in urgent and hushed tones. Constable Ma still stared at her from across the room. Of Philip Ye there was no sign. Mouse was dismayed.

"Mouse, you have done very well," said Superintendent Zuo.

"But the house—"

"Mouse, it is going to be difficult enough to put together the teams to strike at The Singing Moon bars across the city tonight without word leaking out. This house in Longquanyi District will have to wait for another day."

"The cultists may have all escaped by then."

"Then so be it," said Superintendent Zuo. "Not all of them will be murderers. Most, I suspect, will be misguided young people. When the first arrests are made this evening, we will quickly learn who ordered the attack on Investigator Deng, who the really bad people are."

"But what if Prosecutor Xu has been taken from Chongqing, or from wherever she has gone, to this house? What if they kill her when they learn about the raids on The Singing Moon bars in Chengdu?"

"Mouse, we cannot always save everybody," said Superintendent Zuo.

Mouse felt she was about to cry again. "But Prosecutor Xu is a good person...impulsive, I know...but a good person. Maybe if I go—"

Superintendent Zuo put his hand on her shoulder. "Mouse, you have done your part...and you have done it very well. If it is Prosecutor Xu's karma to survive this day then you will see her again."

"I do not believe in karma."

"How about Heaven?"

"No."

"Then how about him?" Superintendent Zuo nodded toward Philip Ye who had just returned.

"Constable Ma, Mouse...you're both with me!" snapped Philip Ye, putting on his raincoat.

Constable Ma jumped up, eager, but the order stunned Mouse. She had assumed she would be allowed to stay safe in the Homicide office for the rest of the day – or, at least, until as many cult members had been rounded up as was possible.

"Mouse, hurry up, we have to move," said Philip Ye, opening the door for Constable Ma.

Mouse looked to Superintendent Zuo.

"Go on – you'll be fine," he reassured her.

Not knowing where she was to be taken, Mouse packed her laptop away and put her coat and hat back on.

CHAPTER FIFTY-FOUR

Sunday

Professor Xiong produced a key from his trouser pocket and opened the door leading to the suite of rooms once occupied by his late wife. "No one is usually allowed in here, Ms. Xu. But I must show you. You must understand everything that she was…and is."

Xu Ya wrinkled her nose at the stale air that assaulted her. She found herself in a sitting-room smelling of age, decay and death – so different to the rest of the house. A long sofa and chairs were set out as if to receive guests. But the floor was uninviting bare stone, and the room was unheated – a perfect habitat for ghosts, she thought, if such children's fantasies existed. From one wall, a large portrait of Mao Zedong looked down on her. There was not an ornament to be seen, nor a window to the outside world. If this room was representative of Yi Li's outlook on life then hers was a very stark perspective indeed.

"I used to joke with her," said Professor Xiong. "I said she would rather live in rooms reminiscent of the caves the Party leadership had to hide away from the Nationalists and the Japanese in the old Communist capital at Yan'an. I offered her every comfort. She refused all. Her purity, her commitment to the cause was everything to her. Come, Ms. Xu, here is her study."

He opened a door to what Xu Ya had assumed to be a cupboard to reveal what was little more than a box room. It also had no window. Professor Xiong switched on a dim electric light. There was a small writing-desk with a hard stool, a few bookcases stuffed with paperbacks and a pile of minutes from ancient Party committee meetings stood in the corner almost waist-high. Xu Ya had seen more attractive prison cells. She glanced down at the faded spines of some of the paperbacks, seeing the writings of Lu Xun – a favourite of Mao Zedong – and also the novel *Red Crag* by Luo Guangbing and Yang Yiyin, a favourite of her own from her childhood.

Out of place, incongruous, standing proud on the writing-desk was a photograph in a silver frame. Not only was it too big for the desk and would impede anyone working there, Yi Li had not seemed the sentimental type. Xu Ya had the distinct impression that it had been placed there just prior to her visit. Professor Xiong picked it up and passed it to her, anxious for her to see. It was a faded wedding shot, in black and white, two young people staring out of the distant past, both very serious, as if the future of China depended on their union. Both were dressed in the ubiquitous Sun Yat-sen suits of the time, standing close together, almost at attention in the military fashion. The young Yi Li held a tired-looking bouquet of flowers in her hands. The scene made Xu Ya feel sad, depressed even, though she knew she was not one to judge; her wedding photographs, all destroyed now, had been much worse.

"When was this taken?" she asked.

"Autumn, 1960 – we were both twenty-one."

"She was very beautiful," Xu Ya lied, thinking Yi Li had made the right decision to hide herself away in her 'cave'.

"You remind me of her."

Oh, I certainly hope not, thought Xu Ya, conscious that Professor Xiong was standing a little too close to her. She passed the photograph back to him and stepped away slightly, but not so quickly he would notice. He placed the photograph back gently on the desk.

"Yi Li and I were very different people, of course," he said. "I was born of an old aristocratic lineage. We had a grand estate in Longquanyi District. My father was a patriot though. He died fighting the Japanese. I do not know what he would have thought of Yi Li. He would have expected me to marry someone more traditional, someone less revolutionary." Professor Xiong laughed at his own words. "It was her passion that attracted me to her. She was, in many ways, the female embodiment of the revolution. Her parents were both long-time activists for the Party. Her father had studied abroad, in France and in the Soviet Union during the 1920s. Her revolutionary instruction began sitting on his knee. And she was to suffer for the revolution. Her parents were both arrested by the Nationalists in Chongqing in 1946, never to be seen again."

"How did Yi Li survive?" asked Xu Ya, feeling more sympathy for her now.

"It pains me to say it, Ms. Xu, but I do not know. It never occurred to me to ask. I suppose she was taken in by relatives and friends. But I only told you about her parents to make you understand that for Yi Li the revolution was a matter of blood. She had always understood what was at stake, whereas I only joined the Party to further my own career. Ms. Xu, you have revealed to me the extent of your self-centredness through your futile search to find the ideal romantic partner. But, though criticism is due to you, you should always remember that my crimes have been far worse. I paid only lip-service to the Party. I treated my wife badly. Though through my designs and inventions I have contributed to the defence of China, my motivations have always been personal, self-aggrandising. Even the lecturing I undertook here in Chongqing and in Chengdu was more about the needs of my own ego than that of the students. With the coming of the Reform Era, despite my wife's protestations, I set up a private company and utilised every military contact I had made through the years to make more money than I could ever spend or even properly count. For me, Ms. Xu, as you can see, it was as if the revolution never happened."

"But you did suffer, Professor...in the 1960s...during the Cultural Revolution."

"Ah, that old tale, Ms. Xu. Indeed, I was attacked and crippled back in 1966, but I was not really damaged, if you understand me. I was the same flawed man after that I had been before. It was my wife who really suffered during that awful time. It was not the Red Guards that bothered her. She was fully supportive of their cause, if not always of their methods. When she was caring for me she would happily tell me that I had brought my injuries upon myself. You see, Ms. Xu, being a woman of wisdom and far-reaching insight, Yi Li had already seen the need for the Cultural Revolution. She knew the Party had been taken over by monsters and snakes: the black-hearted capitalist roaders. She took full blame for what had happened to the local Party committees in Chongqing, their leaning to the right. As a senior Party cadre she could do no more than offer her resignation. After helping me recover, as the good wife she was, she then took to her rooms and began a period of introspection, self-criticism and a study of Mao Zedong Thought that would last until the end of her life."

More likely she resigned her posts to save her own skin, mused Xu Ya, thinking it politic not to mention this suspicion.

•   •   •

What was the Cultural Revolution?

Even now, fifty years later, Xu Ya found it difficult to say – or even to explain how it had come about.

The simple explanation – and to many the most compelling – was that following the failure of the Great Leap Forward and the cata-strophe of the resulting famine that had led to the deaths of upwards of thirty million people, Mao Zedong had feared that his leadership of the Party and the dominance of his thinking in regard to the future of China was soon to be challenged. Mao Zedong also feared – correctly, many would conclude – a rightward shift of the Party. So Mao Zedong turned to those *outside* of the Party – the masses – and launched the Great Proletarian Cultural Revolution: essentially another civil war, with the Party this time adjudged to be the enemy. Hypnotised by Mao Zedong's carefully manufactured 'cult of personality', the masses, primarily the youth, believing Mao Zedong could do no wrong, named themselves 'Red Guards' and began to attack all symbols of authority – which included very senior Party officials, teachers and anything that smacked of China's heritage and tradition, the 'four olds': old customs, old culture, old habits and old ideas.

This explanation, though comforting to those – mainly in the West – who liked to demonise Mao Zedong and to imagine the Chinese people as his puppets and poor victims, does not really satisfy. For example, it is fine to say that the leader of a cult is evil, but does that absolve the people from being attracted to, and dependent on, the leader of the cult in the first instance? Yes, there is 'brain washing', and yes there is the destruction of the personality once within the cult so that the leader's wishes are never contradicted; but, as human beings, are we not all responsible for what we think, say and do? Xu Ya did not blame her husband for seducing her into a loveless marriage; she blamed her own character for attracting that seduction to herself. Should then the Chinese people not shoulder the blame for their personal failures in being swept up by the fever of the Cultural Revolution and perpetrating all manner of violence and destruction?

And so, more nuanced, more feasible interpretations – and there-fore more attractive to Xu Ya – could be made for the Cultural Revo-lution. In the early 1960s there had been simmering and longstanding factional disputes within the Party dating back to the 1930s and 1940s, especially between those based at the Party capital at Yan'an and those who had worked selflessly and tirelessly incognito for the cause throughout the rest of China under the most dangerous of conditions – old hatreds and ideological differences that could no longer be suppressed at that time. There were also the social problems and tensions that had created a toxic mixture of anger and bitterness among the people, a powder keg waiting to explode. And, finally, there was the peculiar international situation, the strained relations with the Soviet Union, the expanding American military effort not far away in South-East Asia, and a growing sense of isolation the people felt from the rest of the international community.

Whatever the truth, the Cultural Revolution was in many ways – but, surprisingly, not in all ways – a cataclysm. China descended into violence and madness. The local Party infrastructure was attacked by the Red Guards and effectively dismantled. The police were ordered to stand aside. Worst of all, to Xu Ya's mind, the entire legal system was destroyed, the law being denounced as a bourgeois form of restraint designed to hold back the revolutionary masses.

It took two years of chaos before an ecstatic Mao Zedong decided he had achieved all his aims, including that of preserving his position at the head of the Party, and been persuaded by those closest to him that enough was enough. It could be argued that the Cultural Revolution continued – albeit, in a less destructive form – until Mao Zedong's death in 1976. But it was back in 1968 that he sent in the military to reassert control across the country. Ironically, a large number of Red Guards died in clashes with the army, or in the internecine conflicts that had broken out between different Red Guard groups. Also millions of young people, who had made up the backbone of the Red Guards, were sent into the countryside to 'learn from the peasants'. And yet, through it all, Yi Li, the Red Harridan herself, had hidden herself away in the safety of her husband's house.

Xu Ya kept this to herself but she felt nothing but contempt for Yi Li.

"I confess, Ms. Xu, I did not understand my wife until after she had died," said Professor Xiong. "Unlike you and me, she was never tainted by self-centredness. She thought only of the people. I saw her lose her temper only once, back in 1978, when she spoke of the announced reforms of Deng Xiaoping, saying, 'That black-hearted demon has betrayed us all.' As you would expect, Ms. Xu, I laughed at her. I could not predict the future as she could. I could not see that a beast had been unleashed among the people, that individualism would soon run rampant, that the people's lust for power and wealth would soon be insatiable. We have become a capitalist country in all but name. Is it any wonder so many are being treated for depression these days? Is it any wonder so many have gone insane? But, do not look so sad, Ms. Xu. Did I not promise you that I was about to heal your broken heart? When my wife died, I was bereft, Ms. Xu. I was consumed by bitterness and grief. I had never treated her with kindness or seen her for what she was. I could not eat or drink. I took to my own bed for many days. Do you not agree that we do not realise how much we cherish a person until that person is gone?"

"I suppose," replied Xu Ya, unconvinced, the memory of her husband no kinder for his passing.

"Early one morning, Ms. Xu, three months after her death, after I had wrestled with my conscience through another sleepless night, I sat up in bed to find my wife standing beside me, a ghost, a luminous being, her beauty restored, the ravages of her final illness all healed. It was incredible, quite incredible. As a scientist and engineer, if anyone had come to me beforehand and told me such a story I would have laughed in their faces and thrown them out of the house. But it was true, Ms. Xu. My wife was really there. Her appearance before me overturned everything I had ever believed."

He paused to weigh Xu Ya's reaction. She tried to keep a straight face, trying neither to laugh nor furrow her brow in condemnation.

"Ms. Xu, you are a lawyer. That I accept. Your job is to weigh evidence. I should have realised you would not be so easily persuaded. But remember, I am not one of the common people. My mind is not full of childish tales of hungry ghosts, fox-spirits and demons. I tell you she was standing before me as real as you are now. As her husband of fifty years, how could I not recognise her?"

"I believe you had a dream – a nice dream," she said, not wanting to anger him.

"It is evidence you need, isn't it, Ms. Xu?"

She nodded, wishing she had not come, that she'd had the good sense after hearing from Philip Ye the story told by the witness Yao Lin about the Professor crying in public over the death of his wife, to realise that all was not right with him, that grief and guilt had disturbed his mind.

"Then it is evidence you shall have, Ms. Xu," he said, pulling open the top drawer of the desk with a dramatic flourish.

CHAPTER FIFTY-FIVE

Sunday

Before Thursday, Captain Wang Jian of the People's Armed Police Force had never heard of Philip Ye.

Born in Beijing, Captain Wang had lived an itinerant life. As a boy, he had moved from garrison to garrison as his father's career had advanced, but never to Chengdu. And then, after he had followed his father into the PAP, he had only had the chance to visit Chengdu on occasion, for short periods of time, for rest and recuperation after testing tours of duty working diplomatic protection in Iraq and Afghanistan, and, much more recently, as a company commander in the Tibet Autonomous Region. During these tours he had learned as best he could how to deal with incomprehensible and recalcitrant peoples, as well as with the extremes of heat, cold and altitude – the last having severely debilitated him at times, giving him headaches, nausea, breathlessness and the occasional bout of dark depression. In the deserts of the Middle East and the high passes of Tibet, he had had little time, and certainly not the inclination, to concern himself with the history and politics of Chengdu. He had never heard of the family Ye or the arrival of the Shanghai Clique. And he had had no idea that Mayor Ye had sired a *hùnxuè'ér* son whose features were so Western that if one were in the midst of a drunken haze he could easily be mistake for a full-blood *lǎowài*.

The municipal police of Wukuaishi Station, sympathetic for the most part, had done their best to educate him after the fight with Philip Ye. They had cleaned him up, taken his uniform to be laundered and pressed, let him sleep off the effects of all the alcohol he had imbibed, and, after feeding him, had patiently explained to him all he needed to know. They showed him the footage of his one-sided fight with Philip Ye being repeated again and again on TV. They also explained that the same footage had been uploaded onto the internet and would be available for viewing until the end of time. This, the constables found very amusing. But they had consoled him when his father would not take his calls from the station. Fathers could be like that, they said. They also got angry on his behalf when it was discovered that all of the fellow PAP officers he'd been out drinking with had got safely back to the barracks after abandoning him. The constables told him not to worry, that some good would come out of all this. He would not be a bachelor for long. Every woman in Chengdu who was single – and many who weren't – would have studied the footage of the fight with great interest. He had a great media profile now, they explained. They told him that for the short time he had been standing upright squaring off to Philip Ye, he had looked quite dashing. The many women who had tried and failed to get close to Philip Ye, would surely make a play for him instead.

Mister Ye.

That's what the municipal police called him.

His rank was unimportant.

Don't mess with Mister Ye again, the young constables advised him.

By late afternoon, he was sober enough to be taken through to the office of Superintendent Tan.

"Captain Wang, you must be fined for your disgraceful behaviour, of course."

"Superintendent, I acknowledge I was at fault. I apologise for the inconvenience I have caused you and your officers."

"Captain, I appreciate that you wished to blow off some steam as you have just returned from a difficult tour in Tibet. But I must warn you never to disturb the peace in Wukuaishi again. Also, do not attempt to take revenge against Mister Ye. It would not go well for you. Forget the Shanghai Clique. They may hold all the important posts in Chengdu, but the underbelly of the city is still very much owned by the family Ye. Pick a fight with that family and you will wish you were back in Lhasa dousing the flames of burning monks."

"I have no argument with Mister Ye."

"I am glad to hear it," said Boxer Tan, most relieved.

As both Captain Wang and his father – Major-General Wang, the newly promoted commander of all PAP units in Sichuan Province – were to be based in Chengdu for an extended period of time, his father had rented an apartment for them both in the central Jinjiang District. At a strained dinner that Thursday evening, his father had chosen not to chastise him. That pleasure awaited a Board of Inquiry set to convene on Monday morning. Until then he was to be confined to the barracks or his father's apartment – his choice. He had chosen the apartment.

"I have spoken to Superintendent Ye today," said General Wang, in between mouthfuls of delicious dry-fried chicken. "He has apologised to me. It seems a number of PAP uniforms have been stolen recently and hoodlums have been masquerading about the city in them. With you drunk and out of control he could not tell the difference. It suits me to believe him. You are to attend a meeting at the Procuratorate in the morning. There you will shake hands with Superintendent Ye while Chief Prosecutor Gong endeavours to explain away this idiotic fracas to the people."

"Yes, Father."

The handshake at the Procuratorate – in reality a photoshoot directed by the smarmy Chief Prosecutor – was not a pleasant experience for Captain Wang. He had tried to engage Philip Ye in conversation, only to be cold-shouldered. That evening, over a more convivial dinner, very pleased with the press release, his father had asked him, "What was he like?"

"Who, Father?"

"Philip Ye."

Captain Wang considered the question carefully for a moment and then said, "He is an enigma."

"How so?"

"His features are predominantly Western, but search deep into his green eyes…really deep…and you will see that he is very much Chinese. He has the eyes of a cat but the soul of a dragon…a very dangerous dragon. Outwardly he is cool and charming, but beneath the façade – and it is a façade, Father – he is a volatile and unpredictable man, maybe even a fanatic of some kind. He plays the game very well. But anyone who thinks Philip Ye is not his own master is blind. As a friend I would never turn my back on him, as an enemy I would never underestimate him."

Major-General Wang took a sip of beer. "I would rather you were friends with Philip Ye than those buffoons you were running around with the other night. I hear there are parties at his father's house. His father may be in disgrace but many men of influence attend those parties. These men could be good for your career."

"I don't believe Philip Ye to be the friendly type."

"The family Ye is famous in Chengdu."

"Or infamous, Father – depending on your point of view."

Major-General Wang grunted, conceding the point.

That weekend, Captain Wang occupied himself by reading a history in English of the development of gunpowder in China. Mid-Sunday afternoon, the book almost finished, feeling one of his black Tibetan depressions lurking nearby, Captain Wang received a phone call from his father.

"Captain, as of this moment, a Special Tactical Unit has been mobilised. You have been personally requested by the People's Police – outside of the usual channels, I should add – so you shall lead the unit. Do a good job and this will do much to influence the Board of Inquiry's decision on Monday. Expect visitors at the apartment within the next hour. They will brief you."

His father was gone before Captain Wang could frame any useful questions. He quickly showered and changed into his uniform, thinking it must be a drill of some kind. But soon enough he began to think otherwise; for drills to be properly effective, extensive planning had to be done. He had heard of no such plans being made. He switched on the TV but all seemed relatively quiet in Chengdu. There was a lot of police activity up in Wukuaishi following a stabbing, but that was all. He was mulling all this over when there came a knock at the door sooner than expected. He examined himself in the mirror, saw his uniform was immaculate, put his best fighting face on, and opened the door.

"Captain Wang, are you recovered?" asked Philip Ye, with a grin.

Dumbstruck, Captain Wang had no adequate reply. Philip Ye walked past him into the apartment, followed by a scowling giant of a woman, she whom Captain Wang remembered very well from the shooting of that old man on the Yusai Road. Her fierce expression told him there was nothing wrong with her memory either. He tried to shut the door, wondering what sort of evil trick life might be playing on him now, when he heard a squeal. He had almost trapped a woman in the doorway – a woman so small she could have easily been mistaken for a child.

"Forgive me," he said.

"It happens a lot," replied Mouse, scurrying inside.

Captain Wang thought her very attractive, except her hat and coat were too big for her, and the bag she was lugging about too heavy.

He shut the door, properly this time, the depression he'd been resisting all weekend forgotten.

"Quickly, Mouse – show the Captain what he's up against," said Philip Ye.

Captain Wang stood idly by as the tiny woman set up the laptop on the table and switched it on. He was disturbed by the big woman's large, unforgiving eyes boring into him. He tried to estimate her height, weight and strength, not liking the conclusions he came to.

"Captain, please concentrate," said Philip Ye. "I must be brief as I cannot linger. Mouse is about to show you building plans and photographs of a house situated in a remote area of Longquanyi District. The plans you must treat with caution, however. We believe the new construction is substantially different. Copies will be left for you on a memory stick. We believe this house is being used by a small religious cult that is responsible for two homicides during the last few days as well as an attack on a procuratorate investigator. A prosecutor is also missing, possibly kidnapped. The decision has been taken to round up as many cultists as possible, not only as part of the ongoing homicide investigations but also to discover more about this cult's beliefs and motivations. We have only enough available manpower at short notice to hit addresses within Chengdu – which includes local SWAT and PAP units. Mouse here has been collating intelligence reports about this house in Longquanyi District. She has identified a lot of unusual activity there. Unfortunately the intelligence reports dried up last summer. This leads us to presume either that the house has fallen into disuse again or that the local police have been paid off. I suspect the latter."

"So you wish me to assault the house?"

"Yes, Captain, this evening."

Captain Wang swallowed, his mouth dry. In the photographs he could see barbed wire mounted on the surrounding high walls, sturdy metal gates and metal grills over the windows. It was not going to be easy. "Is this all the information you have?"

"I'm afraid so."

"Weapons?"

"Unknown – most likely knives."

"Numbers at the site?"

"Unknown."

Captain Wang stared at Philip Ye in disbelief. "What *do* you know?"

"I know that your father told me that you were always up for a challenge, that you'd done one tour of duty with a Snow Leopards hostage-rescue team, and that there a Board of Inquiry will sit on Monday morning that it would be useful for you to impress."

"My father says a lot of things."

"You were my choice, Captain."

"Do you want to get me killed because of my stupid behaviour the other day?"

"No, Captain – but you do seem to care about how we enforcers of the law treat the people. Most of these cultists will be no more than misguided youngsters. I am sure you will do what you can to minimise injuries and loss of life."

"Is that so?"

"I also know you can't handle your drink," said Philip Ye, grinning again.

Captain Wang resented Philip Ye needling him, especially in front of the women. But the operation was a chance to get out of the apartment. And, if the operation proved a success, the Board of Inquiry would indeed be impressed. If not....

"Who's leading the raids across the city?" he asked. "I will need to coordinate with them."

"Commissioner Ji – I've given his number to Constable Ma Meili here," replied Philip Ye, indicating the big woman. "She will accompany your team."

Captain Wang was about to protest, but it was Constable Ma who spoke up first.

"Superintendent, please let me go to Chongqing with you," she begged.

Philip Ye raised an admonitory finger. "No, Sister, we have discussed this. You will go with Captain Wang. You will follow his orders. He will keep you safe. If Junjie is anywhere, he will be at this house in Longquanyi District. I feel it in my bones. Junjie is important to this cult. They need him to paint The Willow Woman again and again. If I were the cult, this house in Longquanyi District is where I would hide him. So, go find Junjie. Fulfil the promise you made to Old Man Gao."

"But—"

"When I am done in Chongqing, I will come and get you, Sister. I give you my word."

As Captain Wang had discovered a few days before, Philip Ye was not a man to argue with. Constable Ma shut her mouth, though he could tell from her expression she was far from happy.

Philip Ye then addressed him. "Thank you, Captain – good luck and good hunting."

In a whirl of motion, the tiny woman packed up her laptop,

thrust a memory stick in his hand, put on her hat and coat, and with a brisk wave and a bright smile chased after Philip Ye who was already out of the door. Captain Wang looked down at the memory stick in his hand. If casualties were to be kept to a minimum, among his own men and women as well as with the cultists, more information was needed than he'd been given. Aerial photographs were required, and quickly. He looked over at Constable Ma who was glowering at him suspiciously.

"Ever been up in a helicopter?" he asked her.

The flicker in her eyes gave him some enjoyment. So the big girl felt fear. That, at least, was good to know.

CHAPTER FIFTY-SIX

Sunday

I t was a mystery to Xu Ya why it had taken her so long to realise that Professor Xiong was no longer the man he had once been, no longer properly sceptical, no longer wonderfully and condescendingly acerbic, no longer one of China's greatest exponents of rational and scientific thought.

What had happened to him?

The death of a spouse, after fifty years of marriage, must always be affecting, but in all the years Xu Ya had known Professor Xiong, she had never heard him utter one affectionate remark about Yi Li. He had never stated it unequivocally, but he had made it clear nevertheless to all who knew him that he considered his marriage a mistake. But something had kept them together all these years. They had had ample opportunity to divorce. And, as Xu Ya could attest to from personal experience, it was always difficult for those on the outside of a marriage to comprehend what really passed between husband and wife.

For whatever reason – it could simply be overwhelming guilt – Yi Li's death had undermined Professor Xiong's personality, his sanity. Or maybe all she was seeing in him was nothing but the upsetting depredations of old age. Regardless, her old friend no longer stood before her. This was not Professor Xiong. This stranger's eyes were too bright, his manner too insistent, his shifting facial expressions too odd.

"Professor, it is impossible for you to provide evidence for the existence of your wife's spirit. Spirits do not exist; therefore your evidence cannot exist."

A circular argument, intellectually useless, but it would have to suffice. Nothing else came to Xu Ya's mind.

Professor Xiong continued as if she had not spoken at all. Out of the desk drawer he took a flat square object wrapped in a protective black silk cloth. Xu Ya had no doubt what it was: yet another photograph, yet another 'surprising find'.

"What you have there is not evidence," she reasserted.

Again, it was as if Professor Xiong had not heard her.

"Ms. Xu, it is hard for me to describe to you how shocked I was when my wife's spirit appeared to me. At first I did not know what to make of the visitation. I wanted to tear my eyes out for deceiving me, for giving me false hope. But, as dawn broke, and the sun rose higher in the sky, it became impossible for me to deny what I had seen. At last, able to eat and drink properly again, renewed as I had been by her presence, I spent the remainder of the day in deep thought, struggling to understand what her reappearance in my life meant. I eventually came to the conclusion that my wife's period of introspection and self-criticism had come to an end, that she was ready to place herself once more in the vanguard of the revolution. So, that evening, understanding what I must do, I got down on my knees and prayed to her as the stupid common people would pray to an imaginary god. I wanted to hear her voice, receive her instructions for me. I was ready to obey her, Ms. Xu, as I had never obeyed her in life. I prayed for many hours and expended so much effort that sweat burst forth from my head. But it was worth it, Ms. Xu. The notion eventually came to me that I should visit her rooms. I had had them sealed off after her death. And so it was, in breaking the seals, that I discovered our wedding photograph in her study, proof if that is what you want, Ms. Xu, that we are bound in death as we were in life. And then, here in the drawer of this old desk, I found this."

Professor Xiong pulled away the silk cloth and let it fall to the floor. He did indeed hold another old photograph in his hands, though, from where she was standing, Xu Ya found it hard to see the detail of the photograph properly.

"I took this picture while we were courting," he continued. "It had always been my favourite of her but I thought it lost many years ago in one of our house moves. So smitten was I by Yi Li when I took this picture, I made a vow to follow her wherever she might lead me. To my great shame, after our marriage I soon forgot that vow. But, in being led to rediscover this photograph again, it became clear to me what she was now teaching me: that my vow still stood, and that this time I should honour it. My wife may well be in the afterlife, Ms. Xu, but in this world, under her direction, I shall speak for her. In her name, I will gather the young revolutionary-minded people about me. In her name, we will hunt down those capitalist roaders who oppose us. In her name, we will purge China of all its poison, of the twin demons of greed and selfishness. In her name, the cause of socialism will finally be victorious!"

"Please let me see," said Xu Ya, reaching out for the photograph, wanting to humour him, to keep him calm, and then to get out of the house as quickly as she could.

His face aglow, he put the photograph in her hands. Her stomach turning over, strangely dreading what she might see. Like the wedding photograph, this too was in black and white and faded, a portal into China's depressing past. It was a rural scene – they must have been out for an unchaperoned walk – Yi Li in her Sun Yat-sen suit, sitting on the bank of a river under a tree, doing her best to look suitably determined, political and revolutionary. For the life of her, Xu Ya could not see in Yi Li what Professor Xiong had seen in her. Even in such an idyllic setting, Yi Li looked every inch a miserable cow!

Professor Xiong spoke softly.

"What was that you said?" Xu Ya asked, thinking she must be hearing things.

"The Willow Woman," he repeated.

Xu Ya looked back down at the photograph, suddenly recognising the scene for what it was and simultaneously realising what Junjie had done. He had painted an *interpretation* of the photograph – Yi Li, the river, the willow tree – making of it a religious scene. By sheer natural talent and a great dollop of artistic licence he had turned a dull, hard-faced woman into a goddess worthy of worship. It must have been this 'interpretation' that Junjie had been practicing in his sketch book, wanting for some reason to impress Professor Xiong. And, as reward for his success, Junjie had been taken from his loving father and made to paint the same picture over and over again. She looked up at Professor Xiong and saw the depth of his madness within his eyes. She looked down at the desk and knew that in this house, somewhere nearby, Junjie had been held captive and made to paint, his sad face soon to be caught by Madame Xiong's camera. So she hadn't imagined him after all.

Xu Ya let slip the photograph from her fingers, forgetting that it was evidence. The glass smashed as it struck the stone floor. Professor Xiong's mouth opened in horror.

Xu Ya, enraged, reached into her jacket pocket and pulled out her procuratorate badge and ID without thinking, holding it up to Professor Xiong as one would a ward against evil, her words spewing from her mouth like hot lava from an erupting volcano.

"Professor Xiong Yu, you and others yet to be named, are to be charged with membership of an unlawful religious cult pursuant to Article 300 of the Criminal Law. Furthermore, you and others yet to be named, are to be charged with the unlawful detention of the youth Gao Junjie and thereby depriving him of his freedom, pursuant to Article 238 of the Criminal Law; and you, and others yet to be named, are to be charged with unlawfully coercing the youth Gao Junjie to paint religious pictures for you, pursuant to Article 244 of the Criminal Law; and you are to be charged with ordering, or conspiring with others to order, the homicides of Zhu Yi and He Dan – also known as Poppy – pursuant to Article 232 of the Criminal Law and as such—"

She got not further. His walking stick, swung with surprising speed and viciousness, smacked into her wrist, knocking her ID from her hand, making her yelp with pain. She turned to flee, to get help from others in the house. But the walking-stick caught her again, hard, on the side of the head, sending her sprawling onto the hard, stone floor. As the room darkened around her, she heard a voice in her ear.

"The Willow Woman told me not to trust you. She told me you were a demon in disguise. Like a fool, I ignored her. I could not believe it of my old friend Xu Ya. I had hoped you would stand at my side, join with me and the many, many followers of The Willow Woman, and help me set about the rebuilding of the perfect socialist society. You could have been an asset to me, a future leader. Instead, you have proved yourself worthless, and as such you must die."

CHAPTER FIFTY-SEVEN

Guilt assailed Mouse as she had been driven away from Captain Wang's apartment. She had caught herself daydreaming about Captain Wang rather than worrying for Deng Shiru. But, in her defence, Captain Wang had been unexpected. When Philip Ye had told her and Constable Ma where they had been headed, neither of them had been pleased.

"I do not like him," had said Constable Ma.

Mouse had kept her thoughts to herself. But, from what she remembered of the drunken PAP officer from the TV she imagined he must be a ruffian.

"I do not like him," Constable Ma had repeated, as if she had expected Philip Ye to change his mind and turn the car around.

"Sister, we do not judge a man on a first encounter," he had replied.

"I do," she insisted.

"Sister, I need you to accompany Captain Wang to Longquanyi District."

"No, I do not like him."

"I need you to find Junjie."

"No."

"Sister, I do not ask this of you lightly."

"I want to stay with you."

"Today, it is not possible."

"Superintendent, you must make it possible."

"Sister, this is not a debate."

"I debate with no one."

And so on.

This seemingly bad-tempered back and forth between Philip Ye and Constable Ma had continued until they had reached Captain Wang's apartment. Mouse could not believe a simple constable would argue with a superintendent so. But, from what Mouse could see, Constable Ma worshipped Philip Ye. When Constable Ma wasn't staring at him directly, she was peering out of the corner of her eye at him, watching his every move. This Mouse could understand. He was Philip Ye, after all. However, what he saw in her – coarse, ungainly, prejudiced, suspicious, untrusting and apparently lacking a sense of humour – was anyone's guess. However, all thoughts about this odd relationship had been washed out of Mouse's mind by the unexpectedness of Captain Wang. She had found him to be no ruffian at all.

He had stood tall, slim and strong. In his uniform, he had almost taken her breath away. Though not much more than thirty years of age, there was an air of hard-won wisdom about him, a sense that he had been many places and seen many things – not all of them pleasant. Definitely a man of action, she saw a more introspective side to him. Books filled the apartment, some even written in English. It was possible that they could have been his father's, but Mouse thought not. Captain Wang, she decided, was quite the educated man. And, after the unfortunate incident where he had almost trapped her in the door, he had kept casting surreptitious glances at her. This was a good sign, a very good sign. She was going to have to call her good friend Jinjing in PAP Personnel to find out more about him; treading carefully, of course, so as not to stir up any gossip.

However, now speeding away from his apartment, Mouse remembered Deng Shiru was struggling to live and felt herself the worst woman who had ever lived. To distract herself from her misery, she asked Philip Ye, "Who is Junjie?"

"The beginning of all this…and hopefully the end," he replied.

Which was not very enlightening and all quite mysterious.

Mouse allowed herself to be swallowed up by guilt again. She had carried a torch for Deng Shiru for so long it was incomprehensible to her that on the day he lingered at the border of life and death she would discover another man to fall in love with. That is, if it was love. She had never believed in love at first sight. Her attraction to Captain Wang had to be a reaction to the stress of the day, a passing fancy, an escape from reality, something to be laughed about in days to come.

By the time Philip Ye had stopped the car outside the flower shop, Mouse had concluded that she had suffered in Captain Wang's apartment a meaningless rush of blood. Furthermore, she was certain she could never be seen out with a man who sometimes got so drunk he would abuse the police out on the street. And yet she was still searching for excuses for him, about to clamber out of the car, when Philip Ye spoke up.

"Mouse, what happened the night that Prosecutor Xu's husband died?"

Mouse almost forgot to breathe. She turned away quickly from Philip Ye's intense inquiring gaze, wishing she were far away.

"So you *do* know."

"I'm sworn to secrecy," she whispered, refusing to face him.

"I don't like secrets."

Now she turned to him, angry, feeling the need to speak up for her missing friend. "You are not one to judge. The family Ye has enough secrets of its own!"

For a moment she feared for her life as his eyes widened in astonishment. But then he began to smile. Ashamed of her unbelievable show of temper, Mouse began to smile in return. Thankfully he did not press her again. For all of his foreignness, and his intensity, and his spikey unpredictability, it was hard not to warm to Philip Ye. It would not have taken him long to break her defences down.

As she opened the car door to get out, she said to him, "Please do what you can to find Prosecutor Xu. She does not always think straight and people are often a puzzle to her but there is no braver person under Heaven."

Whether he didn't believe her, or merely had nothing to say, Philip Ye kept his silence. He gave her a perfunctory wave and then the sleek black Mercedes was gone, merging with the traffic, to vanish around the corner.

With a heavy heart, already missing Philip Ye's exciting and yet disturbing presence – what a strange feeling that was! – Mouse considered her own sad reflection in the window of the flower shop. The lights were off. As it was a Sunday, Madame Qi, the owner, would be out visiting her son in the east of the city. The concrete steps up to her apartment were situated to the side of the shop. She bleakly contemplated the chilly home that awaited her. In the presence of Philip Ye and Constable Ma, intimidating as they both were, she had forgotten her fear of the cultists. No police raids had been carried out as yet. The cultists remained at large, possibly even waiting for her at the top of the steps or hiding in her apartment. There had to be other options. She was considering whether to make a run for a nearby restaurant or teashop, to keep in the company of others, or even to check herself into a cheap hotel, when a hand touched her shoulder. She almost jumped out of her skin.

"Mouse…I'm sorry," said Philip Ye. "I wasn't thinking. I've parked up around the corner. I didn't mean to abandon you. Superintendent Zuo would never forgive me. He has taken quite a shine to you – as has Captain Wang, I noticed. Superintendent Zuo told me you live alone. Is that true? Do you have any family you could stay with?"

"No, but I'll be okay, Superintendent."

"Are you sure?"

She nodded, wanting to be brave.

He took her laptop bag from her. "Come, little mouse, let me take you somewhere safe."

She dutifully followed him to the car. She assumed he would drop her back at PSB HQ but soon they were heading into the heart of the affluent Wuhou District and before she realised quite where she was, large heavy gates were parting for them, and they were rolling down a long gravel drive with first tall trees and then immaculately maintained English-style gardens on either side. Before her arose a majestic house that could easily have graced the cover of any one of her English Victorian novels.

"Welcome to the House of Secrets," said Philip Ye, with an amused sideways glance at her.

"I did not mean—"

"No, Mouse, the accusation is very fair."

A grinning man in a black suit, a pistol beneath his jacket at his waist, opened the door for her. "And who might this be?"

"Day Na, this is Mouse," said Philip Ye. "She is to be our guest tonight."

Philip Ye led her into the house. It was all she dreamed it would be, the light, the colours, the magnificent furniture, the priceless displays of what had to be Ming and Qing porcelain, and the paintings, which included examples of exquisite calligraphy mounted on the walls. The house might well be English on the outside, but it was definitely Chinese on the inside.

"This house is you," she said to Philip Ye, forgetting herself.

"No, this is my father's creation," he replied, though it was obvious to her that she had pleased him.

He took her to the kitchen. Expecting to find a score of maids at work, Mouse was astounded to be introduced to Ye Zihao, the former mayor of Chengdu, apron tied tightly around his waist, pipe in his mouth, busy preparing food.

"So, who is this you have brought me, Philip?"

"Father, may I introduce Ms. Hong Jia of the People's Procuratorate. She has been very courageous today and a great help to me. Tonight she is to be our guest."

"Well, well…it is a pleasure to meet you, Ms. Hong," said Ye Zihao, holding his hand out to her.

Once the most powerful man in Chengdu – a man never to be underestimated – his hand was hot to the touch. To Mouse, he seemed unchanged by his long house-arrest, just as dynamic as ever, a man to be feared, respected still and – she could not help herself – to be adored.

"I cannot stay, Father," said Philip Ye.

"You are still intent on going to Chongqing?"

"Yes, Father."

"Then I disown you for being a fool."

"As you wish, Father."

The two men exchanged a glance and then Philip Ye was gone. Ye Zihao took Mouse's hat and coat from her as he did her laptop bag, placing them in the hands of another suited guard who appeared out of nowhere.

"Have you eaten, young lady?" Ye Zihao asked her.

"No, Mayor Ye."

Another man might be occupying his office but no other form of address seemed appropriate. Ye Zihao did not protest.

"Well, Ms. Hong, since my son is determined to risk his life on a fool's errand, and it will be a long evening awaiting his return, you and I must entertain ourselves. Red-braised beef with radish is on the menu tonight. And, as it is a special occasion – he so rarely brings me an interesting woman to speak to – I shall prepare for us each a gin and tonic. How does that sound?"

She nodded, speechless, unable to comprehend what was happening to her. Here she was, in a house many spoke about but relatively few had ever visited, and speaking to her, as if she were a friend of many years, was the larger than life, the hugely talented, the charismatic, the temperamental, the flawed, the always controversial, Mayor Ye Zihao. How had her life of comfortable tedium suddenly been transformed into this?

He sat her down at the table and mixed the drinks for them both. He placed the glass before her, the colourless liquid poured over ice, a slice of lime in the glass. One sip of the bittersweet cocktail and she screwed up her face. Ye Zihao laughed at her. Determined not to be defeated, she sipped some more. Her palate suddenly clean and refreshed, her head beginning to spin, she thought it the most marvellous drink ever.

"This is wonderful," she said.

"Slow down, Ms. Hong – we have an evening to enjoy ourselves."

"Please call me Mouse."

"Oh no, Ms. Hong – I cannot abide nicknames, not in my house. Now please tell me why my son is so insistent on going to Chongqing."

"He is going to find Prosecutor Xu."

"Is she in danger?"

"For her life."

"And is she worth rescuing, Ms. Hong?"

"She is my friend – a good person."

"That, at least, Ms. Hong, is good to know. My son imagines himself a romantic hero reborn from one of the ancient stories. I am his father and yet he listens to not one word I have ever said. He was like this even as a boy: headstrong, always a great worry to me. But we shall not fret this evening shall we, Ms. Hong? He will return, I am sure, with your friend in his arms. But if one hair of his head is harmed I swear I will raze Chongqing to the ground. No one will escape my vengeance. You do believe that don't you, Ms. Hong?"

"I do," she replied, honestly, trembling.

"Good, then that is settled. You and I understand each other. Now let me tell you a story about that vulgar cretin Chief Prosecutor Gong. This story goes back a few years, and the scene is the House of the Golden Lantern in Ziyang – a brothel, if you didn't know – where Chief Prosecutor Gong once made a most embarrassing mistake."

It seemed that Mouse drank, ate and giggled her way through the entire evening. Whatever Mayor Ye Zihao's personal failings, whatever his crimes, these soon became meaningless to her. He was the perfect host, the perfect gentleman. And could he cook! By the time she was on her third gin and tonic – she had refused the red wine he had offered her to accompany her meal, asking for more cocktails despite his amused disapproval – she had fallen in love for the second time that day. When, worn out by all the laughing, she found her eyes closing, he showed her to her room. Silk pyjamas had been laid out for her as well as an assortment of toiletries. As she got under the covers, feeling safer than she had in years, the fragrant aroma of pipe-smoke in her nostrils, she thought she heard Mayor Ye Zihao speaking on the phone. She hoped it was good news, that Philip Ye had saved Prosecutor Xu from the cultists, and that he would return with her soon. His father did worry so. As she closed her eyes she said a little prayer for Deng Shiru. There had been no word from Wukuaishi Hospital. But when she slept, she dreamed she was walking down by the river, talking books with Captain Wang Jian of the PAP.

CHAPTER FIFTY-EIGHT

Sunday

Bad as some of her days had been during her marriage, Xu Ya had always had the sense that somehow she would come through the experience relatively unscathed. Similarly, if she were honest with herself, she had never expected to be in any danger from The Willow Woman cult. She was an important official, a public prosecutor, not some idiot youth or lovesick student. Prosecutors do not go missing. Prosecutors do not come to harm. But, with Madame Xiong's knife at her throat, Xu Ya felt, for the very first time, the hand of death around her heart.

Xu Ya had awoken to find herself bound tightly with thick cord to a chair facing the window in what she took to be Yi Li's bedroom. There was a bed against one wall and the floor, as in Yi Li's other rooms, was bare stone. The window looked out onto a rain-swept inner courtyard, the same courtyard she had seen in the photograph back in Madame Xiong's apartment. It also might have been the very same window Junjie had been staring from when the photograph had been taken. There was some evidence of his presence: a table set up by the window, paper and pens laid out upon its surface. However, Xu Ya could see a layer of dust upon the table and guessed that Junjie had been gone for many weeks, either dead or taken elsewhere.

Nauseous, her head throbbing from the blow she had received from Professor Xiong's walking-stick, Xu Ya had no idea how long she had been unconscious. Glad at least she had not been gagged, she now wasted a lot of breath crying out for help. But, as the sky darkened into evening and the rain beat with ever-increasing ferocity upon the window, she realised that not only had she lost most of the day but also that no one was coming to save her. Either she was out of earshot of the household staff, including the female security guard manning the main entrance, or else, more likely, they were all under the sway of Professor Xiong.

Xu Ya despaired. She began to sob. She knew her outlook was bleak. She had learned too much about the cult, seen too much, and, like Zhu Yi and Poppy, would not be suffered to let live. The law meant nothing to cults. That was their danger to society. A cult only existed to fulfil the will of its leader. And by leader, in regard to The Willow Woman cult, she did not mean the ghost of Yi Li. Ghosts, spirits, phantoms, spectres – whatever one wished to call them – did not exist. By leader, she meant the senile, the grief-stricken, the guilt-ridden, the tormented and the deranged Professor Xiong.

The reasoning she had applied the last evening that had seemingly left her no choice but to try to effect Junjie's rescue all on her own now seemed ridiculous and contrived. She had let her resentments toward Philip Ye and Investigator Deng, and her natural prejudices against the police, cloud her judgement. With hindsight she should have sat down with Philip Ye and Investigator Deng again. She should have explained that she believed she had seen Junjie's face in a photograph taken at Professor Xiong's house. And she should have revealed her past association with Professor Xiong, how she considered it impossible for him to be involved with a cult, but then let them comment, perhaps even take charge and develop a more sensible and considered plan of action.

Oh, Philip Ye, she thought bitterly, her face wet with tears, you have had such a fortunate escape from me. I would have made you the most useless wife. And, as a mother—

From behind her she heard the lock turn in the door. Xu Ya sat still, no longer squirming against her bindings. She held her breath and tried to clear her mind of Philip Ye, of all extraneous and useless thoughts. She had her wits still – and her voice. Maybe there was time yet to talk herself out of her predicament. A light was switched on and Xu Ya blinked, trying to adjust to the new brightness of the room. She heard footsteps cross the stone floor. Xu Ya tried to twist her head to see behind her. But she soon stopped moving when she felt the touch of sharp steel against her neck.

"From the moment I laid eyes upon you, Prosecutor, I knew you would be trouble," said Madame Xiong. "Men are always fooled by a good figure and a pretty face. But me, never. From the beginning I could see that you had a black, treacherous heart. A demoness in high heels, that's what you are…out to destroy my brother…you and the fat man. Well, the fat man is now dead, left bleeding in the road like a stuck pig. And you will soon follow him into the grave. Not that they will ever find your body. When my brother phoned me and told me you were here I could not believe my luck. He was shocked that you'd come to betray him. She is mine, I told him. Let me slit her throat."

"Release me or pay the penalty!" spat Xu Ya, trying to twist her neck away from the knife. But Madame Xiong gripped Xu Ya's neck with her free hand, holding her fast, lifting her chin so the knife cutting into her skin could find better purchase.

"I am not like you, Prosecutor. I do not show a false face to the world. I do not lie like a snake. No one is coming for you. No one knows where you are. I have checked up on you. I have phoned the Procuratorate, pretending I had some more information for you. They told me it was your day off. I almost laughed out loud at your arrogance, your belief you could take on my brother alone. I told my brother that fortune is smiling upon us, that no one will ever see you again."

"How can you believe in The Willow Woman?" asked Xu Ya, fighting for breath, the cord burning into her arms and legs as she tried to free herself. "You hated Yi Li."

Madame Xiong suddenly released her hold on Xu Ya's neck. "I did hate her. It was the happiest day of my life when I heard that she had died. She was a spiteful—"

"But Yi Li *is* The Willow Woman," said Xu Ya. "Your brother has gone insane. He imagines he speaks with her ghost."

Madame Xiong caught Xu Ya on the side of her head with the flat of her hand. Her ear ringing, Xu Ya gasped with pain.

"My brother is a genius – it is only a ruse."

"No, he showed me a photograph of her sitting on the river bank under the willow tree. He actually believes he speaks with her. He is not in his right mind. He arranged Junjie's kidnap. He made Junjie paint picture after picture of her, making her out to be some kind of goddess the people should worship."

"You have been fooled," said Madame Xiong, moving around in front of Xu Ya, the knife idle in her hand.

Xu Ya looked for pity in her beady eyes but saw none. Xu Ya held her tongue as Madame Xiong sat down on the bed, the frame groaning under the weight.

"Prosecutor, you think you are clever but, compared to my brother, you have the mind of a child," said Madame Xiong. "The

Willow Woman is but a trick. Yi Li was always a nasty piece of work. I did not like her from the start. I was a young girl when my brother brought her to our family home in Longquanyi District. I told him not to marry her. But it did no good. She had spun such a web about him he could not escape. I had my chance then. I should have run a knife across her throat. But I was too slow and she saw my intent. I was forbidden from ever visiting their house in Chongqing after. I regret my lack of fortitude back then. It was my fault my brother suffered such a terrible life with her. Yi Li was always carping at him, always undermining him, always holding him back. But not even she could smother true genius. And she could never kill the affection that he had for me. My brother has always looked out for me, as I now look out for him. There is no greater man in all of China."

"But Madame Xiong, he really believes—"

"No, Prosecutor, my brother has fooled you as he has fooled everyone else. The Willow Woman is a charade. He fooled me also for a day or two until I figured out what he was up to. Oh, did I laugh then. My brother had to find a way to bring the people back to their senses. We live in dark days, Prosecutor. China has gone to hell. All common decency, all morality, has been forgotten. The Party is full of gangsters now. All that interests them is money and power. They have sold the people the 'Chinese Dream'. But what does that mean, Prosecutor? No one knows. We are back in the old days before the revolution when the rich got richer and the poor were left to scrabble about in the dirt and fend for themselves."

"Madame Xiong, you must—"

"No, it is you who must listen, Prosecutor! You must see why you have to die. Yi Li always thought herself more revolutionary than most, as if she were Mao Zedong's long-lost daughter. It was all rubbish. When the Red Guards hurt my brother she ran through the streets for her life, to hide in her rooms like a frightened rabbit. She could spout Mao Zedong Thought all day but she was good for little else. But, as she had spun a web about my brother trapping him into marriage, she spun another web about all who knew her, convincing them that only she properly understood Mao Zedong Thought and that after Mao Zedong's death only she knew how to progress the revolution. So, when she died, my brother took his opportunity. I did not see it at first. I thought he was grieving for that heartless hag. In the days after her death I really thought my brother had lost his mind. And then when he said he had seen her ghost I almost lost my own mind with worry.

"But then he began speaking of what the ghost had said to him, relaying her instructions from the afterlife about how to put China back on the road to creating the perfect socialist society. And when I saw people actually listening to him, it struck me like a flash of lightning. I saw what my brother was doing. You see, Prosecutor, the people are lost. The Party has squandered any right it has to give the people moral guidance. So naturally, the people, needing leadership and reassurance, have returned in droves to the temples and the churches. My brother saw the opportunity. Rather than fight superstition and religious stupidity, he has decided to use the people's gullibility to steer them back onto the correct socialist path.

"He speaks directly to the young people as only he can. He tells them that The Willow Woman says this or that…blah! blah! blah!…and the people lap it up just because they think the word comes from the ghost of a revolutionary leader. Once our revolutionary message has been spread throughout China and turned the Party inside out – yes, you should know we do have Party members within our fold – then my brother will discard all this Willow Woman foolishness and reveal himself to be the true architect of China's future."

"That is nonsense!"

"It is the truth, Prosecutor!"

"You are as insane as he is."

Madame Xiong leapt up from the bed. Xu Ya thought she would die then. She saw a murderous impulse take possession of Madame Xiong, and the arc of the knife as it moved toward her throat.

"Madame Xiong, not here!" cried a male voice from behind Xu Ya.

In the nick of time, Madame Xiong returned to herself and stopped the movement of the knife. She contented herself with a sharp slap across Xu Ya's face instead. Xu Ya rode the blow as best she could, afterward tasting blood upon her lip.

"I almost forgot myself," said Madame Xiong to the unseen man.

Xu Ya tried to turn to see who else was in the room, but a hood was suddenly thrown over her and strong hands restrained her while her bindings were loosed. She tried to fight them, to cry out, but received another stunning blow to her head for her trouble. She came to when she was thrown down onto a hard surface, winding her. Bound again at her wrists and ankles, she was thrown about as an engine barked into life and the vehicle she was in lurched forward.

They are taking me to the place of my death, she thought.

CHAPTER FIFTY-NINE

Sunday

With the fading light of day in his rear-view mirror and, according to the radio, a stormy night in Chongqing ahead of him, Philip Ye pushed the Mercedes as fast as he dared along the expressway. Four hours to Chongqing at lawful speeds, he knew he had to do better than that. With the concealed blue and red lights strobing on the car and the military registration plates the Na brothers had quickly swapped for his own no one was going to stop him. And yet, Philip Ye could not but feel that whatever his speed he would be too late. Prosecutor Xu had been missing the whole day, her phone switched off. Mouse had even fielded a phone call, redirected from the Procuratorate, from Prosecutor Xu's parents in Chongqing. They had also been repeatedly trying to contact her. Mouse had fretted when he told her that she had to lie, requiring her to explain that their daughter was caught up in a major investigation and could not be contacted right now. It was true enough, but, if he was on his way to Chongqing to recover a body rather than stage a rescue, then her father – as someone senior in the Central Organisation Department – would find a way to exact his revenge.

Philip Ye couldn't help but look back upon the last few days with regret over missed opportunities. If he had interpreted the visitation from Old Man Gao's ghost properly, if he had understood and taken advantage of the odd chronology and put himself between Old Man Gao and Ma Meili before she had had time to take a shot, then maybe all that had come to pass would have been prevented. He could have spoken to them both, learned of Ma Meili's concerns about Zhu Yi, how she suspected Zhu Yi had something to do with Junjie's disappearance. He could have detained Zhu Yi, squeezed the truth out of him, learned everything he needed to know about The Willow Woman cult, thereby preventing his murder – and probably Poppy's too – without Fatty Deng or Prosecutor Xu ever having to get involved. One simple error of judgement on his part, one moment of hesitation, had resulted in the deaths of three people; and, with no word yet from Wukuaishi Hospital and with Prosecutor Xu still not answering her phone, maybe two more before the day was done.

He had told all to Wolf before leaving Chengdu.

"Philip, you cannot save the world," Wolf had said. "Listen, I'm in and out of interrogations all evening. Remember the little girl from the pond? The whole family did it, I'm sure of it. I've pulled the lot in. As far as I can tell the family had a meeting and decided they didn't like the girl and drowned her. There's a lot I've got to figure out. But, against my better judgement, I'll do what I can to help you find Princess Poison. If you can't reach me, don't worry. I'll contact you when I can."

Philip Ye had given Wolf multiple addresses for Professor Xiong, including the Professor's main residence, all lifted from Mouse's research. However, with no good reason to enter any of those addresses, and with State Security to worry about, all Wolf would be able to do is look for any suspicious activity from the *outside* – that is, if he could free himself from his own work. Philip Ye had pressed Mouse for more information about State Security's protection of Professor Xiong but she had had no more to give.

"What if State Security agents have been recruited by this cult?" Wolf had asked.

"I don't know," Philip Ye had replied, honestly.

Philip Ye hadn't heard from Wolf since. Two hours on the road and he was beginning to think that his father was right, that he had really embarked on a fool's errand. Prosecutor Xu might never be found.

The shikra.

I have lost her again, he thought.

He had been thirteen years old. The new family home had just been built: a facsimile of an English Victorian country manor house, erected on a plot of land in the Wuhou District of the city at tremendous expense. Even at that age, Philip Ye had thought his father mad, the house an obscene waste of money, a bizarre testament to his father's obsession with all things English – an obsession, sadly, that did not extend to spending much time with his half-English son.

In the days following the completion of the house, his father had decided upon a house-warming party. He had wanted to show off his great wealth, his fine taste, his *international* credentials – the Mayor's Office then firmly in his sights. Make me mayor, he was saying, and I will build Chengdu as I built this house. Hundreds had been invited and they all came bearing gifts, all anxious to attach themselves to Ye Zihao's rising star. But, for Philip Ye, only one gift stood out.

A Thai businessman, Nattapong Mookjai, had strolled into the house, grinning from ear to ear, a small hooded bird on his gloved hand. The main reception room had fallen silent, all eyes upon him and the bird – as no doubt he had intended. Philip Ye, who, despite his natural shyness, had been the darling of the party until then, felt aggrieved at first that his thunder had been stolen. But, when Nattapong Mookjai had removed the bird's hood, and the little hawk had stared about the room with its honey-brown eyes, Philip Ye had discovered himself, for the first time, to be in love – as were most of the other people, if the collective sigh that travelled around the room was anything to go by.

Realising the power of the moment, that he had but one chance to bend his father's iron rule, Philip Ye asked out loud, "Father, can we keep it? Can we keep the bird?"

With steely eyes on Nattapong Mookjai, Ye Zihao had replied, "Of course! Of course! How could I ever refuse my good friend Mookjai's generosity?"

In the garden, in the sunshine, away from the clamour of the party, Nattapong Mookjai had talked in all seriousness about the proper upkeep of the bird. Not fluent in Mandarin, he had spoken in halting English instead.

"Philip, a hawk is not a…ah…stupid dog or a cat…you understand? You must care for it. It is like a…ah…a thoroughbred…a racing horse…you understand? Everything must be perfect…food… exercise…housing. Such a bird is…impulsive…excitable. This hawk is better than most. It is a joy to train. And, for its size…it is very brave. But you must never forget, Philip…never…no matter how many times it comes to the fist…that it is a wild creature…never really tamed."

"I will take care of it, I promise," said Philip Ye, determined to do right by the little brown-feathered hawk. "What is it called?"

"If you mean its name…ah, that will be your honour to name it. But if you mean what type of bird…the…ah…species…then in

Mandarin you would say *hè'ěr yīng*: the little banded goshawk. But in India, where it is most common, they call it...in the Hindi language...shikra...which means 'hunter'."

"Shikra." Philip Ye liked the sound of the name as it rolled off his tongue.

"By the brown feathers you see it is a female," said Nattapong Mookjai.

"A real lady."

"Ah, yes, Philip – a real lady indeed."

Contractors had arrived soon after, at Nattapong Mookjai's expense, to construct a small aviary in one of the house's outbuildings. Secretary Wu and his wife, Wang Jiyu, took photographs of Philip Ye with the shikra on his gloved fist, with Nattapong Mookjai looking on, giving reassurance, advising Philip Ye not to look directly at the bird, no matter how much he wanted to admire it.

"Philip, you must give the shikra time. Let her stare at you...let her get used to you. She must learn to trust you."

Philip Ye had never had a better day in all of his short life.

The party in full swing until the early hours, Philip Ye had taken a quilt from his room and had slept in the outbuilding with the shikra.

The next morning he had taken a bus into the city to scour the bookshops in search of texts on falconry – a lost art in China, he had thought mistakenly. The few books he did find were of poor quality. But the owner of one of the bookshops had directed him to a narrow street in the south of the city. There he had discovered, sitting outside a teashop drinking and smoking cigarettes, the old men of the Chengdu Hawking Club, their magnificent goshawks, sparrowhawks, saker falcons and merlins arrayed on movable wooden perches for the passers-by to see. It had taken Philip Ye some time to find the courage to approach these men and their birds. When he did he told them breathlessly of his own.

"A shikra, you say!"

"Well, I never!"

They had made fun of him. They had told him to run along back home to his family. But when he had produced the polaroid instant photograph Secretary Wu had taken of him standing with the bird, all the old men had marvelled at it.

"You must join us," had said one of them.

"Yes, it is about time our club had some fresh blood," had said another.

Philip Ye had assured them that he would join their club, certain that these old men would become better friends to him than the bullying boys and girls at his school. It was his shikra these men were interested in, not his stupid, foreign looks. The old men had told him they would take him out of Chengdu, up into the hills and forests, where he could learn to hunt his shikra. Not large game, they told him. No rabbits, pheasants or duck. The shikra was good for small birds, lizards and mice only, the shikra a good starting bird for a novice falconer, very easy to train, and – as Nattapong Mookjai had said – very, very brave.

Philip Ye had returned home to the new house in high spirits, his new books under his arm. He had whistled to himself as he traipsed along the gravel drive. Until, that is, he saw his bird, his shikra, somehow escaped from the aviary, darting up into the sky, streaking away to the west, over the high wall that surrounded the estate, to be lost among the nearby roof tops. It had vanished so fast, in the blink of an eye, he had immediately begun to believe his eyes had fooled him. It could not have been his shikra. The aviary was secure. The contractors had assured him it was. So it had to be another bird, perhaps a local wild sparrowhawk. But, when he had run to the outbuilding and looked inside, he found his father within, pipe in mouth, smoking contentedly, dismantling the aviary, the shikra gone.

With a gun or a knife in his hand, even at that tender age, Philip Ye knew he would have done murder. As it was, he had thrown himself at his father, punching and kicking and screaming, knocking his father's pipe from his mouth. Lack of filial piety, one of the ten abominations of dynastic law, always punishable by death, his father had only held him at arm's length and given him a resounding slap across the face to bring him back to his senses.

"No pets!" his father had snarled at him, retrieving his pipe and stomping away.

Philip Ye had fled the house in tears. He had caught the bus again, staring out of the windows all the way, hoping to see the shikra perched safely on a roof or in a tree. He had arrived, as evening fell, at Secretary Wu's house. Secretary Wu was at work still, so it was Wang Jiyu who had taken him in, dried his tears, comforted him, fed him, and promised him that all would be done to recover the bird. Later, when Secretary Wu had come home, they had each taken his hand and had walked the streets of the city with him until very late looking for the shikra.

In the days that followed, Philip Ye had continued to live with Secretary Wu and Wan Jiyu. While Secretary Wu was at work, Wang Jiyu had taken him all over the city, to the parks, to the zoo, and finally to the old men of the Chengdu Hawking Club to ask their advice.

The old men had been sad for him.

They had warned him not to expect good news.

A captive bird, they said, that had been just transported to Chengdu, that had not been exercised properly, that was not at its correct weight, might not be fit enough to hunt for itself. Its survival in the wild, therefore, was very much in doubt.

They had patiently explained to him the way of such birds. As predators, the lives of hawks were full of action, violent, often very short. Their fierce natures and their bravery often got them into trouble. To be a good falconer one must get inured to loss, they had said.

After two weeks of searching, his energy and resolve spent, Philip Ye had returned home to his father. It was Secretary Wu who had negotiated his return. Wang Jiyu, in tears herself – Philip Ye had overheard her telling Secretary Wu that she wanted 'her Philip' to stay – would not come with them, wanting nothing more to do with 'that awful man'. No compromise was needed on Ye Zihao's part. Philip Ye, however, had been forced to apologise to his father for his loss of control, to shake his father's hand, and to promise that he would now knuckle down to his schoolwork. As for the shikra, it was never to be mentioned again.

Had it survived?

Despite the grimly realistic outlook offered by the old men of the Chengdu Hawking Club, Philip Ye liked to imagine so. As the months and then the years went by, he had got over its loss. And, as he matured, he had also begun to see that the commitment needed to properly care for such a bird would have been beyond him as a boy. Also, as he began to understand himself better, he had begun to wonder if he would ever have been properly able to enter into that unholy alliance between a man and a hunting-bird. Not only had so much devastation already been done to the fauna of China through the years – it seemed that the Chinese killed everything that swam, crawled, walked and flew for food – but he doubted he had the stomach for the continuous shedding of blood, no matter how natural to the bird it might be. He would certainly get no enjoyment from it. The hunting for murderers he did these days, he considered very different, and never a sport.

Philip Ye had also come to view Nattapong Mookjai in a different light. Ye Zihao had a well-known aversion to animals, thinking them unclean. The gift of the shikra by Nattapong Mookjai had then, at the very least, been irresponsible, at worst highly provocative. What then had Nattapong Mookjai been up to?

Unfortunately it was far too late to enquire with him. Nattapong Mookjai had died violently, in mysterious circumstances, barely a year after the house-warming party, stabbed to death in a seedy bar in downtown Taipei. No one had ever been charged with the crime.

In bringing Prosecutor Xu to Chengdu, had Secretary Wu been as irresponsible as Nattapong Mookjai had been with the shikra? Secretary Wu had described Prosecutor Xu as 'vulnerable', and yet he had not properly caged her, or exercised her, allowing her the freedom of the sky.

Stupid, thought Philip Ye.

It was the nature of hawks to hunt. They could not help themselves. Fit or not, they would always attempt to make a kill.

Rain began to splatter the windscreen as he urged the car on.

CHAPTER SIXTY

Sunday

No one would miss her. That was the sad truth. Her parents, both busy people, dedicated to their careers, would carry on much as they had always done. She would be no great loss to their lives. Never explicit with Xu Ya, they had nevertheless shown through the years that they would much rather have had a son. She had been a disappointment to them from the beginning, her inability to mix properly with the other children at school an embarrassment, her choice of subject, of career, and husband to be treated with obvious contempt. Even if her body was to be recovered, her parents would not bother to tend her grave. Being loyal Party members, atheist to the core, not only didn't they believe in the afterlife, they went further than most by not affording the dead any proper respect at all.

Xu Ya's teeth chattered with the cold. Trussed up, hooded, and thrown into what she now knew to be the back of a truck, she was tossed from side to side, unable to protect herself from the vehicle's erratic motion as it careered around corners and seemingly found every bump in the road. She was on her way to her doom. She supposed her destination to be some isolated field outside of the city where she would be slung into some hastily dug shallow grave. Or perhaps they would cast her down some disused well, her body left to rot in the dark, to be forgotten, her disappearance a mystery never to be solved.

She did not fear death. Like her parents, she did not believe in the afterlife. But, unlike them, she felt the darkly romantic need for a grave and an ornate marble headstone, a place where people could come and mourn her passing – Philip Ye, if only! – and speak to each other about the good works she had done. Or at least one good work. She would have liked people to know she had died trying to rescue a youth with learning difficulties, a youth who had been cruelly taken from his loving father, and that she had been trying to take the law among the people, to be a mother and father to the people, as, in her vivid dream, Huang Liu-Hong had asked her to do. She also would have liked people to know that her bad marriage had changed her for the better. She had become a much more compassionate person, more understanding of the difficult lives of the common people – a better human being.

Yes, she would have liked people to know that.

She would have liked Philip Ye to know that.

She wondered how many would mourn the passing of Investigator Deng. For such an affable man, a man who could talk to any and who intrinsically understood the difference between right and wrong, she expected crowds to gather at his funeral – and that *his* mother would be inconsolable. One would not think it from listening to the Western media, but China was made of such decent men – and women – who, in spite of the many failings of policy and governance, would turn up early to work every day, give their utmost for the greater good, and sometimes sacrifice their lives in doing so.

I hope you have a long, peaceful slumber, Investigator Deng, she thought.

It was her fault he was dead, of course. She should either have confided in him her plans, or ordered him to take the whole day off. She should have known, like a good hunting-dog, he would not give up the chase until exhausted, or until his prey had stopped, turned around, and attacked and murdered him.

I'm so sorry, Investigator Deng.

I really am.

The harsh grinding of brakes brought the truck to a sudden stop. Xu Ya prepared herself for her death, hoping it would be painless, quick. She reminded herself that dying was nothing but falling into an eternal, dreamless sleep, with all the suffering of life, all the hopes and the fears, all of the unrequited desires, left behind for good. She had come from nothingness and was about to return to nothingness – what could be wrong with that?

She began to shake violently when bolts were pulled and the tailgate of the truck was dropped with a clang. Strong hands reached in and grabbed hold of her. Pulled from the truck, gusts of wind buffeted her and sheets of rain soaked her instantly from head to toe. The hood was ripped from her head, painfully taking strands of her long hair with it. She did not complain. Nor did she cry for help. There was no point. She saw she was still in the city, but in the middle of a large expanse of poorly lit waste ground – an abandoned building site on the bank of the black expanse of the Yangzi. There was no one to be seen. Even if someone had been staring out into the night from one of the apartment blocks in the middle-distance, her predicament would have been obscured not only by the darkness but by the many squalls of rain that raced toward her from across the river. Her parents' apartment was somewhere on the far side, one of the many thousand pinpoints of white light that illuminated the bright city, the apartment where Beloved Mister Qin had come to visit her and teach her from his wheelchair, smoking steadily, intense as always, wanting her to understand, needing her to learn.

Oh, Beloved Mister Qin, look where I have ended up.

It struck her then, as one of the two men supporting her bent down and sliced through the binding around her ankles, that it must have been a similar patch of waste ground on which Beloved Mister Qin had been beaten half to death by a gang of brutal police for having the temerity to try to properly defend a client of his.

They began to half-drag her, half-carry her then, one man either side of her, with Madame Xiong, knife in hand, leading the way, dressed like an evil clown in a pink, plastic raincoat with matching hat and boots. They propelled her toward the river, her bare feet slipping and sliding in the mud, her lovely shoes gone, lost somewhere. Another fierce squall struck her, filling her ears and eyes with rainwater, temporarily blinding her. To escape, her mind reached back into the past, to the law, to Beloved Mister Qin.

"Ms. Xu, you must concentrate," he said, lighting a cigarette. "We will begin today with definitions, specifically what is meant by *rule by man*, *rule by law*, and *rule of law*."

She had made notes, his teaching as intense and passionate as ever.

Rule by Man
a system of governance where a leader or government acts arbitrarily, not subject to law, having complete discretion in how and when decisions that affect the people are made

Rule by Law
a system of governance where a leader or government governs the

people using a set of laws but without those laws applying to the leader or the government itself

Rule of Law

a system of governance where a leader or government governs the people using a set of laws that have been drafted with the full consent of the people, laws that not only contain a moral component but also properly acknowledge the rights of the individual, and – most importantly – apply equally to the leader or government

"So, Ms. Xu, do you think you can remember the distinctions I have drawn between these three systems?"

She had nodded, certain of it. When Beloved Mister Qin spoke, it was as if he was communicating directly with her soul. She forgot nothing he told her.

"Then, Ms. Xu, would you please tell me, under which of these systems are we governed today in China?"

There had been a twinkle in his eye when he had put this question to her. Xu Ya had laughed out loud in response. She had been flummoxed and amused and entertained – forced, for the very first time in her life, to properly consider the society in which she lived. She stumbled and stammered and coughed and laughed and coughed some more and then finally held up her hands to admit defeat.

"And this is why, Ms. Xu," he said, in all seriousness, "you are destined to become a great lawyer one day!"

She had been so pleased, she had become quite tearful. No one had ever told her she would amount to anything before.

Of course, as intended, the question Beloved Mister Qin had posed had no easy answer. Even in post-revolutionary China, thousands of years of history and culture and ingrained attitudes towards authority and governance could not be so easily swept aside. It was also far better to see *rule by man*, *rule by law* and *rule of law* not as discrete, mutually exclusive systems of governance but as points on a sliding scale, on which the Party might, from year to year, move back and forth.

It was perhaps easier to point to those times when *rule by man* was predominant: the chaotic and violent years of the Cultural Revolution for instance, when all law had been suspended, and all that mattered was whatever Mao Zedong had said, had written or had thought.

More problematic in modern China was making the distinction between *rule by law* and *rule of law*. The Mandarin for *rule of law* –

fǎzhì – could, because Mandarin lacked prepositions – also be translated as *rule by law* – a subtlety that sometimes confounded Western legal observers and was perhaps used by certain politically astute Chinese legal scholars *to purposely confound*.

Though Xu Ya would eventually spend many happy hours of many happy days arguing with Beloved Mister Qin – both in English and Mandarin – the precise definitions of all three systems, she had rapidly come to the conclusion that she could live, with certain reservations, with either *rule by law* or *rule of law*. It was only *rule by man* to which she took real exception. People were human, and therefore never perfect. Even if leaders were well-intentioned, mistakes would always be made. For all the good he had done – and there had been much – there was no doubt Mao Zedong had made significant errors of judgement. The Party understood this now. It was accepted that the Party had to have a leader, a figurehead, but the thinking of that leader could never again be allowed to dominate, to be beyond criticism. There had to be consensus. This, Xu Ya believed, with all her heart. This, the Party of the 21st Century must surely believe also.

There was no place in China anymore – in her China! – for those charismatic people who would place themselves above the law, regardless of their reasons or intentions: people like the insane Professor Xiong who cared little about the young people he bewitched, manipulated and sometimes murdered while seeking to remake China under the supposed guidance of a ghost; people like Ye Zihao, who had thought he could govern Chengdu as his personal fiefdom, doing as much to enrich himself as he had the city by fair means and foul, even if he was yet to be brought to trial for his crimes; and people like his son, Philip Ye, to whom Heaven had granted far too many gifts, even if his only proven transgression so far was the capture of her heart against all her good sense and then his treatment of her as if she were no more important to him than a fly crawling up a wall – which, if not contrary to the law as written, *should be*.

On the bank of the river, the wind howling across the sky, the two men forced Xu Ya down to her knees. Madame Xiong waved her knife in Xu Ya's face, shouting vile abuse at her.

In one last act of defiance, Xu Ya raised her eyes to Madame Xiong and shouted above the wind, "Cut me and I will bleed only law!"

Enraged, the two cursing men encouraged Madame Xiong to hurry as they were soaking and freezing. Madame Xiong moved behind Xu Ya, yanking her head back by her long hair. She placed the knife against Xu Ya's throat, laughing as she did so.

Expecting a sharp pain and then darkness, Xu Ya glimpsed, through the rain and the murk, a man stumbling across the waste ground toward her. For one fleeting moment she thought it might be Philip Ye, come at the last moment to save her. But then she saw it was not him at all. It was an older, bearded man. It was her Beloved Mister Qin, become a ghost, his legs healed, no longer in a wheelchair. He was shouting, words she could not discern above the wind and the driving rain. She closed her eyes, content now that there was indeed an afterlife, that Beloved Mister Qin had come to take her there and that she would be able to argue law with him once more.

CHAPTER SIXTY-ONE

Sunday

Philip Ye found the house on a rain-drenched street in the outskirts of central Chongqing. Within, the lights were burning brightly. The gate to the property was wide open, a long line of cars – some of them official-looking limousines – were parked nose to tail on the drive. There was no sign of Wolf's car nearby, no word from him either. Which was a great pity. Philip Ye did not attempt to call him. If Wolf could have extricated himself from his own ongoing cases, he would have. He was not the kind of man to let any personal antipathy toward Prosecutor Xu get in the way of doing what was right.

Philip Ye turned off the engine of the Mercedes. He listened for a time to the rain pounding down upon the roof, pondering whether this gathering at the house – business, social or cult-related – would serve to help or hinder him. He had not expected Professor Xiong's main residence to be empty. There was always going to be opposition of some sort. He had just hoped there would not be too many, not too much blood to be potentially spilt.

He closed his eyes.

Inhale for eight beats; hold for four; exhale for eight.

In breath, there is life; in breath, there is serenity; in breath, there is clarity.

He reached out to the house with his mind. He looked for her there. It was a technique he had practiced a number of times in the past few years but with inconsistent results. He searched and searched, looking for the tell-tale point of light in the darkness. But he found nothing. He may not have perfected the technique, may not have been sure why it worked some days and others not, but he was certain, if she had ever been here, Prosecutor Xu was now gone. Whether she had left of her own volition or she had come to harm in that house, he could not tell – but he had to assume the latter. He had tried her phone again and again but with no reply. An inexplicable wave of sadness washed over him, a sense that his long drive to Chongqing had been in vain. Well, if true, Philip Ye determined he was going to make Professor Xiong pay.

He opened his eyes. It was almost nine according to the clock on the dashboard.

His phone rang. It was Superintendent Zuo.

"Philip, the teams are in position – we're about to move."

"I understand."

"Philip, are you okay? Are you there yet?"

"Yes, just arrived…don't worry about me."

"I should have travelled to Chongqing with you."

"You know we both do our best work alone."

"But Chongqing is a—"

"I know."

"Stay safe."

"And you."

Philip Ye switched off his phone and slipped it into his raincoat pocket. What is happening to me? he asked himself. I have become a mithering, sentimental old woman.

He gritted his teeth. It was time to dispense Chengdu justice. He pushed all sadness about Prosecutor Xu from his mind. There would be time for reflection later. He opened the car door and stepped out into the storm.

The wind, coming down from the mountains, howled along the street like an express train. It almost lifted him off his feet. The rain, glacial cold, bit into his exposed hands and face. He raised the collar of his raincoat and made a run for the house. Out of breath by the time he reached the main door, he banged upon it with his fist. He didn't notice the two shadows that detached themselves from a car parked further down the street only to clamber over a wall and disappear into a neighbouring garden.

The heavy wooden door juddered as it was yanked open with some force. The wet night had caused it to expand and wedge tight in its frame. A young woman stood glaring at him, her eyes remorselessly looking him up and down. In her mid-twenties, with a short, military-style haircut, dressed in a smart navy blue skirt and a matching jacket that only just covered the pistol on her right hip, her presence dismayed Philip Ye.

"Who are you?" she asked, brusquely. "You're not on the guest list."

Philip Ye thought she looked harried, uncertain – unusual for a State Security agent. They usually prided themselves on being masters (or mistresses) of every situation.

"Forgive this intrusion," he said. "I know my arriving uninvited is the height of rudeness…but I'm a physicist from England…a great admirer of Professor Xiong. I am only in Chongqing for a short while…flying back to England tomorrow morning, in fact. I was hoping to pay my respects to the Professor if at all possible."

If she had been a Chengdu native and recognised him, or pulled her gun because she didn't like the look of him, or just slammed the door in his face, he didn't know what he would have done. As it was, after a brief moment's hesitation, she told him to come inside out of the rain – though it sounded more like an order than an invitation.

She indicated he should raise his arms, which he did. She patted him down quickly and expertly for weapons. Satisfied, she thrust her hand out to him. "ID?"

He had hoped that both Wolf and Mouse would have been proved wrong, that State Security would have lost all interest in funding a protection detail for Professor Xiong now that he had been forced into retirement and was no longer considered the important asset he had been. As he handed his passport to her, he wondered whether she (or anyone else from State Security) had any knowledge, or even involvement, in The Willow Woman cult – and if she had any idea of what had happened to Prosecutor Xu. Only time would tell.

Her intelligent eyes flicked back and forth between his face and the photograph in the passport.

"A man can never have enough fake documentation," the Na brothers had told him when they had presented him with the passport as a gift on his last birthday. How they had managed to forge what appeared to him to be a genuine UK passport they refused to tell.

"Philip Lao," she muttered to herself.

"Yes…from England," he confirmed again, worried she might spot some discrepancy in the passport he had not picked up himself.

"How is it your Mandarin is so fluent and you speak it with a Sichuanese accent?"

"I was raised for a time in Chengdu."

"You look familiar to me."

His heart skipped a beat. "I've been told that my features are more Western than Chinese…that all Westerners look alike."

"Your father is Chinese, your mother English?"

"Yes."

"An unhappy combination."

"It proved so," he replied.

She offered no apology for her unkind observation. She returned the passport, apparently satisfied, but stared at him for a few long moments as if considering whether or not she should throw him back out into the storm. He breathed again as she said, "Wait here," and he watched her walk down the marble-floored hall, her movement lithe, athletic and perfectly balanced. She would be a handful, her feet and hands deadly weapons, her prowess with that pistol on her hip second to none. It was far too late to regret not bringing Ma Meili with him.

As he waited for her to return, he looked about him, the ruling aesthetic of the house pleasing to the eye, the décor restrained and ordered – the expression of a disciplined and cultured mind. There was not a painting of The Willow Woman in sight. He was tempted to think he had made a mistake, that he had accused Professor Xiong unfairly. But as he opened all his senses to the house, delving beneath its perfect surface, deep into the psychic fabric of the structure, he felt misery at the house's core – madness too. He sensed nothing about Prosecutor Xu, not even a whiff of her expensive perfume on the air, but he had definitely come to the right place. All was not well here. He would have liked Fatty Deng to have seen this place, to see for himself where all his good work had taken the investigation.

When she returned, unsmiling as ever but the swing of her slim hips a touch more pronounced as she approached him, she said, "You are a fortunate man, Mister Lao. Not only will Professor Xiong receive you but an extra place is being set for you at his table. Just take care you mind your manners and only speak when spoken to. His dinner-guests are all important men."

"I understand," he replied, nodding like a fool as if he were both grateful and excited.

She took his raincoat from him and his phone, explaining that so many visitors to the house in the past had been disrespectful enough to take photographs without permission that the Professor had banned them from his presence. She opened a door off the hall. Looking in, he saw it was a cloakroom partially converted into a small security office. On a desk sat a small monitor, receiving a grainy CCTV feed from the street outside. He could see his car clear as day despite the foul weather. He cursed himself for not noticing the camera on the outside of the house. She had probably been watching him since his arrival. He was fortunate that the cameras resolution was not good enough to pick out his military plates. She hung his raincoat up on a rack and placed his phone down on a desk next to seven others.

"That's quite a collection you have there," he said.

"Your phone will be returned to you when you leave," she replied, shutting the door, and closing off any further attempts at conversation.

She took him through the house in silence. At the open doorway to the dining-room she stopped, waiting to be noticed, to be invited within.

From over her shoulder, Philip Ye could see a bevy of maids bustling about a long banquet table that ran almost the entire length of the room. Seven men sat at the table, three either side, facing each other, and one at the head. Prosecutor Xu, as expected, was nowhere to be seen. Mouse had shown Philip Ye a photograph of Professor Xiong taken a few years ago accepting a technology award. This was indeed the man sitting at the head of the table, though looking much older and frailer now. Philip Ye recognised none of the other men. But by the cut of their bland suits and their even blander faces, they had the look of low-level Party cadres or local government functionaries. Their attention was wholly on Professor Xiong and he was in good voice. He was speaking loudly and fervently, clearly on a subject dear to his heart.

"Gentlemen, if we are to compete with the best in the world, the management for state funding of research must change. There is too much stupidity, too much waste, too much corruption, and far, far too much replication. If I hear again of separate government depart-ments funding similar projects in two different institutions run by scientists who supposedly had never heard of each other then—"

Professor Xiong stopped in mid-sentence, noticing he had a fresh audience standing in the doorway. "Mister Lao, please come in and join our little soirée. I am afraid we are putting the world to rights. Your unexpected arrival is most timely. A physicist all the way from England...fancy that! You can tell all my learned friends about how research funding should be properly managed."

Her job done, Philip Ye's escort turned away to return to her little security office, giving him one last puzzled glance as she did so. Philip Ye ignored her, quickly crossing the floor to effusively shake hands with Professor Xiong, telling him that it was an honour to meet him but he had not wished to disturb such an important dinner.

"Nonsense, young man – you must eat with us," said Professor Xiong. "I have been feeling all day that we should be a party of eight this evening. So your arrival is most fortuitous. Sit! Sit! Make yourself comfortable."

Philip Ye nodded toward the other guests in greeting, swiftly studying each of them in turn, seeing pale skin, disinterested bloodshot eyes and flabby bodies – none of them a threat to him. As he took his seat, the maids buzzed about him, competing with each other to pour him wine and serve him the latest course of food. It smelt good. Braised fish and garlic. He smiled at every maid in turn.

"Tell me, Mister Lao," said Professor Xiong, "you purport to be English but you speak like a native...and with a Sichuanese accent. How is this miracle possible?"

"My father is an international businessman, originally from Chengdu. I attended school there. And I come back often to see friends and maintain my language skill."

"And your mother?"

"English – a university lecturer in Chemistry."

"Ah, excellent, excellent...but did your father support your choice of career?"

"He did not, Professor."

"But you went ahead anyway?"

"Science is a calling, not a profession."

Professor Xiong slapped the table with the flat of his hand. "Did you hear that, gentlemen? What good is it if our schools and universities produce a horde of scientists if the only concern of these scientists is to make as much money as possible? What kind of society are we creating? Is this what we all fought to achieve? Is this really what the Party now wants for us?"

He spoke on and on, hammering home his point, that the China that was being made now was not the China any of his generation had envisaged. The Professor's speech was moralising, sentimental, emotional, and from any other man Philip Ye would have found it boring, if not distasteful – words from a bygone age. But Professor Xiong's force of personality was overwhelming, his conviction bordering on messianic, his personal magnetism utterly captivating. It was impossible *not* to listen to him, pointless trying to take one's eyes off him, ridiculous not to accept that everything he said was right.

So this is what it is like to be under the gaze of a rearing king cobra, thought Philip Ye. And he himself was a mature adult, with a trained mind and a strong will and years of political cynicism under his belt. He was also well used to being around powerful men, his father being a case in point. He could walk away from Professor Xiong any time he chose, and given solitude and time, he could dissect everything Professor Xiong had said and find nothing new, nothing that hadn't been said before, nothing that hadn't been tried before, nothing that hadn't resulted in the long run in tremendous suffering for the people. But for young students, especially the lonely, the lovelorn, those down on their luck or those just looking for a purpose in life, Professor Xiong would prove to be irresistible.

How was it that people such as Professor Xiong arose?

How was it that a human mind could develop in such a way as for all self-doubt to be extinguished?

Philip Ye had no idea. He thought it possible that some people came into the world with minds so afraid that the only mechanism by which they could continue to live was to cling to certain ideas and beliefs so tightly, so rigidly, that all competing or contradictory ideas and beliefs became invisible to them – or, if encountered in other people, something to be fought against and hopefully destroyed. This was the mind-set of the fanatic, he thought – a very dangerous person indeed. And, paradoxically, it was toward such fanatics that so many vulnerable people were attracted, seeing in the fanatic the security of absolute certainty that they would wish for themselves.

Of course, it was only a half-theory, hardly explaining how some fanatics had the charisma of a slug with an astounding ability to alienate their own families, and how some charismatic individuals spoke out against entrenched beliefs and dogma, and only sought to do good in the world. It could be that charisma was a quality of spirit, the mind – dark or clear – only the lens it shone through. He did not know for sure. But, if Isobel's death had taught him anything, it was that to live properly one had to learn to cope with uncertainty, to accept a measure of fear and self-doubt as part and parcel of being human. One never knew when there would be another illness, another death. One never knew when a treasured shikra would be lost to the open sky. And one never knew when another earthquake would come along and turn the whole world upside down.

He had also learned that it was foolish to cede one's mind to any external authority. Not that Isobel's death had taught him this. This was a lesson he had learned all by himself.

"Mister Lao, you must tell us all about yourself," said Professor Xiong, his lecture finally over. "Which university did you attend in England?"

"York, where I read theoretical physics."

"Ah, and then?"

"A doctorate, a few years in industry and then back to York as a research associate."

"Excellent, excellent…and your chosen field?"

"I'd rather not say," replied Philip Ye, feigning modesty.

"Oh, come now, Doctor Lao, one area of research is as good as any other. Do not keep me and my friends on tenterhooks."

It was now or never, Philip Ye thought. Enough time had passed and there was nothing he could do now about the State Security operative in her little office. And soon enough the phones would begin ringing with the news of the raids taking place at every Singing Moon bar in Chengdu and at the old house deep in the remote countryside of Longquanyi District.

He stared deeply into Professor Xiong's complex and hypnotic eyes and said, "My chosen field of research is the potential for the continuation of life following the death of the physical body."

First a moment of shocked silence, and then a ripple of laughter ran around the table. A glass was raised in mock salute to him. Someone almost choked on their food. Philip Ye heard the snap of a zippo lighter as yet another cigarette was lit. But Professor Xiong was not laughing or eating or smoking. His crooked teeth bared, his good humour evaporated, his eyes were hardening in the painful realisation that an enemy had somehow inveigled their way to his table.

"From my initial research," continued Philip Ye, "I have come to the conclusion that ghosts do indeed exist. There are too many instances where ghosts have appeared to people to discount. What then are ghosts and what is the mechanism by which they appear to us? I cannot answer either question yet to my satisfaction, except that I do believe the spirit does indeed survive the death of the physical body and that this consciousness…which is what I think the spirit is…continues its existence elsewhere – a place I am happy to describe as the afterlife. So instead of struggling to answer the most difficult questions, I have satisfied myself so far with trying to answer why ghosts appear to us and, specifically, why ghosts appear to some and not to others. The latter is easier to explain. I believe some are born with a natural sensitivity to that which is just beyond the physical. I also believe that very occasionally, especially in extremely heightened emotional states, those without this natural sensitivity can perceive that which they would normally overlook.

"As to why ghosts appear, I am developing two working hypotheses. The first is that if the conditions are right – I am as yet unable to say what those conditions might be – a person might become attuned to the psychic memory of a landscape or structure and open up a window into the past. The ghost that is then seen is an image from another time and there will be no interaction at all with the observer. And then there are what I refer to as 'true visitations': those rare instances when ghosts appear *to us*, having something of importance to impart. From the data I have compiled, this information always seems to be of a personal nature, a communication that would aid someone in trouble, an offering of forgiveness, or a gift of closure to a dispute or problem left unresolved at the time of the spirit's passing from the physical body. You must understand that I have never heard it said that a true visitation encourages someone to commit a crime, or wishes to be worshipped as a deity, or hopes to promote a new and potentially bloody revolution. Ghosts do not seem to be concerned with such things as politics, religion, or whatever passes for morality these days. They have no judgement to offer. So, Professor, I am intrigued to learn what it was your wife told you when she appeared to you as a ghost. Or would it be more respectful of me to call her The Willow Woman?"

"Demon!" roared Professor Xiong, struggling to stand, his eyes bulging, hatred burning from every pore.

"No – not a demon, police," replied Philip Ye, laying his badge and ID open upon the table. "Though I will concede that many find us very hard to tell apart."

CHAPTER SIXTY-TWO

Sunday

As a deep silence descended upon the room, and the eyes of the king cobra burned into him with rage, confusion and disbelief, Philip Ye reflected on the fact that the majority of his friends and acquaintances – if not all of them – thought him immune to fear. Not only had he been born into the wealth, power and influence of the family Ye, with the confidence that these things bring, but he was also a son of the East and the West, and therefore in possession of a superior, enlightened and educated perspective, unburdened by the humiliation of what it was to be a full Chinese these last one hundred and fifty years, China too weak to stand up to the foreign powers. And, mostly, what was thought of him was true. He *was* confident. He *was* untroubled whenever he encountered the rich and the powerful. He *was* able to communicate without any sense of inferiority with those who originated on the other side of the globe. But what his colleagues did not see was the inner tension, the constant anxiety, the anguish of having to live between two worlds and not being fully part of either, trapped not only in some limbo between the East and the West, but also between the living and the dead. It was all very well being comfortable with the trappings of wealth and power, but if one lacked certainty over one's position or identity, if staring into the mirror every day brought only confusion, and if the very definitions of what it meant to be Eastern or Western, or alive or dead, meant so little, then one felt one was permanently adrift on an ever-changing sea.

As Philip Ye coolly returned Professor Xiong's stare, he could not help feeling envious of the old man. It was an odd feeling, he knew, inappropriate when considering that Professor Xiong was someone who saw the lives of others as dispensable, as pieces to be used in whatever game he was playing. Philip Ye suspected that at no time in his life had Professor Xiong not known who he was or where he belonged, or had ever suffered the excruciating agonies of self-doubt. That Philip Ye knew such mental certainty to be the height of folly, that identity was nothing more than those concepts about the world or about oneself that one chose to adopt, did nothing to alleviate the envy he felt. It would be nice, just for one hour in every week say, to possess the mind of a fanatic.

"Policeman, you are not welcome in my house," said Professor Xiong, struggling to stand, reaching for his walking-stick.

None of the dinner guests rose with him. The maids were also frozen to their respective stations, too frightened to move. Philip Ye wondered if the State Security agent had sensed something was amiss yet, if she was already on her way. He willed himself to relax, to remain in his seat.

"Professor, whether I am welcome or not does not concern me. As police, I am charged with keeping the peace, with protecting the people from those who would harm them. This evening you are to be detained for your many crimes."

"You have no authority in Chongqing!"

"I beg to differ."

"Get out! Get out!" roared Professor Xiong, enraged, flecks of spittle flying from his mouth.

"Tell me what has become of Prosecutor Xu and it will go better for you back in Chengdu."

"Guard! Guard!" Professor Xiong looked about him in a panic. "Where is that stupid girl?"

One of his maids, braver than the rest, detached herself from the others and made a run for the doorway. But she was brought up suddenly by the appearance of a man dressed head to toe in black, a balaclava obscuring his features, a modern military issue assault carbine cradled in his arms. In fright, the maid covered her eyes and dropped to her knees. The stranger surveyed the room quickly and with a curt nod showed his satisfaction with what he saw.

"Boss, the house is secure," he said.

"And the State Security agent?" asked Philip Ye.

"Reconsidering her future with the Professor's protective detail. There's no sign of the Prosecutor. But there's a locked room down the way that's probably worth checking out."

"No!" screamed Professor Xiong, losing all control of himself now, stumbling forward.

"Can I shoot this old fool?" asked the man in black.

"Not yet, but feel free with anyone else," replied Philip Ye, taking Professor Xiong by his shirt collar, keeping him upright, and pushing him out of the room.

It did not take long to identify the door in question. But any decision on effecting an entry had been rendered moot. The lock had already been smashed and the door was hanging off its hinges.

"The Willow Woman will punish you all!" Professor Xiong cried out in dismay.

Philip Ye pushed him roughly into the room. His crippled legs giving way beneath him, Professor Xiong fell onto the stone floor, scraping his knees as he did so. He let out an anguished moan. Philip Ye ignored him. They were in the first of a suite of rooms, a dingy sitting-room if it could be described as such. If this was the real heart of the house – and Philip Ye thought it was – then it was cold and empty. The air was stale, devoid of the smells of cooking and incense that filled the rest of the house. But in this stagnant air, tainted by dust and mould, he finally caught a whiff of Prosecutor Xu's perfume and a sense – no more than a faint echo – of her despair. He had not led himself astray. She had been here.

Out of another room of the suite, another figure dressed in black emerged, assault carbine at the ready in his hands. However, he had removed his balaclava to aid his search.

"There's something in here you should see," said Day Na, gravely.

Philip Ye promised himself he would display no emotion if he was to be shown Prosecutor Xu's body. But as he walked into what he found to be a bedroom, he saw a single chair placed in the centre of the room not far from the bed, pieces of cord lying on the floor.

"My guess is she was held here," said Day Na. "There's a few specks of blood on the floor but whatever they did with her I think she walked or was carried out of here alive. One of the kitchen boys told me she arrived this morning but he hasn't seen her since. The others told him to shut up then. Believe it or not, the household staff are more afraid of this old man here than of me. This was also lying underneath the desk by the window." He handed Philip Ye a shiny black leather wallet. "The other door leads to a small study. I couldn't see anything of importance in there. Doesn't look like it's been used for years."

Philip Ye flipped the wallet open, not surprised to see the gleaming procuratorate badge. Prosecutor Xu stared out of the small

ID photograph, trying to act all professional and serious and failing. There was a faint smile about her lips and her eyes were shining with happiness. The day she had been appointed to Chengdu People's Procuratorate must have been joyous for her, he thought. In her face he also detected a sense of fun, something he had missed in her the night he had met with her back at The Silver Tree. But then again, he wondered if he had seen her properly at all that evening. She had hidden so much from him.

"Boss, time to go," said Day Na.

But Philip Ye's attention had suddenly been drawn to something else. He moved across to the table by the window.

"It's just an old photograph," said Day Na.

Philip Ye picked it up, letting the protective cloth it was wrapped in fall away to the floor. He heard Professor Xiong moan again. The glass of the photograph was smashed but the faded photograph itself was undamaged. A woman dressed in a Sun Yat-sen suit sat under a willow tree by a river.

"This is The Willow Woman," said Philip Ye.

"If you say so, Boss – but we have to go," said Day Na. "We may have tripped a silent alarm."

"I need to question some of the maids."

"Boss, this is Chongqing not Chengdu. We shouldn't be here. A State Security Quick Reaction Team might already be on their way. We have to go. Prosecutor Xu is not here. You cannot save everyone."

"Wolf said the same."

"He's a wise man."

Philip Ye nodded, despondent. He thought back to the wasted days trailing around Chengdu with Wang Jiyu looking for his missing shikra. He could scour Chongqing for ever and find no trace of Prosecutor Xu – unless Professor Xiong talked under questioning. And there was no guarantee that he would talk or, if he did, make sense. Philip Ye looked over at him. Day Na was keeping the old man upright. Professor Xiong's face was ashen, his eyes blank, rolling listlessly in his head. Philip Ye put Prosecutor Xu's badge and ID in his pocket. They would have to be returned to her parents sometime. He would shoulder the blame. He would deliver them himself.

"You taking this old fool with us?" asked Day Na.

"Yes."

"There may be repercussions from State Security."

"That is true," said Philip Ye, uncaring.

Day Na laughed and said, "Life is never dull with the family Ye."

Day Na led the way, lifting the unprotesting Professor Xiong up and putting him across his strong shoulders. They collected Night Na from the dining-room. All the maids and dinner guests had been made to lie down face down on the floor. They stopped off at the security office. The State Security agent was sitting down on the floor, gagged, arms behind her wrists, bound by plastic cuffs. She was conscious, staring up at him, eyes full of hatred.

He wasn't going to say anything, but anger got the better of him. He took out his own ID and showed it to her. "Tell your masters that I've taken Professor Xiong. In time he will be charged with murder, with leading a superstitious religious cult, and maybe sedition too for good measure. You should pray he doesn't implicate State Security in his crimes."

He took his raincoat off the rack and picked up his phone from the desk. About to sweep the other phones onto the floor to smash them with his shoe, he suddenly decided against this. One of the phones might have belonged to Prosecutor Xu and useful intelligence might be gleaned from the others. He rummaged in the drawers of the desk, found a plastic bag and threw the phones inside. With a last look at the young woman sitting staring up at him from the floor, her expression more puzzled now than anything, he walked out of the house. The storm had worsened. The wind was gusting harder and lightning now crisscrossed the sky. He fought against the gale to get back to his car. Day Na and Night Na were already there. They had secured Professor Xiong with more plastic ties. Philip Ye opened the boot for them and they threw the Professor inside. With the Professor lying as if comatose, Philip Ye threw a blanket over him. He then threw the broken photograph of Yi Li, The Willow Woman herself, in the boot too and slammed it shut. He would keep Professor Xiong in the boot until they were safely out of Chongqing. He couldn't take the risk of the Professor's face being picked up on any street cameras. As the Na brothers ran back to their own car – an identical black Mercedes – Philip Ye spun his car around. He drove away at high speed, not quite sure where he was, but looking for an ideal location to park up for a while. Spotting a dark and deserted side street, he braked and switched the engine off. It was time for the Na brothers to discard the false military registration plates the cars had worn and replace them with genuine police plates. Philip Ye used the slight hiatus to phone his father.

"Did you find her?" Ye Zihao asked.

"No, Father."

"Mouse will be upset."

"I know."

"Wolf has been trying to reach you."

"When?"

"Just now – your phone was switched off."

"What did he want?"

"To apologise – he said he'd dropped his own phone in a puddle. He wants you to drop by his apartment."

"That's all he said?"

"Yes."

Philip Ye sighed. "Any word from Wukuaishi Hospital?"

"The Director is keeping me apprised. Investigator Deng is out of surgery. He is doing better than expected."

"I am relieved – he is a good man."

"Philip, was your hunt successful? Did you trap your prey?"

"Yes, I have him."

"I am glad."

Philip Ye checked his messages then. There were two. The first was from Lucy Fu, wanting him to know how overjoyed she was to see him again, that both she and her father were prepared to over-look his barging into Tranquil Mountain Pavilions, that she was looking forward to meeting up with him on her return from New York; the second from Superintendent Zuo, to apologise, to say that Madame Xiong was not at her apartment at the university, her current whereabouts unknown.

He quickly closed his eyes and breathed, needing to keep his temper under control.

Day Na tapped the window to indicate that the work on the regis-tration plates was done, that it was time to go.

Philip Ye dropped the window. "I need to see Wolf first."

"Is that wise, Boss?"

"He has information for me."

Day Na bowed to the inevitable and hurried off through the rain to tell Night Na the bad news that they would not be leaving Chongqing just yet.

CHAPTER SIXTY-THREE

Sunday

Her heart at peace, glad that she had been proved wrong, that there was indeed an afterlife and that her Beloved Mister Qin had come to escort her there, Xu Ya lifted her face to the night sky. Neither the freezing rain beating down upon her face nor the screaming wind troubled her anymore. However, the expected sharp pain to end her life had not come. Instead the screaming rose in intensity. Opening her eyes, she realised it was not the wind at all. It was Madame Xiong, crying out in warning, pointing to the figure of Beloved Mister Qin moving unfalteringly across the waste ground toward them. The two men holding Xu Ya down let her go. They set off, knives appearing in their hands, to intercept Beloved Mister Qin before he got close.

You cannot kill a ghost, thought Xu Ya, laughing to herself, finding some bleak humour in what these men were hoping to do.

But then a series of reports, muffled by the wind, reached her ears. She saw the two men go down in the mud, writhing as if in pain, Beloved Mister Qin then standing above them, pistol in hand, pumping bullet after bullet into them. Only it was not Beloved Mister Qin at all. Her eyes – or her most fervent wishes – had served to deceive her. It was a man she did not know, some unknown saviour brought to her by the storm.

Hope and life suddenly came back into her body, and her heart began to thud again in her breast. Philip Ye's handsome face came back to mind, as did the vow she had made to bring the law to the people. She twisted around to look up at Madame Xiong. There was still murder in Madame Xiong's eyes, and, with the knife held tightly in her hand, the capacity to do it. Madame Xiong reached down to grab at Xu Ya's hair again, to hold her still, so the knife could do its work before the unknown saviour could reach them. But with a last vestige of energy that Xu Ya did not know she possessed, and impelled by her rediscovered desire to live, she threw herself from the kneeling position against Madame Xiong's stocky legs.

Unprepared for this assault from below, Madame Xiong was knocked off balance by the impact. She stumbled, slipping backwards on the mud, her arms flailing like a crazy person as she tried in vain to maintain her footing. She fell onto the bank of the river. As Xu Ya watched on in horror, Madame Xiong failed to find a firm handhold and slid off the bank into the icy, black water. She bobbed to the surface spluttering, but went under again, never to reappear. All that remained of her was that stupid pink, plastic rain hat as it floated off downstream.

Xu Ya was grabbed from behind, lifted onto her feet.

"Prosecutor, did she cut you? Are you hurt?"

Xu Ya turned to focus on her saviour. With a short beard and moustache covering a grizzled face, and tired eyes that had seen far too much, there was indeed a passing resemblance to Beloved Mister Qin. But it was definitely not him. Xu Ya did not know this man at all. She could not speak. She began to shake violently in his arms, her teeth rattling in her skull.

He swept her up in his arms. He carried her back across the waste ground, his steps slow and measured, careful not to drop her. When he put her down it was next to a dented old BMW parked a short distance behind the truck that had brought her to this desolate spot. He opened up a rear door and pushed her inside and onto the back seat. He threw a blanket over her and slammed the door shut.

Xu Ya pulled the blanket about her, grateful more for the comfort it brought her than for the added warmth. She expected her saviour would now drive her to the nearest police station. But he did not. She watched, through windows blurred by the rain, his dark figure cross the waste ground again. He stood on the bank of the river for a few moments as if lost in thought and then tossed something far out into the water. His pistol, she thought, but could not be sure. Then, one by one, he dragged the bodies of the fallen men to the rear of their truck.

She shook her head, inwardly protesting. The bodies were evidence and evidence always had to be preserved.

She watched him pick up each body and roll it into the back of the truck, his strength impressive. Then she lost sight of him as he went around the side of the truck. He was gone some time. Xu Ya became frightened, fearing he might not return. But then he came hurrying back. As he jumped into the car, his breathing hoarse and laboured, she saw the first lick of flame curl around the truck.

"What have you done?" she cried, aghast.

"You're a public prosecutor," he replied, starting the engine. "If you want to keep your job no one must know you were ever here."

Xu Ya was jolted in her seat as he reversed at speed. He then spun the car around and accelerated hard away from the scene. As she looked back through the rear windshield all she could see was a yellow-orange fireball.

"We must call the police," she said. "The law requires that—"

"I am the police."

"But—"

"Prosecutor, this isn't your city anymore. In truth, I don't think it ever was. Chongqing plays by its own rules – always has, always will."

Furious, her mind beginning to function again, she asked, "Who are you?"

"Nobody – just an ageing, brain-damaged, cross-eyed monkey."

Xu Ya had no idea what that meant or why he seemed so angry with her. She slumped back in her seat. The thought of the bodies of those two men being consumed by the fire began to prey on her mind, as did that final memory of Madame Xiong as she slipped forever under the water.

He drove her to a part of the city she did not know. He parked outside a large, old apartment block. When he opened the door to let her out, her legs would not work. He had to carry her inside and up a few flights of stairs. A door to an apartment was opened to them. He put her down on her feet and into the waiting arms of a woman of mature years; his wife, Xu Ya supposed. A doe-eyed teenage girl stood nearby, looking on.

As the woman and the girl took her through to the bathroom, she glanced back and saw him pick up a phone. In the bathroom, the women stripped off her sodden clothes, tutting at her injuries, at the mud and scratches on her feet. They pushed her under a steaming shower. Xu Ya stood shaking for the longest time, the hot water thawing her out, cleansing her, healing her. When she was finally done, they dried her with thick towels. She began to sob, unable to stop herself.

"My daughter's clothes should fit you," said the woman.

Xu Ya nodded, wiping away her tears, wanting to thank her, to embrace both her and her daughter.

"Prosecutor, you must be strong," she said. "Put away your tears for later. My husband has managed to get a message to him. I don't want you to lose face in front of him. He doesn't deserve to see you like this."

"Who are you talking about?" Xu Ya asked, confused.

"Philip Ye, of course. But leave him to me, Prosecutor. I have a few choice words for him. How he could let this happen...." She left the bathroom, shaking her head, visibly angry.

Xu Ya thought on what she said, unable to believe it. Philip Ye coming for her? What did it mean? How did he know where she would be? She quickly examined herself in the mirror. There was a slight cut on her neck where Madame Xiong had held the knife against her. One side of her face was swollen and bruised. And the back of her head still throbbed from the blow Professor Xiong had dealt her. She looked a mess.

"It is because of you I am going to study law," said the teenage girl.

Xu Ya turned to her, puzzled.

"Years ago, when I was little," the girl continued, "my father sneaked me into court to see what it was like. You were presenting a case. It was a murder. I will never forget it...ever. A man had beaten his wife to death. You shone like the sun. You laid bare to the court everything that evil man had done – so simply, so clearly, so cleverly."

"Your father doesn't like me."

"He's police – he doesn't like anyone." The girl giggled. "But he really hated you. I remember him cursing you all the way home from the court. My mother says it is because you were so good at your job."

"Who is your father?"

The girl looked surprised Xu Ya did not know. "Supervisor Lang, Homicide. But Uncle Philip always calls him Wolf. Some years ago Uncle Philip saved my father's life."

"You call Philip Ye, uncle?"

The girl nodded, her eyes shining. "Isn't he the best man in all of China...and the most handsome? All my friends want to meet him one day."

Xu Ya wiped at her eyes again, trying to smile, trying to understand what all of this meant.

CHAPTER SIXTY-FOUR

Sunday

Feeling drained of all life, Wolf shed his clothes. His shoes, though covered in mud, could be recovered. His suit, an old favourite, was a different matter. He didn't want to see it again. It was stained with the blood of the men he had killed, the transfer made when he had hauled them off the ground and rolled them into the back of the truck before setting it alight. His coat and shirt were also ruined. He bundled the clothing up into a plastic bag. On the way back to work he would drop the bag off with a friend of his for burning. As for the men's deaths, that had been unavoidable. He had had to finish them off while they had lain wounded on the ground. They may have died regardless. Wolf didn't know. But he could not take the chance of them living to tell their tale. If Prosecutor Xu was to avoid another scandal, and if he was to keep his job, there had to be no witnesses. A dirty business, but that was how it was sometimes in Chongqing.

He looked up and saw his wife staring at him. He had assumed he had been alone with his thoughts.

"I did not realise how beautiful she is," she said.

"Appearances can be deceptive," he replied, searching in the cupboard for a new shirt.

Han Yue came over to him and touched his arm. "Husband, you have done a good thing this evening."

"I'm not so sure – you know what I think of her."

Han Yue lowered her voice to a whisper. "She is no murderer."

"And how do you know that?"

"I have looked into her eyes."

"Then you should take my police badge and go down to the station and do my job, for you are a much better judge of character than I am." Wolf tried to shake Han Yue's hand from him, pretending he neither needed nor wanted her attention.

Han Yu gripped him all the more tightly. "She may have had good reason to kill her husband."

"That wasn't her decision to make."

"And this evening?" she asked, archly.

"I did this for Philip, not for her. I did this because I owe him... we owe him...and will continue to owe him until the day we die."

"I think they're a good match," said Han Yue, slipping past his half-hearted attempts to fend her off, hugging him.

"Who?"

"Philip and Prosecutor Xu, of course."

"You are being foolish."

"No, I am serious. You told me how brave she was facing certain death. And you should have seen her reaction in the bathroom when I mentioned his name. How about a wager? You and me. A wedding before the year is out."

"I want nothing to do with you, crazy woman."

"Pah! Without me, you'd be nothing, old man."

They both heard the knock at the door. Han Yue extricated herself from his arms to run and open it, planning to give Philip Ye a piece of her mind for allowing Prosecutor Xu to get into such difficulty. But, as Wolf pulled on some trousers and buttoned up a fresh shirt, he heard her squeal with delight – not quite the reaction he had been expecting. When he got to the sitting-room, he found the Na brothers taking turns to hug her and lift her up in the air.

"What are you two pirates doing here?" Wolf growled at them.

"Wolf-man!" the Na brothers cried out in unison, putting down his wife and bounding over to him to shake his hand.

"The boss is not far behind," said Day Na.

"He had to make sure the package we're taking back to Chengdu is still breathing in the boot of his car," added Night Na.

They were about to say more when Lang Xiu, Wolf's daughter, led Prosecutor Xu by the hand into the room. Wolf had to catch his breath. Prosecutor Xu had almost twenty years over Lang Xiu but wearing her clothes they could have been sisters.

"Baby Wolf, how big you've grown," said Day Na, bowing to Lang Xiu.

"Any trouble with boys, Baby Wolf, and you just give us a call," said Night Na, also bowing. "We'll sort them out."

Lang Xiu let go of Prosecutor Xu and hugged each Na brother in turn, giggling as she did so. Prosecutor Xu looked to Wolf in confusion.

"May I introduce the brothers Na," he said, failing to make the situation any clearer.

"Police?" asked Prosecutor Xu, baffled.

The Na brothers doubled up in laughter.

"Certainly not," replied Wolf, horrified at the thought, wanting everybody to stop hugging each other and let him get out of the apartment and back to the station. He had work to do. And he needed a rest. It never ceased to amaze him how anything to do with the family Ye was so wearing on the nerves.

The Na brothers bowed to Prosecutor Xu too.

"Lady, we are factotums," said Day Na, with a mischievous grin.

"Absolutely, nothing but factotums," agreed Night Na.

Thankfully, this ridiculous charade was stopped by another knock at the door. This time, with a shake of his head, Wolf indicated to his wife that he would answer it. When he opened the door he found Philip Ye wiping rainwater from his face with a silk handkerchief, for the first time ever looking older than his years. It wasn't the face. That was as handsome and unblemished as ever. It was the green eyes. They seemed to have dulled in the year since Wolf had last seen him. There was defeat in them, resignation even. Wolf chose not to prolong his agony.

"I have her," he said, simply.

Those eyes suddenly brightened and the set of Philip Ye's shoulders loosened, the years falling away from him again. "She is well?"

"A few cuts, some lumps and bruises and a little shaken up. But Princess Poison is more resilient than she appears. I didn't want to say anything on the phone to your father."

"Because you don't know who's listening in?"

"Don't mock me, Philip. Now step inside. And keep your temper. I insist on harmony in my home."

"You have my word."

Wolf shut the door, thinking on what his wife had said, about a wedding being in the offing. From the change in Philip Ye's demeanour when he had heard that Prosecutor Xu was alive, Wolf thought it might just prove true. His stomach turned at the prospect.

At first Wolf expected the encounter to go smoothly, Prosecutor Xu to be handed over and him to be able to get on with his life. But when they came face to face with each other, it seemed that neither Philip Ye nor Prosecutor Xu knew what to do. After nodding and smiling to Han Yue and Lang Xui, Philip Ye just stared at Prosecutor Xu as if unable to think of something to say. And she, apart from a slight reddening high on her cheekbones and an absent flick of her hand to remove a lock of hair that had fallen across her face, kept her jaw firmly shut. The pregnant silence between them would have made good theatre if Wolf hadn't been so fed up, so distressed by the killing of the two men, and so fearful that Philip Ye was about to make the biggest mistake of his life.

"Professor Xiong has been detained," said Philip Ye, finally.

Prosecutor Xu lifted her chin to him. "By Chongqing police?"

"No, by me."

"In Chongqing, you do not have the authorisation to—"

"I'll not argue law with you, Prosecutor," replied Philip Ye, raising his voice.

Wolf was forced to intervene, ruining the spectacle for everybody, especially the Na brothers who were looking on with a mixture of awe and amusement.

"I insist on civility in my home," said Wolf. "If you two want to debate rights and wrongs, you can do it down at my station."

Prosecutor Xu proudly lifted her chin even higher but kept her silence. Philip Ye ran his hand through his slick hair in exasperation. "The Na brothers will take you anywhere you wish to go, Prosecutor," he said, as if wanting to wash his hands of her.

"Absolutely," said Night Na.

"That's what factotums are for," added Day Na.

Prosecutor Xu looked to Wolf who nodded, indicating that she would be quite safe. Without so much as a glance at Philip Ye, Prosecutor Xu then embraced Han Yue and Lang Xiu, thanking them for their kindness and the loan of the clothes. She then held a hand out to Wolf, which he took, surprising himself.

"I do remember you, Supervisor Lang," she said. "Well, not you exactly. I remember your paperwork. I did once describe you as a brainless cross-eyed monkey. You had made unsubstantiated assumptions in one of your cases. I stand by my words. But you should know that yours were the best case files that ever crossed my desk from any policeman anywhere in Chongqing."

Confused to be damned and praised in almost the same breath, Wolf replied, "No more adventures, Prosecutor – leave the fighting to the police. It's what we're good at."

As the Na brothers began to usher Prosecutor Xu out of the apartment, she turned to say some quick words to Philip Ye.

"Superintendent, I am not the little fool you think I am. There was a photograph in Madame Xiong's apartment...proof that Junjie was alive at the New Year and being held captive at Professor Xiong's residence here in Chongqing. I thought I could rescue him. I regret that I did not find him. And I especially regret that my actions could have contributed to Investigator Deng's death."

"Fatty Deng's not dead," replied Philip Ye.

Her mouth dropped open. But the Na brothers hurried her out and Wolf shut the door quickly before anymore could be said.

Han Yue ran over to Philip Ye and punched him on the arm, saying, "How could you let that beautiful girl get into so much difficulty?" She then hugged him tightly before he had the chance to reply.

"Let the man breathe," said Wolf. "He and I need to speak for a few moments...alone!"

Wolf directed this command also at his daughter, but, as was usual in his home, it took them longer than it should to obey. His daughter especially lingered in the doorway, mooning at Philip Ye as if he were some movie star.

"Out!" Wolf snapped at her.

"She has grown much in the last year," said Philip Ye, when Lang Xiu had gone.

"She has decided she wishes to study law...at Wuhan."

"Is that so bad?"

"She wants to be a prosecutor."

"Better than police."

Wolf nodded. There was that.

"I feared you hadn't been able to extricate yourself from your own investigation," said Philip Ye, taking a seat.

"It was close...too close. Someone is watching over Prosecutor Xu."

"A spirit?"

Wolf shook his head. "I don't know...maybe just an auspicious star. When I finally got away from the station I was delayed again because I had to change a flat tyre – in the rain, mind you. Then, when I was nearing Professor Xiong's house, a daft old guy in a wheelchair, out in this weather if you can believe it, runs out in front on me in the road. I couldn't fucking believe it. Disabled or not, I was going to get out of the car to give him a word or two when I looked up and saw this red delivery truck go trundling by. I remembered what you'd told me about the attack on Investigator Deng. This truck had the same delivery company emblazoned on the side. Maybe I wasn't thinking straight. Maybe that guy in the wheelchair had given me an awful shock. But I jumped back in the car and began to follow the truck. It took me all over the city. I thought after a while they had figured out I was tailing them. But then I followed it down to this deserted spot by the river. When they pulled this body from the back of the truck…two men and a woman…I thought Prosecutor Xu was already dead. I tried to call you but I slipped trying to get a better look and dropped my phone in a puddle. That's the third phone I've broken this month. Anyway they took her hood off and I was amazed to see she was still alive. They dragged her down to the riverbank. I never heard her cry out. She didn't plead for her life. Whatever her past sins, she's got courage, Philip – I'll grant you that."

Wolf then described what happened next, how he had scrambled over the mud and building detritus to get to Prosecutor Xu, how he had been spotted, the two men rushing him with knives, how he had then shot them both down, finishing them off on the ground, emptying a whole fifteen round magazine into them before slipping again in the mud as he tried to feed in a new magazine into the pistol, realising he wasn't going to get to Prosecutor Xu in time before her throat was slit, and then watching in astonishment as Prosecutor Xu roused herself and pushed her female captor backwards, toppling her into the river.

"Who was the woman?" asked Philip Ye.

"When I reached Prosecutor Xu, she was mumbling about a Madame Xiong. Does that mean anything to you?"

"Professor Xiong's sister."

"Ah – anyway she'd sunk without trace by the time I got to the river."

"Dead?"

"I'm not sure how she could have survived. Only time will tell. I'll keep an eye out for reports of bodies being washed up downstream."

"Witnesses?"

Wolf shook his head. "Visibility was bad. I didn't notice anyone in the vicinity. They chose their spot well to dispose of Prosecutor Xu. I didn't use a service pistol…it was the other you gave me. I threw it into the river. I set light to the truck after throwing in it the bodies of the two men I'd killed. I can't see forensics wasting too much time on what appears to be a gangland killing."

"Your phone?"

"In the river also."

"Thank you, Wolf."

"I told you Prosecutor Xu had the stomach to make a kill."

"So you did."

"Philip, part of me wanted to leave her to her fate."

"We don't really know what went on between her and her husband."

"Have you fallen under her spell already?"

Philip Ye smiled. "You told me she was only good at pissing people off."

"Did I say that?"

"You did."

"Well, just watch yourself, Philip. Think about why she has been hired by the Chengdu Legal and Political Committee. They may finally be about to go after your father."

"I haven't forgotten."

"Anyway, what happened with Professor Xiong? Did he really see his wife's ghost?"

"I believe so. And, though it troubles me to say it, the visitation from his wife – or I should say Professor Xiong's misinterpretation of that visitation – was the beginning of The Willow Woman cult. From what I have learned their marriage was complicated, very troubled. I suspect she appeared to him as an offering of forgiveness. He, in his senility, or just from fear and intense guilt, interpreted the visitation quite differently. I think the appearance of her ghost fright-ened him so much it overturned everything he had previously believed to be true. He suddenly discarded his life of science and took on her extreme political views with a vengeance, elevating her to the status of goddess in his mind, believing that in creating the cult he was actually doing her will. Naturally the cult was still a projection of his grandiose personality, the young people flocking to him rather than anything his dead wife might have believed or stood for."

"Are you sure she didn't come back to try to scare him to death… to take her revenge?"

Philip Ye smiled. "No, I believe my theory still stands: ghosts do not appear to seek justice or vengeance as many might think, but only to offer forgiveness and consolation to those mourning them, or to pass on information needed to prevent hurt to a loved one."

"Philip, if ghosts are the spirits of dead people then why can't they be as evil in death as they were in life? How do we know that the Professor's wife might not have wanted him to act in the way he did?"

"I have no sensible answer for you," replied Philip Ye, with a weary shrug of his shoulders.

"You want to believe only the good in us survives death."

"Maybe."

"Philip, I don't know how you've survived in the police so long, being such an optimist."

"Perhaps I just hope the afterlife to be better than this."

Wolf checked his watch. "I have to get back to the station."

"The drowned girl?"

"Yes."

Philip Ye stood and held out his hand. Wolf gripped it tightly, sad that they'd had so little time to talk. Before Philip Ye left the apartment, the women hugged him some more and made him promise to return soon for a proper visit.

As Wolf showed him to the door, Philip Ye said, "Remember, Wolf, that you are family. If you need anything...."

"Not family, Philip...I'm your friend."

"Is the distinction so important?"

"It is to me."

When Philip Ye was gone, Wolf returned to the sitting-room and found his wife and daughter holding hands, grinning like a pair of idiots.

"What?" he asked.

"Husband, it is good news," said Han Yue.

"The best news, Father," said Lang Xiu.

"Prosecutor Xu has promised to help our daughter get into the law school at Wuhan," said Han Yue. "She is still in touch with the Director of Teaching there. She has even offered to tutor our daughter."

Wolf stomped off to the bedroom to complete his dressing so he could go back to work. Soon he felt his wife's eyes upon him again. "What?"

"It *is* good news, Husband."

"Is it?" he replied.

CHAPTER SIXTY-FIVE

Sunday

"Is it true?" asked Xu Ya, hardly daring to believe, as she got into the car with the Na brothers. "Is Investigator Deng still alive?"

The Na brothers, sitting up front in their black Mercedes, the car identical in every way to Philip Ye's car, down to the red and blue flashing lights when needed, twisted around in their seats to face her.

"He's at Wukuaishi Hospital," said Day Na.

"And out of danger," said Night Na.

"So don't worry."

"He has the best care."

"The very best."

"The boss insisted on it."

Xu Ya frowned, trying to take this wonderful news in. "By 'boss', do you mean Superintendent Ye?"

"Ah," said Day Na.

"Sometimes," said Night Na.

"It depends."

"In this instance we mean Mayor Ye Zihao."

"You mean the *former* mayor, Ye Zihao," Xu Ya said, sharply. She pointed at each of them in turn. "You, Day Na...and you, Night Na... you both work for the family Ye, don't you?"

"More or less," admitted Day Na.

"In a manner of speaking," said Night Na.

"It's complicated."

"Very complicated."

The brothers glanced at each other, delighted. Xu Ya had surprised them. She had identified each of them correctly, and without hesitation. After all this time, both Philip Ye and Ye Zihao still made mistakes. And they had yet to figure out that the brothers often swapped shifts. Even their mother, long in the afterlife now, had got them confused at times.

"Where would you like to go?" asked Day Na of her.

"To your parents' apartment or back to Chengdu?" asked Night Na.

"Chengdu is my home now," she replied.

This delighted the brothers further. Day Na passed a phone back to her as Night Na started the engine.

"Speak to your parents," he said. "They have been trying to reach you at the Procuratorate. They are very worried. Mouse has told them you've been carrying out a secret assignment and therefore could not be reached."

"Mouse?" Xu Ya had forgotten all about their proposed dinner engagement for the evening.

"Yes, a clever little mouse," said Day Na.

"A surprising little mouse," said Night Na, with a laugh.

Xu Ya did as they suggested. She spoke to both her parents, one after the other. She apologised for worrying them. In return they spoke to her as they would to a child, a child that could now never be trusted after the disaster that was her marriage. She was glad to soon terminate the call, glad to be on her way back to Chengdu. In truth, after the events of the day, she'd be glad never to see Chongqing ever again. If her parents were that worried for her, let them visit her in Chengdu. Though she suspected she would have to wait until the end of time for that to happen.

She found a blanket next to her on the back seat, wrapped herself in it, and lay down. Heading out of Chongqing, the great storm began to abate. She surprised herself by falling asleep with two strange men for company. She dreamed of flying again, soaring high above the landscape, above the mountains and forests, and above the cities also, far away from the concerns of humankind.

When she awoke, they were not in Chengdu. The dashboard clock read midnight. Not yet halfway. The brothers had managed to find a restaurant in the middle of nowhere.

Realising she was famished, and that she had no idea where her handbag and purse were, she said, stupidly, "I have no money."

"Our treat," said Day Na.

"Yes, indeed," said Night Na.

Whether it was because she had just survived a close brush with death or merely the irrepressible good humour of the brothers, Xu Ya could not remember when she had enjoyed a meal out so. The restaurant was quiet and that helped. But the atmosphere of the place did not really matter. It was just good to be alive. The brothers talked and talked, not about the family Ye – that appeared to be a forbidden topic – but about their lives growing up in Dalian. They were rude. They were outrageous. They flirted with the exhausted waitresses. They demanded that the chef come out of the kitchen so they could congratulate him personally. Xu Ya had never met such jovial, big-hearted men. Not that she let this observation fool her. She noticed things about them, how attentive they were always to their surroundings, how disciplined they were in their movements, how straight were their backs.

"Where did you serve in the military?" she asked of them.

"Sorry, not allowed to say," replied Day Na, with a smile.

"Some stories are not to be told," added Night Na.

"Then tell me at least why you work for the family Ye."

The brothers glanced at each other again, as if trying to decide together on the best response. It was Day Na who spoke first.

"You must see, Prosecutor, that life, in general, is quite boring."

"But with the family Ye," continued Night Na, "there is no such thing as a boring day."

Not satisfied with this reply, Xu Ya said, "But Ye Zihao is under house-arrest and the family Ye…." She left her words hanging. She did not want to ruin the dinner with the airing of unproven suspicions.

"Prosecutor, sometimes bad families do good things," said Day Na.

"And sometimes good families do bad things," said Night Na.

"But there are very few families that are always interesting—"

"—no matter what they do."

Xu Ya gave the brothers such a hard stare that they each raised their hands to cover their faces before collapsing into the chairs in convulsions of laughter. She was forced to shake her head, to give up her interrogation – for now.

Back in the car, she slept again. But when she woke this time, a little before three in the morning, they had arrived outside Tranquil Mountain Pavilions.

"Journey's end," said Day Na.

"And, as the Wolf-man said, no more adventures now," said Night Na.

"Maybe not for a few days," replied Xu Ya, delighting the brothers further.

Both the brothers got out of the car and Night Na held her door open for her. As she stepped out into the chill Chengdu night air, the mist lying heavy again about the city, there was something else she needed to ask, something that had been troubling her since leaving Chongqing.

"How is it that Supervisor Lang and Superintendent Ye know each other?"

"The boss saved Wolf's life a couple of years back," replied Day Na.

"It was a bad business," said Night Na.

"That was when Wolf learned the boss's dark secret," said Day Na

"His very dark secret," said Night Na.

Xu Ya's stomach turned over. "What secret?"

"That the boss is a spirit-medium," said Day Na.

"A very talented spirit-medium," confirmed Night Na.

"Spooky stuff."

"Extremely spooky stuff."

"He thinks we don't know."

"But we do – nothing much gets past the brothers Na."

Xu Ya shook her head. They were making fun of her, trying to befuddle her. She would have to do some digging of her own. Without thinking – was it her exhaustion or the emotion of the night? – she kissed each brother on the cheek, which unexpectedly silenced them both for a few moments.

Day Na passed her a small business card. She thought it was blank until she turned the card over and saw a single telephone number.

"What's this?" she asked.

"Call that number if you need help," replied Day Na.

"Day or night," said Night Na.

"But I thought you only worked for the family Ye," she said, tears in her eyes, not quite knowing why.

"We like you," said Day Na.

"Absolutely," said Night Na.

"And besides, Chengdu has become a much more interesting place now that you've arrived."

"And who is to say that the fortunes of Prosecutor Xu and that of the family Ye are not one and the same?"

Before she could respond, they had jumped back in the car and with a squeal of tyres raced off into the night. Still staring at the telephone number they had left her, she stumbled through the door of Tranquil Mountain Pavilions, to be greeted by the night concierge

Mister Ni.

"Welcome home, Prosecutor Xu," he said.

"It's good to be home at last, Mister Ni," she replied, meaning it.

At about the same time as the Na brothers were dropping off Prosecutor Xu at Tranquil Mountain Pavilions, Philip Ye was pulling up outside Wukuaishi Station. Professor Xiong had said nothing the entire journey from Chongqing. Professor Xiong was no longer the same man. His body rigid, his king cobra eyes no longer threatening, his charismatic presence diminished beyond all recognition, it was easier for Philip Ye to carry what was nothing more but a frail old man across the threshold of the station.

At the reception, Baby Wu was fast asleep, his head down on the counter. Ma Meili's ginger cat, Yoyo, was curled up next to him, snoring peacefully. Fortunately, Philip Ye had phoned ahead. When he had placed Professor Xiong down on one of the seats in the waiting-area, Boxer Tan came out of his office to meet him.

"So, is this him?" asked Boxer Tan, pointing at Professor Xiong, full of fury, remembering what had been done to Fatty Deng.

"May I introduce Professor Xiong," said Philip Ye.

Professor Xiong sat with his hands on his bony knees, looking down at the floor, refusing to acknowledge either of them.

"He looks unremarkable," said Boxer Tan.

"You would not have thought so in Chongqing a few hours ago."

"Is he the reason Old Man Gao lost his daft kid?"

"Yes."

"He's got a lot to answer for."

"Indeed."

"Mister Ye, the cells are full from the raids on all The Singing Moon bars this evening. You should see them all, not much older than children most of them, none of them making any sense. This Willow Woman cult has really taken hold of their minds."

"Casualties?"

"A couple of the cultists are screaming about police brutality… but that's nothing new. No police got hurt tonight. But someone's been killed in the PAP operation down in Longquanyi District."

"Who?"

"Don't know, Mister Ye – that's all the information I have. So what do you want me to do with this evil old bastard? Squeeze him into the cells with the others?"

Philip Ye shook his head. "No, he has to disappear for a time."

"The Black House?"

"Yes, no one is to know where he is...not the Procuratorate...not even State Security if they come sniffing around."

"State Security?" Boxer Tan scratched his head, wondering how one old man could cause so much trouble.

"It's a long story. Just tell the guys at the Black House to keep him under wraps for the time being. I don't want anyone spiriting him away. If anyone asks...as far as Chengdu PSB is concerned...we've never heard of Professor Xiong."

"Very good, Mister Ye – and Prosecutor Xu?"

"Back home, safe and sound."

Boxer Tan broke out into a grin. "I'm glad to hear it. It would have upset the boys to take her picture down from the office wall. Oh, and Mister Ye, did you know Fatty Deng's out of surgery?"

"I've heard. How is he?" asked Philip Ye, anxiously.

"The nurse who called me said it was looking positive, though the next forty-eight hours are crucial. She said he died twice more on the operating table. Twice more, Mister Ye! What do you think it means?"

"I don't know."

"I had an uncle who fell into a pond as a boy. When they pulled him out he was no longer breathing. They pumped his chest and out came a bucket full of water. When he came to he swore to everyone he had been walking about in a different land."

"What kind of land?"

"He would never say."

"Is he still around?"

Boxer Tan scratched at his scalp again. "No, he died for real a few years back. Car crash. I'm just wondering whether Fatty Deng, when he gets better, will have a similar story to tell. Maybe, if you're in Wukuaishi again in the next few weeks, we can go visit Fatty Deng together."

"Maybe – and maybe next month when my father has another party you can put a suit on and come down to the house and enjoy yourself for once."

"Only if Wukuaishi Station can do without me for a few hours," laughed Boxer Tan, parties really not his style.

Philip Ye left Professor Xiong in Boxer Tan's very capable hands and returned to his car. He was very relieved about Fatty Deng. Three times dead! He hoped Fatty Deng would make a complete recovery. He very much wanted to speak to him. Before he started the car to drive the final few miles home he made one last phone call.

"This is Secretary Wu."

"She is safe," said Philip Ye.

Secretary Wu sighed with relief. "How is—?"

"Well enough and, though she almost died this night, seemingly unrepentant."

"I am very grateful, Philip…and Professor Xiong?"

"The Black House."

"Ah, I suppose that's for the best…for now."

"State Security will be looking for him."

"Leave them to me."

Philip Ye steeled himself. "Secretary, I have a favour to ask."

Silence.

"It does not concern my father," Philip Ye added.

"I'm listening, Philip."

"It is a trifling matter only, hardly worth your attention, but it is important to me."

"I will do what I can."

Secretary Wu listened as Philip Ye laid out what was required; or, to be more exact, what it was he wished.

"That is fair," said Secretary Wu, after Philip Ye was done. "Before you go, there is someone who would like to speak to you."

Philip Ye could sense Wang Jiyu's presence next to Secretary Wu. She had been listening in to every word of their conversation. But he wasn't ready to cross that particular bridge yet. Wang Jiyu had been more of a mother to him than his birth mother in England had ever been; more so, in fact, than even his compassionate 'little mother', his step-sister, Ye Lan. But Wang Jiyu had wanted him to renounce his father after his father had been removed from office, to come live with her and Secretary Wu – and that he had been unable to do. Nor had he been able to forgive her for suggesting it.

"Perhaps another time," he said to Secretary Wu, quickly ending the call.

He switched his phone off and dropped it onto the passenger seat. He breathed deeply for a few minutes, letting all of the emotion go, letting the rhythm of his heart return to normal.

Fatty Deng.

Dead three times.

What did it mean?

And what stories, if any, would Fatty Deng have to tell about the land of the dead?

Might he have even glimpsed Isobel?

Philip Ye started the car and drove slowly home.

CHAPTER SIXTY-SIX

Monday

The morning broke warmer and brighter than of late. The sun soon burned off the night mist, the sky a hazy azure blue. Philip Ye was surprisingly cheerful. Not only had he had a full five hours uninterrupted sleep – PSB HQ could wait for him today – but when he got down to the breakfast table a beautifully handwritten thankyou note had been left for him by Mouse.

"She and I have become the best of friends," said Ye Zihao, pouring the tea.

"You mean you have discovered that she works in the Procuratorate archive where many, many secrets are kept."

Ye Zihao was not affronted. "Philip, it is going to be a long war against the Shanghai Clique. We need as much help as we can get. Besides, there are so few witty women left in Chengdu. Those who remain need to be cherished."

Mouse was still on Philip Ye's mind when he pulled into the carpark of the PAP barracks. Captain Wang, looking resplendent in his full dress uniform, was waiting for him as Philip Ye climbed stiffly out of the car. After they had shaken hands and commented like happy schoolboys about the change in the weather, Philip Ye presented Captain Wang with a small slip of paper on which he'd written a number.

"What's this?" asked Captain Wang.

"That number will bypass the switchboard at the Procuratorate and take you direct to the archive."

Captain Wang rubbed his freshly shaved chin, embarrassed. "So, Superintendent, are you a mind-reader and matchmaker too?"

"Just be aware that my father considers Mouse family."

"And that I'll end up in a hole in the ground if I am anything less than a gentleman?"

"Something like that." Philip Ye smiled. He was warming to Captain Wang. Unusually for the PAP, he appeared to have a sense of humour.

"Has she any outstanding ties?" asked Captain Wang.

"I only met her for the first time yesterday. I know very little about her. You're going to have to do some of the work yourself. Anyway, enough of romance, are you set for your Board of Enquiry later this morning?"

"I am – it appears after last night's exploits in Longquanyi District I have been elevated to the status of hero again. I expect to be fined, nothing more."

"I am glad to hear it."

"I am in your debt, Superintendent."

"No, you were the right man for the job."

"I am grateful, nevertheless."

"I understand there was a death."

"Not one of ours, thank Heaven. And Constable Ma was quite unhurt if you were worrying. I should have called you but it has been such a busy night."

"How did Constable Ma fare?"

"She was a revelation," replied Captain Wang, shaking his head. "Where has Chengdu PSB been hiding her all these years?"

He guided Philip Ye through the door into the main barracks complex. "Constable Ma is not keen on flying but on the ground she's hard to keep up with. The assault was tricky. I flew over the location myself and we even sent a few drones up to have a closer look. We couldn't approach by road. We would have been seen for miles. And we couldn't easily rappel down by ropes, certainly not down onto the roof of the house. It was still being refurbished and there were just too many unknowns. We were forced to resort to basics, deciding to drop down outside the perimeter of the house, sprint across the open ground and then blow the gates with explosives.

"However, I'm not sure Constable Ma quite understood the plan. As soon as we were off the helicopters, she outran my forced-entry guys and wrenched the iron gates off their hinges with her bare hands. I've never seen anything like it. Then she barrelled through the main entrance to the house and a few minutes later it was all over. There were a few knives wielded by the cultists…and one idiot rushed one of my men with an axe. We had no choice but to put him down. And that was that. We detained thirty-five cultists, a mixture of men and women, most no more than twenty years of age. Constable Ma found that missing kid…the one that's soft in the head. The cultists had chained him like a dog to a wall in the basement. Again, she just wrenched the chain out with her bare hands. The kid was in a bad way. From what I can understand the cultists told him that his father was sick in hospital and that he needed to keep painting those Willow Woman pictures to pay for his father's medical bills. Heartless bastards. The kid's nothing but skin and bone, frantic with worry for his father."

"Has he been informed his father is dead?" asked Philip Ye, solemnly.

"No, he got so agitated when we took him away from his painting that we had to sedate him. I've put a call into social services. They're supposed to be sending someone out to assess him today. I expect you are desperate to interview him. Before we sedated him he was babbling to Constable Ma about a friend of his called Poppy, about how she'd taken him on a long bus-ride to Chongqing to see a great man, how she had given him a photograph to draw and then tricked him. The poor kid has really been through the wars."

"I'll have a chat to him in a day or two when he's recovered somewhat – not that it's my case anymore."

"Not invited onto The Willow Woman task force?"

"No – but I don't mind. Homicide detectives prefer to work alone."

Captain Wang suddenly put out an arm to stop their progress down the corridor to the refectory. "Superintendent, before we meet up with everybody, may I speak to you about Constable Ma. I understand that she is to be transferred back to Pujiang County because of that shooting the other day."

"This is true."

"Look…I may be speaking out of place, but she really impressed us last night. The Special Tactical Unit would like to offer her a secondment, a full transfer if all goes well. It's unusual I know, but a rural backwater would be a waste for such a woman. Earlier, before breakfast, she lifted one of our physical training instructors above her head. And then she out-shot me on the firing range. She is a marvel."

"Have you spoken to her?"

Abashed, Captain Wang nodded.

"What was her reaction?"

"Positive, I think – though it's hard to tell. Those big eyes of hers are like mirrors."

"What about the shooting of Old Man Gao?"

"You mean my feelings about her opening fire before considering other options?"

"Yes."

Captain Wang shrugged. "I've reviewed the footage. I now believe that that old man was determined to die no matter what. If she had not opened fire immediately he would have found a way to force her hand."

"She knew him."

"Ah," said Captain Wang, shaken.

"They had been friends."

"Then I am sorry for her. But, and call this perverse if you wish, that knowledge makes me want her more. The Unit needs people who can make the difficult decisions, take the most heart-rending shots under immense pressure if necessary."

With that last comment, Captain Wang resumed their progress down the corridor, stopping just at the glass doors leading into the refectory.

"The other members of the Unit really like her," he said, pointing through the glass.

Philip Ye saw a boisterous group of young men – and a few women – still high on the adrenalin of the night before, drinking tea at a long table in the middle of the refectory, chattering away, exchanging stories, and, in the midst of them, the very centre of attention, was Ma Meili. It was a far cry from the other morning when he had left her in the canteen at PSB HQ and no one would approach her, let alone speak to her. Here, she was laughing and chatting with the other officers as if she had known them all her life. She was dressed in one of their black combat uniforms. Maybe she belonged with them. The thought unexpectedly saddened him.

"Superintendent, would you stand in the way of me offering a secondment for Constable Ma?"

"Of course not, Captain."

"She has told me, because of the shooting the other day, there is an ongoing Procuratorate investigation that—"

"That has been resolved."

"It has?"

"As of this morning, the Procuratorate has lost all interest in Constable Ma. PSB Personnel will be able to process your second-ment request at once."

"Are you sure I have your blessing?" asked Captain Wang, looking at him closely.

"I will not stand in the way of anyone's good fortune."

Captain Wang was overjoyed. "Come, you must meet everybody before you take her away."

"Forgive me, Captain, no...maybe another day."

"Are you sure?"

"May I see Gao Junjie instead?"

Hiding his disappointment, Captain Wang took him to one of the dormitories. Inside, Junjie was fast asleep on one of the bunks, his thumb in his mouth, a female sergeant on guard nearby. She stood to attention when she saw Captain Wang. Junjie's face was indeed pale and there were dark circles about his eyes. It was a pity his father was not alive to see him, thought Philip Ye, he would have been so happy; Fatty Deng too, without whom the investigation would not have got so far, and so quickly.

"Call me if you have any problems with social services," said Philip Ye.

"I will," replied Captain Wang.

"If you don't mind I'll now wait for Constable Ma in the car. Send her out to me when she is ready."

"Of course, Superintendent...and if you are free one evening, my father and I would like to invite you to dinner. We are not the most scintillating company but—"

"You do know who *my* father is, don't you?"

"Superintendent, local politics do not interest me or my father."

"It should."

"Regardless, we should like you to come to dinner."

"Then I accept," said Philip Ye, cheered by the invitation, extending his hand.

Back in the car, he sat patiently, feeling the need to breathe, but choosing not to, content for the first time in many years to wallow in his melancholy. He knew he should have been happy, his part in the investigation into The Willow Woman cult done, his duty to the ghost of Old Man Gao discharged. But he could not help feeling smothered in gloom and afraid for what was to come. Maybe Wolf's instincts were right and Prosecutor Xu should have been left to die by the bank of the Yangzi. The family Ye could yet rue that decision.

The opening of the passenger door surprised him. He had not noticed Ma Meili's approach. She was back in her awful faded smock and shapeless jeans. She had also returned to her normal self, no longer the laughing, gregarious woman he had seen in the refectory.

Deep, troubling emotions whirled about her and Philip Ye felt a dull ache begin at the back of his head.

Was it him?

Did he inspire these dark emotions in her?

"Captain Wang was very impressed with you," he said, trying to lighten the mood. "He wants to take you into the PAP."

"I tried to tell him I was not real police but he did not understand," she replied, glumly.

Ah, so that was the problem.

"Sister, don't be concerned," he told her. "Your file says you are police and that's all that matters. As for the PAP, they will want to retrain you anyway, make you over in their mould."

"This would be a good thing?" she asked.

"For you, I think, yes." He started the engine, hoping this would satisfy her.

"But the Procuratorate—"

"Have lost all interest in you, Sister."

"Can it be so?"

"I would not lie to you."

He pulled out of the carpark and exchanged a wave with the guard manning the gate. As he turned left onto the road leading back into the city he began to feel a constriction about his chest. If anything the tension in the car had heightened not lessened.

"Is Fatty Deng—?"

"Alive, Sister – proving remarkably difficult to kill."

"That is good," she replied. "And Yoyo?"

"Safe with Baby Wu."

She was silent for a time, then said, "And Prosecutor Xu?"

"Back at her desk at the Procuratorate, I assume."

"I do not like her."

"I know, Sister."

Her breathing became ragged and irregular. He looked over at her and saw her staring aimlessly out of the window, engaged with some inner dilemma.

"What is troubling you, Sister?" he asked, needing to clear the air before he suffocated.

"What will happen to you?" she asked, blurting the words out.

"Do you mean what comes next for me?"

She nodded, her big eyes curiously welling up.

"There are cases that are outstanding on my desk and soon enough more trade will come my way."

She brushed a filthy sleeve across her eyes to remove the tears. "What do you mean...trade?"

"In Homicide it is what we do, Sister – death is our trade, our business. Not that this should concern you. Soon you'll be tracking smugglers through dense forests, climbing mountains in search of drug dealers, and jumping out of helicopters onto the roofs of high-rise buildings to rescue hostages and other such exciting things with the PAP."

She bit her lip, unable to smile. One good sleep, he mused, and he'd already forgotten how much work she could be.

"Listen, Sister, before I take you back to The Silver Tree to collect your things, I thought we might stop off at a small temple that I know. We could make an offering for Old Man Gao, light some incense, pay our respects to him, tell him that Junjie is safe, and wish him well for his onward journey through the afterlife."

"I do not believe in such things."

"It is not about belief, Sister – it is about showing respect. Then we'll visit Fatty Deng in hospital and pick up Yoyo from Wukuaishi station. And after, maybe we could—"

"Superintendent?"

"Yes, Sister?"

"Thank you for helping me."

"It is my pleasure, though in reality I have done very little."

His words did little to satisfy her though, or to lift the atmosphere in the car. Unable to take anymore, he pulled over to the kerb and confronted her.

"Constable Ma, what is troubling you?"

Silence.

"Speak to me!"

"I cannot say," she mumbled, unable to face him.

"I have given you an order, Constable."

Her tears flowed freely now. "I want to do this trade with you… this business of death."

Philip Ye was astonished. Would he ever understand this giant of a woman? "Are you certain?"

She nodded, again brushing away her tears with the filthy sleeve of her smock. Irritated beyond measure by her lack of care for herself, he passed his own silk handkerchief to her to dry her eyes.

"Homicide is not for everyone," he said.

"I would not get in your way, I promise."

"I will make you study…and not just policing, but history, law, and science too. It will not be much of a life for you, Sister. There will be none of the excitement that Captain Wang is offering you."

"All I have ever wanted is to be police…a detective…to catch bad people."

He took his phone from his pocket and passed it to her. "Then you had better call Captain Wang."

"But—"

"Be kind, apologise to him and tell him you have just discovered that, as of this morning, you have been formally transferred from Robbery to Homicide and that this order cannot be revoked or amended for at least a year."

He expected her mouth to drop open in surprise as usual, but instead she covered up her face with her massive hands so he could not see her emotion. He thought it might be an hour or so until she was ready to make the call so he steered the car back into traffic and turned on the radio so she could, until then, hum along to the tunes.

CHAPTER SIXTY-SEVEN

The little sleep Xu Ya had managed had been difficult, full of nightmares. Over and over again she had watched Madame Xiong slide beneath the black waters of the Yangzi, never to be seen again; and over and over again she had awoken, believing Philip Ye to be sitting nearby, watching her, judging her.

It had not helped her state of mind to learn that Philip Ye had been in her apartment. On her arrival back at Tranquil Mountain Pavilions she had raged at Mister Ni, the night concierge, when she had found her clothes folded neatly on her bed and her papers and books disturbed on her desk. Mister Ni had been suitably regretful. He had told her that he had heard that the legal department at FUBI International Industries would be drafting a letter of complaint to Chengdu PSB. Xu Ya had demanded another apartment. Mister Ni told her that one might be available in a month or two. She had raged at him again. Mister Ni had made her a cup of tea. She had refused the tea and stormed off to bed.

Well before dawn, giving up on sleep, she had got dressed, made herself a large mug of coffee, and gone down to the lobby and shed some tears as she apologised to Mister Ni. A very decent man, Mister Ni told her not to worry. Both he and Mister Gan, the day concierge, were both just glad she was back from Chongqing safe and sound.

"You gave us all quite a scare, Prosecutor Xu," he said.

She went into the Procuratorate early. She wanted time to think upon all that had happened, to organise her thoughts before being called to account for her actions of the weekend. But, on arrival, she found the Procuratorate abuzz with the news of the many police raids across the city in pursuit of a new and highly dangerous religious cult and Chief Prosecutor Gong in a terrible temper. She was summoned to his office immediately. He was not alone. Secretary Wu and Party Chief Li were with him. Xu Ya nearly fainted on the spot. She took the chair that was offered her, crossed her legs and folded her arms, and did her best to conceal the fear she felt.

Chief Prosecutor Gong wasted no time in launching into a venomous tirade, demanding to know why she had had the temerity to commence a major Procuratorate investigation into The Willow Woman cult without the proper authorisation, how her special investigator had nearly been murdered by this cult, and what had possessed her to run off to Chongqing without telling anyone.

"I was trying to save the life of an unfortunate youth," she explained, meaning Junjie.

Chief Prosecutor Gong was contemptuous. "Trying to save the life of an unfortunate youth? Have you gone mad, Ms. Xu?"

She felt like a naughty child.

"So, where is this unfortunate youth?" asked Chief Prosecutor Gong, tartly.

"I did not find him."

"So you could not even do that right?"

"No, sir."

Chief Prosecutor Gong had more to say but Party Chief Li raised a hand to silence him.

"Ms. Xu," said Party Chief Li, "you ought to be dismissed for your extraordinary conduct these last few days. If Chief Prosecutor Gong chooses to waste his weekends playing a ridiculous Western game a thousand miles away then we should hope that there is at least someone with a modicum of sense left in the Procuratorate able to properly respond to what has been the worst threat to civil order in Chengdu in years."

"I was available...by phone," said Chief Prosecutor Gong, meekly, his face suddenly ashen.

"However, Ms. Xu," continued Party Chief Li, ignoring Chief Prosecutor Gong, "somehow, you have survived your ordeal in Chongqing, and somehow the raids across the city and out in Longquanyi District were very successful, and somehow harmony has been restored to Chengdu. Whether any of this success can be attributed to you, I very much doubt. But I do have a soft spot for survivors. To survive even one's own stupidity is important, don't you think?"

"Yes, sir."

"I need a complete statement regarding all your actions of the last few days. This statement will be for our eyes only. You are not to have anything further to do with the investigation into the activities of The Willow Woman cult, nor are you to allow yourself to be interviewed by the task force that has been set up by the PSB or by anyone in the Criminal Procuracy Section. Your interest in the family Xiong is over. Is that understood?"

"Yes, sir."

"Now run along – we have work to do."

She retreated to her office and locked the door. She switched her computer on and hastily wrote out a resignation note. But she deleted it just as quickly, unable to face a future without her work as a prosecutor, unwilling to run back to her parents.

She stared out of the window.

She phoned Wukuaishi Hospital. Investigator Deng was unconscious but stable. More would be known in a few days.

She stared out of the window some more.

She phoned the archive but Mouse was not at her desk. She was told by another clerk that Mouse had been temporarily attached to the Criminal Procuracy Section task force and was currently in a briefing.

She had still written none of her statement when some time later there was a tap on the door. Hoping it was Mouse come to cheer her up, she opened the door, only to be stunned to find Secretary Wu himself come to call on her. She offered him a seat but he refused, preferring to stand at the window and look down upon the city.

"I think we have finally left the winter behind us," he said.

She wanted to run and hide. "Secretary Wu, please forgive me. I have let you down and—"

"You may be pleased to hear that the youth Gao Junjie – an artist of some considerable talent, so I am led to believe – has been recovered safely from a house in Longquanyi District. He is in the care of the PAP as we speak."

"That is wonderful news," said Xu Ya, struggling not to cry.

"But let us not speak of him or that odious cult," said Secretary Wu. "You have important work ahead of you. As of this morning, Commissioner Ho has been removed from his post as head of PSB Robbery. He has made a full confession of his crimes to Commissioner Ji. An example has to be made of him. You have the responsibility of drafting the Bill of Prosecution and will present the case in court. There will be much media interest."

"I understand."

"Unfortunately, you will be working very much alone until Investigator Deng regains his health."

"I will cope, Secretary Wu. Who is taking over at PSB Robbery?"

"Supervisor Maggie Loh – soon to be promoted to Commissioner Third Class. She will be our first female police commissioner in Chengdu. It will be quite an event."

"I met her the other evening. I liked her. She seems very energetic."

"She is the future, Ms. Xu – as are you."

"Thank you, but—"

"There is one little matter that must be cleared up, Ms. Xu. Do you have your file on Constable Ma Meili?"

Xu Ya picked it off the top of her pile of paperwork. "I have it here."

"Good – I need you to rewrite your conclusion into the shooting of Old Man Gao. Constable Ma is not to be transferred back to Pujiang County. She is to remain with Chengdu PSB."

"But—"

"I am aware the shooting did not play well in the media at the time but Constable Ma should not be punished for that. She was only doing her job. Besides, the media is now much more concerned with a dangerous cult running wild about the city."

"Secretary, I beg you to reconsider. There are serious discrepancies in Constable Ma's file…in her application to transfer to Chengdu PSB last summer. And you said yourself that—"

"Ms. Xu, regardless of the law or even one's own feelings, when the wind blows sometimes one has no choice but to bend. We are not perfect. We are a society in flux – a country in search of its future. Concessions often have to be made, deals have to be struck. This is how it is – for now. Take the rest of the day off. Go home, relax, find some inner peace, and come back tomorrow revitalised so you can begin the necessary work on bringing Commissioner Ho to trial. Leave your statement regarding the cult until the end of the week. You may have gained a better perspective by then. And maybe, next weekend, you might join me and my wife for dinner. My wife gets lonely at times. We all need friends, don't we, Ms. Xu?"

We all need friends….

After Secretary Wu had left her, Xu Ya, in a fit of temper, threw Constable Ma's file across the office, the papers spilling out all over the floor.

This was Philip Ye's doing.

She knew it.

She did not go home as ordered. Her handbag lost the day before, probably burned up in the fire that had consumed the red delivery truck together with her purse and credit cards, she went to the bank and argued with the manager until he had released some cash to her. She then went shopping. She bought herself a new handbag, some shoes she fell in love with at first sight, and then, quite by chance, came across a small boutique down a side-street selling – she was assured – genuine Hawaiian shirts. She sought out the largest size they had, hoping that would do, and bought the most colourful, the most garish shirt she could find. In shades of red, orange and yellow, the shirt was decorated with pineapples and flying parrots. It was hideous but she thought Investigator Deng might appreciate it.

"Ah, you are a woman of taste," said the shopkeeper.

She gave him a foul look while handing over the cash.

She drove to Wukuaishi Hospital. Because of who she was, she was whisked on arrival into the Director's office and assured that everything that could be done for Investigator Deng was being done. She was advised not to visit Investigator Deng, that his condition was such that she might get very upset.

"I am not so delicate," she replied.

But when a nurse took her to Investigator Deng, when she saw his sleeping face – which was swollen and had a greyish hue and looked nothing like him at all – and saw all the tubes sticking out of him, it was all she could do not to fall to her knees in despair. The nurse helped her to a chair and brought her a cup of tea. The nurse then told her that only an hour earlier the son of the former mayor had come by, accompanied by the biggest woman she had ever seen.

"Āiyā!" exclaimed the nurse. "Philip Ye is so handsome I thought my heart might stop."

Philip Ye.

Xu Ya wondered if she would ever escape his shadow.

When the nurse had left to go about her other duties, Xu Ya listened to Investigator Deng's assisted breathing for a while, trying to understand all the displays on the monitors. On the bedside table she noticed a small package. She picked it up and was surprised to see it was addressed to her. She quickly tore off the wrapper and inside found her missing procuratorate badge and ID, together with the phone she thought she had lost forever back in Professor Xiong's house. She also found Investigator Deng's badge and notebook inside. There was no note but she guessed who had left the package for her, cursing Philip Ye for his lax attitude toward security. Anyone in the hospital could have walked away with the package.

Tears welled up in her eyes when she opened Investigator Deng's notebook and saw the paper spotted with his blood. She read what he had written and learned much about what he had been up to while she had been en route to Chongqing, how he had re-interviewed the student Pan Mei and singlehandedly discovered the true purpose behind The Singing Moon bars. His notes also solved a mystery for her, how it was that Supervisor Lang had been able to lock onto her trail in Chongqing. Investigator Deng had described a red delivery truck parked outside The Singing Moon bar on the Siguan Road. This description must have been communicated to Supervisor Lang by Philip Ye, so that when Supervisor Lang spotted the truck he knew to follow it. One little paragraph in Investigator Deng's notebook, one neatly written detail, had saved her life. It was almost too much to believe; almost too much of a burden to carry.

"Prosecutor?"

She snapped the notebook shut and looked up. An old man, not too dissimilar in appearance to Old Man Gao, was standing before her. "Yes?"

"Forgive me for disturbing you but my name is Ho…Uncle Ho… a friend of the family. My wife and I are visiting with Deng Shiru's mother. She is quite depressed. She has been placed in a bed in a room just down the corridor. A nurse told me you had arrived. Would you come and visit with Madame Deng? You would cheer her up, I am sure. Deng Shiru spoke so highly of you…said you were a real lady. It would be good for his mother to meet you. It would really make her day. Maybe we could all play *májiàng* together. My wife cheats a little, but she means nothing by it."

Xu Ya shook her head. "No, I cannot stay."

But Uncle Ho would not take no for an answer. He held out his hand to her. "Prosecutor, this is not Chongqing. You are in Chengdu now and here it is understood that it is good for the soul every now and then to idle away a few hours of the day, to sit, to laugh, to joke, to drink tea, to play *májiàng* – to spend time with people."

"I am not very good with people," she said.

"And I'm not very good at *májiàng*," he replied, "but that doesn't stop me playing."

"It is not the same," she said.

"Ah, Prosecutor, some would consider me a fool to pick an argument with such a clever lawyer, but I beg to differ."

Uncle Ho made her laugh.

Uncle Ho lifted her spirits.

Xu Ya recalled Huang Liu-Hong from her dream instructing her to take the law to the people, which meant mixing with the people and sharing in their ordinary lives. So she accepted Uncle Ho's invitation. There was much emotion to begin with, Madame Deng taking hold of her hand and refusing to let go. But, when they had all sat down at the table to play, it was laughter rather than tears than echoed around the table. Madame Deng told some humorous stories from her son's time in the police; Uncle Ho sang a couple of ancient folk songs, much to the delight of the passing nurses; and Aunty Ho tried to scare them all with a ghost story from her home village, assuring them, in spite of their sniggering, that the story was quite true.

Uncle Ho was proved correct. Spending a few hours wasting time playing *májiàng* and drinking tea was indeed good for the soul. Xu Ya allowed many of her concerns to fall away from her and felt a lightness of heart she had not experienced in years. However, to do honour to the memory of her late mentor, Beloved Mister Qin, who had laboured long and hard to teach her the importance of the Rule of Law, when Xu Ya caught Aunty Ho cheating by hiding tiles in her lap, she found she could not overlook the indiscretion. She gave Aunty Ho a smart slap on the hand, and said, very sharply, "For rules to be meaningful, they must apply to everyone."

Madame Deng put her hands to her mouth in shock. Uncle Ho almost spilt his tea. But Aunty Ho swiftly countered with, "I'm not sure what rules you are speaking of, Prosecutor, but in my home village this is how we've always played. At my great age you wouldn't expect me to learn something new, would you?"

THE END